A
BARNSTORMER
IN OZ

A NOVEL BY
PHILIP JOSÉ FARMER

A BARNSTORMER IN OZ

or
A Rationalization And Extrapolation Of The Split-Level Continuum

BERKLEY BOOKS, NEW YORK

A limited first edition of this book has been published by Phantasia Press.

A BARNSTORMER IN OZ

A Berkley Book / published by arrangement with
the author

PRINTING HISTORY
Berkley trade paperback edition / September 1982

ISBN: 0-425-05641-4

A BERKLEY BOOK ® TM 757,375
The name "BERKLEY" and the stylized "B" with design are trademarks
belonging to Berkley Publishing Corporation.
PRINTED IN THE UNITED STATES OF AMERICA

To L. Frank Baum, to Fred M. Meyer, to the International Wizard of Oz Club, to Lester and Judy-Lynn del Rey, to Judy Garland, to all the Scarecrows, Tin Woodmans, Cowardly Lions, and Dorothys this side of the Yellow Brick Road, and to John Steinbeck, who said that, more than anything else, he would rather be "the ambassador to Oz."

A
BARNSTORMER
IN OZ

1

Kansas winked.

That was the second unexpected and disconcerting phenomenon. The first had been a few seconds before when a green cloud had ballooned from emptiness about two hundred feet in front of him. He was flying at one thousand feet altitude in his Jenny, a Curtiss JN-4H biplane, when the emeraldish haze had spurted from an almost cloudless sky like a genie from a bottle. It had grown in two eyeblinks to a thick mist about eighty feet wide and thirty deep. It was a transparent light-green at the edges and the front and an opaque dark-green elsewhere.

He had been so astonished that his trained reflexes had deserted him. His left hand did not move the huge wooden control stick, and his feet did not move the wooden rudder bars. The Jenny shot into the outer limits of the cloud. It was then that the state of Kansas winked at him, disappeared, reappeared, then was gone.

Fort Leavenworth, the Missouri River, and the fields and trees vanished.

This was no cloud formed of tiny drops of moisture. He felt no wetness on his face.

The sun was in the same position as when he had plunged into the cloud. The sky, however, which had been partly cloudy on this April Fool's Day, Easter Sunday, and first day of Passover of A.D. 1923, was now pure blue.

He glanced at his wristwatch. Eleven A.M. He knew what time it was, but he did not know where he was.

Below was a tawny desert with big outcroppings of dark rock.

Ahead, two miles away, was the edge of a green land that extended to right and left as far as he could see. The desert ended abruptly at the borders of the land as if it were an ocean breaking against an island. The land sloped up gradually for a mile, then it became high cliffs supporting a plateau.

He glimpsed twinkling towers, houses, and fields beyond the trees on the edge of the plateau.

He twisted his neck to look behind him. The cloud was dwindling, and then it was gone as if it had been sucked into an invisible vacuum cleaner.

Hank had been heading north by northwest towards Muscotah, Kansas, to deliver the personal effects of John "Rube" Schultz, his late flying partner in Doobie's Flying Circus. Hank had dreaded telling the widow how Rube had died in the accident, why the funeral would have to be a closed-casket ceremony, and his probably inadequate attempts to console Mrs. Schultz. It seemed now that he would not be landing on a meadow near the widow's home. Not within the time he had planned anyhow.

The compass needle on the instrument panel had swung crazily. Now it had steadied. He was still going north by northwest.

Hank Stover said, *"Sacre bleu!"* Then, "Holy smoke!"

His heart beat as fast and as hard as a woodpecker's bill against oak. His palms were wet. He felt slightly disoriented and number than he had been when drinking brandy while on leave in Paris. He was as frightened as when that black-and-scarlet banded Pfalz had been on the tail of his Spad.

He stiffened. To his right, what looked like lightning—it was hard to be sure in this bright sunlight—had spurted between two tall and sharp spires of dark rock. And then what seemed to be a flaming ball had rolled from the tip of one spire and exploded.

"I drank a lot last night," he muttered. "I've got a drophammer of a hangover. But I'm a long way from delirium tremens."

A ball of something shimmering and transparent rolled up from a ravine, shot ahead of the plane, got to a few feet from the vegetation-lined border, and disappeared in a bright expanding gout.

Small figures, birds, surely, rose in clouds from the trees near the desert.

He was over the greening land and approaching the cliffs. The plateau would be five hundred feet below him, but he pulled back on the joystick to climb. There would probably be an updraft from the cliff-face, but he was not taking any chances. Even though the JN-4H had an engine almost twice as powerful as the JN-4D, she was not as responsive to the controls as an Army pursuit. Besides, he wanted to get a wider view of the country. Which was what and where?

Even then, the truth was like a finger on the pulse of his mind. It felt a slight throb, but he could not believe that he was not deceived.

During his twenty-two years, Hank had had many surprises and shocks. The worst had been when his proposal of marriage had been rejected and when a Pfalz flown by one of the Kaiser's knights of the air had gotten on the tail of Hank's Spad and when he had slipped while transferring from the wing of a Jenny to the back seat of an automobile during a show outside Nashville, Tennessee. There was also the shock when his mother had removed the make-up from her forehead and taken her eight-year-old child into a dark room and showed him the very faint glimmer of a round mark on her forehead. That, however, had been delightful.

This was the worst because it was so unexpected and because it could not happen.

Yet, contradictorily, he now was not as shocked and surprised as he should have been. He thought he knew where he was though he just could not believe it. And if he was where he unbelievingly believed he was, where, as far as he knew, only two persons from Earth had preceded him . . . no, it could not be.

Two miles to his right was a thin cataract falling down the face of the cliff. It would have been much larger if it had not been for a dam north of which was a lake. On both sides of it were trees, meadows, and farms. Many irrigation ditches limbed it. Most of the trees looked like those in Illinois, oaks, sycamores, walnuts, Osage oranges, pines, and others. But there were also palm trees here and there.

The farmhouses were rectangular and had high pitched roofs. His mother had told him about these and commented on the difference of their structure from that of the country to the northwest.

Though the houses and barns were painted with many colors, red seemed most popular.

All had thick lightning rods.

The fences, made of split logs or stone, seemed to be property markers. They were not high enough to keep the sheep, goats, and cows from jumping over them.

Below was a road running more or less parallel to the edge of the cliff. It was of red brick and the only paved road for as far as he could see.

He turned the Jenny to the left and flew above the road. A farmer driving a loaded wagon stood up, opened his mouth, and pointed at the plane though there was no one else around. Yes, there was. The two cows pulling it were looking up.

As he passed the wagon, Hank saw that there were no reins attached to the harness.

Ahead, almost on the edge of the plateau, was a castle and west of it a village. It was of some white stone, about three hundred feet high, and surrounded by a wall one hundred feet high. No castle on Earth, though, had a huge watertower on its top or walls set with huge red precious stones, rubies. Of course, he could not be sure that the stones were not glass, but he didn't think they were. This building was also equipped with lightning rods.

Zooming over the top of the castle at an altitude of two hundred feet, he saw that the walls did not completely enclose the castle. They were shaped like a U with ends that curled back, horseshoe-shaped, and the opening faced the desert. The castle was X-shaped.

Hank flew over the village, noting the many people running about and gesturing excitedly at him and to others. He turned and came back along the road. Now men and women were pouring out of the great open gates of the outer wall of the castle. He left them behind, turned, headed into the southwesterly wind, and began descending. He made a three-point landing on a meadow, the wheels and the tail skid touching at the same time, taxied to near the fence, and turned off the engine. The cattle and sheep on the meadow had run to a far corner and were huddled together facing him. The people from the farmhouse were standing in front of the porch and probably arguing about whether or not they should approach him.

They could think that the Jenny was a winged monster. And Jenny must appear especially fearsome. Her fuselage was yellow, and her wings were scarlet. Two big blue eyes were painted on each side below the exposed engine, the propellor hub and part of the area around it was painted to look like a nose, and below it was a mouth with a red Cupid's-bow mouth and white pointed teeth.

It was warmer here. The temperature when he had left Kansas City was about 24 degrees Fahrenheit. It seemed to him that it was close to 39 degrees here.

Twelve bald eagles flying in V-formation flew over him at a height of twenty feet. Squadrons of goshawks, chicken hawks, and peregrine falcons followed them. Bringing up the rear were twelve golden eagles. All the birds were about one-third smaller than the species he knew on Earth. They wheeled and landed on the branches of some trees at the edge of the meadow. There, silent, scarcely moving, they eyed him steadily. But a lone peregrine circled above him, then sped toward the castle.

The engine was hot enough that he could start it again without having someone spin the propellor. Perhaps he should do that and taxi to the northeast corner to face the wind and so be ready for a quick takeoff.

"What the hell," he said, and he climbed out of the rear cockpit and got down to the ground.

He was conscious that he was flamboyant and handsome in his barnstormer's garb: black leather helmet with green-rimmed goggles shoved up on it, a long white scarf, black leather jacket, black-leather fur-trimmed gloves, yellow puttees, and black shoes. However, instead of the conventional rabbit's foot attached to the jacket to ensure good luck, he wore a housekey on a gold chain.

There were by then many people along the road, all staring at him. The eyes of most of them were on a level with his bellybutton. He was not surprised.

The men and women jabbering in an unknown language—yet it sometimes sounded like English—wore tall conical hats with tiny bells hanging from the wide brims. The women wore dresses with low-cut necklines and hems just below the knees. Their boots were really wooden shoes to which were attached leggings of wool. The men wore sleeved shirts, vests, pants, and boots like the women's except that they had a fat roll at the tops. The older men were full-bearded; the younger, clean-shaved or moustached.

Only the women wore make-up, and that was just rouge.

All were Caucasians, though deeply tanned. The faces looked like those he had seen when in occupied North Germany.

After a while, the animals in the corner of the meadow approached him, their number swelled by those from adjoining farms. These were, like the people, about one-third smaller than their Terrestrial counterparts.

Hank was shocked when a sheep spoke to another. The language was undoubtedly that of the humans, but the voice was unhuman. Its Victrola-record quality sent chills over him.

Yet, he should have been prepared for it.

Deciding that he would probably be leaving the meadow soon, he took out his anchoring equipment from a recess in the rear turtle deck. Just as he finished staking the Jenny down, he saw a train of chariots bearing armed women stop by the fence. Chariots! Pulling them were diminutive moose. These, like the cows he had seen, lacked reins. And the charioteers carried no whips.

He should have expected that.

The female soldiers got down from their vehicles, and assembled in formation at the directions of an officer. Their steel helmets were conical and had gold arabesques and bore on the front a horseshoe shape enclosing an X. Long scarlet feathers stuck from the peaks, and red cloth chinstraps secured the helmets. They wore stiff red shirts over which were hip-length woolen jackets, scarlet with gold braid. Their knee-length scarlet skirts bore yellow, blue, and green designs: the horseshoe and X, hackenkreuzes, ankhs, and owls' eyes. Their boots were like the farmers' but were scarlet with golden clockwork.

Stover looked at the blonde, blue-eyed commander and said, "A real doll! A peach!"

There was nothing peachy about the sword she held in one hand or her troop's long spears. She gestured that Stover should leave the plane. He did so, and he suddenly found himself surrounded by sharp steel spearheads.

Smiling, he gestured that he came in peace. If the commander understood Indian sign language, she did not indicate so. He was marched to the road and then down it towards the castle. The chariots, with the rest of the soldiers, followed them, and behind them came the crowd of civilians. The bodyguard and he walked a mile before coming to the castle. Here a large crowd of people, animals, and birds, waited to see the giant who had flown in a huge bird from somewhere. It was kept from pressing close to him by soldiers, males who also wore skirts.

Hank went across a drawbridge over a fifty-foot-wide moat, passed through the outer walls, across a courtyard with marble paving, and up twelve marble steps forty feet or so wide. These were flanked by ramps for the animals. He had no chance to examine the rubies, large as his head, set in the walls by the entrance.

He was seeing much but noting little in detail. He went through high-ceilinged and wide halls furnished with statuary, paintings, and other artifacts of various kinds. The floors were marble set with colored mosaics. At the end of a hall, he was conducted up a broad winding staircase and arrived, out of breath, at a door on the ninth floor.

He walked stooping through the doorway into an anteroom. The next room had a steel door with a small barred window. He was urged through that, and the captain and two soldiers who had accompanied him into the room left it. The door was closed, and a big steel bar clanged shut on the outside. He was in a very large room with furniture too small for him except for the enormous canopied bed. A door led to a bathroom. It did have running water, however, though the toilet was too small for him to sit comfortably on—his testicles would fall into the water—and he would have to bend far over to wash his face. The only light he'd have at night would be lamps burning oil of some kind.

2

What Mr. H.G. Wells, Mr. Roy Rockwood, and Mr. Dante Alighieri had overlooked in their journeys to other worlds was how shocked their heroes would be. To leave Earth was to suffer a physical and emotional blow similar to that which the newborn baby felt on being ejected from the womb. However, the baby had no idea of what had happened, whereas the adult journeying to the moon or Mars or Hell had some notion of what he was to encounter and had willingly launched himself into the unknown. Also, Mr. Wells' characters in *The First Men In The Moon,* and Mr. Rockwood's in *Through Space To Mars,* and Mr. Alighieri's in *The Inferno* had voyaged within the relatively narrow limits of the solar system and their destinations were not unmapped. Mr. Alighieri's hero, Dante himself, had a clear image of what Hell would be like, though the reality must have shaken him to the center of his being. Surely, the heroes of all three fantasists must have been numb and disoriented for a while. Lesser men might have died from the shock.

Well, maybe not. After all, they had had some sort of conditioning for their voyages, some degree of preparation.

But to be suddenly propelled into another universe—that was something that Hank Stover had not read about or even heard of. Well, yes, he had. Hell, Purgatory, and Heaven were other worlds in the sense that they were in another universe. Or were they? Weren't they in the solar system also?

And, in a sense, he had been conditioned, prepared, for this universe by his mother's stories and Mr. Baum's books. So, he had not been completely shocked.

8

Also, though he was in another universe, he was still, somehow, in the solar system of Earth.

There was a big ornately carved pendulum clock in the room. Its face bore twenty-three single characters or bi-characters. These were numerals, many of which looked like they had been derived from the Greek alphabet, some from the Latin, and a few from what he thought was the Runic. He was not sure, but they seemed to be like those he had seen in a book on the Gothic language.

The clock was obviously a twenty-four-hour chronometer. The day, indicated by the zero mark, started at noon. The zero mark at the top of the face was not the zero he was accustomed to. It was a short horizontal line with a large dot in the middle. These people, if they or their ancestors had come from Earth, would have come before Arabic numerals had been introduced. But one of their geniuses had invented a symbol for zero.

When the clock struck noon, Hank's wristwatch indicated 12:04:08 P.M. The moon was full, as on this date on Earth, and, though it was pale in the daylight, its markings seemed to be like Earth's moon. There was a morning star, which would have been Venus on Earth. Sunset was at 6:25 by his watch, just as it was supposed to. Also, the constellations were what he could have expected on this date as seen from the Midwest.

What was not on Earth was the sudden appearance and rolling charge across the desert floor of huge glowing balls and their silent explosions as they neared the fertile borderland. Something at the edge of the desert was discharging them.

On April 2, the moon, now beginning to wane, rose at 8:00 A.M.

He was sure that this desert and the green land were not on Earth somewhere. Even though there were in A.D. 1923 unexplored territories, this could not be one of them. Wherever the green haze, some sort of entrance, had sent him, it had not transported him to a remote spot of his native planet. He had passed into another universe.

The two universes formed a split-level continuum. Earth and this planet shared the same extra-atmospheric space but yet were walled off from each other. Or they were two different floors in the same planetary building, as it were. When he had gone through the green haze, he had ascended from the first floor, Earth, to the second floor, *Ertha*.

Ertha. That that was so similar to the English word was no coincidence. Not when the language used *lamb* for lamb, *fotuz* for foot, *manna* for man, *kald* for cold, *arm* for arm, and *herto* for heart. The people of this desert-surrounded land, called Amariiki, "Spirit-Kingdom," spoke a tongue descended from some Germanic language. He suspected that it was Gothic, but he did not know enough to be sure.

There was also a nation to the north which was called Oz. This was not a word which these people had brought in from Earth.

Hank Stover had had many questions, still did, but he could not ask them until he learned his captors' speech. Since they started his language lessons an hour after he was in his luxurious cell, they were eager to communicate. Most of his daylight hours were spent bent over by the window in the door. His instructors, all wearing gauze masks for the first two weeks, stood on the other side. Hank learned much, but he got a hell of a backache and, sometimes, a headache.

"What am I?" he yelled now and then. "A skunk? A pariah? Something unspeakably filthy and degraded? A leper? A Socialist?"

Four men, four women, and a child taught him, each for about an hour and fifteen minutes. One was the blonde pipperoo, Captain Lamblo, "Little Lamb." Like the others, she had no surname but had a nickname or cognomen. Hers was "The Swift."

They started out by pointing to and naming parts of their bodies. He repeated their words until his pronunciation was perfect or, at this stage, acceptable. If he could have seen their lips, he would have learned faster.

They brought in objects and named these. After five days, he was taught simple sentences.

"Sa-her'z ain sko." "This is a shoe."

"Sa-thar'z ain hilm." "That's a helmet."

"Ii sai thuk." "I see you."

"Sai thu mik?" "See you me?"

"Ain, twai, thriiz . . ." "One, two, three . . ."

He was able to relate many words to three branches of the Teutonic language. His Swedish governess had taught him some of her language, and he had learned German in prep school, during the Occupation, and at Yale. This enabled him to relate some of the words to English.

But how had the Teutonics gotten into this world? And why had they become pygmies?

In the meantime, he had managed to get a building erected around the Jenny to protect her from the weather and wind. He could not see the plane because his windows, the *augdor,* literally, eye-doors, faced the south. He had also gotten his captors to deliver his luggage, which was kept in the recess under the rear turtle deck. This had been brought to him wrapped in sheets and carried by men with gloves. The sheets were removed, and the cases were pushed through the door at the ends of long sticks. He supposed that the sheets and gloves would be burned later.

He was happy about this. He had had to wash his underwear, shirt, and socks in cold water and with the strong soap. Then he had had to go without them until they had dried. Now he had a change. He also had a carton of Camel cigarettes and a quart of bootleg booze, Glenfiddich scotch, smuggled in from Canada. He'd had to smoke the local tobacco, a strong burley, in a pipe. He did not like to smoke a pipe. They'd given him beer, which was tastier than any he'd ever had, but he preferred hard liquor. The stuff they'd given him was grain alcohol mixed with water and the juice of berries.

Also in the luggage was a Colt .45 New Service revolver and two boxes of ammunition. These people had no idea what they were, but he did not intend to use them.

There were also copies of a farmer's almanac, Sinclair Lewis's *Babbitt, Civilization In the United States,* edited by Harold Stearns, and two *Current Opinion* magazines. The latter had been taken from a Kansas City boardinghouse, and, though they were the April, 1920 and April, 1921 issues, Hank had started reading them. They had many interesting articles. Besides, he would read anything, even the labels on a can of Campbell's soup, if he had nothing else.

He also exercised vigorously for an hour, and he spent some time observing the celestial phenomena and the hundreds of fireballs that went up in flashes like shells from Big Bertha.

He asked Lamblo what they were called.

"*Fizhanam.*" "Enemy-ghosts."

When he asked her to explain their nature, he got no answer.

At the end of the third week, his captors must have concluded that he was *rain,* clean. The inner door was unlocked, and Wulfla (Little Wolf), a teacher, entered. But two guards stood at the door.

"Why did you treat me as if I had the . . ." he said. What was the word for plague?

"*Unhaili. Zha, sa Aithlo* (Yes, the Little Mother) had you locked up until we could find out if you were carrying some evil thing which might make us sick."

"What diseases do you have? After all, if I can give mine to you, you can give yours to me."

"You'll have to ask Little Mother. She commanded that you be kept here untouched. But I think that you giants have some sort of loathsome illnesses which might make us sick and die."

"You don't have those kinds of diseases?"

"*Ne*. We die of *gund* (cancer), heart failure, stroke, and other self-diseases, but, except for some skin diseases, we have little that one person transmits to another."

More questioning told him that these people did not even have the common cold, though they could get pneumonia. And the childbirth fatality rate was low, one in ten thousand. Some of his questions were readily, if not fully, answered. Others were referred to his scheduled meeting with *Sa Hauist* (The Highest), another of the many titles of the female ruler.

He was puzzled by the tobacco. If these natives were descendants of Dark-Age Goths, how had they encountered tobacco? That was indigenous to America; the Goths were Europeans. Also, there were many other North American plants: canned squash, pumpkin, and Indian corn or maize. Potatoes and tomatoes were lacking, but the former had come from South America and the latter from Central America to Europe and then to North America.

There were many illustrated books on the shelves, and these showed animals that were a mixture of European and American. They included the lion and tiger that Baum had written of and his mother had told him about. The lion looked much like the African counterpart, but the cub spots had not entirely faded away in the adult. It was much larger in proportion than the African lion would have been if it had diminished in size. It seemed to him that it must be descended from the "Atrocious Lion" that had once roamed the southwest U.S. but had become extinct about 14,000 years ago.

The tiger, which his mother had never seen but had heard of, was not the Asiatic cat. It was what was called the sabertooth tiger or smilodon, and its fur was tawny and unstriped. It, too, had perished on the North American continent about the same time as the American lion.

Apparently, the giant ground sloth and the short-faced grizzly also dwelt in the forests and plains along with the humpless camel, the mammoth, and the mastodon.

Where were the dog and the horse? The ancient Goths would have had these when they came into this universe. What had, boojumlike, snatched them all away?

And what had caused both animals and humans to shrink in size? And what . . . ?

He tried to keep from thinking of the questions that crowded at the windows of his mind like ghostly peeping toms.

Sometimes, he stared out the huge French windows or from the balcony. His apartment was in the southeast arm of the X-shaped castle. He could see part of the southern land, the farms, the forest, and the desert beyond. He could also look into many windows on the lower levels of the arm. There was one vast room which aroused his curiosity, though he had never seen anyone enter it, not even to dust.

Its windows were huge, and its curtains were always open. The floor was of wood, and the walls had many various designs including pentacles and nonacles. There were many tables, large and small, bearing what looked like laboratory equipment. When the sun shone into it, he could see much of the room clearly. At night, only one light burned, a giant torch set in the middle of the room on top of a sphinx of highly polished black stone which was pointed southward. The head had four female faces. At least, he thought it did since he could see the profiles of those in front and behind and the full face of the one looking to the south. Its seven-pointed crown was set with jewels. The couchant body was not a lioness's but a bear's.

3

On the 28th day of his imprisonment, the late afternoon sun was shrouded by thick black clouds. The wind slowly strengthened until it had a voice and then was howling. The branches of the trees flailed, and their tops bent. Thunder snapped out lightning as if it were a whip on fire. Rain came at nightfall and spread over the windows of his apartment. Out in the desert, the white arcs increased their number and the distance they spat from point to point. The gigantic fireballs seemed to pop out from everywhere. They rolled like a charging army, like thundering surf, toward the edge of the sands, where they blew up.

''The devil's laying down his artillery barrage,'' Stover muttered.

Cold skated over his skin. After the barrage, then what? Zero hour? The onslaught?

Also, his theory that the spurts and balls were some kind of St. Elmo's fire was untenable. That could not exist in this wet atmosphere.

He went to a table and poured out a tall glass of the local liquor which had long ago replaced his scotch. This was different from the first bottle he'd been given. It was some sort of barley vodka, strong eye-watering stuff. He drank down two or three ounces and turned, full of Dutch courage, to face the fury from the south. He had not been afraid of lightning storms before; in fact, he had flown through them, and, though nervous, had not been frightened. But there was something about this fury that made him far more uneasy. Perhaps it was those arcs and fireballs. His instructors had not been able to explain them. They had said that they had always been out there, but they did not know how they originated.

14

Stover had almost gotten used to them. Now . . . they seemed determined to get over whatever hidden barrier it was that kept them in the desert.

"I'm anthropomorphizing," he said. "But what else can an *anthropos* do? It's his nature to commit the pathetic fallacy. Commit?"

The wind seemed to get even stronger, rattling the windows and hurling solid slices of the rain against the glass. The tall grandfather clock in the living room, the case of which was carved with grotesque goblinish faces, gonged twelve times. Midnight. And before the final note sounded, the rain and the wind stopped. It was as if a switch had cut off the power that was driving the elements.

He opened the French windows and stepped outside. There was silence except for the drip of water. The fireballs, the "enemy ghosts," exploded as they hurled themselves against the desert boundary. Their flashes reminded him of artillery barrages at night on the distant front. The farmhouses were not illuminated, and the clouds covered the sky. But the intense glare of gouting fireballs as they went up punctuated the darkness as if God were a crazy writer whose finger was stuck on the asterisk key.

Far off, thunder rumbled sullenly. It sounded like an angry bear whose attack had been beaten off and who had decided to go elsewhere.

The glowing spheres became more numerous. The desert was suddenly alive with them. Where there had been an estimated four or five per acre, there now seemed to be a hundred. They wheeled towards the forest across the sandy marsh in ragged phalanxes; the rumble of their advance was like the wheels of an ancient British chariot army.

Suddenly, to his left, a glaring sphere slipped through whatever it was that had prevented its mates from penetrating. He saw it in its full splendor, then could see only flashes now and then as it sped through the heavy forest.

He jumped. The room holding the sphinx, previously lit only by the single torch, had flared with a great light. It blinded him when he turned to look into it, but, as the illumination died down, he saw that someone had come into the room. At first, he could not make the figure out distinctly. The bright light had faded, leaving the torch to push back the darkness, a task it could not handle. Then, a hundred lights sprang out, making the vast room bright but not dazzlingly so. They came from many hemispheres set in the walls.

Stover swore. How could all those lamps have been lit at once when there was only one person in the room?

He forgot about that. The person was a woman, nude except for high-heeled shoes of some glittering silverish metal and a tall conical white hat with outspread bird-wings. Her long hair hung down almost to the back of her knees, and its dark auburn seemed to catch the light, compress it, and shed it as if it had become jewels. Her face was beautiful but with just enough irregularity, a nose a trifle too long, lips a trifle too full, eyes a trifle too far apart, to make them nonclassical but highly individual. Her body was perfect, long, slim but well-rounded legs, hips narrow but not too narrow, a slim waist, a big ribcage, full upstanding breasts with tiny aureoles but big nipples. Her skin was very white.

Hank despised peeping toms, but he could not force himself to go back into his room. Surely, if she did not want to be observed, she would have closed the curtains. Moreover, what she was doing had made him curious. He forgot about decency and gentleman's behavior.

She had taken the torch from the hole in top of the four-faced sphinx's head and had stuck it in a wall-holder. Then she went to a table and put her arms around a glass or crystal sphere twice as large as a basketball. She carried it to the sphinx and placed it on the top of the crown, where it fit snugly.

Stover glanced southwards, the corner of his eye having detected another breakthrough. Two more flaming balls had rolled through, leaving their exploding companions behind. The first was halfway through the forest, flitting phantomlike among the trees and bushes, and it would soon be out of view below the plateau edge.

He looked back at the red-haired woman. She was dancing counter-clockwise around the sphinx. In her left hand was a shepherd's staff, the shaft of which was carved with a spiral. She raised and lowered and stabbed it in and out as she spun, leaped, shuffled, whirled, sidestepped, bent, raised, and moved her lips. Now and then she seemed to be catching the neck of an invisible enemy in the hook at the end of her staff.

Lightning challenged the earth to a duel by slapping it in its face. He jumped, and his heart hammered. The bolt was unexpected; he had thought that the electrical fury was over. Also, the discharge had seemed to come so close to him that a cat's whisker could have measured the distance. Following the bolt, thunder rumbled as if the sky were trying to digest the spirit of anger. Lightning bridged cloud and ground again, though farther away this time.

The clearness of the sphere was gone. Something dark roiled inside it.

At the same time, the corners of the vast room darkened as if shadows were breeding in it. The blacknesses expanded like a cloud of ink shot out by an escaping octopus. It floated to the nearest lamps and passed over, but he could see the burning wicks faintly through the darkness.

A chill passed over him. His hairs felt as if they were rising.

"Jesus!" he muttered. He went back into his room and got his binoculars. Returning to the balcony, he directed the glasses towards the sphere, focussed them, and saw that there was within the sphere what looked like a miniature of the scene outside the castle. There were little black clouds and tiny threads of lightning shooting among them and down from them.

Suddenly, six little glowing rolling balls formed on the lower part of the sphere.

The blackness filled half the room now and was sweeping towards the center where the redhead still danced like a maniac around the sphinx.

He could not keep the binoculars on her face; she moved too swiftly and erratically, though he had the impression that her movements were not erratic for her but were rigidly patterned.

He put down the binoculars and looked out over the forest. Seven fireballs gleamed now and then in the trees.

No. Eight. Another had burst through.

He looked back at the room and put the binoculars up. The sphere now held eight fireballs.

The redhead stopped before the sphere, arched her back, which was towards him, her left arm raised, and the corkscrew-shafted staff pointing upwards. Then the staff came down, and it was pointed at the sphere.

For some seconds, thirty perhaps, she held the staff steady. Then it stabbed at the sphere but stopped a few inches from it. The blackness, which had been a few feet from her, closed in. He swore. Now he could see her only dimly. But he saw clearly the dazzling light that spurted from the end of the staff and struck the sphere.

The darkness oozed back a few feet. He used the binoculars again. There were only seven fireballs. He looked out at the forest and counted seven.

Again the staff jabbed. A twisting bolt of light shot from the tip of the staff and struck one of the balls inside the sphere. It vanished in a gout of flame. He looked out at the woods. Six were left. The one that had been in the lead was gone.

Again and again, the red-haired woman threw light from the staff. Each time that a tiny ball in the sphere was discharged, a giant ball among the trees disappeared. The darkness shrank back towards the corners. When the final minute ball was gone, the shadows had also gone to wherever they had come from.

The rolling spheres on the border burst as if they were signals sent up for a retreat, and the spheres behind them rolled away. The thunder also moved away. Silence except for his heavy breathing enclosed him. He was cold and sweating; his pajamas were soaked. The odor of his fear was heavy around him.

As swiftly as they had been lit, the flames in the hundred lamps went out. The red-haired woman took the sphere from the top of the sphinx's head and put it on the table. She placed the tip of the single torch into the socket hidden on the sphinx's head. Stover used his binoculars to zero in on her face. Her expression was so forceful, so triumphant, and so savage that it scared him. He went into his room, closed the French windows, and drank more of the barley vodka. Even it did not make him go to sleep quickly, however.

The morning of April 30th, he showered and shaved and, after some consideration, put on his barnstorming outfit instead of his civilian go-to-Sunday-meeting clothes. He felt that a uniform of some sort would be best. This was a state occasion.

His breakfast was not brought in as usual. Shortly after the clock had struck nineteen—7:00 A.M. by his watch—Captain Lamblo and six women soldiers entered. He was marched down the hall and descended the winding staircase to the ground floor. Here he was conducted into the central part, the axis of the castle, and along a high-ceilinged, very broad, red marble hall with gold statuettes on silver pedestals by the walls and thence through an arch set with rubies as large as cabbage heads into an enormous room. Its domed ceiling was at least one hundred feet high at the apex, and it was one hundred feet wide. The floor and walls were of white marble, and gigantic tapestries bearing what seemed to be historical scenes hung from the walls. There was also much gold filigree on the walls.

A crowd, perhaps three hundred people, animals, and birds, was lined up to form two sides of an aisle. The humans were dressed in uniforms or splendid formal clothes, the women wearing long ankle-length gowns and the men colorful kilts. As he was to find out later, though males wore trousers for work or everyday dress, they donned kilts for formal occasions.

At the end of the aisle, near the far wall, was a platform of marble white with seven marble steps leading up to it. Its edges were set with rubies even larger than those in the hallway. In the center was a throne carved from a giant ruby. A woman sat on a cushion on it.

This was the queen, the highest, the wise-woman, the witch-ruler, Herself, Little Mother.

The soldiers lifted their spears in salute but did not accompany Stover and Captain Lamblo toward the throne. The little blonde led him to the foot of the platform, gave the queen a sword-salute, and stepped to one side.

No one had spoken while he had walked down the aisle; no one had even coughed or sneezed or cleared his or her throat.

Hank recognized the tiny, exquisitely beautiful, auburn-haired woman on the throne. He had seen her dancing naked in the enormous room during the storm. Now she was covered from ankle to throat in a loose white gown, and, instead of a conical hat, she wore a gold crown with nine points. Inset in its front were small rubies which formed the outline of an X inside a horseshoe-shape. Her hair was now coiled around her head. Her very dark blue eyes were fixed on him. The corners of her lips were slightly dimpled as if she were thinking, "You saw me that night."

Of course, she would have known that he had witnessed that strange frightening ritual or whatever it was. She could have drawn the curtains if she had not wished anyone to see her.

Stover felt awkward bowing to her, but he thought that he should.

She inclined her head slightly in acknowledgement.

He said, "Glinda the Good, I presume?"

4

"Goodness is a relative quality," the queen said.

They were breakfasting on the balcony of her apartment. She sat on a chair and ate from dishes on a small table before her. He was in a chair and at a table which had been specially constructed for his size. Even the plates and the spoon, two-tined fork, and knife, had been made for him.

"Goodness is relative to what?" Hank said.

"Not to evil but to other goodnesses," she said. "However, I shouldn't be speaking in abstract terms. There is no such thing as goodness or evil in themselves. There are only good and evil persons. And in reality there are not even those. There are what humans have agreed among themselves to define as other good and evil persons. But the definition of good and evil by one person does not match, though it may touch or intersect, the definition of these by another person."

Stover was silent for a moment. In the first place, he was not fluent enough to be sure that he understood everything she was saying. In the second place, he was wondering if she was trying to tell him something without being specific about it.

He ate a slice of hard-boiled egg and a chunk of buttered bread. Since he'd come here, he'd had plenty of vegetables and fruit, wheat and barley, cheese, eggs, nuts, and milk. But no meat, fowl, or fish. Though he craved steak and bacon, he'd not complained. If he voiced his desires, he'd be regarded as kin to cannibals. His hosts would be disgusted and horrified.

He glanced at the male moose standing by the side of her chair and the female bald eagle roosting on a wooden beam sticking out of a wall. They had said nothing so far, but it was obvious that her bodyguards understood what their mistress and her guest were saying.

"In any event," he said, "Your Witchness must be highly respected by your people. Otherwise, they would not call you the Good."

"I'm a very good witch," she said, smiling. "In fact, I'm so good that I should be called the Best."

He started to say that she must be pulling his leg, but he restrained himself. That phrase, literally translated, would probably not be understood in the American sense.

"You're having fun with me," he said. "I'm sure that that is not what they mean by the Good."

Glinda drank some milk, and she said, "You shouldn't be so sure of that. Or of anything. As yet. And perhaps never."

She could just as well be called Glinda the Ambiguous, he thought. Glinda. That meant both The Shining One and The Swift One. Glinda must be related to, have come from the same primitive Germanic word, as the English "glint."

He sipped the warm unpasteurized milk, and he shuddered a little. It stank like a cow, and he disliked its taste. But milk was healthy for him, and he would have to change many of his habits and tastes if he stayed here. Since it did not seem likely that he would get back to Earth, he might as well start now with his naturalization.

A woman servant picked up a napkin and patted Glinda's lips with a napkin. A woman standing by Stover started to do the same for him, but he said, *"Ne, thungk thuk."* It irritated him to be waited on, literally, hand and foot. He'd been raised in a house with ten servants, but he did not like this close, intent, and hovering attention.

Glinda popped several walnuts into her mouth—thank God, the servants did not feed her, that would have been too much—and she said, "You say that you're Dorothy's son. You do have her big dark green eyes, and your face reminds me of hers. But how do I know that you really are her child?"

"Why would I lie?"

"I don't have many enemies, but they're very powerful," she said. "And very clever."

"You mean that they might import me from Earth so that I could assassinate you," he said. He laughed. Uneasy lies the head that wears a crown . . . no . . . paranoiac is the mind of the ruler.

She laughed, too, looking so beautiful that his chest ached. God, what an enchantress! Even if she was only four feet four inches tall.

"It is ridiculous, isn't it?" she said.

He held out to her the steel key and gold chain which he had removed from his leather jacket that morning.

"My mother gave me this to wear as a good-luck charm."

Glinda took it and turned it over and over. When she handed it back to him, she said, "It looks just like the key she had when she came here."

"It's the same one. I don't know if the house in which she rode the tornado into this world is still standing. But if it is, this key would unlock the front door."

"It's a state monument, and many Munchkins go to see it every year."

"I'd like to see it, too."

"You may be able to. Some day."

The servant asked softly if he was through eating or if he wished more. He told her that he was full. She probably agreed with him, since he had put away three times the amount she would have. After the table was cleared, Stover asked Glinda if he could smoke.

"Not in my presence," she said, smiling to take the sting out.

Stover put the pipe and tobacco pouch back into his jacket pocket.

"Now," she said, "you have told Lamblo your story of just how you entered into our world. But I would like it from you."

He obeyed. When he was finished, she said, "Apparently, you have no idea at all of why this happened."

"No. Does Your Witchness?"

"Not at the moment. Tell me what happened to Dorothy after I sent her home. Tell me of yourself."

That was not easy to do. He had to stop often and explain just what his references were. However, she understood more than he had thought she would, since Dorothy had explained so much to her. What a memory Glinda had! Tight as a banker's fist. She had apparently forgotten nothing his mother had told her.

Dorothy had been carried off in the farmhouse by a tornado, not a cyclone. Her uncle's farm had been a few miles out from Aberdeen, South Dakota, on that day of May 23, 1890.

"Not Kansas," he said. "South Dakota. Kansas is further south than South Dakota."

"What has South Dakota, whatever that is, to do with this?"

Stover sighed, and he said, "I wished I could sail a straight course. But we're going to be wandering through the Unexplained Seas."

"South Dakota?" she said firmly.

"What I have to explain is that an Earthman, an American, wrote a book about Dorothy's adventures here," he said. "But it was fiction or purported to be. Actually, much of it was fiction. And the parts that were true were bowdlerized. They had to be because he was writing a book for children."

"Bowdlerized?"

"Censored. Expurgated."

He had a hard time finding words which were the equivalent of censored. Finally, he gave up and defined the term.

"Mother was gone for six months, but, in the book this man, Lyman Frank Baum, wrote about her, she was here for only a few weeks. This man Baum was a fiction writer but at the time was the editor of a newspaper in Aberdeen. He heard about the little girl whom everybody thought had been carried off by the tornado. Her body was searched for but not found. People thought that she'd probably been dropped into a ravine or woods many miles from Aberdeen. Maybe the coyotes had eaten her.

"Then my mother showed up with a tale of having been transported to some unknown land beyond the desert in the Arizona Territory. At least, that's where she then thought she'd gone to. Of course, nobody believed her story about talking animals and people no taller than an eight-year-old child and an animated scarecrow and a woodman made of tin and witches and flying monkeys and all that. They thought that she was either lying or crazy."

"And so your mother quickly realized this and claimed that she had been delirious. Or something like that."

"How did you know?"

"Your mother was an extremely tough and adaptable child. Very matter of fact. She would have understood the best course to take once she saw that she was not believed."

"That's Mother all right. Rough and ready. A loving and sympathetic heart but very little sentimentality or soaring imagination. A brain as quick and tenacious as a wolf trap. Her attitude is: This is the way the world is, no matter how strange and unjust it seems, and I can handle it."

"An excellent character analysis," Glinda said. "But then what happened?"

"Baum heard about the child's story and went out to the farm to talk to her. Though he did not—probably—believe her, he pretended to. He took notes after his three conversations with her, but he did not print a word of it in the newspaper. That would have embarrassed Dorothy and her aunt and uncle and caused even more ridicule and doubt about her sanity or veracity. But he did not forget her fantastic tale, and, later, he used his notes as the basis for *The Wonderful Wizard of Oz*.

"It was very successful, a best seller," Stover said. "Mother was very surprised when she read it and also angry because of the liberties Baum took with her story. She thought about writing him and telling him so. But she cooled off quickly—Mother is very stable—and she decided to ignore it. After all, what else could she do? She did not want publicity. She wouldn't like it nor would her husband and his parents, and she'd be accused of being insane. So she did nothing about it."

Dorothy did, however, read *The Wonderful Wizard of Oz* aloud to her son when he was five. He was entranced by it, and, when the sequels came out, he read them over and over again.

"When I was eight, my mother told me that she had been to this world and that she was the Dorothy in Baum's books. At least, that she was the child on whose adventures Baum had based his first book. The sequels were all fictional, of course, except for a few items like personal and geographical names. I was both stunned and delighted to find this out, though I was disappointed, frustrated, because she'd made me swear never to tell anyone about her revelation."

Though he was often tempted to tell his playmates that his mother was the Dorothy of Oz, he did not. Then, when he got older, he lost his belief in the existence of Oz. He decided that his mother had been fantasizing. But he was not sure. She was not the joking kind nor would she have lied to her child. To anyone, in fact.

One day, when he was eleven, he brought the subject up. He asked her if she had indeed been telling him the truth or was she merely entertaining him and making him feel important because his mother had been the heroine of a child's book?

She had gotten angry, though not for long. She had taken him into her bedroom and unlocked a little bureau. Out of the drawer she took a small iron box. She unlocked that and took from it, not the treasure he had expected, jewels or gold or a dagger, but a common steel housekey.

"Mother said, 'This is the key to the door of the house that was carried by the tornado to the land of the Munchkins.' "

Stover had gazed awestricken at it.

" 'I wish that Uncle Henry and Aunt Em were still alive,' Mother said. 'They could tell you that, after I'd returned from the Quadling country, I had a shining spot on my forehead. It was visible at day, and at night it gleamed brightly. That was the mark that the witch of the North set on my forehead to indicate that I was under her protection. That mark was the main reason why my aunt and uncle believed my story. But they were not dumb. They knew that I'd be subject to all sorts of publicity and pestering by curiosity-seekers and newspaper reporters and that I'd be ridiculed and mocked or exploited. They made me put face-powder on it. They also told me to keep quiet about where I'd been. But I couldn't help telling other children. They told their parents, and word got around. Of course, I was bound to be a celebrity, since everybody thought that the tornado had carried me and the house off, and I was a seven days' wonder when I showed up. But Uncle Henry put out that I'd been wandering around all that time and that I'd had amnesia—forgot who I was—and had also suffered from brain fever. That's what he told Mr. Baum when he came out to see me.' "

Stover continued, "Uncle Henry had assumed that Dorothy was dead, and he wanted to hold services for her. But Aunt Em told him that they wouldn't consider her dead until it was proven. She had faith that Dorothy still lived, and she prayed a lot for her."

"Surely the newspapers would at least have reported that she had appeared after she was thought to be dead? The reporters would have wanted her story of how she'd survived."

"Yes, especially in that small community where even a tea party was a hot item. The story about her seemingly miraculous escape from death and her amnesia and all that was printed. My mother kept it in a scrapbook and showed it to me."

"Why did this Baum put Dorothy in the state of Kansas?"

"I don't know. Maybe he didn't want to be sued by my mother. As I said, he fictionalized her story, put stuff in it that didn't happen."

He told Glinda about the chapter in which Dorothy and her companions on the quest, the Cowardly Lion, the Tin Woodman, Toto the dog, and the Scarecrow, discovered a city of living dolls.

"Even Baum's most ardent admirers feel that that chapter had no place there, that it was contrived and didn't work. But he did other things, too, all accountable by his desire to write a children's book. It had to be quick and simple reading, and the action had to move smoothly and swiftly. Thus, he ignored the fact that the people of your world would not speak English. He didn't tell the truth, which was that Mother didn't set out at once on the Yellow Brick Road. She had to stay where she'd landed for a month in order to learn the Munchkin language. She's a whizbang at picking up foreign tongues. I'm pretty good, but she outshines me by far."

"All this is interesting," the queen said. "But you still haven't told me of her later life."

"Sorry. I have to fill in the background. Otherwise, you won't know what I'm talking about."

Glinda smiled and said, "I may know more than you think I do."

Hank stared at her for a moment.

"I wouldn't be surprised. I'll ask you some time what you mean by that."

5

His mother had lived the hard struggling life of a Dakota farmgirl until she was almost sixteen. She'd gone to the local grade school and high school and also read much whenever she had the chance.

"Which wasn't often, since she helped with the house chores and even with the plowing and reaping."

But life as a whole was easier and better than before her visit to the other world. Dorothy was hardheaded but not so much that she wasn't also somewhat superstitious. She attributed the improvement to, one, the blessing the North Witch had given her and, two, to the housekey. That had become a semimagical token. But when Uncle Henry was killed by the kick of a mule and, two weeks later, Aunt Em died of a heart attack, Dorothy thought her luck had run out.

"However, she realized some profit from the sale of the farm. She couldn't get her hands on the lump sum because she was a ward of the court, and it was doled out to her for her living expenses and education. She quit high school and went to a business college in Iowa. Then she told the lawyers handling her affairs that she was going to New York to be a stenographer and secretary. They objected, but she went anyway. She got a job by lying about her age. At the same time, she looked for openings in dramas or musical comedies. Mother was—is, even at forty-one—a good-looker."

He was going to say that she had legs almost as good as Glinda's, but he decided that that might not be discreet.

His mother got a job as a dancer in a chorus line in a very successful Broadway production. Shortly afterwards, she met Lincoln

Stover, the only child of a wealthy stockbroker. Lincoln was ten years older than Dorothy, and he was a regular stage-door Johnny.

Hank explained this term.

"His parents came from distinguished families, Massachusetts pioneers who came from England in the early 1630s."

Lincoln Stover, Hank's father, was born in Oyster Bay, Long Island, an area where great estates were owned by such as Louis Tiffany and F.W. Woolworth and where Theodore Roosevelt had a home, his summer White House. Lincoln's parents expected him to follow in his father's footsteps, and so he did—except that he did not marry a daughter of a wealthy New York family. Instead, he fell almost violently in love with Dorothy and proposed marriage.

Mr. and Mrs. Robert Stover, Hank's grandparents, were both affronted and aghast. Lincoln just *could* not—could *not*—marry the penniless and pedigreeless daughter and niece of poor dirt farmers. Though threatened with disinheritance, Lincoln ran off with Dorothy to the wild state of Nevada, where the parson who married them failed to ask the age of the bride.

Perhaps it was the fait accompli that caused the Robert Stovers to tell Lincoln Stover and Dorothy to come home, all was forgiven. A second and lawful marriage was made. And, after Lincoln's father and mother had gotten to know Dorothy well, they not only accepted her, but came to love her.

"Which was pretty good for such snobs," Hank said.

"Your mother was a remarkable person," Glinda said. "Also, very lovable."

"If I weren't so modest, I'd tell you how much like her I am," Hank said.

Both laughed.

Ah, he thought, if only you would love me, Glinda. You'd find me a giant not only in size but in love.

He resumed his biography. When the United States declared war on Germany, August 6, 1917, he was in prep school. He'd quit during his last semester to enlist in the Army Air Service in February, 1918. The previous summer, he'd taken flying lessons. In September he was transported to France, and he flew a Spad pursuit from September 20th until November 11th, the day of the Armistice. He'd been in five dogfights but had shot down only one plane, and he'd had to share that victory with his commander.

When he was discharged, he'd bummed around in Sweden, Denmark, Germany, Italy, and Spain. On returning, he'd finished his prep school education and had started at Yale. But he was passionately in love with flying, and he was too old and experienced to enjoy being a freshman. The summer of 1921 he'd told his parents that he wasn't going back to college. Not for a while, anyway. He wanted to be a barnstormer. Lincoln and Dorothy objected very much, but he was as bullheaded as they. Off he'd gone with the Jenny his father had purchased for him, promising to pay him back from the money he made on his tours.

"Dad refused to have anything to do with me until I gave up all that romantic idiocy, as he called it. Mother had begged me to finish school first and then go, as she put it, skylarking. She was mad at me, too, but she did write me long letters. Oh, yes, I forgot. The housekey. She gave it to me just before I embarked for France. She said it had always brought her luck, and maybe it would for me. I certainly would need it, she said."

Glinda handed the key back to him. "It has been in many far-off places."

He then told her again how he had happened to pass through the green cloud into this world.

"Very rarely," she said, "there is a brief opening in the walls that separate our two worlds. Usually, they occur far above ground, though at one time there must have been some at surface level. They are a natural unpredictable phenomenon, and, for some reason, it is much more difficult to get from your world into mine than the other way around."

"I can't go back?" Hank said. "But my mother . . ."

"It's not impossible. Just hard. As I was about to say before you interrupted, stories handed down by our ancestors indicate that they passed through some openings into this world about 1500 or so years ago. More than one tribe and parts of tribes and some individuals came through. Animals, birds, and reptiles, too. And, of course, insects.

"At that time, the openings must have lasted longer than they do now. Perhaps they moved more swiftly and swept some areas, scooped up, as it were, areas containing living beings. We really don't know what happened.

"In any event, it seems that the openings, from what little we know about them, drifted westward. But, regardless of their location on

Earth, their other side, that which gave access to this world, has always been fixed in this area, Amariiki.''

"May I interrupt again, Your Witchness?''

"Zha, thu mag.'' ("Yes, you may.'')

"What if the openings were partly below the surface of the earth? Would they, when they ceased to be open, quit operating, remove the earth from the other world, too? And the vegetation?''

"I don't know. I think that something, perhaps the Earth's radiations . . .''

Hank thought, Earth currents?

". . . prevented the openings from existing below the ground and water levels of your world and mine. However, when my ancestors got here, they found some humans who spoke a different language. They were tiny, and very hairy, white-skinned, had huge supraorbital ridges, weak chins, breadloaf-shaped skulls, and thick bones.''

Neanderthals? Hank thought.

Glinda said that these were either exterminated or absorbed by her ancestors. During this long process, her ancestors borrowed words from the languages of the vanquished. Thus, names such as Quadling, Winkie, Munchkin, and Gillikin were derived from the firstcomers.

In about ten generations after entering this world, her ancestors had shrunk to their present size. About this time, other tribes came in, and there was war. But these newcomers also shrank in ten generations, and eventually Glinda's ancestors absorbed them. According to the tales, they called themselves the People of Morrigan.

Morrigan? Hank thought. A goddess of the ancient Irish?

Glinda said that there were still some villages in mountainous northeast Gillikinland which spoke dialects descended from the invaders' speech.

Glinda continued. The third people to come were also giants, very dark, and had straight black hair, broad faces, high cheekbones, and big bold noses. They, too, shrank while they were warring with their predecessors. Eventually, they established residence behind the mountain range that cut off the northwestern area of this giant oasis.

"What really bothers me, Your Witchness, is, uh, well, how can an inanimate object, the Scarecrow, for instance, become alive? Not only that, but how can it be intelligent, able to speak? How can something made of cloth and straw, something that lacks a skeleton, muscles, nerves, blood, how can that walk? How can it talk when its mouth is only painted on, how see when its eyes are also painted on? How . . .?"

He jumped, startled, when a bird shot in and then floated to a landing on the back of a chair.

Glinda gave a start, too, and spoke angrily to the bird.

It was a goshawk, and it answered in the voice that still made him uneasy when he heard it. He just could not get used to animals and birds talking, especially when the voices sounded as if they were issuing from a gramophone. They all sounded much alike to him. It made no difference if a small-throated hawk or a large-throated cow spoke. The pitch remained the same, though the loudness differed. The one should have been piping, the other bass. But they were not.

"Pardon, Little Mother," the goshawk said. "I would have announced myself to your guards, but I bring very important news!"

"The pardon depends upon the importance of what you bring me," Glinda said. "What is it?"

"A small green cloud suddenly appeared out in the desert, and a flying machine, something like the giant's, shot through. But it did not continue to fly. Something had cut it in half, and it fell to the ground. It is burning on the ground now."

6

Hank Stover shot out of his chair.

"Exactly where is it?" he cried.

The goshawk looked at Glinda. She nodded.

"Exactly south of the castle. About three miles straight from here."

Glinda rose and said, "Eight miles by the road. Stop!"

Hank turned. "Yes, Little Mother?"

"I can understand your impatience to get there. But you do not walk out in my presence unless I grant permission."

"Sorry, Your Witchness."

Glinda rapidly gave some orders, and she walked out with her bodyguard and Stover trailing. He wanted to run, but he had to walk, and he could not even do that quickly. Glinda's legs, though long in proportion to her trunk, were short compared to his. Fuming, jittering, he matched his pace to hers as they went down the hall and then the stairway to the ground floor. The goshawk had flown ahead to transmit her commands. By the time the party got to the front entrance, it found chariots awaiting it. Hank got into the vehicle driven by the blonde, Lamblo, and bent down so that he could grip the railing. The two moose pulling it would have a heavier load than the others. His weight was over three times Lamblo's.

Presently, the queen, sitting on an attached bench in the lead chariot, gave the word to proceed. Her driver, standing up, shouted at the moose to go at top pace. She did not use reins and was not so much the driver as the director. Sentient animals did not need these and would have resented them.

They raced across the drawbridge and out through the enormous gateway of the outer walls. The people caught unawares scattered before them. Then they were going east on the red brick road and were quickly past the walls. Hank, looking south, saw the black plume of smoke from the burning aircraft.

A mile from the castle, the chariots turned south onto a dirt road. It soon left the plateau and began winding down the face of the cliff. It was just wide enough for two small wagons to pass each other, but the moose took the inner curves as if they were sure that they'd not meet anyone coming from the other direction. Hank hoped they were right.

Lamblo had to shout several times at her animals to slow down, and once she pulled on the brake handle by her side. Somehow, the whole cavalcade—cervuscade?—got down to the bottom without accident. Here, Hank thought, the animals would slow down, take a breather. But no. Now they were going even faster. The trees on the sides of the road flashed by. Eventually, his weight began to tell on Lamblo's beasts, and the chariot dropped behind the others. Glinda, looking back, shouted something, and the others checked their pace.

They came from the semidarkness of the heavy woods into bright sunlight. The desert lay before them. Tawny sand and red and black rocks of from house-size to egg-size. Glinda stopped the chariots. When Hank's pulled near hers, she said, "We'll walk from here."

He did not have to ask her why. Pulling the vehicles through that rugged, ragged waste would have worn out the moose more in a mile than the six miles of racing.

He wondered if that was the only reason when he saw boxes unloaded from the only four-wheeled chariot. They were opened, and the contents passed out. Hank took three of the thin iron javelins Lamblo handed him.

"What're these for?"

The snub-nosed blonde pointed at a white arc springing from one high rock to another.

"They're not dangerous if you don't get in their path. But if any roll at you, throw one of these through it."

She spread her palms up and outwards.

"Gaguum!"

Which was Quadling for "Boom!"

"They explode. Usually, anyway. Sometimes, you have to throw a second one through them."

Javelins were not their only protection. As they walked out slowly, they were joined by a group that had arrived a few minutes behind them. These were archers, male and female, their arrows tipped with round iron balls. The weight of these would prevent long-range shooting, but, apparently, they were thought adequate for their purpose. The archers formed a circle around the queen's party.

They went up a tortured slope of projecting sheets of rocks and pockets of sand. When they got to its top, they could see the wreck burning on the downward side of the slope. Dark marks on the rock showed where the craft had struck near the end of a slanting sheet, had bounced, and then had slid down the bottom half of the grayish apron. Hank wanted to urge more speed; he was vibrating with curiosity. But Glinda walked slowly, and nobody was going to break the discipline of matching the pace with her.

She stopped for a moment and looked around.

"Good!" she said. "No *fizhanam* in sight. They do, however, come up swiftly, Hank."

The searing heat from the flaming wreck kept them from getting closer than a hundred feet. There was nothing to do but to wait for the flames to die and the metal to cool. Or so Hank thought. Twenty minutes later, more soldiers and moose came, hauling with much labor six four-wheeled wagons. These held tanks and pumping machinery. A greenish foam was sprayed from three of them, and this quickly smothered the burning gasoline. Then water was pumped from the other three to dissipate the foam and cool the hot metal.

Hank had thought that the Quadling technology was at about what it had been on Earth in A.D. 1300. But even A.D. 1923 did not have this fire-quenching foam. He had better wait until he was familiar with this culture before he made any conclusions about the comparative advancement of science and technology here and on Earth.

He could now get near enough for a closer look at the wreck. Breathing through his mouth because of the stomach-churning stench of roasted flesh, he walked around the wreck and also looked at the pieces that had been scattered by the two impacts. The hawk had reported correctly. The fuselage had been severed about three feet behind the rear cockpit as if by a giant's sword. The missing part might be out on the desert to the south, but he doubted it. It was probably lying on Kansas soil.

The burned and twisted skeleton of the plane looked like that of a D.H.4B, a two-seater scout and light bomber biplane. The Army Air

Service had over a thousand of them. It usually carried two .30-caliber machine guns in front of the pilot in the front cockpit and one mounted by the rear cockpit. The two fore guns, bent, lay about thirty yards ahead of the wreck. There was no third machine gun visible. Hank thought that it may have been removed from its mounting before the plane took off for the fatal mission.

Normally, the D.H.4B carried two men, but there was only one, the charred mass in the pilot's seat.

However, the crash had hurled from the rear cockpit some cartons of ammunition, a BAR (Browning Automatic .30-caliber assault rifle) 1918 model, a smashed camera, and cases containing film. The BAR was undamaged except for some scratches.

He stood by while soldiers got the body out of the cockpit. When it was laid out on the rock, he forced himself to approach it. Though he had seen some badly burned corpses in France and two at a Missouri landing strip, he felt like vomiting. The gloves and clothes had been burned away, and the boots fell off in strips while the body was being carried. The fingers were missing. The face was smashed in, but it would have been gone anyway. The goggles had been knocked off the head. The ears and nose were gone, and the eyesockets were empty.

He looked into the black mass of the face and wondered what the pilot had looked like when alive. Grimacing, he searched for dog tags but could find none. If the man had identifying papers on him, they had been destroyed by fire. However, the two gold bars embedded in the fried flesh showed that he had been a first lieutenant.

A soldier brought a charred belt and holster containing a Colt .45 automatic pistol. The ammunition in its clip had exploded and destroyed the weapon.

However, some of the boxes thrown out of the rear cockpit held loaded magazine boxes for the BAR, and others contained ammunition which would fit his New Service revolver. And he had plans for making more.

Glinda seemed to be undisturbed by the ghastly stinking thing on the rock. Some of the soldiers, however, were retching, and many were as pale as he probably looked.

Glinda asked him some questions about the airplane. Hank replied that the flying machine was a military one. He was assuming that it had been sent through the green haze on orders.

"Are you thinking as I am?" she said. "That the hazes through which you and this man came through are not natural openings? That they were made by your people?''

''I may be wrong,'' he said, ''but they could be the results of experiments by the Signal Corps. Its headquarters are at Fort Leavenworth. Still . . .''

He did not believe that forcing the openings could have been the goal of the Signal Corps. These had come about as accidental by-products—what was the word?—serendipitous, from serendipity, coined by Horace Walpole in the eighteenth century? At least, the first time had been unforeseen, but the second time must have been on purpose.

''If they were formed by your people,'' she said, ''they don't know how to keep them stable. And you must have accidentally come across one and flown through. I wonder if that was their first attempt or if others had been made before then?''

''I don't know. They must have been surprised when I disappeared into the haze. If they saw me, that is. But I think they did. That would explain why they sent an Army plane through.''

The big brass must be wondering what the hell is going on, he thought. They had probably clamped a security lid on the project. Though they had probably done that from the beginning, before the haze appeared.

Glinda gave some orders. A leather bag was brought from a wagon, and the body was stuffed into it. Six of the huskier troops carried it off and placed it on top of a firefighting wagon and tied it down with ropes. Hank marvelled at Glinda's foresight in bringing the bag. She must have been shaken by the plane's sudden appearance and destruction. Yet she had calmly made arrangements for the disposal of the body. In fact, since she could not know how many men there were in the craft, she'd ordered six leather bags.

At Hank's request, Glinda had the machine guns put on the wagon.

''Is there anything else you'd like brought to the castle? We should be leaving as soon as possible.''

She looked up at the bright blue sky where at least a hundred birds, lookouts, were wheeling. If they spotted a nearby *fizhanam*, they'd notify her.

''Nothing,'' he said.

They walked back through the desert and rode the chariots to the castle. The body was taken on a cart down a ramp into the underground. Hank had expected to be questioned by the queen, but she told Captain Lamblo to take care of Hank. If he wished to go to town or retire to his apartment, whatever he wished, she should see that it was done.

"Within reason, my dear," Glinda said, and she smiled.

Glinda went off accompanied by her high-ranking officers and government officials. Hank looked down at the exquisite little blonde, who was smiling up at him.

She must be tired of looking up my nostrils, he thought. In some ways, it's an advantage to be a giant. In other ways, no.

Though he was twice as tall as she, he did not scare her. Almost from the beginning of their acquaintance, she had been at ease with him, maybe too familiar. She could be a smartass now and then.

"Well, *magla* (little boy), what is your desire?" she said, smiling.

"I think, *mawlo* (little girl), that I'll check up on my *luftskip* (airship)."

"Very well. You may look at it, but the queen said that you couldn't—not yet, anyway—get into it."

"Her trust warms the cockles of my heart. Where did she think I could go?"

But if he'd been in Glinda's place, he would have done the same.

They rode in her chariot to the meadow where the hangar had been built around the Jenny. There were also two guards there at all times to keep the curious from damaging her. Hank was delighted when he saw the plane's painted smiling face. It was like seeing an old friend, his only reminder of Earth.

He gave her a good inspection while Lamblo watched him as she chatted with the two female soldiers. She wasn't the only one with eyes on him. The two cows nearby observed him with their big brown eyes and occasionally made low remarks in the eerie voices. They resembled Black Anguses except for their size. Hank glanced at them now and then, seeing not the living animals but thick juicy rare-done steaks. Though he felt ashamed, as if he were contemplating cannibalism, he could not dissolve the mental image nor stanch the saliva flow.

He would soon have to replace his gasoline with grain alcohol. He would have to increase the size of the jet openings to the carburetor because alcohol was less efficient as fuel. That was no problem. The Quadlings had the equipment to do that. He would also have to advance the spark ignition because alcohol burned slower than gasoline. The engine would give him starting problems, but he could get

ether to put into the carburetor before he started it. His flight range
would be shorter.

There was plenty of castor oil to use for engine lubrication.

Spare parts would be a problem. He would also need replacement
batteries, but he could get these made—he hoped.

There was no rubber for the two wheels, but he could use iron-
rimmed wooden wheels. The landings would be harder, but what the
hell.

He would have to train mechanics . . .

Suddenly, he knew that he was planning on staying here. Why not?
He was like a 20th-century Columbus who'd discovered, not a
continent, but an entire planet.

Yet . . . if a green haze should show up and he could fly back
through it to Earth, would he turn away from it?

He did not know yet. The chances were that he would never have
to make a decision.

Having satisfied himself that the Jenny was ready to fly at a
moment's notice, he left the barn. Lamblo, giggling at something a
guard had said, followed him. They rode into the town, which held
about ten thousand citizens, not counting the animals and birds. Its
red-brick main street ran for six blocks and was lined mostly with
stores selling various goods. The sidestreets near it were mixed
residential and business areas, and these were not longer than four
blocks. The big square was where the farmers and vendors came to
sell their products. The town hall, the military recruiting headquarters,
a printing press, the weekly local newspaper, library, two temples, and
some other buildings also fronted the square.

"Suthwarzha (Southguard) is the largest community of Quadlingland," Lamblo said. "It's as big as the capital of Oz, though not
nearly as splendid, from what I've heard."

Oz, which had an area about equal to Rhode Island's, was the
central sovereign state of this oasis-land. It was bordered on the north
by Gillikinland, on the east by Munchkinland, on the west by
Winkieland, and on the south by Quadlingland. The northwest part of
Gillikinland, however, was where the dark-skinned Natawey dwelt.
Hank's mother had not reported that because she had never heard of it.

Nor was the entire oasis-land called Oz. Readers of Baum's first
book knew that Oz was the small country in the middle of the land and

not the name for the whole area. But in his second book, Baum decided to extend the name to cover the whole land.

Hank had been so influenced by Baum's series that he tended to think of the oasis-country as the Land of Oz, though he knew better.

Now, as he walked under the bright sky through the noisy crowded market of the town square, he thought of many things. It was impossible for him to concentrate on one subject because there were so many distractions. A cross section of an alien culture was around him.

What occupied his mind for a moment was the role and status of animals. He saw a group of men, women, beasts, and birds entering the granite three-story-high town hall. He asked the blonde about them. Lamblo said that they were the elected representatives of the Quadling people. Hank decided that they would be called senators in the U.S. He felt again the slight disorientation and numbness of mind. Cattle, moose, deer, sheep, eagles, robins, cats, and . . . bullsnakes! These were senators?

"Why not?" Lamblo said.

Hank did not answer that. He would have had to describe the difference between American and Quadling political systems, and that would have plunged him into the lack of sentiency in Terrestrial animals, and that would have swept him into only-God-knew-what. He was here to learn, not to teach. At least, he was as of today.

He was told that, though nonhumans were citizens and had the right to vote, they were the descendants of slaves. In many respects, they were still second class. They just were not as intelligent, in the main, anyway, as humans. They had never produced philosophy, music, literature, painting, sculpture, science, technology, and new institutions. They were dominated by instinct much more than their human cousins were.

Hank questioned her further. In this world, all governments except the Natawey's were benevolent despotisms. Though sometimes, as during the reign of the late Witches of the East and the West, the despotism had been malevolent.

However, though the supreme rulership was based on heredity or a coup d'etat or just the very long life of the ruler, there was no nobility and the lower levels of government were quite democratic. The officials of the local and county governments and much of the state government were elected by popular vote.

"How long have women had the vote?" Hank said. He was thinking that in his own country, up until a little more than two years ago, they had been denied suffrage in most states.

"For at least a thousand years," Lamblo said.

In America, Negroes had the right to vote but were afraid in many areas to go to the polls. And Indians were denied the right.

"A philosopher of my world, I forget his name, said that the best government was a benevolent despotism. The main trouble with that system was that the despot died, and usually someone not so benevolent took over the reins of power."

"Is that so?" Lamblo said. "We haven't had that disadvantage in Quadlingland. Our queen has reigned over us for almost three hundred years."

Hank would have been more staggered by this revelation if he had not been conditioned to accept it by Baum's Oz series. Though he had thought that Glinda's longevity was a fiction, some part of his mind had accepted it as true.

"She looks as if she is only twenty-five."

"She's looked that way for two hundred and seventy-five years."

"What's her secret?"

"Witchcraft, of course," Lamblo looked puzzled. "But she is a white witch. Her long life and non-aging come from a different source than that of the red witches."

"Which is what?"

"I don't know. If I did, I'd be a witch, too."

She wrinkled her snub nose. "Maybe. It takes great courage, some say great foolishness, to be a witch or wizard. And, though the advantages are great, there is always a great price to pay."

"What is the price?"

"I don't know. I wouldn't dare ask Queen Glinda, and even the priests and priestesses won't say. Probably because they don't know."

If there was true magic in this world, then its principles of physics were not quite the same as in his world. But he had had evidence from the beginning that this was not just an exact counterpart of Earth.

He shook his head as if his thoughts were drops of water he was trying to shake off. Too much data was coming in too fast. He was confused. To the confused, the world was chaos. He needed time and experience to sort out the facts. He had to organize them into a system his mind could be comfortable with.

He would not, however, be as comfortable as these people. They apparently just accepted what was and did not question it. But then, he was, in his own world, much like them. Why did he accept the ''law'' of gravity, for instance? Or the principle that all people were, in theory at least, politically equal? Or that he had a right to eat meat because cows and pigs could not speak?

Yes, but what about the carnivorous domestic creatures, the cats and hawks? What did they eat?

He sighed. He must be patient, take his time.

Nevertheless, he could not stop asking questions.

7

Hank knew from the maps his instructors had shown him that this oasis-land was about the area of Alaska. People had been here for thousands of years, yet it was not crowded. There were many large forests and comparatively uninhabited mountain areas. Why was the land not jammed with humans? Especially when they seemed to be much healthier, much less disease-ridden, than those on Earth?

"The wise rulers of the past knew that they would soon run out of land on which to grow crops for the ever-increasing people. The trees would all be cut down. The rivers and lakes would be poisoned. There would be terrible wars for the land and the water. In time, this green land might become like the desert surrounding it.

"So they used a medicine made from a Natawey plant. This made males sterile while it was being taken. And laws were passed that only so many babies could be born, just enough to replace the dead. Of course, the number of babies was allowed to increase until the number of people had reached the estimated maximum. I mean, the maximum that the land could support and still have many woods. Though it was long ago determined that this land could feed and house even more, it was decreed that the limit not be exceeded. That was a thousand years ago, and since then the laws have been strictly enforced."

Hank was skeptical. What about passion and negligence? What happened when the male neglected to take the contraceptive but nevertheless impregnated a woman? What about the babies born from rape?

"No innocents of *Guth* (God) are killed!" Lamblo said. "That would be horrible! Unthinkable! Surely, your people don't murder babies?''

Hank hesitated, then said, ''Only from anger or cruelty or negligence or indifference or madness. It . . .''

''Only?''

Her blue eyes were wide; her mouth open.

''I mean that it's not from policy. It . . .''

He stopped. He did not want to be sidetracked into this kind of conversation.

''What happens to the male?''

''He's sterilized.''

''What if he commits rape?''

The case was thoroughly investigated to make sure of the circumstances in which the crime occurred. Whatever the situation, even if the woman was partly at fault, the male was sterilized. But a man who'd been seduced suffered no other judicial punishment. Where the man had no excuse at all, he was killed.

''How?''

''His head is chopped off.''

''What's the punishment for other crimes?''

If what she said was true, crime was much less frequent here. Maybe that was because of the smallness and closeness of most communities.

Murder and rape and illegal fatherhood were capital crimes. So was the attempted assassination of the ruler. Other offenses seemed to bring light sentences—from his viewpoint, anyway.

Hank was impressed by the comparatively small number of insane and by the therapy they got. But then these people could afford to treat the insane well because of their rareness. However, it said much for their mental health that insanity was so rare.

''But if an unexpected pregnancy occurs, does that mean that someone who might have been allowed a baby has to do without?''

''No. The unscheduled baby is given to the woman who would have been scheduled to have one of her own.''

''That seems cruel to both the mother who has to give up her child and to the woman who can't then bear her own.''

''Life is a compromise,'' Lamblo said. ''Give and take. What hurts one blesses another—perhaps. In any case, the laws try to make sure that there's not too much hurt for some and too many blessings for others. The system isn't perfect. Is yours nearly as good? Better?''

Hank did not reply.

He decided he wanted to return to his suite, take a shower, drink some booze, do some thinking. Lamblo had purchased a bottle of this world's equivalent of Scotch. It had been imported from Gillikinland because Quadlingland did not have the environmental requirements for making it. Since trade between these countries was very limited, the price was very high.

"The Queen is paying for it," Lamblo said. "But I imagine that she'll get from you what you owe her for it. In one way or another."

Much of the business was done by barter, but there were coins of various denominations. Gold and silver, being so common, were not the bases of the money system. Instead, copper and nickel were used.

They started walking toward Lamblo's parked chariot. On the way, Hank wondered what means were used to keep the domestic nonhuman population down. Lamblo said that they, too, used the contraceptive liquids.

Hank said, "But what about the wild animals?"

"They eat each other," she said, shuddering.

Hank dropped behind to look at some tobacco on a stand. But he forgot about that because of the entrancing swing of Lamblo's hips. Holy smoke! Now there was something that was the same on both worlds. And it had been so long, far too long . . .

Lamblo turned when she became aware he was no longer with her. She must have read his expression. She smiled knowingly, and she walked back to him.

"Well, Handsome Giant?"

He cleared his throat.

"Well, ah, I was just thinking. Why haven't I been given this sterilizing drink?"

"Because you've been a prisoner until today. However, the queen has ordered me to put in a supply for you and to make sure that you drink it daily."

"Yes?" he said, studying her.

"You'll get it as soon as you return to your rooms."

"Why would I need it?" he said. He waved a hand to indicate the tiny people around them. "I'm so big. It seems impossible."

She burst out laughing.

"Just how much experience have you had with women?"

His face warmed.

"Plenty."

"I don't really doubt that, *magla*. But they must all have been giantesses. I assure you that little women have no trouble with big men."

How would you know? He did not voice the thought; it would have been indiscreet.

She touched the back of his hand with a finger, an exquisite finger, a child's. The contact made tiny lightning balls roll over him and through him.

"Come," she said in a suddenly husky voice.

She turned and walked to the chariot. He followed her and got into the vehicle. After making sure that he was holding the front rail, she told the two moose to return to the castle as quickly as possible. They started trotting, but one of them turned his head and said, "You promised we could have the rest of the day off."

Lamblo laughed and said, "Very well. But you talk too much."

Hank raised his eyebrows. Had she planned this? Well, what if she had?

He scarcely noticed anything during the trip back. When they were in his apartment, Lamblo at once went to a table on which was a bottle of red-purple fluid, the spermatocide. She opened it, saying, "The other bottles will be in the chest of drawers by your bed."

She poured out about six ounces into a stone cup carved into a gargoyle face. Hank took it by the big flaring ears and gulped the stuff down. It tasted like a mixture of walnuts and cranberry juice, and something unidentifiable, sharp yet pleasant.

"It'll take full effect in fifteen minutes," Lamblo said.

He belched but did not excuse himself. Quadling custom did not require that. Neither did flatulence unless it occurred in the presence of the queen.

Lamblo sat down in the chair used by the instructors. She started to take off a calf-length boot. "I'll take a bath."

"Must you?"

She removed the other boot and then her socks.

"*Himin!* (Heavens!) My feet are so dirty!"

"It's good clean dirt," he said thickly.

She rose and unbuttoned her jacket. "Very well."

"It's been so long that it won't take long," he said. "The first time."

She smiled. "Your conference with Little Mother isn't until after breakfast."

Hank hated himself at that moment, though not overly much. He wished that it was Glinda, not Lamblo, standing before him.

That's not fair to her, he thought. But when had anybody anywhere ever been fair in this situation?

Lamblo's eyes widened.

"You are indeed a giant, *magla*."

8

Hank had always had to have several cups of coffee before breakfast. It was the only way to start the day. He was out of luck here. He could not, however, be grumpy with Lamblo. After their long night, he'd have been a real heel to treat her churlishly. So he forced himself to smile and to chat away lightly, though he seldom spoke a word until coffee had humanized him.

He drank the apple juice instead of the warm milk—he couldn't down that so early—and he ate his egg omelette mixed with walnuts, his delicious brown bread and butter and jam, and slices of a melon. The latter must be indigenous; it tasted different from any he'd ever had.

Oh, God, for coffee and orange juice and bacon in the morning! And for roast beef and ham and chicken and turkey and mashed potatoes, and tomatoes in his salad, and bananas and peanut butter! At least, he had apples. The ancient Goths had been introduced to the apple tree by the Romans, and seedlings had been brought into this world by the ancestors of the Amariikians. They had also brought in lettuce. Which meant that the ancestors were probably Ostrogoths, East European or maybe even Asia Minor tribes. Lettuce had not been grown in western Europe until the Middle Ages.

After eating, they shared a pipe, and then she said that she had to report for duty.

She indicated the bottle of *afseth*. "Don't forget to take it. You should get in the habit of drinking it as soon as you get out of bed. If you should forget it, the previous dosage will keep you sterile for from three to four days. But you shouldn't take a chance."

47

"Yes, dear."

She laughed and kissed him warmly for a long time.

"Will I see you soon?" he said after she had pushed herself away.

"Tonight. I'll be here—unless the queen has something for me to do. She might. There's the Gillikin crisis, and . . ."

"Crisis?"

"The queen will tell you all about it. So long, lover."

She was delightful. Fun. Passionate. He was very fond of her, but he was not in love with her. From her attitude, he judged that he was not supposed to be. She was on a sexual lark, and she was not thinking about marrying him. Or, if she was, she was wise enough not to mention it.

The use of the *afseth* drink had had an effect on mores similar to the introduction of the automobile and the cheap condom in the United States. Actually, its effect had been much greater because it had been a part of this society for a thousand years. It had freed men and women in many respects, though Hank wasn't sure that he approved of some of these. The young adults were expected to have as many sexual partners as they wanted. But, once they were married, they were to be faithful to their spouses. Whether the expectations were more lived up to here than on Earth, Hank didn't know.

These people, though pygmies, were not the simplified childlike characters of Baum's Oz book. That was essentially a moral fable cast in a fairy land. His Dorothy had been looking for a way to get home, his Cowardly Lion had wanted courage, his Tin Woodman had desired a heart, his Scarecrow had wished for brains. They had gone through many adventures to get to the man who was supposed to be able to give them what they wished for. But the Wizard of Oz, though a humbug, had seen that three of them already had what they sought. Unable to convince them of that, he gave the Lion a drink which he said was liquid courage, gave the Tin Woodman a velvet heart stuffed with sawdust, and gave the Scarecrow brains of bran mixed with pins. These material tokens were not magical, but they gave the three the assurance that they had what they thought they had lacked. The Wizard's magic was based on psychology only, but the shrewd old circus showman knew what he was doing.

Dorothy had been wearing something which could have gotten her home shortly after she had arrived in Munchkinland. This was the pair of silver shoes she had taken from the dead and dried-away Witch of the East. The Wizard had not known that. It was Glinda who, at the end of Dorothy's odyssey, had told her that.

The Wonderful Wizard of Oz was a children's classic. And it could also delight and inform adults whose imagination had not been slain by the dragons of maturity.

Dorothy had outlined her story to Baum. It had been simple and swift enough then, but Baum had reduced and speeded it up even more. He was a story-teller artist who left out what he did not think suitable for a young child's tale, and he had added touches here and there that were not in Dorothy's narrative. He was not reporting or writing history even if he did later adopt the title of "Royal Historian of Oz" while writing the series.

Nevertheless, there were things in it which children would skate over while reading the fascinating adventures. There was death in Oz, though there were no gory details, and Baum was right in being sparing of them. The Tin Woodman chopped off the head of a wildcat chasing the Queen of the Mice. Two bear-bodied, tiger-headed Kalidahs were smashed to death when they fell off a log bridge chopped off by the Tin Woodman. The Woodman also killed forty wolves with an axe. The Cowardly Lion sneaked off at night to get something to eat, and Dorothy did not ask him what his food had been. She did tremble for the deer.

Dorothy saw a tiny baby, which meant that there was birth and, therefore, copulation and conception. And all that these implied.

There was, even in Baum's Oz, hate and lust for power and hunger and terror and oppression and birth and death.

Baum had intended to write no more of Oz than the first book. His great ambition was to be the creator of the truly American fairy tale. His fairies and brownies and sentient animals would be indigenous, owing little to the European.

But his readers, the American children, wanted more of Oz. And, since the demand was high and he needed the money, he wrote a sequel, *The Marvelous Land of Oz*. This was almost entirely fictional, though he did use some names and persons Dorothy had mentioned. And he created those wonderful characters, Jack Pumpkinhead, the Gump, the Wooden Sawhorse, the Wogglebug, and Ozma, the long-hidden and true queen of Oz.

His readers were delighted and asked for more.

Though Baum tried to ignore them, he could not. Like A. Conan

Doyle, he found that what he regarded as hackwork was really the jewel in the crown—as far as his readers were concerned. Doyle made his fortune and his reputation from Sherlock Holmes, though he tried, unsuccessfully, to kill him off so he could get back to his beloved historical novels. Baum worked at the genuine American fairy tale as long as he could, but then he did what he must. He ended up writing fourteen in the series.

During the course of this, he decided to make Oz as Utopian as possible. Thus, in his later books, no one could die in Oz nor would anyone grow old. Babies would remain babies forever; people who were old when the great fairy queen Lurline cast her spell on Oz would grow no older.

Even if a person were cut into little pieces, the pieces would still live.

Baum forgot about this from time to time, and his later Oz books contained passing references indicating that there was a possibility of death in that land.

Hank had not noticed the many discrepancies in the series when he was very young. He had liked the idea that no one could die, but, when he got older, he saw that this took much of the tension from the adventures. And, when he became a young man, he realized that a world in which babies remained babies and there was no death, and, by implication, no birth either, was a horrible world.

Still, he could turn off his critical faculties and enjoy the books as he had when a child. Become, during the reading, a child again.

Here, though, he was in the nonfictional world. He could not close a page when he was tired of reading it and walk off. Reality was a novel that kept batting its pages hard against you. You had to read on and on until you died. Even sleep was no refuge; your mind presented other books, even more plotless and footnoted and nonsensical and filled with misprints and dropped sentences than what you read while awake.

Hank put on his barnstormer outfit and then studied the sheet of paper on which he had printed the twenty-eight letters of the Quadling alphabet and the symbols he'd made up to indicate their pronunciation.

He spent an hour reading a child's primer. Then he went to the bathroom, coming out just as a servant came for him. He was led this time into a large room near the throne room. Glinda, clad in a pure white robe but uncrowned, sat in a chair before an oak table. The table legs were carved like sphinx-faces.

There was a long line before her, petitioners of various sorts, he supposed. But he did not have to wait. The servant conducted him by the people and animals. If they resented his being passed by them, they did not show it. They stared at him openly, as the natives did everywhere. But many smiled, and some even said, *"Goth morn!"*

They were noisy, too, not silent in the queen's presence as he had expected. Sometimes, a short phrase or a complete sentence sounded as if it was English. Double-talk English.

Glinda smiled at him, said something to the captain by her side, and waited while the soldier announced that the audiences were over for a while. The petitioners could wait in the hall.

A folding chair was brought in built for him, and Hank was told to sit down across the table. He waved away the glass goblet of fruit juice offered him.

Glinda leaned back in the high-backed, ornately carved oaken chair. "Have you anything to ask me? Is there anything I can do for you?"

Hank was sure that he was not here just so she could find out if his needs were being taken care of. He said, "No complaints. As for asking, well, I have a hundred questions."

"Some of which we may have time for," she said. "You're here primarily so that I can acquaint you with certain situations. And I have a request to make of you."

"I'm all yours, Little Mother."

He thought, I sure would like to be.

"The man who was killed yesterday in the flying machine will be buried this afternoon," she said. "I don't know what religion he was, but if you care to say prayers over him, you may do so during the ceremony."

"My father's an Anglican; my mother, a Methodist. I'm a hard-shelled agnostic."

Glinda looked puzzled.

"It doesn't matter," he said. "I'll say a prayer for him. It couldn't hurt."

"No. But he may be only the first. Others will follow him, I'm sure. What you must know is that we won't tolerate any more. One of you is enough. We can handle one—especially since he is Dorothy's son. One is even welcome. But no more than one. We will not be invaded!''

Hank was startled. The last sentence had been uttered so strongly and with such a hard face and eyes. Glinda meant what she said.

''My anger is not for you,'' she said, smiling. ''But you're intelligent. You must have known from your strict quarantine that we are very disturbed at the prospect of disease from Earth. We had those here once, and they must have killed many. Then the plagues died out. Why, I don't know. Perhaps that was because of something the Long-Gone Ones left here. Some sort of anti-disease protection which fills . . . radiates? . . . over this land.''

''The Long-Gone Ones?''

''The ancient aborigines. The nonhumans who originated on this planet. Or, at least, they did as far as we know. They must have died out or been exterminated or left this world before the first humans came through the openings. We do not know, but the stories that have come down to us, in distorted form, I'm sure, from our ancestors . . . these say that there were no indigenes then. But there are the half-buried ruins of a city of the Long-Gone Ones in the far northwest corner of the land. We don't know much about it since it's in Natawey territory. I have been there, but I wasn't able to make much from what I saw during my brief stay. I had other things to occupy my interest then.''

She paused, looking as if she were contemplating the past. Then she said, ''It was very fortunate that neither you nor your mother were carrying any diseases when you came here. But I know that these foulnesses sicken and kill many of you. And if these are brought in, well . . .''

She grimaced as if she were seeing visions of hell.

''My people would be defenseless. They would be swept away by the thousands, perhaps all or almost all would die. Be honest, wouldn't that happen?''

Hank thought of the American Indians who had died from the diseases contracted from the whites. He thought of the Polynesians who had been struck down by tuberculosis, smallpox, scarlet fever, and syphilis when the whites came.

''I don't think they'd be wiped out, Your Witchness,'' he said. ''But the results might be horrible. Devastating. However . . . you said that there was something here which now keeps diseases away. Why wouldn't that apply to new diseases? Why would your people be infected? Wouldn't they be unaffected?''

"I told you that the ancients suffered from these. It was only after a hundred or so years, if the chronology is right, that the plagues disappeared. There seems to be a certain time required for whatever the agent is that fights disease to assert itself. By the time that it did its work, the diseases would kill us by the hundreds of thousands.

"In any event, I would not want even one to die from these things you Earthpeople carry around as nonchalantly as you do your handkerchiefs.''

"Pardon me, The Highest, but that's an exaggeration. We're not indifferent . . .''

"No?''

"Anyway, what can I do about an, uh, invasion?''

"You're the only one who can interpret for us. We may need you as a go-between. I intend to have some of my people learn English, and I wish to do so, too. Just now, we have more to deal with than Earthpeople.''

She frowned and bit her lip.

Hank waited.

"First, though, the Earth problem. There is more than disease to it. Even if there were none, you people would destroy our society. You'd bring in your religions, your customs, your institutions. You'd change us for the worse.

"And we have so much gold and silver, so many precious stones. Your greed would ravish the land. But, in order to make your piracy lawful, to make the robbery accord with your images of yourself as honest and lawful and God-fearing, you'd find a pretext for declaring war on us. You'd send in your armies and conquer us. Then you'd start the rape.''

9

Hank, his face red, cried, "That's not so, Glinda! It wouldn't be that way! You make us sound like savages, but—"

"Yes? Be honest. Isn't that the way your people have always been? By that, I don't mean just your nation, Hank. I mean all the nations. Haven't they always done just such things if they happened to be powerful enough to do it? And haven't those that weren't powerful enough wished that they could?"

"You seem to know much about Earth!" Hank said. "Very strange for someone who hasn't been there!"

"I didn't say I hadn't," Glinda said.

"When? Where?"

"I'll tell you at another time. Perhaps. Now, Hank, the other crisis. There hasn't been a war here for thirty years. It seems that one is unavoidable now, though. Your mother undoubtedly told you that she was visited by the Witch of the North, Helwedo, shortly after she came here."

"That was in Baum's *Wizard,* too," Hank said. "But he didn't mention her name. My mother didn't tell him that."

"Helwedo was then near a thousand years old."

Hank rolled his eyes. He wanted to ask her how some people could live so long, but this was not the time. When would it be? Events were racing like Barney Oldfield. Like Alice and the Red Queen.

"Helwedo heard about Dorothy's arrival from one of her hawk spies, and she came immediately to see your mother."

The Witch was indeed a witch. She had appeared before Dorothy with a bang of suddenly displaced air, a phenomenon which Dorothy

54

had forgotten to tell Baum. Helwedo had some means of transportation unknown on Earth, unless the witches of old there had had some such power. He did not believe that they did. Maybe "magic" was possible here. Not there.

"Helwedo encouraged Dorothy to wear the dead Witch of the East's silver shoes."

Glinda paused, then said, "At least, they looked as if they were of silver. Real silver would never have stood up under all the walking and running your mother did in them."

I'll bet, Hank thought, that Helwedo told you about Dorothy. Or perhaps one of your bird spies did. I'd mortgage my ass to Rockefeller to get enough to place a bet on that.

It was then that he began to suspect that Glinda may have been subtly guiding Dorothy all through her quests. But he did not have time to dwell on that subject. He had to concentrate on Glinda's words.

"Ten years ago, Helwedo, the Witch of the North, the queen of the Gillikins, died suddenly. I did my best, but I could not prevent a young witch named Erakna from seizing power. Erakna the Uneatable. She is so clever that she even hid from me that she was a red witch until it was too late.

"I felt sorry for the Gillikins. They were as oppressed as the Munchkins had been under the East Witch and the Winkies under the West Witch. But I bid my time, and Erakna made no moves against me. In fact, she sent word that she had no ambitions beyond the borders of her nation. She would be content to stay there and rule. I did not believe her. No red witch can be believed."

Can the white witches? Hank thought.

"However, she had her troubles. Revolts, increasing raids by the Natawey from the mountains, a struggle with another red witch. But she seems to have put down all opposition now, and the ambition she's kept like a hungry wolf in a cage has slipped out now.

"For the past year we've had some border incidents with the Gillikins. Erakna says that the troublemakers are outlaws, but I know that the incidents were instigated by her. Also, she has taxed her subjects heavily to build up a big standing army, and they're holding maneuvers now on the borders of Winkieland and Ozland. It's evident that she's ready to invade."

"I'm sorry to hear that," he said. "But . . .?"

"What does that have to do with you? You'll find out. I want to confer with the Scarecrow and the Woodman. Very soon. I could send messages by hawk, but I prefer to see them personally. *Andaugi bi andaugi*. Face to face."

"You want me to fly up there and get them?"

Glinda smiled. "Very good. Lamblo's lover is not only a handsome giant, he is intelligent."

Hank blushed.

Glinda laughed again and said, "How long will it be before you can leave in your flying machine?"

Hank told her what had to be done. The engine of the Jenny had to be altered slightly to burn ethyl alcohol. He had to ensure that there were supplies of fuel along the route on places flat and long enough for a plane to land. He needed maps, too. Those he'd seen were not good enough.

"A hawk who knows the way will ride with you," she said.

"Is there likely to be trouble on the way?"

"There is. Erakna, I'm sure, knows about you. That you're working for me is enough excuse for her to attack you. However, she may not have an opportunity."

Glinda sent for a female hawk named Ot, a purple-and-bronze feathered bird he had seen before. Hank made sure that they understood exactly what he required. They discussed the distances between the supply depots, the purity of the grain alcohol, and many other requirements.

Lunch time came. Food and drink were brought in. Ot only fed once a day, and she passed up lunch. Hank asked her what she ate. In that weird gramophone-like voice, she said, "When I'm among the tame ones, nuts and insects. These are prepared for me in a meatlike consistency. But when I'm in the wilds, I eat mice, rats, rabbits, and anything not too big to fight back."

That answered several questions. One of them had been whether or not sentiency extended to the insects.

Hank concluded that he could take off for Winkie country in ten days. Glinda told Ot that there was no need to spend more time with them. The hawk launched herself from the chair and flew through the open door.

"Why, Glinda," Hank said, "don't you just transport the Scarecrow and Woodman here? If Helwedo could whiz from one place to another in practically nothing flat, you must be able to do so. And if you can do that for yourself, why not others?"

Glinda stared at him for a moment before speaking.

"You're still strange to our customs and laws," she said, "so I'll forgive you. However, in the future, remember this. No one asks a witch about her professional secrets."

"I beg your pardon," he said coolly.

"Granted. However, I don't mind telling you some things. One is that it takes an enormous amount of energy for the transportation via . . . how shall I name it? The word is not in the vocabulary of the people and the word itself has power. Only witches know it. This power does not come without hard payment, and it is used only when absolutely needed. I could bring those two here quickly after certain preparations. But it is not necessary.

"You, however, even if you'll take ten days to get ready and six for the trip, will have them here long before they could get here by ordinary means."

Glinda stood up.

"You'll have all the blacksmiths and millwrights and labor and materials you need. You will begin at once. Be ready at four o'clock, though, to attend the funeral for the dead flier."

A half hour later, Hank met the dozen men summoned by Glinda. He spent two hours organizing them and making sure they understood exactly what he wanted. He helped them draw schematics and diagrams on paper made from rags. At fourteen o'clock, he went back to the castle. Lamblo came for him a half hour later. She wore a uniform he'd not seen before, all-black garments and a scarlet shako bearing a silver death's head emblem.

"I only put these on when I'm in the honor guard of a funeral," she said. "Sit down, Hank. I have to ask you some questions. I know the answers, but the forms have to be filled out."

He sat down. "Shoot."

"What? Oh, I see. Very well. What is your name?"

"My God! You know it!"

"That's a funny name," she said, and she giggled. Then, her face smoothing out, she said, "Just give me the right answers. It's required, and if you clown around, we might be late. Little Mother wouldn't like that."

"My name is Henry Lincoln Stover."

"Are you related to the dead man?"

"No."

He wondered what the reasons were for this interrogation. It was probably required by the government bureaucrats. Even Quadlingland had these.

"Are you a friend?"

"Of yours?"

She smiled slightly but said, "Of the dead man."

"No. I never heard of him before."

"Would you be willing to act as a bereaved?"

"You mean a mourner?"

"Yes."

Hank twisted one side of his mouth and looked sharply at her. "What is this? What do I have to do if I say yes?"

She told him.

He paled, and he said, "For God's sake! What kind of barbarism is that?"

"It's our ancient custom."

"Hell, I wouldn't do that for my own mother!"

She shrugged and said, "Very well. The professional mourners will earn their pay."

She stood up. "Let's go."

Hank followed her. He felt uneasy, and his stomach seemed to be turning over. If he could have refused the invitation to attend the funeral, he would have done so. But then both his courage and finer sensibilities would be doubted by these people, not to mention by himself. Besides, his curiosity was driving him.

Lamblo's company met them at the north main entrance to the castle. They formed around Hank, and presently he was marching in their midst, his stride cut down so that their short legs could keep up with him. They went west on the road through the town. It was deserted. Apparently, everybody, including the animals and birds, was at the cemetery. This, like all burial places, was on the western edge of town and on a hill. West was where the souls of the dead went, the far west beyond the land of the living, somewhere out beyond the desert.

Hank had been told this late one night by Lamblo.

"There, so the priests and priestesses say, is another green land where God and His angels instruct the dead on their errors and faults.

Then the dead are sent back in the form of *amaizhuath* (mind-lights) or *fonfoz* (firefoxes). They come back across the desert and possess the bodies of animals and birds and sometimes human beings or even inanimate objects.''

Hank had had a flash of that stormy night when he had seen the nude Glinda going through that weird ceremony or battle in the vast room of the sphinx and the shadows.

''How can they possess a body that's already possessed?''

Lamblo had said, ''I don't know. They just do.''

She had looked very uneasy.

''What happens to the dispossessed soul?''

''It goes back to the land of God, where He and His angels explain what the soul did wrong. Then it is sent out again to the land of the living.''

''Sounds like a game of musical chairs for spirits,'' he had said and then had had to explain what ''musical chairs'' meant.

''Do you believe what you've told me?'' he had said.

''Do you have a better explanation? Let's not talk about such things. Let's try the *saitigzhuz-nyuh* position.''

God was called either *Guth* or *Chuz*. Hank thought that the *Chuz* came from *Tius,* and was related to the Old Norse god *Tyr* and Old English *Tiw*. An angel was *anggluz,* a word that had come from the Greek and indicated some early contact with Christianity. But, somehow, an angel had become confused with a *slanchuzar,* a semi-divine maiden something like the Old Norse Valkyrie.

The ancient confusion was also evident in the crosses on the gravestones in the cemetery. There was the simple cross, the Celtic cross, the saltire or X, and the swastika, called the *thyunz-hamar,* Thor's hammer, the symbol used worldwide on prehistoric and historic Earth.

Most graves had monuments, sculptures representing not only humans but many types of nonhuman life. Next to a woman's grave was a deer's.

Though he had been verbally prepared by Lamblo, he was still shocked when he saw the priests, priestesses, and the professional mourners. The holy men and women looked more like African witch doctors than anything else. They wore tall headdresses of varicolored long feathers; their faces were streaked with black and red paint, necklaces of bones and teeth flapped on bare painted chests, their naked genitals were shaven, and their legs were painted like black-and-red barberpoles. They danced like medicine men, shaking rattle-gourds, ringing tiny bells, and whirling bullroarers. The mourners, men and women, were naked and gashing their naked flesh with stone knives.

He had stepped out of a quaint, even "cute," village into the Old Stone Age.

Lamblo ordered her troops to halt. Hank stopped also. The soldiers stepped aside for him, and Lamblo gestured with a sword that he should go on. Feeling numb, he walked towards the coffin, a lime-stone hemisphere. Its lid was off, and the charred body lay unclothed in the recess on top of the dome-shape.

Before it was a round open grave. Beyond it, Glinda sat on a marble throne, but an old black blanket protected her naked buttocks from the hard cold stone. She wore only a feathered headdress and was painted from neck to toes with alternating white-and-black stripes that spi-ralled around her. She held in her left hand a long wooden shepherd's staff.

Hank stopped before her and bowed, his eyes on the ground. He was embarrassed. The mourners howled, the crowd hummed like a dynamo, the gourds rattled, the bells rang, and the bullroarers roared.

"Look up!" Glinda cried. "Look up, stranger!"

Reluctantly, Hank raised his gaze. Glinda was half-smiling, and her blue eyes seemed amused. Did she know how shocked he was at this savagery and her nakedness?

"Look up, stranger!" she said, and she pointed the staff at the sky.

Hank obeyed. The sky was unclouded. What was he supposed to see, even if only symbolically? He glanced to his right and saw that everybody was also looking upward.

"Silence!" she shouted, and the wailing, humming, rattling, tin-kling, and roaring ceased. But a baby held by a woman near the front of the crowd screamed.

"Face to the west!" Glinda cried. "Look west!"

He turned with everybody else except Glinda.

"There we all go!" she said. "Whether you live a day or a

thousand years, you go there! Naked you came into this world; naked you go there! As it was, so shall it be!''

She paused, then said, ''But it shall not always be thus!''

''It shall not always be thus!'' the others shouted.

''There is an end even to endlessness!''

''There is an end!''

Silence for a minute. The baby was nursing now and quiet. Glinda shattered the silence.

''The dead should not go home without blood!''

''Not without blood!'' the crowd shouted.

''The dead man is a stranger! He is not of our blood! Yet even the stranger shall not go hungry! Is there no father or mother, no brother or sister to give him blood?''

''There is none!'' the people yelled.

''Is there no one of his blood to give him blood?''

''There is one!''

''Then let him share his blood! The dead shall not go hungry!''

A priest and priestess ran up to Hank. The woman grabbed Hank's right hand and turned it over to expose the palm. The man raised a flint knife and slashed down. Hank cried out from the pain. He had not expected to be cut so deeply.

''Jesus Christ!''

''Turn towards the dead!'' another priestess shrilled.

Hank was urged to face the coffin and then was pushed towards it. The crowd also moved to look at the red granite dome. The holy men and women began dancing again, the gourds rattled, the bells tinkled, the bullroarers hummed, the mourners began howling and cutting themselves.

The tiny priestesses pulled his hand so that it was above the ghastly face of the corpse. Then she turned it, and the blood dripped on the black charred skin and into the half-opened mouth.

Glinda rose from the throne and pointed the staff at the dead man and then to the west.

''Drink so that you may be strong! Go! Go west to your home!''

This is no place for an anemic, Hank thought. He looked at the blood and the corpse and hoped that he would not faint.

Glinda had opened her mouth to say something. Now she was staring, not at him but at the south. Those facing him on the other side of the coffin were also staring and crying out. Even in his numbness, he knew that this was not part of the ceremony. He turned to look out across the desert.

High in the sky, but falling, was a bright light.

It looked like a Very flare, the burning magnesium signal light he had seen so often in the night skies over the battlefields of France.

10

Before the still glaring though tiny light reached the ground, an object appeared above it. It came from a green cloud that looked no larger than Hank's hand. It twinkled, the sunlight bouncing off its silvery material.

"A parachute?" Hank murmured.

Almost immediately after it, another flashing object shot from the cloud and drifted down.

And then another light flared out.

The green cloud dwindled into the blue sky.

Glinda said something to the hawk perched above her on the right corner of the throne. It flapped off toward the descending light.

Hank wanted very much to leave at once for the desert, but Glinda had other ideas. That she could keep the curious crowd from stampeding for the desert showed her iron control of herself and her people. She said loudly that the ceremony would continue, and it did, though even Hank could see that it was being rushed. At Glinda's request, he said a prayer over the corpse, the "Our Father," the lid was put on, and the heavy coffin was lowered by straps into the grave. Hank was then directed to bleed a few drops onto the coffin, and the shovelers started filling the hole. The holy people danced nine times widdershins around the grave, and then Glinda took off her feathered headdress and put on a long loose white robe.

A doctor bandaged Hank's hand. A few minutes later, he was on a chariot headed for the desert. When the procession was halfway down the cliff-road, the hawk lit on the railing of Glinda's vehicle. The two conversed, but Hank was not near enough to hear what they said.

When they were on foot and within half a mile of one of the fallen objects, they stopped. Lamblo, by Hank's side, said, "God save us!"

A glowing ball perhaps twelve feet wide appeared suddenly on a tall twisted rock spire. Glinda shouted an order, and a company of male archers trotted out ahead of the main body. The shimmering sphere, through which Hank could see the sky beyond it, rolled straight down, perpendicular to the ground, and then shot towards them. But it did not seem aware of them. Its path, if continued on a straight line, would have led it about thirty feet past them.

At the barked commands of a captain, the men raised their bows. Another order. The arrows sped into the ball, and it exploded like a French .75 shell. Hank jumped and blinked. The ball was gone, but the wooden shafts of the arrows were burning.

They proceeded warily but without incident until they got to the thing that had come from the green cloud. It was a large wooden box covered with small mirrors and attached to a huge collapsed parachute, painted silvery.

The cords of the chute were cut, the silver-painted leather straps were unbuckled, and the lid was opened. Hank looked inside it. Enclosed in thick insulation were other boxes. He removed and opened these. There was a movie camera, four canisters of movie film, a Kodak and ten rolls of film for it, two instruction manuals, tablets of writing paper with many pencils, pens, and bottles of ink, a pencil sharpener, a twelve-inch ruler, erasers, protractor, materials for developing film, an instruction book with procedures for using the developers, a flashlight, a stopwatch, and a large manila envelope. The envelope bore the emblem and title of the U.S. Army Signal Corps. Also on it, in large printed letters, was his name.

"Now how in hell . . .?" he muttered.

Before he could open the envelope, he heard a cry from around the spire. A hawk flew around it and announced that another box was being brought in. Hank decided not to open the envelope until he determined the contents of the second box.

Opened, the other container revealed a radio transmitter-receiver with headphones and extra batteries. There was also an envelope with his name. As it turned out, it contained an exact copy of the letter in the first envelope.

Glinda must have been curious about their find, but she wished to get her people out of the danger zone. A minute later, they were marching towards the green land. When they reached it, they loaded the boxes into a moose-drawn wagon. Hank did not open the envelopes until he was in a room on the first floor of the castle.

Glinda's first question was about the things in the boxes. He told her what they were and who or what had sent them.

"Read the letter," she said. "Then give me the essence of it. Then read it aloud, translating for me."

There were six pages of single-spaced typing. Though the missive came out of the office of a Colonel Mark Sampson of the U.S. Army Signal Corps, it was also signed by the General of the Armies and the chief of staff, John Joseph Pershing.

"Black Jack himself," Hank murmured.

He had great respect for Pershing's abilities during World War I, but he also loathed him. It was, so he had heard, Pershing who had refused to permit American fliers to wear parachutes. The reason: they might abandon their craft during combat if they were in extreme danger. In other words, Pershing did not trust the courage of his aviators.

It was also Pershing who did not mind wasting thousands of soldiers to gain a position but who thought that whorehouses for his men were wicked and did his best to close them down.

"A genuine prudish prick."

"What?" Glinda said.

"Nothing. O.K. Here goes."

"O.K.?"

"An American phrase. It means all right, fine, yes, hunkeydorey, copasetic."

"Hongkiidorii? Kopasetik?"

Hank read the letter to himself, but there was no silence in the room. Though the queen was evidently impatient to learn its contents, she wasted no time. She conferred with several people and birds, gave orders, dictated a short letter, and went once to the toilet. When she came out of it, she found that Hank had read all of the letter.

"First, there's not a word about how they were able to identify me," he said. "But it would not have been difficult."

He wondered if Intelligence agents had visited his parents. Probably not yet, since everything about this would be a top-secret priority. They would have thoroughly investigated Mr. and Mrs. Lincoln Stover, though.

And they surely would have notified President Harding about it. Perhaps a few cabinet officials, too.

"This is addressed to Lieutenant Henry L. Stover. I'm no longer an Army officer, and I'm not in the reserve. They're using the title for psychological reasons."

"Why?"

"They want me to do certain things because I'm an American citizen, and they're appealing to my patriotism. Reminding me that I was an officer and a soldier and should act like one."

"What certain things?"

"These will become apparent, Little Mother. They also omit any specific explanation of just how and why the green haze, the opening, was made. However, they do refer to the operation or experiment or whatever as Project Thor. That might mean that it has or had something to do with power transmission. Thor was the god of thunder and lightning to the Norse people."

It would not be easy to explain everything in the letter. There were just too many references lacking in this culture or in his vocabulary.

"I could be guessing wrong, but I think that possibly the Signal Corps was conducting an experiment to transmit . . . oh, hell! I'll have to make clear what the word electricity means."

Glinda surprised him by saying that she had some grasp of the concept. His mother had told her about it and had also described somewhat how lightning power was generated and transmitted and what it could do.

"Yes, but she was an eight-year-old kid. Besides, the science of using it has progressed considerably since 1890. So I'll give you more details and bring you up to date."

When she heard Hank out, she said, "And these Signal Corps people were, you believe, doing what?"

"I think that they were trying to transmit electrical power without wires. Via the atmosphere, perhaps. A famous scientist, Nikola Tesla, has long been interested in trying to do that. Maybe he's the head of the project. I don't know.

"Anyway, I think that the Corps was conducting such an experiment just as I was flying near Fort Leavenworth. And there was a totally unexpected by-product of the experiment. A weak place in the walls between these two universes or a natural channel for going up or down the slope between the two worlds . . . well, this weak spot was opened by the power. Just long enough for me to fly through.

"The Signal Corps people saw me go into the haze and not come out. So they duplicated the experiment, and the haze was made again. I don't know what fantastic speculations they made about this. Whatever they were, they wouldn't match the reality. But they did decide to send an Army plane through. Just how they planned to get it back through to Earth, I don't know either. Probably, they made plans to open the gate again at a specified time. But . . ."

He shrugged, and he said, "Evidently, they don't have control over the dimensions or duration of the opening. And they have no idea what this world is."

He burst out laughing, then said, "If someone told them that this was the Land of Oz, he'd be considered crazy! They'd lock him up! And if, when, I tell them the truth, they'll think I'm out of my head!"

Should he tell them that his mother was the Dorothy of Baum's books? No. Whether or not they believed him, they'd harass her with long interrogations. They'd make her life miserable, give her no rest or privacy. And if by some chance the secret of this project came out, and if he did convince them that he was indeed in Oz, she'd be subjected to worldwide publicity.

Glinda said, "You have the means to convince them."

She pointed at the boxes stacked in a corner.

"They still won't believe me."

"That's not important. Continue."

"Well, after impressing upon me that I must tell no unauthorized person about this—who in hell could I tell, that side of the universe? —they demand that I cooperate to the fullest extent. Obey every order. Do my utmost to get information about this world to them."

"With the films?"

"With those and maps and data about the population, if any. . . . They don't even know if this world—they call it the Fourth Dimension—has sentient beings or life of any kind except for me. . . . If there are sentients, then they want to know all about them. Particularly, their . . . your . . . military potential. Also, diseases, the natural resources, by which they mean fertile land, bodies of water, wood, iron, copper, bauxite, oil, gold, silver, and so on. I'm supposed to make motion and still pictures of everything significant, record data about this and that, give them as complete a picture as possible."

He looked up from the letter.

"They aren't even sure I'm alive or, if I am, that I'll be around in this area to get the message. They admit they're taking a chance."

"When will they open the way again?"

"It'll be opened briefly seven days from now. At ten in the morning their time. They don't know, of course, whether the time here corresponds to theirs. I'm supposed to go by the time on the watch they sent. But they're taking a chance. It's all highly chancy."

"The way will be open briefly?"

"So that I can acknowledge receipt of this. After that, thirty days before I am to pass through the films and data."

Hank interpreted the message word by word, interrupting himself or being interrupted by the witch to clarify various references. When he was finished, Glinda said, "I wonder what would happen if you failed to send your reply seven days from now? Would your people then just give up?"

"Not at all. They'd try to send through another pilot as soon as they could get the needed control over the gateway."

"Maybe they won't be able to do that."

"That's possible. But I doubt they'll give up. Their curiosity will be too great. They'll believe that this world might be as big a danger to theirs as you think theirs is to yours. They can't stop trying. If things from my world can come here, then things from yours can go there. They'll be thinking of the novel by Mr. H.G. Wells. That was about an invasion from Mars . . ."

He outlined briefly the plot of the book. Then he said, "They'll think the worst. They can't afford to take a chance that there might not be any danger to them here. You can understand that, can't you, Your Witchness?"

"Oh, yes. So . . . this is not a problem which can be ignored. I will allow you to send your first message, but I want you to read it to me. And don't lie. I will know if you are."

Hank felt his skin warming. "I wouldn't think of it!"

"Yes, you would. You're thinking of it now. Not that that means that you would lie. Now, just how do you intend to get the message through the opening?"

He told her that he would fly above the green cloud and drop the message through.

Glinda smiled and said, "What if the cloud is large enough to admit your airplane? Will you desert us then?"

Hank bit his lip.

"I'll be honest. I don't know. I doubt that the cloud will be large enough. Apparently, it takes a lot of power to generate it, and it probably won't be very large. It also won't last long. I'll have to act fast and be accurate on the first passover. Otherwise, I won't make it. Also . . . well . . . I don't think the Army bigshots would like me to return. Not just now, anyway. They need someone here who can, uh, feed them information. Or be their ambassador, you might say.''

Glinda laughed and said, ''Perhaps act as their agent for whatever plans they have or will have. I'll trust you not to leave us. I can't do otherwise. If you find that you can't resist the temptation, you'll go. And that's that.''

''I do get a little homesick now and then,'' he said. ''But I'm also very curious about this world. Besides, as I said, it's my patriotic duty to stay here.''

''Very well. It's only by thinking of the here and now that one can survive three centuries. Though it's always necessary to keep in mind the near future if you don't want to die. Sometimes. . . . Never mind. Get your flying machine ready, and make your first report. Be sure that that is brief. And do not put in either report how old I am, nor even suggest that others have lived as long or longer.''

Hank started to ask why he shouldn't, but he said, ''Telling them that would ensure that they would try to get here. They would want your secret of longevity. That, more than gold and jewels and more territory and the marvels of another universe, would bring them here. Everybody wants to live forever.''

''Yes, that would be the irresistible lure. However, not everybody wants to live that long. And few will ever have the means to do so. I could allow you to explain that, but they would not believe you.''

11

The morning of the seventh day after the message from Pershing, Hank was summoned to Glinda's apartment. She told him to sit down.

"You do that so often I'm beginning to feel like a dog," he said.

"Toto," she said, and she laughed. "Yes, I can remember that curious creature. Well, a dog, I assume, does not resent being ordered to sit down. Not if it loves its mistress. Here, Hank. Hold this in your hand."

A little man with a long gray beard extended a round whitish-gray object the size of a large plum.

"The Black Pearl of Truth," Glinda said as Hank took it. "It's not a genuine pearl; it just looks and feels like one."

There were no oceans or oysters known to this land, but apparently, there were river mussels which had pearls.

"My mother told Mr. Baum about this. She said that you had shown it to her. Baum used it in his second book. But he assumed that you wore it next to your body. I suppose that he was wrong."

"Right. Wrong," Glinda said. "You, the one being tested, must hold it or wear it next to your skin."

He thought that it probably detected the shifting electric potential of the holder's skin. It would turn from gray to black if the holder lied. But what if the wearer believed that he was telling the truth, though he was not?

As if she'd read his mind, Glinda said, "It couldn't be depended upon if you were insane. But you're sane, at least, I judge you to be so. Relatively speaking, that is. No one is completely sane. A person that is would go crazy."

Hank held the ''pearl'' up between his thumb and forefinger.

''This also represents a danger to my world. If these could be manufactured and put in every court of justice, in every home, society would crumble.''

''I know that,'' she said. ''That's why you won't mention it. As yet, anyway. However, it is unique. It can't be duplicated. No one knows how to make another like it. It's something the Long-Gones left behind them. It was found seven hundred years ago and has been owned by the Quadling witches ever since.''

At her command, he interpreted the message he had written the night before. The Pearl did not change color.

''Good. What I expected,'' Glinda said.

The report was placed inside a very thick insulated envelope, and that was placed inside a disc-shaped receptacle. This had a framework of spring steel and a triple-fold covering of tough leather. An accidentally drowned cow had provided the leather. The interior of the case and the insulation of broken walnut shells would hold the report and some photographs Hank had taken with the small camera, and some Quadling artifacts, including a tiny solid-gold statuette of Glinda. She looked at these before permitting them to be put into the case.

''Too bad you don't have film that shows color,'' she said. ''They won't be able to see the auburn of my hair.''

Hank grinned.

''If Your Witchness would cut off a lock for export?''

''Don't be a smart aleck.''

What would the Army brass and President Harding make of these pictures? One of the castle from the ground, an aerial view of it and the town, himself standing among a crowd of pygmies, Glinda on her throne, Glinda in a moose-drawn chariot, Glinda by him in front of the Jenny, the open pages of a book, the castle guard on review, a raccoon writing on a pad of paper, a cat reading a newspaper, two views of the cemetery, and many other photographs.

Hank had captioned each. Surely, the mention of Glinda and Quadlingland would cause an uproar. Also, unbelief.

He took off in the Jenny in a cloudless sky at 10:15 A.M., Central standard daylight saving time. The hawk, Ot, rode with him, her talons digging into the right shoulder of his heavy leather jacket. Though Hank knew the approximate area where the cloud had appeared, Ot claimed that she could pinpoint it. She gave him instructions, and

he circled the place where the green haze was supposed to show.
Eleven o'clock came. The air remained empty. Fifteen minutes passed.
Something had gone wrong. The gate-opening equipment had broken
down or was malfunctioning. Or there was not, for some reason,
enough power available. Or the opener-generator had blown up. Or the
brass had decided to call off the operation because of bad weather.

A half hour went by. He observed four of the giant balls rolling far
out in the desert. When he had the opportunity, he would photograph
some of them.

After a while, Hank was both bored and anxious. He was also tired
of circling counterclockwise, so he straightened out and turned and
went on the clockwise path. And then, just as he had noted that it was
11:46:12, Ot startled him by screaming in his ear. He looked up from
the watch to his left. About forty feet below a green cloud was
beginning to form.

He banked even steeper and nosed down. With his left hand, he
picked up the disc by its edge and held it edgewise out into the
airstream. By the time he was above the haze, it had expanded into a
diamond-shaped area the widest part of which could easily enfold the
Jenny.

His heart beat like the pick of a miner who had just seen the start of
a gold vein.

If he dived suddenly and steeply, he could zip through the cloud and
be back on Earth.

But he did not, and he was glad that he had not. The green began to
shrink rapidly. When he flipped the disc in it, the haze was the size of
a large desk, and, for a second, he thought that it would miss the
target. If he had tried to escape, his plane, and, possibly, himself,
would have been sliced.

"They didn't give you much time," Ot yelled in her Victrola-like
voice.

"They would have if they could have!" Hank yelled back.

Evidently, they were having trouble with the machine.

Glinda would be somewhat comforted when he reported that.

When he came to her counselling-room, she did not ask him, as he
had expected, if he had been tempted to pass through. She told him to
do what he could towards his report but not to let that interfere with
the pick-up flight.

"Do you still think that you can return in six days?"

"Give or take a few," he said. "I may be grounded by bad weather or engine trouble. I would like permission to have more time so that I could see my mother's house in Munchkinland."

"I can understand your sentiment," she said. "But you'll have to do that some other time. I have reports that Erakna's armies on the Winkie and Oz borders have been considerably increased. Is it possible for you to leave sooner than planned?"

Hank thought for a minute, and then said, "I could go tomorrow if I forget about mounting the machine-guns on the Jenny."

Glinda smiled. "At dawn then."

"If the weather's good."

"Don't worry. It will be."

He did not believe, as her subjects did, that she could control the weather. But she might have meteorological data brought to her by her bird agents. And, after three hundred years, she must be able to "predict" weather as well as or better than the best weather-forecasters of Earth. Not that that meant much.

Before sunrise, he was flight-checking the Jenny and making sure that all his supplies had been loaded. Glinda, in thick white woolen clothes and boots, was there to see him off and give him some last-minute instructions. Lamblo, also dressed against the early-morning cold, stood to one side, trying not to look sad. She had wanted to go with him, but, even if the queen had allowed her to, she could not. There was no room for her.

Two hawks, Shii and Windwaldriiz, were in the front cockpit. Ot was with Hank so she could navigate for him; Windwaldriiz would leave them when they got to the Emerald City to carry the news to Glinda; Shii, when they got to the Winkie ruler's castle.

The gray light brightened, and the sun rose swiftly from the horizon. Hank said a see-you-later to the queen. Lamblo came up to him and said, "Kiss me, Hank."

He hesitated. She said, "Don't be bashful. Everybody knows about us."

"I'll bet," he said. "Even the Gillikins."

He bent down and lifted her up to the level of his face and gave her a long kiss. When he set her down, he looked at Glinda. She was smiling. He would have felt better if she had looked just a little bit jealous.

He climbed into the cockpit. The motor had been warmed up, so it started quickly and smoothly when a Quadling spun the propellor after Hank yelled, "Contact!" He used the English word, which he had taught the two men assigned to him as mechanics.

The wheel blocks were pulled aside, and he eased in the throttle. The Jenny started moving forward. He taxied to the east end of the meadow, turned around to face the dawn-gentle western wind, then gave Jenny the gas. As his wheels lifted, he waved at the group in front of the hangar.

His course lay northwest by north. He had had to adjust the compass since there seemed to be ten degrees difference in true north here and on Earth. In any event, he did not need the instrument. Ot would notify him at once if he deviated from the flight path. She was standing by his left hip now, jammed into the space between him and the cockpit fuselage wall. Better she was there, even if it crowded them, than on his shoulder. Birds, unlike the animals, could not control their evacuations. Hank had had to clean off his jacket after their last flight. Ot was on a thick cloth now, and, if it was dirtied, it would be thrown away when they landed.

The weather was as pleasant as Glinda had said it would be. At three thousand feet altitude, the Jenny bore through the sky with very little air disturbance. Farms, interspersed by wide areas of woods, dirt roads, small lakes, and a river reeled by below him. At noon, he landed near a small village and refueled. He had plenty of alcohol in the tank, but he liked to have a good reserve. Besides, he needed to relieve himself and to eat lunch. The locals came out in a body to gawk at him, a few daring to speak to him.

Twenty minutes later, he took off again. An hour before dusk, he touched down at a larger village near a small river. His quarters were ready, a room in the house of the Kaizar, the elected leader, the equivalent of a mayor. Hank would rather have slept in a barn and have the people kept away from him. He was far from being antisocial, but he needed time for some hard exercise and eight hours' sleep. The locals were hot to ply him with questions, food, and liquor, give a big party for him, and keep him up as late as possible with their merry-making.

Also, he might as well sleep in a barn since there were no beds big enough for him. When he was in his host's house, he had to stoop to get through the doorway and hunch over to keep from bumping his head against the ceiling. He supposed he'd have to sleep on a pile of blankets.

The questions shoved at him were about equally divided among queries about Earth, the witch-queen, whom few of them had seen, and the rumors of the threatening invasion by the Gillikins. Hank sighed with weariness when he thought that he'd have to put up with these at every stop. But he did his best to be genial and reply as best he could. After all, he was sort of an ambassador to Oz, and he was Glinda's representative.

Also, he liked these tiny people even if the piping voices of a mob pressing on him did get on his nerves. They were, in many respects, alien, but on the whole they seemed friendly and hospitable. The young unmarried women did their best, some openly, others subtly, to get him to sleep with them. He rejected them reluctantly and gently. Though tempted, he told himself that Lamblo was, in a way, his fiancée. She had not asked him to marry her and might never do so. But the attitudes and circuitous comments of the castle people made him think that they were, in effect, engaged.

These people were morally rigid in some of their ways, ways that Americans would have thought peculiar. In others, they were liberal to an extent that would have outraged and repulsed many Americans, especially those in the Bible belt.

However, he told himself, a Quadling in America would have had the same reaction towards different mores. But then so would a West African or Malay.

He and the hawks got up in the morning with hangovers. He ate a light breakfast, which caused his host and family to shake their heads and tsk-tsk. How could he keep his giant body going on such a small amount of food? He did not reply. He wanted coffee badly. In fact, he awoke every morning lusting for steaming-hot black java.

The next day, near noon, he came to the edge of a thick forest, unbroken by tilled land, unmarked by humans. It stretched ahead of him for two hundred miles, if Ot was right. Hank had been told that, long ago, the wise if often draconian ruler-witches had decided that the forests made natural obstacles to war. But what strengthened this decision was the will of the creatures of the forest. They were willing to give the humans a certain space, if they made no attempt to enlarge it at the wild beast's expense. Here, the animals were sentient and could fight back with an intelligence that Earth's animals lacked.

So, by ancient agreement, humans lived within their allotted space with their domestic animals. The wild animals kept to their woods unless starvation forced them to raid the farms. The humans sometimes transgressed on the forest, but they knew the price they might have to pay.

Actually, a certain amount of trade goods and visitors passed through the trees. But most of the traffic was by river. His mother and her companions had used the Gogz River for much of their journey southward to Glinda's capital. Baum had omitted this for story purposes or for reasons known only to himself.

The second touchdown for refueling in the forest was on a slanting meadow at the bottom of a mountain. The party sent in to prepare the way had cut down trees and uprooted the stumps and filled in the holes.

Between Quadlingland and Ozland was a range of mountains many of which were over 14,000 feet high. Hank did not like to take the Jenny over eight thousand feet because the controls became "mushy" then and also because he might not find a path between mountains lower than the service ceiling of the plane. He flew above the Gogz River, staying at five hundred feet above its sometimes broad and placid, sometimes narrow and boiling, course. Doing this added two hundred miles to his flight path and forced him to make extra stops for refueling.

Ozland itself was as flat as Kansas, mainly farmland interspersed with large woodlands. The dirt roads were lined with fruit and nut trees planted hundreds of years ago. A person could walk from one town to another and not have to worry about going hungry, though that person might get tired of the limited diet.

Ot kept up her irritating stream of chatter all the way until she sighted the tips of the towers of the Emerald City. Ot became silent after that. Not because of awe or excitement from the sighting. Hank told her that he would wring her neck if she did not shut up for a while.

The capital, the "city" built by the Wizard Oz, was on a river. Baum had neglected to mention this, though that might not have been his fault. Dorothy may have failed to tell him of it. However, there had once been a flourishing village here because it was by the river and its location on the crossing of four roads made it a natural trade center. Oz had torn down the houses and placed on the site his monument to himself.

As the Emerald City neared, its details became more evident. It was beautiful and exotic, a circular wall enclosing many small houses, and, in the center, the huge palace. The fifty-foot-high wall around the city was of great greenish stone blocks. On its wide top were many slender watchtowers of red stone, each topped by a pole from which whipped the flag of Ozland. The flag had been designed by The Wizard himself; the present ruler, the Scarecrow, had left it unchanged. The country originally had been named *Mizhland* (Midland) but had been renamed after the famous Wizard.

Hank, having plenty of fuel left, circled the city twice and then buzzed it twice. There were enormous emeralds set in the outer exterior of the wall, jewels which Glinda said were undoubtedly the relic artifacts of the Long-Gones.

There were four enormous gates in the wall, not, as Baum had said, only one small one. A single gate could never have handled the traffic of a city of 30,000 and the thousands of traders and tourists.

The houses of the residents were of varicolored stone and, like the Quadlings', rectangular. (Only the Munchkins had round houses.) The streets were of green brick, and there were many trees, parks, and fountains. The palace, which covered at least six acres, was of greenish stone in which were set more emeralds than were in the entire city-protecting wall. Hank grinned when he saw it. Oz had built it to reproduce, though on a larger scale, the Capitol Building of Washington, D.C. The Ozians must have raised their eyebrows when they saw the plans for it. There had been no architecture like that in the whole country.

In front of the palace was a bronze statue of a man sitting on a chair; it was twice as big as that of Lincoln at the entrance to the Lincoln Memorial Building in Washington. It was of the Wizard, dressed in a tall plug hat, a cigar sticking straight out of his lips, and in the evening clothes of a gentleman of the late 19th century. The face was, by coincidence, much like the illustration of the Wizard by Neill. But it also reminded Hank of D'Israeli.

Having gotten a bird's view of the fabulous city of Oz, Hank directed Jenny towards the landing field. This was a wide flat meadow by the river about a half-mile from the walls. It was used as a market for the local farmers and the merchants from foreign lands. But, today, it had been cleared of its tents and wagons and the refuse carted off.

It looked as if the entire city and its visitors had assembled to greet him. Stakes had been driven into the earth to mark a long wide landing strip, and ropes had been tied to connect the stakes. Even so, the police, wearing green uniforms and scarlet coolie-type helmets with black roaches, were having a hard time keeping the crowd from pressing against the barrier.

Hank brought the plane around to head against the wind and began his landing approach.

12

He turned off the ignition and climbed out of the plane. Ot flew into the front cockpit, said something to the hawks there, and Windwaldriiz winged off with her message for Glinda. The babel was deafening with the cries and chatter of people, animals, and birds. Hank waited for the greeting committee. At its front was the ruler, the Scarecrow.

He—it, rather—was a walking question mark for Hank.

According to Hank's mother, Baum had narrated truthfully, in essence, anyway, her meeting with the thing. She had come across the Scarecrow stuck up on a pole by a cornfield. The crows, however, paid it no attention; they were eating the corn not a foot away from it. The Scarecrow had spoken to Dorothy and had gotten her to free him from the pole. And his story of being conscious while the farmer painted eyes, nose, lips, and ears on his face was true. Dorothy, eight years old, tough, yet with the naivete and acceptance of marvels of a child, had not questioned him much. Nor had she wondered how a scarecrow could be alive and speak through painted lips and see with painted eyes. Even his statement that he could see better with the left eye, because the farmer had painted it larger than the right, had gone unchallenged. Nor had she wondered how a skeletonless and muscleless creature could walk. Nor where he, who did not eat or drink, got his supply of energy. Nor how a thing with no infancy or childhood, a thing which had seemed to bloom from no seed, could suddenly talk and quite fluently at that.

There were perhaps a million scarecrows in this land. Every farmer had one. Why was only one in a million able to talk and walk? Why were all the rest just inanimate objects?

Moreover, what Baum, Dorothy, and most of Baum's readers had overlooked was that scarecrows might frighten away crows on Earth, but here the crows were sentient. They would know instantly that the mock-man was a dummy. So, why did the Munchkin farmers make them?

The truth was that every farmer had one, and he had placed it to attract corn-eating birds, not to drive them away.

It was against the law to kill animals and birds, except in special circumstances, but these needed food, and so every farmer allotted a certain amount of his crops to the predators to keep them from the rest. To mark the privilege section, the farmer erected a scarecrow. It was an ancient custom that had become law. The animals and birds, being sentient, usually ate only in the fenced-off area known as the "sacrifice garden" or the "grace field."

The Gillikins, Hank had been told, did not use scarecrows. They set up wooden images called *fuglskarya* (bird-share).

Somebody was responsible for the singularity of the Scarecrow. What these people called "witchcraft" had to be involved. If it wasn't, Hank would eat his helmet unboiled and without salt and pepper.

He might be overly suspicious, but he wondered if Glinda's invisible hand had been and was pushing events in the directions she wished.

For instance, it was not true that Helwedo, the Witch of the North, the Gillikin ruler, had been waiting for Dorothy when she came out of the farmhouse. If she had been, she would not have been able to talk with the little girl. Dorothy did not know the language. But three weeks later, when Dorothy could carry on a simple conversation, she was visited by the witch. After telling her something about the land and the silver shoes of the dead and dried-away Witch of the East, she had taken off her white conical hat. While balancing it on her nose—quite a feat—she had said, "One, two, three." A shimmering enclosed the hat, and when that was gone within a second, it seemed to have changed into a slateboard. In big white chalkmarks was written on it: LET DOROTHY GO TO THE CITY OF EMERALDS.

That was what Dorothy was told that the message was. She could not read it.

Who had written those words? Glinda?

If so, why?

And how had she done it? She was many hundreds of miles away. Did she have not only telepathic powers enabling her to communicate with the North Witch but also telergic powers?

Had Glinda somehow animated and made sentient the Scarecrow so that the little Earth girl might have a protector and advisor?

"Am I being paranoiac?" Hank muttered. "I don't think so. I'm just being logical or trying to be, anyway. However, I don't really have enough information to construct any probable and logical hypotheses. And that is what's driving me crazy. Making me anxious and frustrated, anyway."

He had seen many things to make him feel somewhat disorientated since he'd come here. The Scarecrow perhaps affected him thus more than any thing so far. Even though he had been conditioned to accept it as part of the normal world because he'd read Baum's books, he still felt that the Scarecrow was weird. Weird in the sense of "freakish," startlingly odd, and "suggestive of ghosts, evil spirits, or other supernatural things; mysterious; eerie." He also thought of golems and Frankenstein's monster.

Yet, this thing, its painted smile and big blue eyes, this lurching awkward being, was more comical than sinister. His mother had loved it much, perhaps loved it more than any of the strange beings she'd met.

He also had another adjustment to make. He had unconsciously expected the Scarecrow to be as tall as he. That was because of Denslow's and Neill's illustrations, which had shown both the Scarecrow and the Tin Woodman as tall as Earth adults. They should not have been drawn as such, since it was evident that a pygmy Munchkin farmer would not make a scarecrow any taller than he.

The thing, smiling, approached, its blue-clad sleeves and white cloth gloves—its hands—spread out welcomingly.

"Dorothy's son!" the phonographic voice boomed. "Welcome! Thrice welcome!"

It folded its arms around Hank's waist and pressed its flat face against him.

Hank was moved, and, for some reason, tears crawled out and slid over his cheeks.

"I thank the Little Father," he said. "I wish my mother could be here with me."

The Scarecrow released him and stepped not very gracefully back.

"And how is the dear little girl?"

"In good health and happy spirits, The Highest. But she is, of course, not a little girl anymore."

"Ah, yes. I forgot. They grow. . . . Well, come along with me to the palace, my boy, and I'll show you your room and give you the schedule for today and tonight."

Hank first made sure, however, that the Jenny was wheeled carefully into a barn and that a guard would keep the curious away from it.

"It, too, has a painted face," the ruler said.

Hank did not reply. What could he say except to ask the king what caused his strange remark.

The daylight hours were spent in making a tour of the city and environs. The evening was a long feast with much guzzling of beer and booze by most of the guests. There was no smoking in the room, however. The Scarecrow still feared fire more than anything. With good reason.

Hank sat at the ruler's right and ate and drank. The Scarecrow, at the head of a table seating fifty, had neither plate nor cup. It asked Hank many questions about his mother and Earth. Then it said, "Glinda has sent me information about the attempt of your people to open a way between them and us. She is much concerned about it."

"I don't think there's any reason to be concerned," Hank said, lying. "My people don't seem able to control the opening, and I doubt very much that they ever will."

"Perhaps not. In any event, Glinda should be able to handle it."

Hank was going to ask what it meant by that, but it said, "Of much more immediate concern is Erakna the Uneatable."

Hank wanted to ask it how the witch got her name, but he was afraid to.

"She's even worse than the late Witch of the West," it said. "She's so cruel and oppressive, and she's taxing the Gillikins' pants off. Her excuse for the high taxes is that she must raise a big army for defense. Yet she's the one who's instigated the border incidents, and she's getting ready to invade us."

The Scarecrow tapped its head. "The trouble with this world is lack of brains. If only reason could rule . . ."

"Emotions have almost always governed human behavior, and they always will," Hank said.

"I wonder what the reason for that is?"

Erakna had been comparatively unknown before the old North Witch died. It was unlawful for anyone but the ruler to practice witchcraft, but there were some who did so anyway in the distant rural areas. Erakna had appeared in Helwedo's palace a few minutes after the old woman had died. She had seized power by terrorizing the Gillikins with a display of witchly pyrotechnics and violence that had cowed them. That she had been planning the takeover for a long time was shown by the suddenness with which a band of her followers had moved into the central government. There had been revolts, but she had put them down bloodily.

The main conflict, the deciding one, would probably be between the witches. If Glinda could overcome Erakna, the Gillikins would fold up. If Erakna killed Glinda, she would take all four countries. There might be resistance to her, but her opponents would be psychologically crippled.

After the feast was over, Hank said goodnight to the guests and went to bed. The Wizard had built a monstrously large bed for himself, a sprawling canopied piece of furniture with gold solid legs and alloyed silver frame. This was the only bed large enough for Hank, and the Scarecrow did not mind Hank using it. The Scarecrow did not sleep. He read all night or studied and signed papers or sometimes just prowled the palace.

"A ruler has many decisions to make, much information about his subjects to ponder. I'm fortunate in that I, unlike flesh and blood monarchs, don't have to waste eight hours every night. My people, you might say, get two rulers for the price of one."

Hank laughed and said, "While you're visiting Glinda, Your Wiseness, who rules in your place?"

The Scarecrow's face could not change expression. Yet Hank got the impression of raised eyebrows.

"My prime minister, Azer the Eager. A very wise young man, though he smokes too much."

"Have you checked him out?" Hank said. "I mean, you know his background thoroughly?"

"What?"

Hank gestured impatiently.

"I mean, he couldn't be a spy? Erakna's agent?"

"Why in the world would you think of that?"

"Erakna, from what I've heard, is very subtle, a real snake. Oh, well, perhaps I'm too presumptuous. Too suspicious. But . . ."

The Scarecrow turned its head so that Hank could see only the larger eye.

"Did Glinda suggest that you ask me about Azer?"

Hank nodded.

"She said that she had no reason to suspect him. I hope Your Oneness will forgive me for saying this, but she wasn't satisfied with his story. I mean, he says he comes from a small village on the Winkie border. But you did not verify that."

"Well, I declare!" the Scarecrow said, and it said something Hank couldn't understand. It was probably reverting to its Munchkin dialect.

"I'll be leaving in the morning," it said. "How can I do that if I don't know whether or not Azer is trustworthy? If he's Erakna's agent, then . . ."

"There's no need to be alarmed," Hank said. "Glinda has already sent a hawk to Azer's village. He investigated and reported to her that Azer seemed to be what he said he was."

The Scarecrow waved its white-cloth hands. "Then, what . . .? Ah, I see! Glinda is teaching me a lesson. She thinks I'm too naive—she's right, I must admit—and she's showing me what I should have done. And what I must do in the future. That Glinda! She's the wise one, not me. I'd say my brains were rotten if I hadn't put in some new ones only yesterday."

It's hard to believe, Hank thought, but it's true. This thing replaced the cloths which made up its body, the trousers and shirt and jacket and gloves, the sack on which its face was painted, the straw which stuffed its body and hands, and the boots, the heaviest part of its body.

It also had put into the head a new mixture of bran and needles. What it called its "brains." The mixture that the punning charlatan, the Wizard Oz, said would make the Scarecrow sharp. Bran-new brains mixed with needles. But that was what the Scarecrow wanted, believing that it was unintelligent, brainless. Yet it had had from the beginning a great wisdom, though it was also uneducated and naive.

Hank shook his head. How could this being be alive? Except for the old tattered floppy-brimmed hat, which was not a part of it, it was entirely new. A different entity from yesterday's. Fully replaced in substance. But not in essence.

What was the thing that made the Scarecrow a living continuum? He believed that there was something that made up the Scarecrow and which inhabited his clothes, boots, and head-sack. Was it some kind of energy configuration? A tightly contained invisible complex of electromagnetism? Or some other kind of energy? A combination of e.m. energy with some unknown energy?

He dared then to voice his questions to the Scarecrow.

The round blue eyes looked surprised, but they always had that look.

"You are a profound young man, as philosophical as you are tall," it said. "I have thought and thought about these enigmas, but I just don't know. I'm wise, but wisdom can't go far without knowledge. And I don't have the knowledge I need. Perhaps Glinda could tell you. Us."

"She's very evasive about such things."

"If she is, she must have very good reasons."

A few minutes after dawn of the next day, the Jenny took off. Three miles due west of the capital was a rough circle of heavy woods about two miles in diameter. This, Ot said, was one of the domains of the wild beasts. Humans never ventured there unless they were fleeing justice.

"Go that way," she said, indicating with a foot a southwest direction.

"Why?" Hank said.

"It's only a little out of the way. You'll see something very interesting."

Hank shrugged and turned the Jenny's nose. Very quickly, he saw a clearing in the green mass. Near its edge on the ground was what looked like an overturned balloonist's basket or gondola.

"What's left of the Wizard Oz's balloon," Ot said. "He came down here after he left The Emerald City because he'd been exposed as a fake wizard. He didn't get far, did he?"

Hank had not expected the Wizard to stay afloat for very long. When the Wizard had risen from the city, he'd been in a balloon the envelope of which had been filled with air heated from a wood fire on the ground. As a result, the hot air had soon cooled after the balloon ascended. The Wizard had been lucky to get as far as he had.

"What happened to Oz after the balloon came down?" Hank shouted.

"He went to the northwest," the hawk said. "Very few humans saw him, but reports from animals and birds indicate that he took off for the wild country that way."

Hank wondered if he could still be alive. He'd been an old man when Dorothy met him, and about thirty-three years had passed since then. Surely, Glinda, who had spies all over the land, would know what had happened to the Wizard. He would have to ask her about him when he got back to Suthwarzha.

It took twenty minutes to leave Ozland. Then the plane was over heavily forested, hilly country which became near-mountainous in ten minutes. This was the difficult terrain which his mother and her three strange pals, two animated objects and a self-doubting lion, had crossed. After sixty miles of increasingly rough air, Hank landed at a depot. It was a mountain meadow at the edge of which were three large tents and a group of people.

When Hank turned the ignition off, he said, "Little Father, how do you like flying?"

"I wasn't cut out to be a bird. I felt rather, ah, uncertain."

The Scarecrow unbuckled the belt without seeming difficulty. Hank had not been sure that it had enough strength to do it. It got out of the cockpit and climbed down. When it jumped off the wing, it sprawled forward on its face.

Hank got out. The Scarecrow got up and said, "I must be the most undignified monarch in two worlds."

"Maybe," Hank said. "But you are the most sober."

It looked at Hank, then laughed phonographically.

"Ah, you mean that I don't drink because I can't. Very good. However, the way I stagger, stumble, and fall, people who don't know me must think I'm a drunk."

By then the Winkies were by the plane. They had a two-wheeled cart on which was a barrel of ethyl alcohol, a funnel and a can. There were six of them, men in clothes of various colors but all wearing yellow conical hats. Hank supervised the refueling, did all that was needed before flight, and took off.

The flight was uneventful, and he landed near the huge gray castle formerly occupied by the Witch of the West. The Tin Woodman, notified by a hawk that the Jenny was coming, was waiting with his entourage at the edge of a meadow. He hurried across it and was by the plane just as its propellor quit whirling. Hank and the Oz monarch got down from the cockpits. The Woodman, however, ignored the customary salutations and embracings to blurt out a message.

"A messenger from Glinda said that we should come as swiftly as possible! She says that the invasion might come sooner than expected. Therefore, we should leave at once."

Niklaz Sa Kapyar (Nicholas the Chopper) did not much resemble the illustrations of him by Denslow and Neill. The funnel hat was missing, and the top of his head was in wavy metal, simulating the curly hair he had once had. The face did not have the comically long and thin cylindrical nose, nor was the jaw a separate piece attached by hinges. It was a lifemask in tin, the features of a young man with large flaring ears, a broad square face, bushy eyebrows, deepset eyes, snub nose, wide mouth (set in a grin by the artisan who'd made it), and a prominent, deeply clefted chin. The eyes had once been painted on, but blue glass eyes had replaced them.

The head was set on a horizontal disc above the thick short neck so that Niklaz could turn the head at 360 degrees if he felt like it.

The trunk had a deep chest to which was welded tin nipples and tin hair. It also had a simulation of a navel.

In the illustrations in Baum's books, the arms and legs were attached to the tin trunk by thick pins, and the joints were similarly secured. The real Tin Man, however, had joints which were like those in a knight's suit of armor, and the arms and legs were not flat but rounded in a lifelike manner. Though he could move less awkwardly than Baum's Tin Man would have been compelled to, he still was not graceful or swift.

Like the Tin Man of Denslow and Neill, he did not wear clothes. However, the artisan had omitted the sex organs.

He wore no crown. Why should he? There was only one like him in the land, and everybody knew that he was the ruler of the west country. A servant did, however, carry for him the symbol of the office and the man, the tin ax.

Now that the king had delivered his message, he embraced the Scarecrow. They told each other how glad they were to meet again, and they asked about each other's health (which Hank thought was funny since they never got sick), and then the Scarecrow introduced Hank, which was also unnecessary, since his identity was obvious.

The Tin Woodman spoke in a voice as phonograph-sounding as his stuffed friend. He said that he was happy to meet him, and then he relayed Glinda's message.

"I had hoped you could spend some time in my palace," he said. His right arm swiveled slightly to gesture at the huge somber stone pile on top of a hill.

"But we must leave now."

Hank said they could go as soon as he had refueled and checked the oil supply and inspected for leaks and loose wires. A half hour later, the two kings were in the front cockpit. Hank and Ot got into the back one, the carburetor was primed with ether, the propellor was spun, and the engine coughed, turned, and roared. After taxiing to the far end of the field, the Jenny took off southeastwards.

The rough country got even hillier, then became a mountain range. Hank flew between the mountains, many of which were over twelve thousand feet high. The sun was covered with clouds. Generally, he followed a broad winding river at the bottom of a canyon, but sometimes Ot told him to go through passes to shorten the distance. They had been in the air for an hour and a half when Ot said, "Turn right into that pass there. The first refueling station is two miles from the river."

"Good!" Hank said. "I don't want to get caught in a storm."

Hank brought the Jenny up and out of the canyon, over its edge, and started down above a downward slope. He was at a thousand feet above the ground when Ot screamed, "Great God!"

"What is it?" Hank said. He could see no cause for alarm.

"Hawks!" Ot cried. "About fifty! Straight ahead!"

Hank still could not see anything.

"What about them?"

"They're flying straight for us! They can't be up to any good! It must be an ambush! They're Erakna's, I'll bet! She's sent them here to attack us! She can wipe us out, kill two of her greatest enemies, kill you, wreck the airplane! Oh, my God!"

Hank saw a swarm of dots ahead. He twisted around to look back, and he swore.

"Looks like there's an equal number behind us!"

"See! I told you so! It's an ambush! What do we do now?"

The hawks had planned well. The Jenny was between two precipitous mountains towering over eleven thousand feet. She had about four miles on both sides to maneuver, but she could not turn tail and try to ram through the hawks behind. She might escape them, but she'd run out of fuel before she could get to the next station.

Hank had to fly westward.

He began climbing. He could not gain altitude faster than the hawks and so fly over them. But he was going to need room for maneuvering. He didn't want to smack into a mountainside while he was trying to elude the attackers.

He looked upwards, and he was startled.

There seemed to be several hundred dots up there dropping at terrific speed. Then they became recognizable as hawks as they hurtled down in their two-hundred-mile-per-hour dive.

"Lord, we're done for!" Ot moaned. "Holy Marzha, Mother of Mercy, bless me! Holy Nantho, Mother of Hawks, protect me!"

"How about the rest of us?" Hank yelled. "Say a prayer for us, too!"

Then he said, "What the hell?"

The hawks above had flattened out their dives somewhat. One group was headed towards an intersection point with the hawks approaching from ahead; the second, towards the hawks behind the plane.

Ot screamed with delight.

"They must be Glinda's! She found out about Erakna's ambush and set up an ambush for the ambushers!"

Hank hoped that that was true. He also wished that Glinda had warned him about this so he could have flown another route. But maybe she'd not had enough time.

Hank quit climbing and dived somewhat before leveling out. He pushed the throttle in all the way. He would need all the speed he could get to bull his way through the oncoming enemy. The altimeter indicated that he had almost a thousand feet altitude above the ground below him. He was five thousand feet above sea level, which meant that the engine had less power. It needed more oxygen. He was making only sixty miles per hour ground speed.

Then the Jenny was among a cloud of hawks. Ten seconds before, Glinda's birds had struck the enemy like bolts of feathered lightning. The fifty or so headed for him had suddenly become about a dozen. But these were out to kill him and were checking their speed to match his. They would be trying to board the Jenny as if they were pirates.

The Scarecrow and the Woodman had unstrapped the safety belt and were standing up. The Winkie king held his ax up, ready to chop at the onslaughters. The Ozian was waving his arms about as if he could scare off the birds. Or perhaps he was just expressing his fear.

Hank cursed and howled at them to sit down and belt themselves in again. He could not make any violent maneuvers that might throw the two out of the plane. Then he thought that, yes, he could. The Scarecrow could land almost as safely as if it wore a parachute. The tin man would be battered and bent and maybe his limbs and head might be torn off. But he could be repaired.

However, he had no time nor room for dives, loop the loops, chandelles, Immelmanns, or anything like that. Even if he had, he'd have been followed by the hawks.

A hawk landed on the upper right wing and sank its talons into the fabric. This ripped away, and the dispossessed bird, a screeching frustrated fury, shot by Hank.

Another hawk managed to grip the edge of the front cockpit windshield. Niklaz's ax flashed, and the hawk was split. Blood spattered the windshield and cockpit and covered parts of the rear windshield. Hank suddenly could not see ahead.

That did not concern for the moment. There was a thump, a perceptible jarring and slowing down of the plane. Feathers sprayed by him and pieces of flesh and a severed glaring-eyed head. The plane began to quiver and to shake. And the motor roared peculiarly.

One or more hawks had encountered the whirling propellor.

The vibrations increased; the plane bucked.

Hank cursed once more, and he cut the ignition off. The propellor presently was still, revealing that the outer part of a blade had been broken off.

"What is it? What's happened?" Ot screamed.

"We have to make a deadstick landing!" Hank said. He did not have to yell now. The only sound was the singing of the wind through the wires connecting the wings and the fuselage. And the far-off shrieking of the battling hawks.

He looked behind. Glinda's divebombers had knocked out over two thirds of the enemy, but the survivors were battling hard.

He looked below on both sides. Two miles ahead was the broad though sloping meadow that was to be his first landing on the home-leg. It still was. Fortunately, the wind had not become stronger, and it was only slightly gusty.

The two in the front cockpit were yelling at him now. They wanted to know what would happen.

Hank shouted back at them, but the wind carried his words off. He sent Ot to them with his message.

"And stay with them or abandon ship," he said. "I don't care which. Just get out of the cockpit. I need all the room I can get."

Ot delivered the information. The two sat down, and the hawk did the intelligent thing. She flew away.

The wind was from the west today. Hank glided steeply enough into it to keep the Jenny from stalling but not so swiftly that he would, he hoped, land at such a velocity that he'd run out of landing area. When past the meadow, he banked and came back across it and then turned towards it again. The wheels knocked leaves off from the top branches of a tree. Having cleared that, Hank at once side-slipped the plane to lose altitude swiftly. He had just time enough to straighten it out before his wheels touched. Up went the plane, bouncing, came down on wheels and tailskid, leaped again, landed hard, bounced a little, and then the grass and flowers of the meadow were streaming below them and the trees ahead were racing toward them. He did not have brakes; he could only pray that the Jenny would stop in time.

She did. Under the limbs of a tree, the propellor hub only a few inches from a thick gray-black tree trunk.

Hank sat and said nothing for a while. His breathing and heart slowed down. The two ahead of him also sat quietly. From a distance, thunder rumbled and the cries of men running from the camp came to them. Ot landed on the edge of the cockpit, startling him.

"A bad landing for a hawk!" she cried. "But I suppose it's a good one for a man?"

"Very good under the conditions," Hank said.

The Scarecrow rose and turned around. It had some blood spots on its face and the point of a feather stuck near the edge of its painted lips. Though its face did not lose its smile, its voice quivered.

"Does this happen often?"

"Nothing exactly like it has ever happened before," Hank said. "But I've been in worse situations. Anyway, we Earth pilots have a saying. Any landing you can walk away from is a good landing. So this is very good."

Rain dropped, gently at first, then poured. The Scarecrow got under a wing. If watersoaked, it became heavy and slow-moving. The

Woodman did not mind the rain. Despite what Baum had said, it did not rust. That was a nice touch Baum had made up, as was the Woodman's weeping and then getting rusty joints from the tears. Niklaz had no body fluids or tear ducts.

Ot said, "Glinda has to be notified about this. I'll get a messenger if there's one available. Do you have anything special to tell her?"

"Yes. We may be three days late. Or more. I have to get a new propellor. And I have to take out the propellor shaft and see if it's been bent. If it is, then it has to be straightened. Also, we can't fly if it keeps on raining. We won't take off until the repairs have been made and the weather's good."

"I'll see she gets the message," Ot said, and she flapped off.

By then men had arrived. They were wild-looking, their hair growing waist-length, their beards spreading out like wild mushrooms, their cloth garments tattered, torn, and dirty, and they bristled with daggers, swords, spears, and axes.

According to what Niklaz had said before they'd taken off, these were outlaws. Glinda had made contact via hawk with several groups of "wild men," as they were called. She had offered them pardons if they would act as guerrillas for her. They had set up the refueling stations in these mountains. After the plane had left, they would go northward, slip across the Gillikin border, and terrorize the citizens. Or, if the Gillikins invaded, the guerrillas would harass the armies.

Ot introduced him to the leaders of the band, which numbered exactly forty.

Call me Ali Baba, Hank thought. Forty thieves is right. They could have stepped out, been run out, rather, from *The Arabian Nights* for being too unsavory. I never saw such a bunch of cutthroats, not even on Wall Street.

The two that especially got his attention were Sharts the Shirtless and Blogo the Rare Beast.

Sharts was a giant among his own kind, as tall as Hank's six feet two inches and broader and more heavily muscled. A "Strangler" Lewis. A handsome one, though, the only clean-shaved man in the crowd. He could have posed for a collar ad. His thick wavy hair was sunset-red. His eyes were strange and disconcerting, purplish with aquamarine flecks and with a hint of madness about them. He had a habit of whistling tunelessly while by himself or when someone else was talking to him. This was going to irritate Hank considerably, but at the moment he just thought that it was an eccentricity to note.

Hank did not know how Sharts had earned his sobriquet. He wore a bronze-colored velvet shirt which must have cost him, or the man he robbed it from, much money.

Weird-looking as the giant was, he was like a candle beside a searchlight compared to Blogo. Hank knew at once that this creature's ancestors had not originated on Earth.

Blogo's head was apish but bore on its top a tall fleshy-red rooster's comb. His nose was long and cylindrical and had a big knob at the end. His long rusty hair swirled in the back to make an opening for the third eye there. The eyes in front were small and light blue and looked guileless. His arms, though human enough, were covered with more rusty-red hair and reached to his knees. The torso was also human, though very hairy, and few men were as broad or as thickly boned. The legs were ostrich-like, very skinny, completely hairless and as pale as the belly of a fish. The feet were those of a five-toed bird.

Blogo's chest was cavernous, but his voice was high-pitched and squeaky. It needed lubrication and apparently got it quite often. He carried on a shoulder strap a large stone flask which contained a mixture of water and grain alcohol, easy on the water.

Sharts the Shirtless's voice was like the bass from an organ, deep, honey-flowing, and almost emitting sparks of charisma.

Unreasonably, Hank became jealous. How would Glinda react if she ever met this fellow? And he was glad that saluting, not handshaking, was the custom here. This man could have pulped his hand and probably would have been pleased to do so.

"Even in our mountain fastness we've heard of you," Sharts said. "The fabled Earthman. Tall as our ancestors were supposed to be. Neither of us, however, are as near to the sky as Thago the Ungracious, Erakna's bodyguard and lover. He boasts that he is the biggest and strongest man in the whole land. I hope to get near enough to him some day to test him."

"I'd like to see that fight," Hank said. "*I* wouldn't want to tackle you."

Sharts looked pleased, though he did not smile. He never smiled.

"This," he said, gesturing at Blogo, "is my second-in-command and my bosom buddy."

"At your service, friend of Glinda the Good," Blogo said. "I might add that, excluding Sharts for certain and Thago for perhaps, I am the second strongest man in the whole land. I am also the most courageous."

"Yes, he's afraid of nobody or no thing," Sharts said. "Isn't that right, Blogo?"

Blogo swelled out his chest, and his cock's comb expanded and became a deeper red. "Right."

"Unafraid of anybody or any thing," Sharts said. He paused, then said, "Except for the Very Rare Beast. Right, Blogo?"

Hank could almost see the air spurting out of Blogo. The comb shrank, and it may have been his imagination, but Hank thought that the knobbed nose became slightly deflated.

"Well, yes."

"Who's the Very Rare Beast?" Hank said.

"I don't even want to talk about him," Blogo said, and he strode off on his birdlike legs.

Hank, watching him, said, "Are there any more like him?"

"In spirit or in form?" Sharts said.

"I mean . . . of his kind?"

"A few," Sharts said sadly. "There are about twenty still living. His species is near extinction."

"He doesn't look natural," Hank said. "I mean, he doesn't look like a product of nature, one of God's own creations."

"He's not. His ancestors were, I believe, and I've done a deep study of his origins, made by the Long-Gones."

Hank told him what had to be done. Sharts said that he would see to it that all that was required would be done and very swiftly.

"When I say, 'Go!', the whole universe beats it."

Hank grinned but said nothing. When Sharts had left, Ot said, "You must restrain your quick temper around these people. They don't like badmouthing. They just might run you through with a knife, even though they do have a high respect for Glinda. Also, don't argue with Sharts. He thinks he knows everything, and he gets nasty if anybody contradicts him. Sharts's nastiness is ten times more nasty than anybody else's."

"What was he outlawed for?" Hank said.

"You might not believe it to look at him now," the hawk said. "But at one time he was the greatest scholar and doctor of medicine in

Quadlingland. Except for Glinda, of course. One day, a subordinate had an attack of irrationality or pride or indiscretion. Or all three. I don't know just what Sharts and his assistant were arguing about. I've heard that it concerned whether or not the soul was a physical entity and, if so, where it was located in the body. Sharts claimed that it must be in the brain and it could be located and operated on so that its tendency towards evil could be removed. The assistant said that that was nonsense. Sharts lost his temper and broke the assistant's neck. Then he fled from justice and took refuge in the woods.''

"I'll try to control my temper," Hank said.

"Good idea. Even the Cowardly Lion is afraid of him."

"Why was the Rare Beast outlawed?"

"Oh, him! Hah, hah! Ugly and outre as he is, he thinks he's the world's greatest lover. Maybe he is. Anyway, one of his many women claimed that she was pregnant by him. That's impossible, of course. No human woman could conceive by a Beast. But she pressed her suit in court, and the legally literal-minded judge of the remote rural area where they lived decided that Blogo had to marry her. That so enraged him that he killed the judge and three character witnesses with his bare hands, wrecked the courtroom, and fled through a window.

"When Glinda heard about it, she cancelled the judge's decision, but he's still wanted for murder."

"A nice pair," Hank said.

"If you don't cross them, you'll find them very likeable," Ot said. "If you can stand Sharts's whistling and Blogo's bragging."

13

Sharts might be arrogantly proud of his knowledge, but he certainly had a very keen mind for mechanics. He asked so many questions about the airplane that Hank became annoyed. He was discreet enough to conceal his irritation, however. And, once Sharts had had the principles of aeronautics and internal combustion motors explained, he was a great help to Hank. He assisted Hank in the inspection and repairs. He also rustled up fabric and glue to repair the wing torn by the enemy hawk. And he had Hank explain the operation of the .45 revolver.

"We'd all have weapons like that," he said, "if it weren't for the witches and wizards."

Hank said, "What do you mean?"

"The explosives you call gunpowder were invented four hundred years ago. Maybe earlier. But the rulers made its manufacture and use illegal. Anybody caught with it was hanged. The witches and wizards did not want everybody who'd like to kill them to be able to do so from a half-mile away. Any competent magician can prevent any lay person from killing him within a quarter-mile range by arrows. So . . . no powder and no guns."

"But my mother's farmhouse fell on the Munchkin witch and killed her."

"It was a force of nature, a tornado coming seemingly from nowhere that did it," Sharts said. "The witch was caught off guard. And then there's always the possibility that Glinda had her hand in that."

Hank raised his eyebrows.

"That thought has occurred to me, too. Anyway, you're an outlaw. What's to keep you from making powder and guns?"

"The witches don't bother me as long as I don't bother them. But if I did have guns, both the good and the bad witches would be on me like bluejays on a cat. Like coyotes on a dying bull."

"I would think that a man with your great knowledge and mind would have become a wizard," Hank said.

"I'm too well known, too easily identified. I'd have to find a mistress or master, a teacher, and the moment I applied to one of the big ones, I'd be marked, even if I could find one who'd take me as an apprentice. I wouldn't last long. I could find a minor wizard or witch, but they couldn't teach me what I'd want to know. The small ones are practicing illegally and will be hanged if caught. But the big witches tend to ignore the lesser ones since they're no danger to them."

"What about Erakna? How'd she escape the notice of Glinda and the old North Witch?"

"She didn't. She was Helwedo's apprentice for a while, studying to be a white witch. Then she said that she'd had a change of mind, and she didn't want to be a witch anymore. She resigned and joined a nunnery in the far north. But she had become a red witch; that happens sometimes, you know, a good witch goes wrong. She managed to keep it secret, bided her time, and, when Helwedo died, she struck. She surprised Glinda. Believe me, that takes some doing.

"Why has Glinda allowed you to keep your firearms?"

"I don't know," Hank said. "I wondered about that, but I thought it better not to ask."

"She's probably making an exception because she plans to use you. You'll be more useful because you have this flying machine and your exploding weapons."

"I wouldn't be surprised," Hank said.

He asked Sharts about the rolling lightning balls, the sentiency of animals, and the animation of the Scarecrow.

Sharts's internal struggle was visible. He hated to say that he did not know the answers to Hank's questions. It galled and roiled him so much that he even forgot his obnoxious whistling. Finally, after many grimaces and grinding of teeth and twitching of nose and ears and fisting and unfisting, he acknowledged the truth.

Hank kept his face blank. He did not want to look sympathetic or astonished. Sharts might resent either expression.

"I do have several theories," the giant said, breathing heavily. "But they are such that I can't test them out in a laboratory. The witches and wizards claim that they don't know, but I think they're lying. They know, but they don't want the people to know."

Using the undamaged propellor blade as a model, Sharts carved out of an indigenous wood as light as balsa two blades for the Jenny. Three days after the landing, the plane was ready to go. By then, the sky had cleared up. However, the weather-scout hawks reported that a heavy storm front was moving in from the west. Hank should be able to get to all of his refueling stations before it struck. He might even be able to reach Glinda's capital.

He said thanks and goodbye to the outlaws. He waved to them from the cockpit as the Jenny climbed from the meadow. He had a hunch that he would see them again.

When he landed at the last refueling stop, he got the latest news from a hawk sent by Glinda. Erakna had launched a full-scale invasion. Her armies had overrun the Winkies on the borders and were pushing through the forest between Gillikinland and Ozland.

"What do we do now?" the Tin Woodman said. "We should be home directing our troops. Our people's morale will be low without us to lead them."

"Glinda didn't tell me what to do if such an event happened," Hank said. "But she would have thought about its possibility. Obviously, she wants a conference with you whatever should happen."

A weather scout flew in. The storm front was still one hundred miles away.

The local conditions were strange. There was not a wisp of wind. The air was as heavy as the belly of a hog that had fallen into a corncrib. It was also very dry, as dry as the Prohibitionists had hoped that America would be after the Volstead Act. When Hank rubbed his hand across the patch on the wing, sparks cracked.

The two rulers were uneasy. If they could have rolled their eyes, they would have done so.

"We think that it'll be best for us to stay in camp until the storm is over," the Woodman said to Hank.

"Why? That might mean a delay of several days. A week, maybe. Every second counts now."

"When the air's so dry and there's so much electricity in the air, strange things sometimes happen," the Scarecrow said.

"Like what?"

"The little mind-spirits, the firefoxes, roam freely then. The witches can keep out the big ones, usually, but they can't control the little ones unless they're close to them."

"What do you mean?"

"Sometimes, the little ones dispossess animals and birds and those who were born in, uh, objects.

"You don't have to worry about that. Few humans ever get dispossessed, though it does, rarely, happen. It's said that, when a good witch becomes a bad one, she's been taken over by an evil mind-spirit. I reserve conclusion on that statement. There's not enough information to decide what is the truth and what isn't."

"They're right," Ot said. "We should wait until the storm's over."

"We can get home before it comes."

"You don't understand!" the Tin Woodman said. "It's here! Now! The first wave, anyway. Things'll get worse soon."

"Oh, you're talking about the static electricity," Hank said.

"Yes, of course!"

"He's an ignorant Earthman," the Scarecrow said. "You can't expect him to understand."

"His world must be a good one," the Woodman said, "if they don't have to worry there about mind-spirits."

Hank was exasperated.

"I don't think you know any more about these things than I do!"

"We don't know much about them. But we have experienced them," the Scarecrow said gently and a trifle superiorly.

"Well, what do you want to do?" Hank said. "Stay here or fly on? If you stay, you're going to be late for the conference. Worse, you'll be late getting back home. By the time you do, you might find that the Gillikins have occupied your capitals. Or the war's over, and you're no longer crowned heads. Just royal bums!"

"That wouldn't be a bad life," the Woodman said. "To tell the truth, I'm not as happy as I should be. Being a king is hard work and tedious. I was happier when I was just a woodchopper. There wasn't any glory to it, but I didn't have all those responsibilities, either."

"I would abdicate in a moment," the Scarecrow said, "if my conscience did not force me to stay on the throne. The people need someone with brains to guide them. Though, sometimes, I think that they'd do just as well without me. The system is set up so that . . ."

"This is no time for soul-searching," Hank said. "Or maybe it is. Look. You two are putting your safety ahead of your concern for your people. Royal cowards! Do you think that Glinda even considered the possibility that you might delay the trip because you're scared? She would've gotten a report on what the weather conditions are here. But did she send a message that you should wait until the danger, if there is any, is over? No, she didn't."

"You just don't understand," the Scarecrow said. "You wouldn't go up if there was a thunderstorm. Why should we go on when we'll have to face the equivalent of a thunderstorm, no, something much more perilous than that?"

Hank became even angrier.

"I'm taking off in a few minutes from now! If you decide to stay here, too bad! I'll just have to explain to Glinda what happened!"

The Scarecrow, the Woodman, and the hawk groaned.

Reluctantly, the three got into the cockpits. For once, Ot did not chatter incessantly or, indeed, at all. She was very subdued. Hank would have liked this if he had not started feeling guilty. Perhaps they did have some very good reasons for not going up. If anything they expected did happen, then he would be responsible.

On the other hand, they should leave at once no matter what perils awaited them. He began wishing that a thunderstorm had sealed them in. Then everybody would have had an excuse for not flying.

If every *if* was a drop of water, everybody would have been drowned long ago.

About ten miles from the stop, as they were flying at five thousand feet altitude between two mountains, a form of St. Elmo's fire sheathed the craft. Spires of static electricity rose from every point. When he took his hand from the joystick, flame leaped between its end and his glove. Gouts of fire streamed up from the tops of the heads of the two in the front cockpit. Around the propellor was a flaming circle, a St. Catherine's wheel. Flame ran up and down the wires between the wings. Ot cowered down by Hank and moaned, then stuck her head under a wing.

"It can't hurt us!" Hank shouted. No one besides himself could hear him, but he needed assurance, even if only from himself.

He jumped as the fire on the right wing flowed towards its tip, and then collected into a ball about a foot in diameter. It began rolling back and forth along the right upper wing. Then it shot from the tip onto the left upper wing, drawing the fire there into it.

Hank dipped the left wing in the forlorn hope that the ball would roll off. It did not, of course.

The Scarecrow and the Woodman had disappeared. They must be bending over as far as they could go to escape observation. As if the ball could see them!

Now the sphere rolled inwards along the upper wing. It stopped for a moment at the inner edge of the wing above the front cockpit. Hank watched it while he cursed himself for having insisted on the flight. He was scared. Part of his fear derived from his helplessness and not knowing the nature of this thing.

Suddenly, the sphere leaped out, a fiery missile shot by an invisible cannon. It arced over the front cockpit and landed on the edge of Hank's windshield.

He stared into the bright blaze and could see through it the trailing edges of the upper wing and the clear sky beyond.

A vision of it landing on his head, enveloping it, and then exploding was so strong that he almost believed that it had happened.

He yelled with terror, and Ot, startled, jerked her head from her wing. She screamed, and she leaped upwards, her wings unfolding. She was abandoning ship.

The sphere shot out at an angle past Hank. He twisted his head to see it, but it was gone by then. Where? Ot was dwindling, a dark shape below him. She was, however, no longer flying. Her wings were extended for gliding.

He felt relieved until he realized that he had lost his guide.

There was more to worry about than finding his way back. Again, the plane was wrapped in the eerie electric flames. A glowing sphere formed, but this time on the tip of the left upper wing. It rolled along the plane, sucking up the static, until it had traversed the entire length. Then it rolled back and poised, as had the previous one, above the front cockpit.

Hank pulled the .45 revolver out of the holster and shot it.

He did not think that the bullet would do any good. In the first place, the bullet was lead, not iron. In the second place, even if it had been iron, it was not grounded. Just as he had expected, the sphere was undisturbed.

Firing at it did nothing but make him feel as if he were doing something to protect himself. He was not, however.

He saw the tin head of the Woodman rise above the edge of the cockpit, then duck back quickly.

He pressed his back against the cockpit. So swiftly that he had not seen it even as a blur, the sphere had leaped from the wing to the edge of his windshield.

Hank shot it again. Shot through it, rather. The ball was unaffected, but there was a tiny hole in the fabric of the upper wing.

"It won't get into me!" Hank said aloud. "They say it doesn't harm humans. Well, hardly ever!"

But what if it were just the ordinary Earth-type lightning-ball? It could land on him and blow up, burn him or short-circuit his nervous system and make him insane. He had read about such balls doing just that to humans.

The sphere was gone. There it was! Perched now on the rim of the front cockpit windshield.

The Tin Woodman rose, the upper part of his body visible. He would have to be standing on the seat. His ax rose, lifted by two hands.

Hank waited for the explosion.

It did not come. As if whisked by an unseen hand, the glowing sphere shot back from the cockpit and seemed to disappear into the engine.

A moment later all electrical manifestations were gone.

Far off on the horizon, the black storm raced towards them.

14

The Jenny outran the clouds, though not the wind, in the mountains. Hank had to land her in the hilly country. He found an upland farm and brought her in over a meadow against a strong wind. As he was taxiing towards a barn, the right wings were lifted by a gust. The left wings dipped, and the tip of the lower one would have scraped against the ground so quickly that he would not have had time to use the controls to right the craft. But the tip did not drag against the earth and tear up fabric and bend the framework. The left wing lifted, putting the plane on both wheels.

"That was lucky!" Hank muttered. A gust under the left wing must have straightened her out.

It almost seemed as if Jenny had done it herself.

The farmers ran out of the house, their eyes wide, their arms waving. They had never even heard of the Earthman and his flying machine, and they were frightened, not sure whether the thing was a dragon of legend or a vehicle for a wizard. They knew about the Scarecrow and the Tin Woodman, however. These reassured the farmers, who then pushed the Jenny into a huge community storage barn. Hank tied her down, and all went into the house.

The storm hit a few minutes later with lightning, thunder, and rain. Hank sat on several cushions on the floor in a corner while their hosts served him food and drink. They were awed and pleased by the presence of the two rulers and the giant who was under the protection of Glinda the Good.

With a big if meatless meal and a pint of vodka in him, Hank said goodnight to the farmers and went to the barn to sleep. His two passengers accompanied him. Hank lay down on the hay in a stall.

"Your Shininess," he said to the Woodman, "I've not had a chance to ask you just how you got your, uh, present form. I know what you told my mother. The story is that you were in love with a young woman, but her mother did not want her daughter to marry a woodchopper. She wanted her to marry a rich farmer and town councillor, even though he was fifteen years older than the daughter. But the daughter preferred you. So the mother got a minor witch, an old woman named Mombi, to put a spell on you. Is that right so far?"

The Winkie king sighed, and he said, "That's what I told your mother."

"Is this Mombi the one who's allied with Erakna?"

"Yes. Though 'allied' isn't the correct word. Mombi is a subordinate. She's not Erakna's equal."

"O.K. Got you. Anyway, my mother said that you said that the spell worked this way. First, it made your ax slip while you were cutting wood, and it cut your right foot off."

"That's what I told your mother."

"But you had an artificial foot made and went right on cutting wood. And your girlfriend still insisted on marrying you."

"Those were my words."

"The next time that the ax slipped, it cut off your right leg."

"Halfway down the thigh. I knew then that the 'accidents' were no accidents. How could an ax do that? It would have to be directed by someone, a witch or wizard. I knew that someone did not wish me well, and it didn't take long to figure out who that one was. I accused her mother, but she denied it. So I went to old Mombi and accused her, but she denied it. I would have gone to the police then, but her mother would have been involved, and she would have been hanged with Mombi. My lover could not endure that. She begged me not to tell the police, and she promised that she'd get her mother to call Mombi off. She'd marry me right away, too, and then there'd be no reason to keep the spell on me. So I said I'd keep quiet about it."

"Why would Mombi be executed?" Hank said. "The Munchkins were ruled by the East Witch then. She wouldn't care if there were other red witches."

"Wrong. She didn't want any competition at all, red or white."

"Baum wrote that the woman's mother had gone to the East Witch and promised her two sheep and a cow if she kept you from marrying her daughter. That isn't what Dorothy told him, but he either forgot the details or else decided to streamline and modify the story. Anyway, the East Witch would not be bribed by two sheep and a cow. That'd be too paltry a sum. And animals just can't be given away to others, as we do on Earth. They have rights. Baum overlooked that. Also, if the East Witch had wanted to get rid of you, she'd just have you killed. None of this slow amputation stuff."

"It was Mombi, not the East Witch who put the spell on me," the Tin Woodman said. "But the East Witch would have enjoyed the, as you put it, slow amputation stuff."

"Baum wrote that, the first time the spell worked, it made the ax slip and cut off your leg. So, he said, you went to a tinsmith and had him make you a new leg of tin. Just how would the tinsmith attach the leg to your body? With a pin through the hipbone? Even if he could do that, you couldn't use the leg except as a crutch. And it would have been useless since it would have bent at the knee. You couldn't have walked with it, let alone chop wood and carry the wood."

The Scarecrow said, "I admire the way you use your brains, Hank. You're very logical."

"Thank you, Little Father. So, Baum wrote that the loss of your leg didn't stop you from working or from courting the old woman's daughter. But the East Witch continued the spell. The ax chopped off your right leg. Very neat. But painful, I would think. And how did you survive these amputations? You were alone in the forest when these 'accidents' happened. You must have lost a great deal of blood. It was a wonder you didn't die. Who found you, applied a tourniquet to your stump, took you to a doctor? How long were you in a hospital?"

The Winkie king did not reply.

"And then, according to Baum, the ax cut off your arms, one after the other. By that, 'one after the other,' he must have meant that there was a considerable time between the severing of one arm and the next. But, surely, you would have known long before that that the ax was enchanted by a malevolent witch or wizard. You would have refused to use that ax. In fact, you would have given up using the ax or any dangerous tool.

"So, Baum wrote, you replaced your arms with tin ones. But you would have been able to use these even less than you could use the legs.

"And then, here comes the most unbelievable part, the ax slipped and cut off your head. But, so Baum said, the tinsmith happened to come along, and he made you a new head out of tin!"

"Thinking logically, I would say," the Scarecrow said, "that you would have been dead, Niklaz. The tinsmith could have done nothing for you."

Hank looked surprised. He said, "Is this the first time you've thought about his story?"

"Oh, no! I'm just making some comments. Bolstering the structure of your logical questioning."

"Well," Hank said, "then comes the next event. The ax is supposed to have slipped once more and cut your body into two equal parts. Again, the tinsmith came to your rescue. He made you a torso of tin and attached your other tin parts to it. But you did not love the girl any more because you did not have a heart. You were a hollow man in more ways than one."

"Not really a man," the Winkie king said.

"Yes! Baum was writing a children's book, so he could not have said anything about your lack of genitals. I doubt that he even thought of that. My mother hadn't, not when you told her your story. She was only eight years old.

"Baum said that, once you were in your tin body, you were in only one danger. Your joints might rust. So you kept a full oilcan in your cottage, and you oiled the joints when you thought it was needed. But one day you were caught in a rainstorm, the joints rusted, and you couldn't move. You stood there in the woods for a year until Dorothy and the Scarecrow came along and oiled the joints. Nonsense! Tin wouldn't rust that fast, if at all."

"Very good," the Scarecrow said.

"Baum also said that you had a lot of time to think while you were frozen with rust. You had time to decide that the greatest loss you had known was not losing your sweetheart. It was losing your heart. When you were in love, you were very happy. Love was the greatest thing in the world, and I won't argue about that. To love, you had to have a heart, and you vowed to go to the Wizard Oz and ask him to give you one.

"After that, you'd ask your sweetheart to marry you. Now, I ask you, what kind of marriage would that be? A tin man, no flesh-and-blood organs whatsoever, married to a flesh-and-blood woman? Did you really for a moment think that she'd marry you? Or, if she did, that the marriage would last?"

"Of course not," Niklaz said.

"Well, then, did you really go to Oz to ask him for a heart? Did you need a heart? That is, did you lack kindness and tenderness and compassion and empathy?"

"No."

Hank turned to the Scarecrow.

"Did you really go to Oz to ask him for brains because you thought you needed them?"

"Oh, yes!" the stuffed thing said. "I was stupid; I knew it; I wanted intelligence more than anything."

"But you had it from the beginning!"

"Oh, no! I didn't know anything! Well, very little, anyway."

"You confused lack of knowledge and experience with a lack of intelligence," Hank said. "Well, O.K., so you weren't lying when you told my mother why you wanted to see Oz. But King Niklaz . . ."

"You believe I'm lying?"

The tin mask was expressionless, but the voice was indignant.

"Yes. Your story just won't hold water. It's leaking like a sieve. Just to take one thing, your new tin head. You'd be dead. Your brain would be rotting. But even if it weren't and the tinsmith managed by some surgical miracle to transfer your brains and nervous system to the tin head, how would it be kept alive? It needs blood and food. But you say that even this impossible thing wasn't done. You were given a new head, an empty tin one, and suddenly you, your brain, your spirit, call it what you will, is in the tin head. Baum didn't say that, but it's implied."

"What is your reasoning about this?" the Tin Woodman said. His voice was emotionless.

"I think that you did lose a foot, and that it was caused by a spell—whatever that means—put on you by Mombi. You thought that it was an accident, and you had an artificial foot made of tin. The connection must have been made by a leather ring or sheath, though. Otherwise, the metal would've rubbed your flesh raw. How am I doing so far?"

''You make sense,'' Niklaz said. ''But what seems to be sense is not always so in reality.''

''Then, when you lost the other foot, you knew that someone had enchanted—I hate to use that unscientific word—enchanted the ax. You figured out quickly who was behind the 'accidents.' Your reluctant future mother-in-law and the only known local witch, Mombi. Isn't that right?''

''You'd make a fine detective,'' Niklaz said. ''A fine theoretical one, anyway.''

''But not a good practical one, is that what you mean?'' Hank said, cocking his head to one side. He grinned. ''Let me continue to theorize.

''So, though you might be a simple man who chopped and sold wood for a living, you were smart enough to seek out someone who might protect you. Or, maybe, this someone had had her eye on you, and she came to you. It'd be a hell of a long walk for a man with two good feet, but one who had artificial feet, well!''

''Her?'' the Scarecrow said. ''You said, 'Her.' ''

''A long walk,'' Niklaz said. ''To where?''

''To Glinda in her Quadling capital,'' Hank said. ''I don't think you went to her. She came to you. Or maybe she transported you to her by magical means. In any case, you two met face to face. And she made a bargain. She'd put you in a new body, one that could not be killed, though it could be destroyed. Not easily, however. She promised you immortality or a very long long life, anyway. She probably had to argue with you for some time. You might be immortal and near-invulnerable, but you'd be giving up a lot for that. You'd never taste good food and drink again. On the other hand, you'd not have the daily inconvenience and mess of digestion and excretion. You wouldn't have to worry about bad breath or toothaches or losing your teeth or having cancer or heart failure.

''You wouldn't have a stroke or go blind or have an earache or have to suffer the aches, pains, loss of strength, and sadness of growing old. Need I go on? The profits would be greater than the losses.

''The greatest losses, though, would be that you'd have no sexual pleasure and no children.''

''Those are great,'' the Tin Woodman said. ''But possibly the worst is something you forgot. I'd be a freak. I'd no longer be regarded by humans as being human. I'd always be an outsider. I could be their king, but I'd not be able to share fully the acceptance and warmth that one human can give to another. On the other hand, as you say, how many humans ever do give the acceptance, understanding, and warmth that they should if they're fully human?

"Really, they're all freaks. Well, no, I shouldn't say that. Almost all are. There are some genuine, fully human humans among them. But they're so rare that they're freaks, too."

"Well, I don't think they're as bad as that," Hank said. "But I'll have to admit that there are few of us who get to be what we should be."

"Or even try," Niklaz said.

"You may not have stood for a year with nothing to do but think," Hank said. "But you must have done a lot of thinking."

"I lived alone in the woods."

"Now," Hank said. "Continuing my surmises—or is it deductions? —Glinda did come to you with an offer. And you took it. So she transferred your persona, I don't know how, your soul or your cerebral-neural system to the tin body. Which was made all at once and not piecemeal as in the story you told everybody. I don't mean that she literally transferred your brains. Obviously, she couldn't do that. But she did transfer whatever it is that makes you you to the tin head."

"Why would she want to do that?" Niklaz said. "What would she get out of it? Witches, white or red, seldom do anything just out of the goodness of their hearts. Not when magic is involved. That requires too much magical energy and is very dangerous."

"Just what I was going to ask, rhetorically, that is. She did have a use for you. She wanted you to accompany Dorothy to the land of Oz. You'd be Dorothy's adviser and protector. And, if Glinda's plans worked out, Dorothy and you and the other companions would eliminate the West Witch. And perhaps incidentally, perhaps not, get rid of that humbug, the Great Wizard Oz."

"Humbug?" the Scarecrow cried. "How dare you? He gave me the only thing I lacked! Brains!"

"I won't argue with you," Hank said. "Wizard or not, he was clever and shrewd."

"And good! A good man! Great and good!"

"O.K. But I think that Glinda . . ."

"*If* Glinda was behind this," Niklaz said. "*If* events went the way you say they did."

"Yeah. I think that Glinda wanted to get rid of Oz. Maybe everybody else, including the East and West witches, thought that Oz was a true and powerful wizard. But she knew he wasn't. She knew that his strength was just a front, and it could easily crumble. Which it did. Look at how you two and my mother and the Cowardly Lion exposed him. There was a danger that he'd be overthrown or run—he did run, escaped in a balloon, anyway—and some evil person would take over. So she connived to make him leave, and now there's a good ruler in his place. You, Your Wiseness," he said to the Scarecrow.

"Oh, no. Well . . ."

"You're Glinda's good ally," Hank said. "The Wizard never had anything directly to do with her, though he wasn't dumb enough to oppose her. He knew that if he and Glinda met, she would know quickly he wasn't a real wizard. He kept his distance from her. Just as he stayed aloof from the common people, even the servants and guards of his palace. He ruled, but he hid from everybody. What a lonely life he must've had!"

"If I could weep, I would," the Scarecrow said.

"I, too," the Tin Woodman said.

"You two aren't really freaks," Hank said. "You're more human than most of the people I know."

"Freaks? Me? Us?" the Scarecrow said.

"Your pardon," Hank said. "I mean different."

"You've constructed an impressive theory," Niklaz said. "Is that all it is?"

"Ask Glinda."

"She won't answer most of my questions."

"Then she must have good reasons for not doing so."

The Scarecrow said, "You should get some sleep, Hank. The weather-scouts say that the skies may be clear by tomorrow afternoon."

"Yes, cut the chatter," a cow in a nearby stall said. "Go to sleep. You keep waking me up. Do you want to sour my milk?"

15

As the Jenny flew over Suthwarzha, Hank saw that Glinda's workers had really hustled while he was gone. They had built a larger hangar at the edge of a meadow on the east side of the castle. The meadow was, however, nearer the edge of the plateau than Hank liked.

The wind was coming from the southwest across the desert, bringing hot, dry, and gusty air. Just as he came in for the landing approach, he saw the windsocket turn to point into the northwest. He started to crab the Jenny, intending to turn her nose just enough so that, though the plane would be pointed one way, she would still move on a straight line. But the joystick moved without him, and the Jenny was at exactly the right attitude for the landing.

Hank felt cold run over his skin.

Though he was violating all his training and his pilot's reflexes, he took his hand from the stick and his feet from the rudder bar.

The Jenny straightened out just before her wheels touched, and she made a perfect three-point landing.

Hank swore softly.

He did not touch the throttle, but it moved, and the motor slowed. When the plane had slowed enough, she began turning slowly, and then she taxied into the hangar opening. Inside, with the rudder turned, the ailerons on the left wing lifted, the engine roared, and the Jenny turned to face outward. When that maneuver was completed, the ignition was turned off, and the engine stopped. Hank sat numbed until the propellor had quit whirling.

He got out of the cockpit and assisted his passengers to the floor. Lamblo greeted them and said she was to conduct them to Glinda.

Hank said, "I'll be along in a minute."

"Little Mother wants you now," Lamblo said.

Hank shrugged and said, "O.K."

But he went to the front of the Jenny and stared at the painted eyes, nose, mouth, and ears. The plane stared back.

"Please," Lamblo said. "She stressed that she wanted to see you as soon as possible. No delays."

"I'll catch up with you before you get to the big gate," he said.

Lamblo's eyebrows went up. She looked as if she would like to ask him why he wanted to stay behind, but she said, "You'd better." She and the honor guard marched the two kings out of the hangar. As soon as they were out of sight, Hank turned to the plane.

"Jenny? Are you there, Jenny?"

He felt ridiculous, but he had to say that.

"Jenny?" a Victrola-like voice roared. Though the red cupid's-bow mouth did not move, it was the source of the voice.

Hank was startled, though he had expected some such response.

"Jenny? Is that my . . . name?"

She pronounced it as "Chenny." There was no "j" sound in any of the many dialects.

"Yes, your name is Jenny," he said. He whispered, "Jesus Christ!"

"Chiizuz Kraist?" the painted mouth said.

"I'll talk to you later," Hank said. "I have to go. Listen, stay here. Don't leave the hangar. Don't turn on the engine. Or can you do that?"

"Oh, yes, I can," Jenny said.

"How . . . ?"

He stopped. There just was not time for any interrogation. He slapped her lightly on the propellor hub, and he said, "I'll be back." He ran off, though not without a backward glance. The airplane did not look alive. Or did she? Was there some faint light in those big blue long-lashed eyes?

And how would she know what he meant when he said "hangar" and "engine"?

As he trotted towards the castle, he muttered, "The big brass just won't believe this! I don't believe it!"

Glinda was seated behind the big desk in the conference room. She rose when the group entered, went around the table, and embraced the two kings. They sounded happy to see her.

Specially built chairs were brought up for the visitors. The Scarecrow's was of green velvet, the tall headrest bore a huge golden O (for Oz), and a gold crown set with emeralds was fixed to the top of the headrest. The Woodman's chair was of yellow-painted tin with the Gothic W (for Winkie) painted on its headrest, which also bore a tin crown set with yellow topazes. Hank's was a giant overstuffed chair on rollers. Blue velvet covered it, and it had no monogram or crown.

Food and drink were brought for Hank and set on a small table by his chair. Glinda was given a tall cut-quartz goblet filled with wine.

Glinda inquired about the ruler's health. Hank refrained from snickering. She then told him that she would not need his report of the trip. She knew all about it. Hank wondered if she also was aware of Jenny's animation, but he did not ask her. He would wait until she was alone with him. It seemed to him, however, that she would not know about the airplane. Who could have told her?

"As you all know," she said, "the Uneatable has finally launched her invasion. She did not inform us officially that she's at war with us and probably won't bother to do it. The latest reports I have—I got them thirty minutes ago—are that one army is halfway through the border forest between Gillikinland and Ozland, and another one, Niklaz, is a hundred miles from your capital. There's a third, poised on the Munchkin border, and it may have struck by now.

"The army in Ozland is on the road which Dorothy and you two traveled when you were coming to see me. It's not making much headway. The Cowardly Lion is in command of the animal forces there; he's chewed up the advance forces of men and beasts.

"The Winkies have lost two major battles already, and they're retreating to make a stand near their capital. You should get back there quickly. They need your moral support.

"Wulthag, the Munchkin ruler, tells me that Erakna tried a personal attack two nights ago, but Wulthag repelled her with no injury to either woman. I expect one against me at any time, though I'm not sure that Erakna is brave enough, as yet, to try me."

"What about the Natawey?" the Scarecrow said. "I heard that Erakna was attempting to enlist them. She's promised them loot and women."

"Wasokat, the king of the Pekotashas, is Erakna's ally. But King Tekumlek of the Shanahookas is ready to attack Wakosat if a large Pekotasha army leaves the country to assist Erakna. I've long had an understanding with Tekumlek about that."

Glinda raised her right hand, the first finger and forefinger extended. A white-bearded counsellor who'd been standing with a small iron box in his arms put it on the table. Glinda produced a key from out of the air as if she were a magician—which she was, though Hank suspected palming—and she unlocked the box. She raised the lid; its rusty hinges squeaked. From it she brought out two objects, each of which was attached to a steel neckchain.

They were identical: thin iron ankhs or Egyptian looped crosses with an iron G in the loop. The G looked more like an English lower case "r" than anything else.

"I want you to wear these," she said to the kings. "At all times. They're protective sigils, and they'll help ward off Erakna's powers. Notice that I say 'help.' They won't be effective, or, at least, will be only half-effective, against the Uneatable's greater powers. The G is not an initial for my name. It stands for Ganswabzham, the witch who made these and from whom I indirectly inherited them. Put them on. Now."

"I would have sent them with Hank," she said. "But their force had waned with time, and I had to recharge them. That demanded more energy than I was willing to spare at that time."

She spoke to Hank. "I could give you one, too, but you don't need it. You have your mother's gift, the housekey. I have charged that also."

When? Hank thought. While I was asleep?

She told him that he could leave the conference if he had things to do. The plans for military strategy did not require his presence. He should get his machine ready to fly the two back to their capitals by the day after tomorrow. Hank went to the hangar and checked out the physical condition of the plane. Since there were others around, he did not speak to Jenny. He wanted to be alone with her when he did that.

He also talked with the smiths and other technical experts assigned to him. The machine guns were ready for testing, and two hundred .30-caliber cartridges had been made for them. These were filled with black gunpowder, though other experts were working on cordite. There were also two hundred .45 bullets for his automatic pistol and six-shooter revolver, and the cases for bombs and small rockets were finished. The latter would not be ready, however, by the time he left for the north again.

Hank had had some calipers made so that he could be sure that each bullet fitted his specifications. Part of the afternoon was spent measuring them. He only had to reject twenty, not a big amount. Then he test-fired the machine guns on a stand outside the hangar. Satisfied that they were in good operating condition, he supervised their mounting on the upper wing of the Jenny. It was dark by the time that was done.

Food and drink were brought to him for supper. He ate, then ordered everyone to leave the hangar. The guards stationed themselves outside the building. Hank approached Jenny.

"We can talk now," he said.

"I wondered when you'd want me to talk," Jenny said.

"Why didn't you say something?"

"I don't know what to do, what to say," Jenny said. "I . . . just . . . I really don't know."

Hank sipped some of the mixed berry juice and vodka. Who'd believe a scene like this? He, Henry L. Stover, talking, actually talking to a JN-4H, an inanimate flying machine? No, no longer a lifeless object. An artifact that had become sentient and lingual.

How?

"When did you first become aware?" he said. "I mean, when did you first see, hear, and feel things?"

He could not ask her how she happened to be born.

"I was in the air," Jenny said. "I was not. And then I was. You'll have to excuse me if I can't describe things properly. I don't know everything I should. I don't have the, uh, words that I need. Not all of them."

She hesitated, then said, "But I can learn! I can learn!"

"You have no memory of anything before you, ah, came into existence? I mean, before the moment you found yourself in your body?"

"No."

"Nothing?"

"Nothing."

But she did have a memory. She could speak, which meant that she was drawing on a vocabulary somewhere within her. She had to have had a preexistence even if she did not remember it.

Hank described to her what had happened before the glowing ball had disappeared into her engine. He had to stop now and then to explain various references to her.

"First, I was just a nonliving thing of metal and fabric and wood," Jenny said. "Then, I live and talk and think."

"Have you ever heard of . . . I mean, do you know what Quadling means?" Hank said.

"No. That's a word I don't know."

"Do you know the name of Glinda?"

"I heard it, but I don't know who—she?—is."

"What's my name?"

"Hank. I heard the others call you that. I've learned a lot just by listening."

He told her about the Scarecrow, but she was more confused than enlightened.

"You mean . . . I'm something like the Scarecrow?"

"Not physically. But you two have something in common. You both have a soul?"

"A soul? What's that?"

Hank did his best to explain.

Silence. Did the huge painted blue eyes look puzzled?

"There's one thing we'd better get straightened out now," Hank said. "That is, I'm the pilot, you're the airplane. The pilot runs the airplane. From now on, unless I tell you differently, you don't decide whether *you* go up or down, bank, dive, climb, take off, or land. I'm the master; I handle the controls, unless I tell you to take over. Is that clear?"

"I think so. Only . . . I just can't help myself. When you don't do it right or fast enough, I just must do it. It's a matter of . . . what?"

"Survival. Making sure that you don't die."

"Yes."

"Well, you'll have to use self-control. I don't want you to take over! I don't want you overriding me! Do you understand?"

"Yes. You don't have to shout at me! You don't have to get nasty with me."

Hank threw his hands up in the air. A Jenny whose feelings were easily hurt. An emotionally sensitive aircraft. What next?

"You may not remember your former life," he said. "But you came into this world, into being as a machine, anyway, with a half-grown knowledge of speech and a full-grown personality. You're not a newborn infant."

He was convinced that Glinda had caused this transformation or possession. But how could she, hundreds of miles away, have been watching him and so affected the possession?

"She's got all the answers," he muttered, "and she sure as hell better come through with some. Soon."

Or he'd do what?

He could do nothing.

"We'll have some more heart-to-heart talks," he said. "I have to go now. Meanwhile, uh, is there anything I can do for you?"

"No, thank you, Hank."

"Well . . . listen . . . there is one thing, though. Can you start your engine? If you can, I won't have to get someone to spin the prop when I want to start . . . you."

For answer, the propellor spun a few times but the engine died. Hank poured some ether into the carburetor, then told her to try again. This time the propellor spun slowly, the engine whined, then it burst into explosive coughs, the propellor spun swiftly, and the engine roared.

Hank yelled at her to turn off the ignition. She may not have been able to hear him above the noise, but she understood his gestures. The roaring ceased, and the propellor blades were soon visible, then still.

Hank patted her cowling and, feeling disorientated and somewhat ridiculous, walked out of the hangar. He talked to the officer of the guard for a moment, making sure that the hangar doors would be closed and that soldiers would be stationed inside and outside the building. Then he went to the castle.

Late that night, as he and Lamblo sat in the bed and smoked, he said, "I have a new love."

She sat straight up. Hot ashes spilled from her pipe, and she was busy pushing them off before the cover caught fire. She said, "A new love? You . . . met someone you like better than me?"

"I wouldn't say that," Hank said, grinning. "But she can do some things you can't do."

"That I don't believe," Lamblo said. "Come on, Hank. Don't tease me."

He told her about Jenny.

Lamblo shivered and moved closer to him.

"It's witch-art. Glinda must have done it."

"I'd like to know how. And why."

"You're better off not knowing. And not asking."

"I have to."

"Don't, please don't, anger Glinda."

"Glinda the Good? If she's so good, she won't hurt me."

"Glinda's good is the good of the people. You're just one person, and an alien at that. She doesn't know, no one knows, what's going to happen because you came here. And she can't be sure that you're not a spy."

Hank was indignant.

"I am Dorothy's son!"

"Yes, but that's not the same as being Dorothy. Besides, if your mother came back now, she'd be suspected. She's an adult, and . . ."

"Nuts!" Hank shouted. "Pure essence of horse poppy!"

"Now, now, my little giant."

"Don't patronize me," Hank said. "Look. I've been tested . . . the Black Pearl of Truth, you know. What more does Glinda need?"

"The real test hasn't come up yet. You're going to have to make a choice between us and your country. It's bound to happen. Glinda says . . ."

"Well, what does Glinda say?"

"I have such a big mouth. I'm sorry. I can't say any more on that subject. Glinda will have to deal with that. Please forgive me."

"For telling the truth? Nothing to forgive."

Nevertheless, he was angry with her. How dare anyone doubt his integrity?

Later that night, after much undulation of anxiety, sleepless while Lamblo snored as gently as a cat, he admitted that Glinda was right. She was always right. He hated her for that.

16

Ot, the hawk, had shown up. But she was no longer Ot.

Hank found that out the next day. He overheard one of his "me-chanics" mention her name, and he asked the man to repeat what he'd said.

"Oh, she showed up before you did. I suppose it was instinct that made her come back here or maybe she hadn't, somehow, forgotten everything. The first thing she did after she rested was to kill a chicken and eat it."

The mechanic shuddered. "She was caged, of course. She won't be put on trial, but she can't be let loose either."

"What're you talking about?" Hank said.

The little man looked up puzzledly at Hank.

"She was dispossessed. I thought you knew about it. But then . . ."

"I'm still an ignoramus in a lot of things. Where is Ot?"

He was taken to the front courtyard of the castle. There was a stand there with a large cage on top. Ot, or what had been Ot, was behind the bars. She glared at Hank with wild fierce beautiful eyes. Hank spoke to her, but she screamed at him, and when he put a finger between the bars, she hurled herself at it. Hank withdrew it just in time to escape its being torn off.

"Reverted," the mechanic said. "Her soul's gone."

He crossed himself.

"Where's it gone?" Hank said.

"Only God knows."

"No," Hank muttered. "I'll bet Glinda knows, too."

He had a theory. If it was right, that first lightning ball, or whatever it was, had left the plane to shoot after Ot with the intention of dispossessing the sentient entity in her and occupying her itself. Though it had ousted the original possessor, it had failed to take occupancy. Meanwhile, a second ball had formed. Or, if it already existed, it had been invisible until it used the electrical energy in the atmosphere to form the sphere.

Or had he put all his available data into the wrong theory? Was he wrong because he did not have all the data he needed?

He felt very frustrated. He also felt sorry for the hawk.

"Is she going to be kept in the cage until she dies?" he said.

"I don't know. That's up to Little Mother. The hawk can't be let loose. She'd murder more chickens. Even if she were released in the woods, she'd probably prey on the domestic fowl. Also, since she's non-sentient, she'd be handicapped, she couldn't compete with the other hawks. She'd probably starve to death."

Glinda's hawks got their meat by going to the woods where the wild creatures were, and there they caught mice, rabbits, and other small animals. But, since these were sentient, they were not as easy prey as they would have been on Earth. The hawks never seized enough to satisfy their bellies. They depended largely on the indigenous meatnuts, shelled fruit containing a very high percentage of protein. These filled their guts—they were not stinted on these—but they did not satisfy the hawks' craving for real meat. Hence, they were given leave at regular intervals to go hunting in the woods. The mice, rabbits, gophers, wild ducks, and pheasants did not like that, but their treaty with humans did not include protection from domestic birds of prey.

"Has this happened to other hawks?" Hank said.

"Not very often, but it does happen."

"What was done to them?"

"They were left in the cages for a year. If they were not repossessed by then, they were executed. It'd be cruel to free them. They'd just die of hunger."

"Since this can happen to hawks," Hank said, "it must also happen now and then to other animals. And, I assume, to humans. Isn't that right?"

The mechanic crossed himself and said, "I have heard that it does. However, except for some stories which I do not believe because Little Mother says they're not true, the only ones who've ever been possessed are idiots."

Those who belonged to the main church made the sign of the cross and invoked *Marzha, Hailag Aithii of Kristuz-Thun* (Mary, Holy Mother of Christ-Thor). Sometimes she was called other names, though Nantho was the favorite. Nantho, if Hank remembered correctly, was the name of an ancient Gothic goddess. There was also confusion about Christ, because sometimes he was called Thun and sometimes Ogiiz. Hank did not know the origin of the latter name.

They had a form of the Mass, called the *Kollekta* in some regions and the Bread-breaking in others. It was conducted in a barbarous Latin, the translation of which had been lost.

The Goths must have entered this world with all or part of copies of the New Testament translated into Gothic. But the text had become corrupted and expanded since then, and the religion had also been changed and accreted. The Terrestrial and Orthodox churches would regard this branch of the church as heretical. But then the Amariikians would consider those two to be in grave error.

At noon, Hank was summoned to the conference room. Glinda, the two kings, and the human and animal counsellors were there.

"How soon can you leave?" the queen said.

"In half an hour. The spare wheels are ready, but if the battery goes dead, I'm out of luck."

"So be it. You should be able to get to the third refueling station before nightfall. You'll go to Oz first. After you drop Niklaz off, return to the Oz capital and help out the troops for five days. Do—what do you call it?—strafing. Anything you can do with your airplane. Then, regardless of the situation there, come back here. The next message from your people will be coming through shortly after your return."

"If I return," Hank said. "You surely realize, Glinda, that I might be attacked by Erakna's birds again. Or I could have an accident. Or..."

"Yes, I know," Glinda said. "There's also another danger. I've just learned that Erakna has stolen the Golden Cap of the Winged Monkeys. Do you know what that means?"

Hank nodded.

The West Witch had had the Cap when Dorothy had been a prisoner in the Witch's castle. After Dorothy had thrown water on the Witch and the Witch had become, as it were, puddled, Dorothy had taken the Cap. After Dorothy had used the three wishes—"wishes"?—which the Cap's owner could use to control the Winged Monkeys, Glinda had given the Cap to the Monkeys' king. From then on, it was assumed, the Monkeys would be free. They would not be snatched away from whatever they were doing and be forced to do whatever a non-Monkey Cap owner wished, things which were often inconvenient and sometimes extremely dangerous for the Monkeys. Now they were in servitude again.

Hank thought, How does the Cap work? How could it make slaves out of the Monkeys? Why just three wishes?

"I don't know if the Uneatable would use them against you as yet," Glinda said. "However, I'm sure that she considers you a major threat to her. Otherwise, she'd not have sent those hawks after you. She might send the Monkeys to kill you and destroy the plane. Or she might just use the hawks again. Now that you have those machine guns, do you think you'd have a good chance to defend yourself against those flying simians?"

Hank shrugged, and he said, "It depends upon the situation. Jenny isn't a fast and highly maneuverable military plane. I really can't say."

He paused.

"Maybe I should ask her. After all, she's in just as much danger. She might not want to volunteer for hazardous duty."

Glinda smiled, and he knew that she knew.

"Chenny isn't a free-will agent yet. She'll depend upon you. In fact, she's your subject and you're her king. For a while, anyway. She's like a baby duck; she attached herself to the first living thing she saw when she, ah, came out of wherever she'd been before."

"In that case," Hank said, "why didn't the Scarecrow attach itself to the farmer who made it? The farmer would've been the first living being it saw."

"You're a thinker," Glinda said, smiling. "Ask the Scarecrow."

Hank looked at the thing.

"I was very much attached to the farmer," it said. "I longed to get down off the pole and go with him. But he deserted me, and for a long time I had only crows for company. Then your mother came along and got me free, and I, uh, transferred, you might say, my dependence and my great affection to her. Still, I write—dictate, rather—a letter to the farmer once a year. And I take a great interest in his happiness."

"That's enough of questions," Glinda said. "Leave now."

"Pardon me," Hank said. "This concerns the trip. Will a hawk guide me? As you know, Ot is . . . out of it."

"You shouldn't need a guide," the queen said. "You've been over the route. But, yes, I've arranged for three hawks to go with you. One will stay with you as your guide."

Hank thanked her, bowed, and went to his suite to pack. Lamblo entered just as he had finished. She wrapped his waist with her arms and pressed one side of her face against his stomach.

"Oh, Hank, I have a terrible feeling about this trip. A premonition of death. I won't ever see you again!"

Tears wet his shirt. He lifted her up and kissed her.

"Don't worry. Premonitions mean nothing. I'll be fine."

He sat down on the bed and put her on his lap.

"I'll be gone about nine or ten days. You'll just have to control your randiness until I get back."

"It's not that!" she cried. "You know it's not! I love you, Hank!"

He planted a smacker on top of her blonde hair. He smelled fresh air and a very faint odor of violets. She was beautiful and lots of fun and a great bed partner and exuded outgoingness and courage. He was very fond of her, but he did not love her. Still, in a sense, he did love her. And so he was not wholly lying when he said, "I love you, too."

She got off his lap and turned to look up at him. Those blue eyes were so full of love and trust that he felt guilty.

"Enough to marry me?" she said.

Now was no time to hesitate.

"Sure," he said.

Why not? He would never have Glinda, and he was not certain that, if he did, he would like it. On the other hand—life was so other-handed and underhanded, too—was he a coward? Afraid to hurt her by saying that he did not love her? When she would be hurt much more later on if things soured between them or he regretted having this impulse?

"Sure," he said again, smiling. He had thought of a good reason to delay any wedding.

"Sure. I'd marry you. But, Lamblo, what if I'm faced with having to choose between the Quadlings and my own people? I mean . . . I don't know what's going to happen. For all I know, there may be war, my country might invade this world. Just to keep your people from invading, I'm sure.''

But he was not so sure.

"Your world is an unknown quantity. The Army officials will be afraid that Amariiki might be a danger to the United States. To our whole world.''

Lamblo had backed away from him. She said, "But your people will find out that we're no threat to them at all. We're not, you know, and you'll tell them that.''

"They might not believe me. Anyway, they won't quit trying to get here. They know this world is here, and just because it is, and because they've never been here, they'll come. They have to. It's true that, as of now, no other government knows about this world. But some other nation might find how to open the way. If this happens, then the government of that country will try to get here. My government knows this. They'll want to be the first here.''

"And you'll help them do it?''

"Well, I really don't know. It's my patriotic duty. Still . . .''

"Glinda has told the counsellors what might happen if more Earth-people come here. It would be terrible! Ghastly! Surely, Hank, you have a higher duty! A duty to humanity! You're not some tribal savage who thinks only of his little group and everybody else can go jump off the edge of the world!''

Hank sighed, and he stood up.

"I'm late now. I have to go now. We'll talk about this when I come back.''

A minute later, he was on his way to the hangar. He felt unhappy. He knew that, when he got back, he'd be confronted with the same situation. What would he do then?

He had no idea. However, he could think a lot about it while he was gone. If he had any time to do so.

When he got to the hangar, he found his passengers and Glinda there. He was irked. Glinda had come down to see the two rulers off but had not bothered when he had left for the first trip. After all, wasn't he the ambassador from Earth to Oz? He did not apologize for being late. He put his carpetbag in the storage compartment, and he said, "All's ready. Let's go.''

While Glinda embraced the kings, he went to the front of the plane and spoke in a low voice into Jenny's left ear.

"I changed my mind about you doing the piloting. I mean, I'll let you do it under certain circumstances. Just now, as a test, I want you to turn on the motor, taxi out, and take off. When we land at the first station, I'll teach you some simple signals for use while we're in the air. Later, we should be able to work out a more complicated system."

"May I ask why you changed your mind?" the airplane said.

"Sure. I was letting my pride override my sense of reality."

"What does that mean?"

"I'll explain some other time. Glinda is fidgeting. We'd better take off before the Queen of Hearts has my head chopped off."

"What?"

"Never mind."

The royal band was blaring nearby. Hank could barely hear himself now. He gestured at the two rulers, and they left Glinda and hurried towards him, one of them too stiff in his movements and the other too flexible. Hank helped them get into the rear cockpit. He had transferred the joystick to the front cockpit because he could only operate the machine guns from that position. Two of the hawks got in with Their Majesties, and the other, Listiig, flew to the front seat. Hank got in, waited until the mechanic had put ether in the carburetor, and then yelled, "Contact!"

Despite the band's noise, Jenny heard him. While Hank restrained the impulse to turn on the ignition and to keep his hands and feet off the controls, the propellor began turning slowly. The engine whined, then roared. Hank looked at Glinda and smiled. The wind from the propellor was unravelling her auburn hair and blowing her skirt up to her crotch. She was not trying to keep the skirt down; three centuries had made her indifferent to any code of modesty except her own.

After warmup, Hank checked the water temperature, oil pressure, and tach rate. Then Hank gave the signal for the mechanics to pull the chocks from the wheels. The plane began moving, left the hangar, and headed toward the northwest corner. Apparently, Jenny knew the direction of the wind by looking at the windsocket or she could detect it by her sensory system.

Hank felt uneasy, but he clamped down on his strong desire to take over the controls. Jenny taxied perfectly, did as well as he could, turned, faced into the wind, then began moving forward. Hank, fascinated, watched the stick and pedals move. Were they doing this because Jenny moved them, as he would have done, or did she move the rudder and ailerons first and the cockpit controls followed? He would have to ask her.

The takeoff was fine. When the altimeter registered a thousand feet, he knocked hard twice on the instrument panel. Jenny dipped the left wing in acknowledgment.

Hank had ordered Jenny to level off at three thousand feet altitude. She did so, and he wondered how she knew when she was at that point. Did she have some means of reading the altimeter?

He kept his eye on the indicator instruments and the landmarks for a while, then talked with his hawk-navigator. Hank had memorized the landmarks the first time around, but he asked Listiig about them. It would give the hawk a sense of importance or at least of usefulness.

After a while, Hank said, "There is much I don't understand about this world, of course. I was wondering, for instance, why Ot became dispossessed?"

Listiig, standing on his left shoulder, her talons digging into the leather jacket, the wind ruffling her feathers, screamed in his ear. "I heard about the mind-spirits attacking the flying machine! It's obvious what happened! One of them tried to take Ot over! It ousted the one that possessed her but failed to get into her!"

Hank grimaced with disgust. This was no explanation.

"No, I mean, just what is a mind-spirit or firefox?"

"Why, it's a spirit of the dead that has been cleansed of its sins and is sent out to live again in a body! Or it's an evil spirit that escaped from the Faroff Land and tries to take over a body!"

"Sure," Hank said. Apparently, all he was going to get was a religious explanation. Which was none at all.

"Do you belong to a church?" he said.

"Of course! Doesn't everybody?"

17

Now and then, Hank saw large bodies of armed marching men followed by baggage trains. These were going north to help the Ozland troops. There were also cavalrymen riding on deer and moose. Chariots were used only for the castle guards and for ceremonial parades. Once, a long time ago, they had been ridden in battles that took place on large unforested plains, of which there were few now and even fewer then. They were drawn by bovines or cervines that had been bred for many generations for pulling power or speed.

Hank had wondered why the animals, who were citizens, had allowed themselves to be bred for certain qualities. What if a stag, for instance, had desired a mate that the human breeders did not want impregnated?

Animals, though sentient, were more driven by their instincts than humans. A stag might be fonder of a female than he was of others or a female might like a stag more than she did other males. They were, however, subject to rutting seasons, and when these came their sexual drives overcame their personal relationships.

The humans had solved this problem. They fed the animals they did not want to breed one of two mixtures of plants. The males got one which made them sterile, though it did not cut down on their virility. The females got one which effected a pseudo-pregnancy.

There had been and still were animals who had objected to this. But they had a choice of staying with the humans and abiding by the law or going into the woods and taking their chances there.

This was one of the situations where an animal was a second-class citizen. But it had been established through treaty with the animals' ancestors, and most seemed to accept it ungrudgingly.

The breeding agreement, along with some others, was the only means for animals and humans to live together with both parties profiting. Sheep, goats, cattle, and deer provided wool, hair, milk, and labor. They were not killed for meat, and they could not be worked to death or neglected or be ill-treated. When they died, they were buried side by side with the humans and mourned by the humans and animals who had cared for or loved them. Even if the Amariikian church had conformed in everything else to the Terrestrial Catholic religion, this belief that animals had souls would have made this world's church heretical.

Cats were a special case here—as on Earth. They were pets, some of them, anyway, but they were useful as home guards and as rodent-killers. Though most wild creatures stayed away from the areas marked off for humans, many mice and rats took their chances. They invaded houses and barns and were thus considered as outlaws. A human could not trap, poison, or shoot them unless he got permission from the courts because of special circumstances. Cats were given a license to kill rodents, which they would have taken anyway. But they were not allowed to kill any birds except outlaws.

There were other beasts among the marchers northward. Hank saw some mammoths and mastodons. Though midgets, they were huge compared to the other creatures.

The pachyderms were used to pull great wagons but would become warriors when at the front. There were also humpless camels which carried packs now but would usually fight unmounted and were led by their own camel officers. Sometimes, they carried archers into battle.

When Hank landed at the capital, he found the scene had changed. Now there was a host of tents outside the glittering walls, and men were drilling in the meadows. The riverfront was jammed with boats and great piles of boxes being unloaded. The Emerald City was getting ready for a long siege.

Hank only stayed down long enough to discharge the Scarecrow, refuel, inspect Jenny's wires, fittings, and fabric, and feed himself and the hawks. One of them, Wiin, would get a report on the latest news before taking off for Glinda's capital. A half hour after landing, Hank was lifting off. He had three and a half hours of daylight, plenty of time to get to Niklaz's castle. The sky was clear except for some cirrocumulus clouds, and the headwind was an estimated four to six miles per hour. He would stay overnight with the Winkie king and start at dawn for the return trip to the Emerald City.

Jenny was at two thousand feet altitude and twenty miles west of the Oz capital when a multitude of dots sprang into being ahead. And behind and on both sides of him.

Listiig screamed, "The Winged Monkeys! Holy Marzha, Mother of God! Erakna is out to get our tail!"

Hank's skin chilled. It was not just the danger that caused this. The presence of "magic," the teleporting of these creatures in great numbers from afar to his immediate vicinity, made him shiver. He should be used to such phenomena by now, but he probably never would be.

By now the dots had become silhouettes of winged creatures, a horde distinguishable even at this distance as non-avians. He estimated that there were two hundred straight ahead, and he did not know how many behind him and on each side. All were a thousand feet higher than he and diving to gain speed.

The JN-4H could climb at a rate of twelve hundred feet per minute, three times that of the JN-4D. But the Monkeys were above him, and they would be on him before he could get above them. If he dived, they would dive.

Perhaps his only advantage was speed. He did not think that the simians could go ninety miles an hour on level flight, Jenny's maximum velocity at this altitude with this load. They were probably too big and heavy for that. But he did not know for sure.

He struck the instrument panel three times. Jenny rolled slightly to right and left to acknowledge that he would be in complete control.

He pushed forward on the stick, sending the plane into a rather flat dive. He would pick up some speed. Maybe enough to get him through and past those ahead. He should also leave behind those aft and to both sides of him.

He was glad that Erakna's powers were not able to pinpoint the exact area at which the Monkeys would arrive. At least, he assumed that she had lacked those powers. Otherwise, she would have placed the creatures much closer to him and so not given him any time to react adequately.

The oncoming attackers swelled swiftly, too swiftly. Now he could see the batlike structure of the wings projecting from the monstrously large hump of back muscles. He could see the short and bird-thin legs. The whiteness of teeth, long and sharp. The reddish hair. The long outstretched arms. The hands clenching knives, short swords, and short spears.

Unlike the illustrations of them by Denslow, they wore no clothes. But the head of one was circled by a silvery crown. The king.

Hank kicked right rudder to put him into an intersecting path with the king.

He calculated that they would meet in about forty seconds.

That would be fatal for both of them, fatal for Jenny, anyway, if the king struck the propellor. Hank had a parachute, and the Tin Woodman might be very damaged by a fall, but he would survive.

Hank looked behind him. The monarch was standing up now, his ax ready. The hawk with him was fastened to the edge of the front windshield, interfering with Hank's vision. He screamed at her to get back down, but the whistling wind carried his words backward.

He shouted at Listiig. "Get off! Get off!"

The hawk hesitated, then rose and was snatched away.

Hank pulled back on the stick, lifting Jenny's nose.

The Monkey-King and others near him flattened their dive.

"Are they nuts?" Hank cried. "Trying to commit suicide?"

It would not be easy to shoot a small target like the Monkey-King even if the machine guns had been on the fuselage, just in front of him. But they were mounted on the upper wing. When he fired, he would be depending upon guess to hit his target more than anything else.

His eyes went up, then down. He pulled the cable which actuated the machine guns, and they chattered.

Dark blurs flashed by.

There was a thump, and Jenny rocked.

A Monkey had struck the top of the right upper wing—thank God, it had not smashed into the wing closer to the fuselage or hit the strut wires and parted them—and carried off some fabric and shattered the wooden end. But the damage would not interfere with the flight. Unless more fabric, lifted by the wind now filling that plane, was torn off.

He looked back. The hawks were diving for the shelter of the forest. Some Monkeys were following them, but their chase was hopeless.

Two bodies were still falling. One was the animal that had collided with the wing. The other was the king, crownless now. The silvery symbol was falling, twinkling in the rays of the westering sun.

The others had turned and were flapping mightily. But he could outrun them.

"You've wasted one of your wishes!" Hank howled.

Erakna should have waited until he had landed and then launched the Monkeys. That mob could have torn him and the Jenny apart.

His exultation died. If she tried again, she would probably do just that.

She might want to use the second wish for another attack on him, but it did not seem likely. She surely would save her winged slaves for a more important target. But then he did not know the psychology of witches.

Two minutes later, a hundred hawks or more dived out of the sun. They had been waiting for him, placed so that he would be blinded if he looked at the sun. Halfway towards him, the band split, and half turned towards the west. If he got through the advancing wave, he would then be traveling at a rate which would allow the others to match his. They could fly faster than Jenny; they'd try to board him.

And if he turned away from them to flee east, he'd run into the first wave again.

"*Skiit!*" he said in Quadling.

Now the advancers had turned and were curving away from him. They, too, would try to board Jenny.

Suddenly, they were around him, an envelope of screeches, glaring wild yellow eyes, gaping razor-sharp beaks, and talons ready to rend. They closed in on him.

Hank groaned—it hurt him to hand over the piloting—and he banged the panel twice. But he pulled the cable again, and he had the satisfaction of seeing at least a dozen hawks become feather explosions.

That left only about eighty-eight.

He looked behind him. The Tin Woodman was cutting at a hawk with his ax.

Hank loosed his safety belt so he could turn around if he had to, and he pulled his revolver from the holster. He aimed the .45 at a hawk a few feet from him, but he missed. He had not compensated enough for the wind.

Another shot corrected that.

Twenty hawks had fastened talons into the fabric of the wings and fuselage.

Aiming carefully, Hank blew apart seven with eleven shots. He also put some holes through his wings, but that could not be avoided.

Feathers, bits of flesh, and gouts of blood whirled by him.

All but one of the attackers on the front part of Jenny decided to take Falstaff's prescription re the better part of valor. The sole brave, or dumb, one flew from the midpart of the upper wings at him. It disappeared halfway just above the windshield, spattering blood on Hank's goggles. He pushed them up on his forehead and twisted around.

The edge of the ax was just slicing through a hawk before the Woodman. But another had fastened herself on top of the tin head and was blunting its beak and talons on the metal. Another was sliding off the back of the tin trunk down into the cockpit. Beyond the cockpit were two more, clawing their way towards the Woodman.

Hank shot the hawk off of the tin head. The bird that had slid into the cockpit came into sight again, but the Woodman turned and closed his hand around her neck. She beat her wings and tried to fasten onto his resistant body. Niklaz lifted her up and threw her away.

For the moment, they were free. But the hawks were still chasing them. Beyond them were many dots, the Winged Monkeys, outdistanced but not abandoning the chase.

Presently, the yellowish castle came into view. Also, five miles to the right, beyond the hills, a battle was taking place on a farmland. The invaders had traveled more swiftly than the last report had indicated.

Hank would have liked to make strafing runs over Erakna's forces, but he would be deluged with hawks and monkeys if he did.

Hank shouted at Niklaz. "Strap yourself in! We're landing!"

He brought Jenny in, crabbing against the southwest wind, and taxied as fast as he dared towards a huge community-storage barn. Soldiers ran to greet him. After turning Jenny to face away from the barn, he cut off the ignition. He and the Woodman got out of the plane. The hawk that had ridden with the Woodman was, like Listiig, long gone.

By the time the hawks arrived, they found the Winkies, with the king at their head, in battle formation. Jenny had been pushed backwards into the barn, the doors of which were half-closed. Twenty archers and twenty swordsmen were on the roof of the barn, and two ranks of archers and spearmen ringed the barn. Before the door was the main force, thirty archers and fifty spearmen. All also carried scabbarded short swords.

Hank stood in the front rank of the troops by the barn door. He held the .30-caliber BAR, and a man who'd been hastily instructed to hand him loaded box magazines stood by his side.

A scouting group of hawks flew over the meadow first. Having made their survey, they flew back to a tree outside of arrow range and reported to a big hawk standing on the branch of an oak. This female, presumably the queen or captain, flew up and circled while the others arranged themselves in ranks of twenty. When the formation was completed, the chief led them to a height of about fifty feet, a half-mile away.

Niklaz told his men to hold their fire until the attackers were within twenty yards.

The Winged Monkeys were visible now, dots like a cloud of midges at an estimated three hundred feet above the ground.

"It might be wise to save most of your bullets for them," Niklaz said. "They're bigger targets."

"We'll see," Hank said.

The Woodman was right, but, if enough hawks were killed, the Monkeys might get discouraged before they attacked.

What their enemy should do, Hank thought, was to wait until the Monkeys had arrived, then charge en masse. But if they were too stupid or inexperienced to do that, he was not going to advise them. There was also the possibility that the hawks and Monkeys were jealous of each other, and the hawks wanted all the glory and credit. The situation could be a parallel to the interservice rivalry between the Army and the Navy of the United States or of, for that matter, any nation. The two branches of service often tried to shaft each other, even during wartime.

The hawks dived, coming in at about sixty miles an hour, splitting into a large group and a small one. The majority were headed for the men on the ground; the minority, for the men on the roof.

When thirty yards from the defenders, the hawks checked their speed somewhat. They did not want to kill themselves by a too-hard impact against the larger solidly planted bodies.

Niklaz's voice rang out, and the bowmen fired.

Ten hawks were hit.

The archers immediately drew arrows from their quivers and fitted them to the bowstrings. They were to fire at will now. Hank began firing short bursts, and he killed or wounded ten hawks. But, before the second volley from the bowmen was loosed, the hawks were among them, screeching, wings beating, talons and beaks tearing at the men's eyes and faces.

Hank stepped back, and soldiers formed around him. He continued shooting, aiming over their heads at the second and third ranks of the hawks. His guard chopped at the birds with their swords or thrust with their spears. Niklaz whirled the ax, slicing hawks in half or cutting off wings.

Two men in front of Hank dropped their weapons and fell to the ground, trying to tear away the ravening furies on their faces. Hank wanted to drop the BAR, pick up a sword, and slash at the hawks. But he kept on shooting, swiveling from right to left, then reversing, replacing the twenty-round box magazines as soon as one was emptied. He got most of the second rank and much of the third before he had to drop the hot weapon and defend himself with a sword.

Two hawks fell half-severed to the ground. A third fastened herself on the back of his head, talons digging through his leather helmet and setting on fire his scalp and neck. He fell backwards hard, banging the hawk and his head on the ground. Stars shot before his eyes, but the hawk did not let loose. He leaped up, screaming, and tore the helmet and the attached hawk off. He jumped up and came down with both feet on the bird, crushing it.

He put a hand to the back of his head. It came away smeared with blood. A burning coal seemed to be frying his head and neck. He ignored it, picked up the sword again, leaned down, grabbed a flopping wing, and cut the wing off. The hawk, which had been tearing up the face of a man on the ground, collapsed. But its talons did not come loose from her victim's flesh.

Suddenly, the melee was over. For a while, at least. The surviving hawks were flying away, or, if too badly wounded, were staggering away on the ground.

Hank pried the dead hawk's talons from their grip on his helmet and put it on his head. His goggles were lying ten feet away; he decided that he would wear them to protect his eyes.

The hawks had lost heavily. Fifty were dead or too hurt to be effective. None of the men were killed, but ghastly face wounds had put seven out of action. Four seemed to be blinded in one or both eyes. Several had missing noses and ears.

Niklaz had the badly wounded taken into the barn where the medicos could take care of them.

"I don't hate easily," the Tin Woodman said. "But I hate that Erakna. All this is totally unnecessary."

Hank thought so, too, but he said nothing. He went into the barn to make sure that no hawks had gotten in there and damaged Jenny. Three birds had entered, but they had been killed before they could get to the plane. He went back to the men outside.

Niklaz said, "I wonder how the battle is going."

"What?" Hank said. Then he understood that the king was referring to the conflict they had seen on the plains just before landing.

"If the Gillikins break through," Niklaz said, "it won't take them long to get here. We might be able to hold off the hawks and Monkeys, but we can't stand up against an army."

18

"Will they have hawks, too?" Hank said.

The tin mask smiled fixedly through the blood.

"You're worried that their hawks will reinforce the others. Yes, they'll have hawks and eagles. But not many. They'll be used primarily as scouts, not fighters. Erakna doesn't have thousands at her command any more than Glinda does. Most birds prefer to be wild. Glinda has about five hundred who serve her, and half of these are scattered through the land. I imagine that Erakna has about the same."

"Here comes one of hers now," Hank said, pointing. Niklaz turned to look at a duckhawk which had just landed on the branch of an oak near the edge of the meadow. However, the duckhawk yelled at them not to shoot. He was Rakya, one of theirs. He had come to report on the plains battle.

"Oh, yes, I recognize him now," Niklaz said.

The duckhawk lighted before them. He was missing some feathers and had some blood on his breast. One eye was swollen and closed.

"Sire, I have bad news. Your army is retreating in panic, most of them trying to get to the castle. The Gillikins are hot on their heels, and a cavalry outfit, archers and camels, are heading this way."

"When will they get here?" Niklaz said.

"In about an hour."

Niklaz looked at the rugged yellowish heap on the top of the hill.

"Maybe we should withdraw to the castle."

"No," Hank said. "We can't leave Jenny here."

"Could we take her with us?"

"We'd all be too exposed, too vulnerable," Hank said. "We have to smash them first, make them too discouraged to pursue us."

He indicated the mass of hawks and Monkeys to the east. They looked like a swirling cloud, a confusion, but he was sure that the hawk leader and whoever had replaced the Monkey-King were conferring. The disorder would become order soon enough.

"All right, we'll stand off one, maybe two, charges," Niklaz said. "Then we'll have to make a break for the castle."

"No, I won't leave Jenny. They'll tear her apart."

"You're as stubborn as your mother," the king said. "I esteem your loyalty, but loyalty can become stupidity. I have to consider the welfare of my people, and I won't be helping them if I allow myself to be captured."

Hank went into the barn. A medico washed off his wounds with soap and cold water, patted them dry with a towel while Hank bit his lip to keep from crying out, poured a liquid over the gashes and applied taped bandages.

He went to Jenny. "If things get too bad, take off by yourself."

"It's that desperate?" she said.

"Not yet. It might be. If the enemy kills or captures me or I have to run off into the woods, take off. If I manage to hoof it back to Suthwarzha, I'll see you then."

Jenny's tone was undeniably sad.

"And if you don't get back . . .?"

"Glinda will take care of you."

He had the barn doors fully opened so that Jenny could get out. He also hurriedly requisitioned a soldier to put ether in the carburetor if she did have to take off.

Jenny's voice trembled. "I'm so upset. I don't want to be parted from you. I wish I could be like you humans and weep."

"Don't be sad," Hank said. "Be mad. Gee, I almost forgot! Your wing is damaged. You'll have to watch it; more fabric might tear off. By the way, does your damage—I mean, injury—hurt you?"

"No. I can feel it, but it doesn't hurt. At least, I don't think so. I'm not sure just what you mean by hurt."

It was strange. She, the Scarecrow, and the Woodman had the sensories to locate damage, but they were spared pain. Physical pain, that is. They could feel emotional injury.

He dipped a ladle into a tin bucket of water and drank deeply. Though the air was cool, he had sweat so much that his clothes were soaked. His mouth was as dry as an Army manual.

He went out and told the Woodman what he had in mind.

"I need about twenty men to surround me when I go to the woods. Two won't come back, me and my ammo handler. Do you think it'll work?"

"The hawks have very keen eyesight, but they're about a mile away," Niklaz said. "They might not count you as you go in. But they will wonder why the group went into the trees. They'll check that out."

"Have the men pretend to crap," Hank said. "That'll fool them, I hope. Anyway, from the smell here, I think that some have already filled their pants. Have them shake the stuff out of their pants."

"Yes, it is pretty strong, isn't it?" Niklaz said.

Baum had said that the Scarecrow and the Tin Woodman couldn't smell odors. That wasn't true. They could see with their similitudes of eyes and hear with the similitudes of ears. Since they had similitudes of noses, they could also smell. But they did not have the sense of taste.

By then the hawks and the Monkeys were organizing formations. Hank filled in the men he needed on his plan, and presently he was duckwalking toward the woods so that his head would not be above the group around him. A squint-eyed Winkie named Nabya the Sneezer carried the magazines.

When they reached the massive one-hundred-foot-tall, beautifully flowering, indigenous trees lining the meadow, the group opened out. Hank and Nabya went into the cover of the woods, where their sense of smell almost reeled under the dense but exquisite odor of the blooms. They went south, then east. When they were about a hundred yards from the barn, they walked to a spot about forty feet in from the meadow. They crouched behind a bush and got ready.

They had gotten into the woods just in time. A bald eagle flew over the barn and circled, then flapped northward. It must be a scout sent by the Gillikins. It would soon be telling the cavalry that the Winkie king was here and his route to the castle would be cut off.

Niklaz had seen the eagle, but he apparently was going to stay at the barn.

"Here they come!" Nabya said. He spat out a plug of tobacco.

The hawks were not flying at top speed; they were hanging back so that the Monkeys could keep up with them. Both groups were at a hundred feet altitude. The hawks were three lines deep in the van, and the simians were four lines deep. The birds were silent, but the Monkeys were screaming war cries and shouting insults at the enemies and encouragement at each other.

Hank shook his head. These creatures were unnatural in that they had not evolved into their present form. Surely, they were the products of artificial genetic engineering. The Long-Gones had made them.

They were said to be, pound for pound, the strongest beings in the world. They would have to be to lift their forty pounds or so and fly at an average rate of twenty miles an hour. That two each could have lifted Dorothy, the Scarecrow, and the Tin Woodman was evidence of their powerful muscles. Twelve of them had carried the Cowardly Lion at the ends of ropes to the castle of the West Witch. But it had been a short distance.

The hawks were a hundred yards from the barn. Hank said, "Let's go," and he stood up and walked to a tree on the meadow edge. Stationing himself on one side of it, he raised the BAR and began shooting. Nabya handed him the box magazines.

At least thirty hawks went up in feathers and blood, the bullets going through two or three at a time. Hank then pointed to the left and raked the front line of monkeys. Over fifteen, he thought, were hit, including the big brute leading them.

Hank continued firing into the mass as it swept over the meadow. He wished he had a Thompson submachine gun. It had a 50-round drum magazine and would not have required changing as often as the 20-round box magazine of the BAR. Also, it was much lighter and less cumbersome. It took a strong man to stand up and handle the 18.5-pound BAR. The rifle was fitted with supports attached to the barrel so that the operator could lie prone on the ground and shoot with most of the weight on the support. Unfortunately, Hank's targets were mostly in the air. He had to tilt the weapon at considerable and varying angles.

Nevertheless, he worked carnage and panic over the meadow. There were at least two hundred and fifty Monkey carcasses on the bloody grass and many hawks and eagles.

Then he was out of ammunition.

He put the BAR on his shoulder, making sure that the hot barrel was not on the leather. He said to Nabya, "Follow me!"

About ten Monkeys were brave enough to fly towards him. He had six rounds in his revolver. Even if he got six of the enemy, he would not have time to reload before the survivors were on him.

His long legs left Nabya behind. He stopped when he heard a cry, and he whirled. The pseudo-simians were bounding along on all fours, their wings folded, close behind the Winkie. Nabya, who was burdened with a knapsack holding the empty magazines, had turned to face the attackers. He lifted a sword and stood ready.

Hank dropped his rifle and raced toward Nabya while he took his revolver from his holster. He shouted, "Lie down! Lie down, Nabya!"

The Winkie either did not hear him or was afraid that he would be too easy a prey if Hank missed. He slashed at the first of the Monkeys and cut its paw off. Then he was hurled to the ground on his back by a screeching Monkey.

Hank held the .45 in both hands, and he loosed three bullets. The two behind the simian which had attacked Nabya fell. The Winkie and the Monkey were rolling over and over on the ground. Unable to shoot from a distance without endangering Nabya, Hank ran up to them. When he got the chance, he fired, and the bullet went through the back of the creature's head and blew its face all over Nabya.

The surviving Monkey ran off but collapsed before it got sixty feet away.

Nabya did not move. His throat was torn open.

Hank cursed. He rolled the Monkey off from Nabya and turned Nabya over so he could remove his knapsack. He picked that up and ran to the rifle. He decided that he should reload the revolver before going on. He did that, and then, carrying the sack and the BAR, returned to the edge of the forest.

The Woodman and ten soldiers and medics were the only ones on their feet. Before and around them were piles of dead and wounded attackers. Two dozen Monkeys, about fifty feet away, were jumping up and down, howling obscenities at the defenders and encouragement to each other. They were trying to work themselves into a frenzy for another charge.

Hank emptied the revolver into them, reloaded, and advanced, firing again. By then the Monkeys were running away, heading past the barn into the wind and toward the farmhouse. They went very fast on all fours, then stood up, their birdlike legs moving. Their bone-and-skin wings were flapping hard, but they just did not have a long enough runway. They could never get into the air and clear the farmhouse or the trees behind it.

Realizing this, they stopped, howling, and reversed course. Five of them made it, finally rising slowly and heavily.

Niklaz said, "Erakna has paid a heavy price. But so have we."

"I'm glad she didn't use all the Monkeys at her disposal," Hank said. "If she'd sent the whole horde, we'd all be dead now."

Niklaz said, "Yes. When we were with your mother, the West Witch sent the entire pack against us when we approached her castle."

"How many?"

"Oh, I'd say a thousand."

"Then she has plenty left."

He looked eastward. There were approximately fifty flying away. These had never landed but had turned when they saw their fellows ahead of them tumbling from the air under the fire from the BAR.

"I wonder," he said, "when Erakna will summon them back to her."

"Those? She won't. She'd have to use a second wish to recall them. She's abandoned them. They'll have to get back to their pack as best they can. It'll be a long way, too."

Hank sent two men to get his weapons and the belts. He then said, "What're you going to do, Your Shininess?"

"You may call me Niklaz. What will I do? I could hole up in the castle. It's provisioned for a long siege. But my people would be without a general to lead them. I'm going to retreat into the forest and reorganize my army. I've already sent a messenger to tell the people in the castle to leave it."

"Good fortune, Niklaz," Hank said. "I'm taking off right now. The Gillikins will be here soon."

"What a vast stupidity," the Tin Woodman said. "All these deaths and hurts and suffering. And for what?"

"That's the way it is on Earth, too," Hank said. "Only there, this goes on all the time. At least, you've had thirty-three years of peace and no wars or rumors of wars until now."

"I don't even have time to bury the dead."

"They won't care."

The wounded were being carried on improvised stretchers towards the woods. Jenny had been trundled out of the barn, her path cleared of corpses and carcasses. Hank saluted Niklaz and said, "No time for a leisurely farewell."

"Don't I know it," the king said. He pointed at the north. Hank turned and saw two camels standing on top of a hill a mile away. Presently, one turned and disappeared behind it.

Hank put the knapsack and BAR in the back cockpit and got into the front seat. Ten minutes later, he was airborne. The Winkies had been swallowed by the trees by then. The Gillikin cavalry was racing down the nearest hill, camels in the front and camels bearing archers behind them. Beyond them, people were pouring out of the castle, joining a throng from the north, the beaten and fleeing army of Niklaz the First and Only.

Hank went back to the Emerald City. Jenny badly needed her wing repaired. She was lucky—Hank, too—to get there without folding up. The city and the area around it were unusually crowded. Refugees from the north had come to it with all the household goods they could pack into wagons. As yet, however, the invaders were stalled in the forest. Forced to march in narrow columns, they could not mass for a battle. The Oz army was ambushing them, cutting columns off, shooting from the cover of trees, snipping off pieces here and there. The defenders were greatly helped because the wild animals were their allies. The Cowardly Lion had enlisted the local beasts and birds and also brought with him many lions, cougars, sabertooths, bears, mammoths, mastodons, and wolves from his realm in the forests in the north of Quadlingland.

"Even so," the Scarecrow said, "the Gillikins will break out of the woods within a few days. We won't be able to stop them in their march to the city. The country's too open. Tell Glinda that all I can do now is to prepare for a siege. That ought to tie down most of their army."

"She probably already knows that," Hank said.

"Yes, probably. But she has to get the news officially."

A hawk arrived with an order from Glinda. Hank was to forget about the planned strafing of the Gillikins. He took off three days later. He felt tired and defeated but not discouraged.

19

Stover reported the latest developments to Glinda.

"All bad news, I'm afraid."

"No," the queen said. "Not all. You must have slain almost a fourth of Erakna's hawks, and that means that her intelligence and messenger force is greatly reduced. Also, you dealt a heavy blow to the Winged Monkeys.

"However, the Uneatable will have learned from her two encounters with you. The next time she sets a trap for you, she'll do it differently."

"Why am I so important to her?"

"It's not you so much as it is the airplane. She must have an exaggerated idea of the danger it represents to her armed forces."

Hank winced, but he had to admit that she was right. Jenny's main use was just carrying passengers. She could have been of limited benefit in strafing or bombing the invaders if it were not for the hawks and eagles. But these could bring him down fairly easy. He had been lucky escaping them. Also, the hawks were far superior scouts.

Now, if only he could have an MB-3A pursuit plane. No use thinking about if's, though.

"You're not the only teller of bad news," she said.

"Yes?"

"The day before Erakna sent the Winged Monkeys after you, she killed Wulthag."

"Oh, my God! The East Witch is dead?"

"Yes. Somehow, Erakna got through her defenses and incinerated her. A Gillikin army is marching almost unhindered to the Munchkin

143

capital. Old Mombi is with it; she's to be the ruler, subject, of course, to Erakna.''

"That's terrible!''

"Not altogether. Erakna is spreading her forces too thin. She'll have a hard time conducting a war on three fronts. Four fronts when she starts invading Quadlingland. The Gillikins are already short-handed on the farmlands. She'll probably bring in slaves from the conquered areas to replace the farmers. But they'll have to be guarded, and she'll have to use a lot of soldiers to do that. She'll also have to tie down many soldiers and occupation troops.''

"Could she also have thought about capturing me so she could question me? She must be very curious about me. Maybe she thinks that I have knowledge that she could use, especially of weapons.''

Glinda sipped berry juice, then said, "You're very shrewd, Hank. Like your mother. Yes, I suppose that was in her mind, but she obviously preferred that you should be killed. She is more concerned about how much you might help me than about possible aid to her.''

Hank hesitated, then said, "Pardon me, Little Mother. I . . .''

"Call me Glinda when we're alone. I get tired of titles.''

"Well, uh, Glinda, I wonder . . . that is, when Erakna attacked Wulthag, she must have used up a lot of energy. Wouldn't she be weaker then, her defenses not so strong? Why didn't you take the opportunity then to attack her?''

Glinda's eyes narrowed, though she smiled.

"Erakna used up much energy when she attacked, yes. But by the time I detected that, she'd slain Wulthag. Poor dear. As soon as Wulthag died, Erakna immediately took over Wulthag's store of energy. That not only recharged Erakna, it made her stronger than before. That's why I did not attack.''

"Thank you for the explanation,'' Hank said. "Though it's not really so illuminating. I need a clear and detailed description of both the theory and the practice of magic.''

"You'd have to go through the discipline of witch-art,'' she said. "That'd take years, and it'd be very dangerous. Out of every hundred who begin training, half quit before they get very far. Out of the remaining fifty, only two or three, if that, become full-fledged witches or wizards. The others . . . die.

"I should modify that. A few settle for being minor witches. Like Mombi, for instance.''

"Why don't you attack her?"

"I will when conditions are right."

She told him to make out his report for the Signal Corps and she would read it. When the green haze came again, he should have everything ready. She might wish to censor it, however.

"They just won't believe it," he said.

"Even if they think you're crazy, they'll keep trying. They might attempt to send through another flier. Or, perhaps, many. Once they can control the size and duration of the opening, they'll invade. I'm sure of that."

"I'm not. You're very worried about disease. But they'll be just as concerned about the diseases here. They could be wide open to them."

"But we don't have any. None for them to worry about, anyway."

"They don't know that. You made sure of that."

"Did I?"

"Sure. What makes you think you didn't?"

"I've had three hundred years experience, but I still run across people who are so tricky that even they fool me now and then. Human ingenuity is deep and complex, and it's most ingenious when it's involved with crime or war. You're tricky, and you haven't declared for us. I wouldn't believe you if you did say you were on our side."

She paused.

"I might if you marry Lamblo. But even then I couldn't be sure of your loyalty. You could marry her as a ploy."

"Damn it! I'm not that deceitful! I have integrity! I'm honest! If I was such a double-dealing swine, I'd have jumped at the chance to marry Lamblo!"

"Cool down," she said, smiling. "You're as hot-tempered as your mother. The difference between you two is that her anger was always appropriate. You're not as self-secure. Of course, you might be faking indignation."

"I'm not very good at faking!"

"Hotter and hotter. The point just now is what you would do if there was no danger from your people and your patriotism wasn't being tried. Would you then marry Lamblo?"

"I really don't know," he said. "I'm not in love with her. That is, I'm not possessed with headlong unthinking passion."

"Passion isn't always love. In fact, it seldom is. If you're waiting for that . . ."

Hank said nothing.

"Whom are you waiting for? Anyone I know?"

"There's no woman on Earth . . ."

"Here?"

"I wasn't going to say that."

There was a long silence. Glinda looked at the pile of papers waiting for her to study and sign or not sign. She sighed. Nobody else, he thought, could convey so much in just an exhalation. There was a deep, centuries-deep, weariness in it. Or, perhaps, not weariness but frustration. Or, perhaps, sadness. Or all three, not levels of them but inextricable strands.

He felt as if he needed the relief of tears.

At that moment, he loved her more than he ever had; he ached for her, but he also felt a shadow. And that was the darkness of understanding that he could never have her for mate or wife. She was human and beautiful, but she was also a very very old human. She would as soon take a year-old infant for lover as him.

She raised her eyes and fixed him with them.

"You're in love with me, aren't you?"

"Oh, no," he said quickly.

He hated himself for the lie. Why had he blurted that out? Why was he afraid to admit the truth? Had he thought that he would offend her? Hurt her? A woman who had had three hundred years to form every defense against every kind of emotional hurt? Who probably did not even need defenses by now?

She smiled slightly but said nothing. Those eyes. They looked like the eyes of the Sphinx of Gizeh. Time-worn, they stared out into infinity and eternity, and these looked back at her, and she became part of them. No. Became them.

Glinda came back from wherever she had been. She said, briskly, "Now. It's very doubtful that your people, the Americans, will be able to open a way at ground level. For some reason, the weak places in the walls now seem to exist above the surface of the two worlds. The Americans won't be able to send through ground troops. What are their chances for sending in an army in the flying machines?"

Hank thought for about thirty seconds before speaking.

"The Americans don't have any large transport airplanes, civilian or military. They could buy some from the British, I suppose, but they would have a tough time keeping that from the public. And, as of now anyway, the whole project is highly secret. They could send in two-seater planes and some bombers, but the biggest bombers we have, in the Army, anyway, don't carry more than three men. But the planes would also have to carry supplies, ammunition, and weapons. That means that they couldn't carry the full complement.

"Of course, if they operated quickly enough, they could establish a base which the first wave could defend while shuttle aircraft brought in more soldiers and supplies. But . . . I don't know. If they wanted to keep the operation secret for some time, it'd have to be a small one. The more people involved, the higher the chance of someone talking."

"What if the officials decide to tell the public?"

"They wouldn't, I think, do that until their hand is forced. They don't want other nations to know about this until they're sure they've got a monopoly here. Also, they'd be risking reaction from their own people. There's a lot of sentimentality about the fictional Land of Oz. Many people would be outraged if they knew that the military was invading this world. To tell the truth, I don't know what they're thinking there, what they hope to do."

Glinda, looking very determined, said, "What I want is the cutting-off of communication and travel between the two worlds. At least until the time, if it ever comes, that your world is more civilized."

Hank's face burned, but he said nothing.

Glinda sipped some berry juice, then said, "I've been considering for some time whether or not to tell you a certain thing. I decided this morning to let you know about it. I want you to put it in your report to your people."

She paused. Hank said, "Yes?"

"I've had hawks circling the area where the green cloud has been forming. The next-to-last time that the green cloud appeared, one of my hawks went through it into your world at my order. When the gate formed the last time, she came back through."

Hank said quickly, "Was she still sentient?"

Glinda nodded and said, "Which means that, though your world does not generate mind-spirits, mind-spirits can exist there."

That news would frighten those who knew about the project. That is, it would if they believed him.

But . . . was Glinda telling the truth? Or had she made up this just to scare the authorities?

"There's only one way to convince them of that," he said. "When the gate next appears, send a hawk through. They can't ignore a talking bird.''

Glinda laughed and said, ''But they can't speak Quadling!''

''That won't matter. They can get a Gothic scholar, and he'll be able to work out the sound-changes and grammatical changes and most of the vocabulary. The only trouble is, they'll have to swear him to secrecy. But they might not trust him to keep his mouth shut. Any scholar would have a hell of a time not telling others about an intelligent talking bird.''

''Would your people let the hawk come back after they'd studied her?''

Hank hesitated, then said, ''I don't know. Well . . . I doubt it. Not for a long time, anyway. She'd have to be studied thoroughly, and that would take months, maybe a year. Even then . . .''

''I won't send one of my people into prison,'' Glinda said.

Hank did not say so, but he thought that the hawk would probably be killed eventually. The scientists would want to dissect her after they had exhausted all study of the living creature. They would be very curious about her brain-nerve structure.

''Why can't you just send them moving pictures of you and others talking to the hawk along with a phonograph recording?''

''I can, but they'd think it was faked.''

''If they did think so, they'd have to believe that you were a traitor.''

Hank was startled. After a few seconds, he said, ''Not necessarily. They might, probably would, believe that I was being coerced. And that would give them an excuse for sending in an invasion force to rescue me.''

''And, since we would resist them, declare war on us?''

''They couldn't do that officially, that is, publicly, unless they wanted to let everybody know about this world.''

Glinda smiled. ''Complicated, isn't it? Human affairs are always so.''

Hank did not reply. A moment later, Glinda dismissed him. He went to the hangar and began the disassembling of Jenny needed for inspection and repair. She was long overdue for them. Jenny asked him what he was doing; she seemed nervous about being taken apart. He explained, and then he had to answer many questions about other things. Jenny was always trying to educate herself. When he was not around, she bugged the mechanics and anybody else, human or animal, within range of her voice.

He quit working a half hour before supper, and he gave his helpers some drawings and instructions for gaskets they should make. After eating, he and Lamblo went to the weekly entertainment held in the ballroom. This consisted of jugglers, acrobats, fire-eaters, jesters, clowns, and a two-act play based on a Quadling legend. Hank got bored, but he could not leave before Glinda did. Fortunately, she was even more bored, having seen much the same acts for three hundred years. She left after forty minutes, and Hank and Lamblo retired to his apartment.

A servant, a cute brunette named Mizdo, woke him at dawn. He had left word that he should be awakened then because he wanted to put in a full day on the plane. Mizdo, however, was not just carrying out her duty as alarm clock. She was wide-eyed and a little pale and agitated.

"The queen says that you are to come at once!"

Lamblo sat up, blinking and saying, "What? What?"

"Not you, Captain!" Mizdo said. "Hank the Giant!"

He was out of bed and headed towards the bathroom. Over his shoulder, he said, "What's up?"

Mizdo pointed a tiny finger at the French windows. "There! There!"

Hank whirled, and, the nightshirt flapping against his ankles, strode to the windows. These were locked and barred because of possible attack by Erakna's hawk assassins. He opened them and stepped out onto the balcony. The sun had cleared the horizon. To the south, high in the air, was a green, roughly rectangular shape. The opening. But it was far larger than before. It had to be as big as two football fields put together.

"What's going on?" Hank said. "They're not due yet!"

The haze began shrinking, but, when it was the size of half a football field, it stopped. Hank watched it for two minutes without noting any change in it. Then, remembering that the queen had summoned him and that it was not wise to keep her waiting, he tore himself away from the spectacle. Ten minutes later, he was in Glinda's suite.

"What do you make of that?" she said.

The haze was still of the same dimensions.

"They've found some way to stabilize the opening," he said. "They're conducting an experiment, a test."

"It's a good thing that Jenny can't fly just now," she said. "Otherwise, you might be trying to escape."

"Never," he said.

"They could fly in an army of planes now, couldn't they?"

"Yes, but I doubt they will. As I said, they need secrecy . . ."

"Perhaps they don't now."

"We can do nothing but wait and see."

The cloud suddenly dwindled and disappeared as if it were a green handkerchief pulled back through a hole in the sky.

"It's always appeared at noon before," Glinda said. "Why should it come just before dawn now?"

Hank did not reply.

"Could it be that it's been small enough not to cause much notice?" she said. "But they don't know that people couldn't help seeing something that big during the day? So they're conducting their tests before many are up and about?"

"I suppose so," he said.

He was awakened at dawn again the next day. Mizdo had just entered the suite, but he had been yanked from a sound sleep a few seconds before. Horns were blaring, drums were pounding, and now through the opened door came the yells and shouts of many and the slap of feet against the floorstones.

"What now?" he roared at Mizdo.

"Flying machines! Many of them!"

20

Breathing heavily after his dash to the top of the highest tower, Hank watched the aircraft as they emerged from the green cloud and headed towards the castle. By the time he had gained the top, the lead planes were circling over the castle. The first to arrive were two Thomas Morse MB-3As, pursuit biplanes. These would be armed with two .30-caliber Colt-Browning machine guns.

Behind them were three D.H.4B two-seater scout and light bomber biplanes just like the one which had crashed.

And behind them were three D.H. biplanes. Airmail carriers!

The Air Service must have brought these in to transport supplies and ammunition. Each had a mail load capacity of 550 pounds.

Here came a Dayton Wright Model FP-2, a twin-float two-engine biplane specially built for the Canadians, who used it for patrolling forests. Had the Army borrowed or rented it?

The FP-2 normally carried a crew of four, but Hank supposed that it was jammed with soldiers and equipment now.

Here came a Loening Air Yacht, a flying boat. It carried four passengers and a pilot, but the passengers would not be civilians this time.

Behind it was an E.M. Laird Company "Swallow," a three-seater Curtiss land biplane.

And behind it was an Orenco Tourister II four-seater commercial biplane.

Glinda arrived then. Her short legs had not been able to keep up with Hank's, but she was in better condition than he. She was not breathing hard.

"What do you think they're going to do?" she said.

Hank walked to the other side of the tower and pointed to the northeast.

"See that lake and the big treeless meadow by it? I bet they're going to land there. The seaplanes will land in the lake and the land planes on the meadow. They'll set up defenses there, their base. There's a road there and embankments by the ditch along the road. On the other side of the meadow is a grove of trees. They'll cut down trees and make some sort of log wall behind which they can shoot from. The lake will protect one side; the embankment, another; the logs, the other two."

"And I suppose that some of those flying machines will stay in the air and protect them from attack there."

"Probably while the other planes are landing. After that, I don't know."

An Elias Commercial biplane had joined the widening circle. It was powered by two LeRhone eighty-horsepower engines and had three cockpits. The pilot was in the front, two passengers in the middle, and one in the rear.

Hank was beginning to understand what the Army had done. It had not pulled out squadrons from one unit or base field. It had plucked one craft from here, another from there. And it had arranged to borrow, lease, or rent some commercial craft. That eleven-passenger Aeromarine Airways, Inc. Flying Cruiser, for instance. The Army must have made secret arrangements to obtain one for a short period and had flown it to near Fort Leavenworth, Kansas, where it would have landed in the Missouri River.

Here came another commercial craft, the Huff-Daland "Petrel," a three-seater.

He wondered why the planes were circling above the castle. Was it to frighten the inhabitants? If so, they were doing a good job. Everybody except Glinda was obviously upset. And down below, on the farms and in the towns, everybody was staring upward. If it had not been for the roar of the engines overhead, he would have heard the cries of the mob.

Now the two pursuits were peeling off and heading, as he had expected, toward the meadow. Others followed them, one by one, as new arrivals entered the southern side of the circle.

The pilots had had more in mind than just shaking up the Quadlings.

They had also wanted their passengers to get a good view of the castle and the layout of the land around it and to check them against the maps he had sent. If they attacked, they wouldn't be doing so blindly.

Hank shook his head. "I can't believe it!"

"What?" Glinda said.

Hank pointed. "Ten Jennies. No, eleven. No, twelve!"

Shortly thereafter, he counted a total of twenty. When they banked to circle, he saw that ten carried a soldier each in the front cockpit and ten had seemingly empty front cockpits. He was sure, however, that these held weapons, ammunition, and other supplies.

"It's a big operation," he muttered.

Glinda, standing close to him, looked up.

"I could order an attack," she said. "I've made plans for just such a situation. But I wish to find out just what they intend to do first. You'll have to interpret."

Hank said, "As you wish, Glinda."

While they went down the stairs, she told him what to say to the invaders' commander.

"Stress that they cannot leave the meadow except to return to Earth. I will not have them spreading disease. If they do leave the camp, they'll be attacked. Don't be diplomatic about it. Tell them in plain words, harsh words, if you must. They must not leave the meadow except to fly back. And they must do that as quickly as possible. I will not argue with the commander. He must do as I say."

"I'll tell them," Hank said. "But I don't know if it'll do any good. They have their orders, and they'll carry them out."

They entered the courtyard and got onto the chariots. Riding out through the gates, Hank saw that the castle guards had been reinforced by the nearby garrison. They had formed a deep rank across the road and were keeping back the mob that had streamed out from the town. Other soldiers were moving the farmers out of the houses between the meadow and the town.

A woods to his right seethed with hawks and eagles. They were waiting for Glinda's orders.

When the chariots were a quarter of a mile from the meadow, they halted. Glinda said, "This is as close as we'll come—except for you. Go and talk to them. No, wait. What are your feelings about this, Hank?"

He laughed raggedly.

"How do I feel? We Americans have a saying. 'My country, right or wrong.' Most of us, I'm sorry to say, agree with that. But some of us don't. My mother taught me that 'right' is higher than anything, well, except God; and He's supposed to always be on the side of right. She also taught me that it's not always easy to see what's right and what's not.

"In this situation . . . I'm torn, Glinda. I love my country, even though there are a hell of a lot of things wrong in it. I want it to be always in the right, to do right. But it hasn't always been and isn't and won't. Still, it's the best country, among the best, anyway, that I've ever seen or know of.

"Now, though . . . they're wrong, dead wrong, to come barging in here like this. They, the authorities, the big shots, have been told what will happen here if they come. They'll be bringing something far more deadly than bullets. Knowing this, having been told to stay out, they come anyway. Why? Because of greed and fear.

"They're wrong, Glinda. It hurts me to say that. Worse, they're evil. They would deny that; they think of themselves as good men, doing what they're doing for the good of the country. But their thinking is warped."

"I know all that," she said. "And more. But just what is your position in this? Are you for or against me . . . us?"

"I can't be a traitor to my country!" he said, a near-wail shaking his voice. "I just can't!"

"Which is your country?"

"What do you mean?"

"The land you were born in or the land of the right?"

The two seaplanes had landed and taxied near to the shore. Soldiers had poured out of them, sinking in the lake up to their waists. Then canvas boats were unfolded, and these were loaded with boxes and pushed ashore and unloaded and shoved back to the seaplanes to be loaded again.

While the two pursuits circled high overhead, the land planes touched down one by one and taxied to the area near the lake. Soldiers and pilots got out to help remove weapons and supplies from the craft. Hank saw ten .50-caliber and four .30-caliber Browning machine guns and two light mortars. Most of the troops were armed with BARs.

Guards were stationed at the perimeters. Some men were digging latrine trenches, and a large number were chopping at the bases of middle-sized trees.

The last plane, a Jenny, landed and discharged a soldier and several boxes.

A man in an officer's uniform stood near the embankment, his binoculars trained on Hank's group. Hank wondered what the fellow made of the tiny people and the moose-drawn chariots. He would be verifying that the natives had no firearms, though he had doubtless been told that. What else had he been told?

One man was operating a movie camera, and two men were setting up radio equipment.

One by one, the planes took off, climbing to about two thousand feet and circling while the others caught up with them.

Hank waited for Glinda to tell him to approach the base, but she seemed to be interested only in watching the procedure. That wise old brain behind that devastatingly beautiful and young face must be considering all possibilities, though.

Presently, the circle above broke up as the planes headed in single file towards the south. The two pursuits, however, dived, turned, and flew towards the Quadlings on the road. They were only fifty feet up as they raced along, and they shot roaring and whistling over the Quadlings. The queen's troops must have been frightened, but they held firm. Nobody was going to break discipline, not when Glinda was around.

"They could have killed us all if they'd wanted to," Hank said.

He watched the pursuits pull up and turn towards the others.

"I didn't think they wanted to," she said. "Go to them, now, Hank. But don't touch them. Stay away from them. I don't wish to quarantine you again."

"As you wish," he said, and he walked down the road. When he came to the wooden bridge across the ditch, he turned and crossed it. A guard, a young private wearing the crossed-rifles insignia of the infantry, challenged him.

"Henry L. Stover, late lieutenant of the Army Air Service," Hank said.

The guard had been informed about him. Not, Hank thought, that he could have been anybody else. Who else in this world stood so tall and spoke English? Except for the invaders, of course.

The guard bawled out a summons to a corporal nearby, and the man came running to escort him to the officer with the binoculars. Hank was surprised when he saw his captain's bars. He had expected that an expedition of such importance would be led by a colonel at least. The officer, like all the soldiers Hank could see, had no cloth insignia.

Hank stopped ten feet from him and said, "Henry L. Stover at your service, sir."

The captain was almost as tall as Hank. He was lean and lanky and had a deeply tanned angular face with high cheekbones, pale blue eyes, and straw-colored hair. He did not look over thirty.

"Captain Boone Longstreet," the fellow said in a deep but rasping voice. The accent was Southern, probably Tennesseean or Kentuckian. "Of the United States Regular Infantry."

Longstreet advanced towards him; Hank stepped back. Looking puzzled, the officer stopped.

"I have orders not to get any closer than this to any of you," Hank said.

"Why not, suh?"

"I don't want to catch anything from you."

A flush spread out beneath the tan.

"That sounds insulting, suh."

"It's not meant to be anything but realistic. These people are wide open to Earth diseases."

The captain looked startled. Hank thought, Good God, didn't the brass tell him anything about that?

"Also, of course," Hank said, "you and your men are very vulnerable to the diseases of this world."

Longstreet paled. The fellow was a regular chameleon.

Why had he lied so spontaneously? Why? Because he did not want them here. They had no right to be here.

But these feelings did not mean that he was a traitor or ready to be Glinda's agent for whatever she wanted him to do.

Even so, he felt guilty. Somewhat so, anyway.

"I'd like to know your orders, Captain," Hank said.

"What? You're a civilian, suh. You have no need or right to know them. Not all of them, anyway."

Hank said, "Look, Captain, I've been authorized to act as an interpreter and a sort of ambassador at large. Surely, you must know that. I have to know your intentions."

"I was told I must deal through you. To a certain extent, that is."

Longstreet stared over Hank's shoulder. Hank turned. The green cloud was back now, and the planes, which had formed into a circle, were dropping out of it, one by one, and flying into the cloud. As soon as the last disappeared, the haze shrank and was gone within a few seconds.

The sight of that, Hank thought, must make the captain feel alone and isolated. Perhaps, helpless. Or maybe he was attributing some of his own reactions to the man.

Hank had counted seventy-five men, enlisted and officers. That did not seem many, but they must be confident that their rapid-fire weapons and their superior stature were the equivalent of an army of pygmies armed only with swords, spears, and bows.

A number were cutting down trees with two-handled saws. Others were digging a shallow trench near the lake. They meant to erect a three-sided log palisade in front of the trench. The lake would be to their backs.

Hank said, "Captain, would you mind telling me just how much you were briefed on?"

"That is not your concern, suh," Longstreet said, looking him straight in the eyes. "I have been ordered to tell you my orders, suh, so that you may transmit them to the chief authority of this place."

Hank pointed at the small but regal figure in the chariot. Her hair shone redly in the sun.

"There she is, Glinda the Good."

Apparently, Longstreet had never read the Oz books. He looked at her through his binoculars, then lowered them.

"Here's what you'll tell this Glinda," Longstreet said loudly and determinedly. "One, we're not here to make war unless we're treated as hostiles. We're here on a peaceful mission."

"Yes, looks like it," Hank said, gesturing at the heavy machine guns.

"You with us or against us?" Longstreet said, but he did not wait for Stover to reply.

"Two, the United States of America is prepared to protect this country against any enemies from Earth."

At least, the captain knew that he was not in his native universe.

"The United States of America offers its aid against any enemies along its border. It is prepared to make a treaty of alliance with Queen

Glinda of Quadlingland and to use its armed forces in her struggle against any and all invaders.''

Hank had expected Longstreet to read from an official letter. But the brass were being cagey. They had issued only verbal orders.

''Three, the United States of America asks permission to establish a base from which its soldiers may operate against the enemies of the Quadlings and which will eventually house diplomats, scientists, and other agents which the United States may see fit to send to Quadlingland, provided, of course, that the reigning authority of Quadlingland agrees to these. Terms will be worked out at the appropriate time.''

''You can stop right there, Captain Longstreet,'' Hank said. ''There's no use wasting time telling me all that. I have a message from Glinda. She told me to tell the commanding officer that you all must get out, leave, scat, scram, immediately. Toot sweet. She won't confer, discuss, or argue about that. She did not invite you here, and she wants you out. *Now!* She doesn't care if your intentions are good or bad. Your mere presence here is a hideous danger, a terrible peril, to the people of this land. After you leave, she'll have this meadow and the woods along it burned to destroy the bacteria and germs you may have left here. And nobody will be allowed to use the lake for three months. She won't talk about it, she isn't open to compromise or temporizing or anything except your instant departure.

''Moreover, she does not want the...uh...gate to this world opened ever again once you've returned to Earth. You will take that message back to your superiors.''

21

Longstreet's face was expressionless, but his cheeks were red.

"My orders are to hold this base until otherwise ordered! Also, I am to defend this base if I'm attacked!"

"Then you won't leave?"

"No! How can I? I depend upon the Air Service for transport! But that has nothing to do with it! I have my orders, and I will carry them out!"

"Look, captain, this is not an ordinary military situation. The U.S. hasn't officially declared war on the Quadlings. Very few people even know that this universe exists. I'll bet that you're a bachelor and an orphan. You have no family ties. Am I right?"

Longstreet looked amazed. He said, "How'd you know?" Then, "What's that got to do with anything?"

"I'll also bet that all your men are bachelors with no kin. Right?"

"What about it?"

"You're part of a very secret project. All of you volunteered for this duty, and you were not told much about it. Maybe you were told that it was part of a scientific experiment and that it involved an expedition to another world."

"The fourth dimension," Longstreet said. "A different universe."

"Sure. Anyway, it's very secret, as I said. The American public doesn't know about it. Very few people do. Some of the Signal Corps, some of the Air Service, President Harding, a few cabinet members, maybe even a few high Republican Congressmen.

"Why all this secrecy? Why keep a lid on the greatest discovery in history? I'll tell you why. Look at that castle, Captain!"

He pointed his finger at the reddish building with the walls set with thousands of twinkling objects.

"Those aren't glass, Captain. Each one is a genuine ruby worth several millions of dollars. This land is lousy with rubies, diamonds, emeralds—up north is a whole city studded with emeralds—topazes, turquoises, tourmalines. And there's gold, Captain, more gold than in a thousand Klondikes and a hundred South Africas. And there's silver enough to build the Great Wall of China.

"I tell you, Captain, the men who get their hands on this wealth will be super-Croesuses. But they'll have to keep a tight control on it. Otherwise, Earth'll be flooded with precious stones and metals, the bottom would drop out of the market, and Earth would be in financial chaos.

"So, it's greed that's behind this. The big shots who sent you here to die don't care about you. If you're wiped out, they'll have a good excuse to send in more poor devils to fight and die for them. For the wealth they want. I wouldn't put it past them to send in men suffering from smallpox and cholera and all the sicknesses in Pandora's box. They'd spread their diseases, and just about everybody in this world would die. I . . ."

"No!" Longstreet shouted. "We were given very thorough medical examinations. There's not an unhealthy man among us. We're clean!"

"You may be. But if military force can't get them what they want, then they'll use disease. Anyway, you're all expendable. If you die here, you'll be buried here, cremated so you won't spread disease. Your deaths will be announced in America, but the truth won't be told about where or why or how you died. There'll be fake reports, you'll be supposed to have died of accident or illness."

"Shut up!" Longstreet said. "I was told that you might not be trusted, and, by God, I see that they were right! You're a traitor!"

"You son of a bitch!" Hank said. "I'm not a Benedict Arnold! I'm just trying to talk you out of this insanity, show you why you're here! I don't want this tragedy! I want to save you!"

"I have my orders," Longstreet said. "Now, I haven't given you the message to deliver to the queen yet."

Hank only half-listened to the rest. But when he went to Glinda, he repeated the captain's words almost verbatim.

"Did he say when the gate would be opened again?" she said.

"No. He said that that was classified information."

"It's a pity, the whole thing. Very well. What must be must be."

She commanded that the party return to the castle. Stover climbed to the top of the highest tower and looked with his binoculars at the meadow. The log fortifications would soon be complete. Pup tents were being put up within the enclosure, and there were four large bonfires. Dawn would see the base completed. What would happen next? Would the soldiers stay inside the base or did they have orders to attack?

There was nothing he could do about them except to plead with Glinda. That would be futile. She had determined her course with logic that he could not prove false.

He went down to the hangar and worked for five hours on Jenny. She was then ready for flight, but he had nowhere to take her. Jenny wanted to talk, but he was not in the mood. He walked away from her while she plaintively asked what was troubling him.

He had hoped to talk to Glinda about the soldiers. She, however, did not invite him to dine with her. He ate in his suite alone, Lamblo being on guard duty. Afterwards, he left the castle and walked down the road until the queen's guards stopped him. He could see the fires and the figures moving around them and could hear, faintly, the singing. The words were indistinguishable but the melody was recognizable. They were singing a popular tune from 1922, "Toot, Toot, Tootsie, Goodbye." He felt homesick for a moment; tears welled. He also felt a desire to go down and join the soldiers.

"Here I am, an American. I'll stand by you even if you're wrong."

That was succeeded by a momentary rage against the men who had sent them here. They should be exposed, punished. Perhaps, if he could somehow get back to Earth, he could publicize their crime and see to it that those fat old men were disgraced.

Now the men were singing Julia Ward Howe's "Hymn to the Republic." That must be making their Southern captain angry. But, immediately thereafter, "Dixie" came to him. Longstreet should be pacified by that.

There was a flare of light, the sound of scraping feet, and the flap of cloaks in the wind. He turned. Glinda and six guards were there. She came to his side and stood silently for a while. Now the soldiers were singing George M. Cohan's "Over There."

He looked down at her profile. The achingly beautiful face was expressionless. She said, "It's sad. Such things should not have to be. I should be hardened to them, but I'm not."

She was not talking about the songs. She was thinking of what would soon be done to them.

"Couldn't you use your 'magic' to transport them back to Earth?" he said. "That would convince the chiefs that they were up against an invincible force, someone with powers they couldn't understand or cope with."

"No, I can't. There are too many. I would have to use special tools, and I don't have nearly enough. Besides, they'd have to cooperate with me if I did have the means, and they wouldn't. Also, it would exhaust me, leave me wide open for an attack from Erakna. And I doubt very much that the chiefs would just give up."

"When are you going to attack?"

"It's better that you don't know. Don't think about trying to warn them. It wouldn't do any good. I can, however, understand why you would want to do that."

He walked away without saying goodnight.

Lamblo did not come to bed; she sent word that she had been ordered to attend Glinda all that night. Hank tried to sleep but could not. He got up and drank some of the expensive imported Gillikin liquor which was much like scotch. After smoking several pipes and downing half a fifth, he reeled to bed. He did not drop off at once, however. He could not find a comfortable position, and he was about to get up again when he became aware that someone was shaking his shoulder. He sat up. Dawn light was flooding the room. Mizdo, looking tired, black under the eyes, had awakened him. His head hurt, his eyes were gummed, and his mouth tasted like the bottom of a chamber pot.

"The queen wants you."

"O.K., O.K., give me a minute."

Despite the urgency, he took his time. He shaved and showered and brushed his teeth with salt and drank some berry juice. Then he dressed slowly. He knew that he was not going to like this day, and he was putting off the inevitable as long as he could.

Glinda was not, as he had expected, waiting for him in her suite or in the conference room. Lamblo, who looked even more worn and pale than Mizdo, met him at the foot of the staircase on the first floor.

She greeted him but did not ask him how he was. She said, "We'll take the chariot to the meadow."

They rode out on a road empty of people and animals until they got to the meadow. Here were many soldiers, male and female, and hundreds of hawks and eagles. Some of the birds were stained with dried blood.

Hank looked around. There must have been a great noise late last night, screaming, shouting, rifles, and machine guns firing. He had not heard it; his suite was on the far south side of the castle and the walls were thick. Now there was silence except for the shuffling of feet, the clink now and then of metal against metal, and the occasional soft orders from officers.

Glinda stood on top of the embankment by the ditch. Hank went to her side and looked down on the dead. Most of the Americans were lying behind the log palisade, but some must have tried to escape across the meadow and into the woods. They had been caught by the birds and their faces and throats torn out. Dead hawks and eagles lay by them, but most of the slain birds were among the corpses behind the logs. Several dozen of the defenders had arrows sticking from them.

"The attack was launched an hour before dawn," Glinda said. "It caught most of them asleep. I sent in archers in the third wave, and they finished up those still fighting and the wounded."

Soldiers clad in white baggy clothes and face masks were pouring methyl alcohol and oil over the bodies. When this was completed, the torches were applied. Black smoke rose from the flames. Even though the wind was from the southwest, Hank could smell the burning flesh. Hank fought against getting sick. He had never before seen wholesale carnage close up. He had been far above the bodies lying on fields churned up by artillery barrages.

The white-clothed soldiers carried in branches and narrow logs and set them over the bodies. Then they threw buckets of alcohol and oil on the wood.

The wounded birds were being treated with watered alcohol. Some of them screamed with pain.

"I don't think that's necessary," Hank said. "I doubt very much if any . . . of my people . . . were diseased."

"I don't want to take any chances."

Hank returned to his suite in the castle, put paper, ink bottle, and pen on the desk, and then walked for a while around the room, his lips moving. Having composed his text roughly, he sat down and began writing.

> July 10, 1923
> Henry Lincoln Stover
> American Citizen
> Castle of Queen Glinda
> Quadlingland, Amariiki

Warren Gamaliel Harding
President of the United States of America
White House
Washington, D.C., U.S.A.
Earth

Dear Mr. President:

Doubtless, you will know in a few days what happened to the soldiers who invaded this world.

As commander-in-chief of the armed forces of the U.S.A., you are responsible for the invasion and their deaths.

You were ill-advised to permit this, but you are the one with the final responsibility.

Surely, you were fully informed of the possible, indeed, inevitable, consequences of this invasion. My report must have been sent to you, sir.

I just cannot understand why the project was not terminated, why there was not only a failure to cease communication but why this criminal invasion was ordered.

I am very angry, and I am very ashamed, and I grieve deeply.

I feel that the officers and the civilian scientists and the government officials who have participated in this project are guilty of a crime. But their guilt is little compared to yours, sir.

I have always been proud of being an American, though I realize that we Americans have done and are doing certain things that we should be deeply ashamed of. But I've always felt that, though we are far from perfect, there is something in the American spirit that is always struggling to rectify the evils in our society. I've always felt that we were not the only ones distinguished by these evils. That is, that all other nations have their evils, some like ours, some of a different nature.

My mother taught me that, though I like to think that I would have been objective enough to realize that myself when I became an adult.

I am speaking, of course, of the position of the Negro, of the treatment of Chinese, Japanese, and the American Indian, of the vast and deep corruption in our government, federal, state, municipal, of the corruption and deaths and ruined lives resulting from the stupid Prohibition law, and . . . but why go on?

These are our problems, and I have faith enough in our political system and in the spirit of the times to feel that, with time, we'll solve them.

It's what's going on now with this world that concerns me.

I have tried to find excuses for the invasion, but I have absolutely failed. There are no acceptable ones. They are unacceptable to me as an American and a human being. There should not be any differentiation in those words, to be an American should mean to be a human being. Sometimes the two terms are synonymous; more often, they're not. But I am an individual, a person, my own self, and I strive to be both. That means that I don't support the slogan, "My country, right or wrong." I want it to be always right, and, if it sees that it's wrong, to become right.

I would think the same if I were a Frenchman or a Russian or a Chinese or a British citizen or a Siamese.

Queen Glinda does not want you to enter this world. She wants all entrance and communication stopped. She does not want, and I don't want it, either, plagues that will kill hundreds of thousands, perhaps millions, of the citizens of this world. She speaks only for one of the nations here, but I am one hundred percent certain that the other governments here would feel exactly as she does.

I am not a traitor because I oppose you or whomever might succeed you. I had no part in the destruction of the invasion force that you sent, and I did my best to find some other way of dealing with the force. I still think of myself as a citizen of the U.S.A., a loyal citizen. But one who's deeply ashamed and grieved because of what his country is doing now.

I beg you, sir, I beg as an American and a human being, that you close down this project. That all activity concerning it cease.

The dangers are not only for the people of this world. If you persist, you may open America—the world—to things which would be even more dangerous, fatal, to the people of Earth.

The implications of these dangers are in my reports. I have not exaggerated or lied. Please, I beg of you, consider them.

Respectfully and sincerely,
Henry Lincoln Stover

While the ink dried, Hank paced back and forth. Were his efforts to be wasted?

He sent a hawk with a message to Glinda. A few minutes later, the hawk returned and said that Glinda could see him at once. When he got to the conference chamber, he told her he had written a letter, and he translated it aloud for her.

She said, "I hope that it will convince your leader to change his mind. I doubt it, though."

"I suppose you're right," he said. "I wish it could be delivered now before they try something else."

Glinda smiled and said, "I'll deliver it. Tonight."

Hank was startled. "But . . .?"

"Oh, it'll cost me, but I know that Erakna is in no position, at this moment, anyway, to attack me while I'm weakened. Besides, it'll be easier and so cost less to me to go through the opening your people made. The more the passageway is used, the less energy needed to go through it."

Hank thought that he need not have been so surprised. She must have a barrel of tricks up that sleeve.

"Do you know exactly where to place the message?" he said.

"I have the letters and other items they sent you. These will enable me to track back to the senders."

"How . . .?" Hank said. He stopped because her smile made it evident that she would not answer him. It seemed to him, however, that the letters and the items must leave some sort of vibrational spoor behind them during their passage in space. Psychic tracks?

He sighed. He would probably never know unless he became a wizard.

To do that, he would have to stay here and to become a citizen. Abandon his American citizenship and apply for naturalization papers to Oz.

In that moment, he knew that that was what he intended. What his unconscious had intended for some time. That is, he had wished to be a citizen. He was not sure that he cared to be a wizard.

22

The next day, Hank Stover was eager to ask Glinda if she had delivered his letter. He was told, however, that she had left word that she was not to be disturbed until three o'clock that afternoon.

"The queen is sleeping," the messenger said.

One hour after the sun had reached its zenith, the green haze appeared. The aircraft that shot from it was a D.H.4B, probably one that had been used to bring in supplies or a soldier. This time it carried a pilot and a photographer. It circled low over the meadow for two minutes, then it circled the castle.

Hank half-expected that a message for him would be dropped from it, but he was disappointed. The plane flew back across the desert and into the haze, which had reappeared two minutes before the craft reached it.

If the big brass thought that he was lying, they would have to believe otherwise when they saw the photographs. They would show some graves filled in, others half-dug, and burned bodies stretched out waiting for burial.

What did the lack of a message mean? That they had not yet written a reply or that they were planning another attack?

He spent an hour in the room where birds and humans brought verbal reports for Glinda. These were taken down by the scribes, and the pages piled in a basket on her desk to be taken to her suite. Nobody objected to his listening in. He did not think that that was an oversight. Glinda, who never missed a thing, must have given orders that he would not be denied admittance.

The Emerald City was under siege, but, so far, the Gillikins had not tried to storm it. The Scarecrow, however, had had a narrow escape. Eagles bearing burning torches had tried to drop them on it when it was inspecting the guards on top of the walls. One had landed only a few inches from it and frightened it. Of the few things it feared, fire was the greatest.

Most of Ozland was occupied by now, and the survivors of the defending army had fled into Quadlingland.

Erakna was in Munchkinland but planned to return to her capital soon.

The chief of the Pekotasha nation had agreed to furnish an army for Erakna. It was not as large as Erakna had asked for because Wasokat was forced to keep a large standing army on his borders if the Shanahooka nation should attack him.

The Tin Woodman and his guerrillas had retreated even deeper into the Winkie hills. A Gillikin army was making an all-out effort to track him down. But they were suffering heavy casualties because the Winkie wild animals were actively allied with the Woodman.

There was much disaffection and resentment among the Gillikins. They were unhappy about being ruled by a red witch, and they saw no reason for the war. Erakna had issued orders for savage reprisals against all suspected of anything but absolute loyalty.

A tornado in northwest Gillikinland had wiped out a battalion of soldiers, and the Gillikins were asking each other, secretly, of course, if the tornado had been generated and directed by Glinda.

The news was, like news everywhere in both worlds, both good and bad.

At 4:15, Hank was summoned to the conference room. He found a Glinda who was pale and a little blue and puffy under the eyes but energetic.

"Your letter was placed on a desk in the Signal Corps headquarters," she said. "It should have caused consternation, panic, and doubt. Not because of its contents but because they will know that I can penetrate their guard. They will wonder how I was able to do that. For all they will know, I could transport not only myself but an army into the strongest fortress."

"Could you?" Hank said.

"No. You know I can't. But there is one who can place an army within a castle, though she could not do it in your world. That is the red witch, Erakna the Uneatable. No, I'll modify that. She could place the Winged Monkeys in the area of my castle. She can't pinpoint their place of arrival, but, if she were lucky, she might get some within the castle near my suite. The others would be scattered within a quarter-mile area.''

"Whoever controls the Golden Cap controls the Monkeys. You'd like to have that control, so you'd like to get hold of the Cap. But Erakna knows that, and she will have taken measures to prevent anyone getting her hands on it.''

Glinda sat back and smiled. She looked so beautiful that a tiny lightning bolt pang shot through his chest.

"You are indeed your mother's son!''

"I take that as a high compliment. You wouldn't be bringing this up unless you had an idea for getting the Golden Cap. And you wouldn't waste your time telling me about it unless I figured in your plan.''

"Very good. You figure prominently. In fact, you are the axle man, the one who holds the wheels and without whom the wheels could not turn.''

"My people would say that I'm the big wheel.''

She gestured impatiently. "Almost all of the arrangements have been made. One thing is lacking. Will you volunteer? I cannot order you to endanger your life.''

Hank thought that she had done a pretty good job of ordering before now, but he did not say so.

"I'll have to know what kind of hot water I'll be in before I can answer that. However . . . you wouldn't have gone to whatever lengths you have gone to if you were not certain that I would volunteer. I'm not so sure that I like being so predictable.''

"No one is one hundred percent predictable. If you should refuse me, I can replace you. To a certain extent, that is. I will still need you to transport the man I'd substitute for you.''

Hank sighed.

"You're appealing to my pride. No, call it vanity. You're saying that no one else can fit into my boots.''

"Not to my satisfaction.''

Hank looked around the room. He, Glinda, and Balthii, a goshawk, were the only ones present. Not even a mouse could have hidden there, and if it could, it would have been smelled out by Balthii. No spy would report on this meeting.

He was silent while Glinda outlined her plan, then described it in detail. When she was finished, he said, "Why did you choose me? You need someone who's relatively inconspicuous, someone who can pass for a Gillikin. The same objection to me goes for Sharts the Shirtless, too. He's as tall as I am. And how many Rare Beasts are there?"

"You won't be walking around the city in daylight and among the crowds. The main reason I picked you and Sharts and the others is that you have the best chance of pulling this off. I *know* that you are the best. I can read character, and I can calculate probabilities to a degree you might find incredible."

Hank sighed again, and he said, "Very well. But what if the Americans invade again?"

"I'll handle that. I didn't need you the last time. Though I was, of course, grateful that you were available if I did need you."

"I can't leave until the day after tomorrow. I have to flight-check Jenny, and I have many things to get ready."

Glinda smiled and said, "And you should have more time with Lamblo."

Later, Hank wondered if Glinda could tell what Lamblo was going to do just by the subtle attitudes of her voice and body or if Lamblo had confided in Glinda. He certainly had had no warning that the little blonde was going to propose marriage to him.

"In my country," he said, when he had rallied from the shock, "the men ask the women to marry them."

"But you're not there," Lamblo said.

They were clad only in robes and slippers and were eating a snack before returning to bed. She was sitting in the high chair which had been built for her. Even so, she had to look up at him across the table.

"Anyway," she said, "that's beside the point. You're dodging my question. Don't do that just because you don't want to hurt me. You surely know whether or not you want me as your wife. You can't tell me that you haven't thought about it."

Hank put down the half-eaten piece of buttered bread smeared with honey. He would choke if he took another bite.

"Don't be afraid to admit that you're in love with Glinda. All the men are. But they can't have her. You can't have her. If you had any sense, you'd know that by now. You'd also know that if you could be her husband, you wouldn't be happy very long. She's three hundred years old, Hank, and she's a witch. You'd never be equals. You'd be her shadow. Or a mortal coupled with a goddess. You'd..."

"I know all that!" he said. "I have more sense than you credit me with."

He drank some milk, and he said, "Only..."

Lamblo was not smiling now; her eyes were slitted.

"Only... if you can't have her, you don't want anybody?"

"No. That's not it."

"I love you, Hank."

Something that had been hard and cold within seemed to soften and melt. He broke up inside, and, though it hurt him, it also made him sob, just once, but violently. It was as if something had torn itself loose from deep within him and had flown up through his throat and out of his mouth. Almost, he could hear it wailing as it flew out into night.

"I love you, Lamblo, but..."

She waited. She was smiling now, her eyes were wide, but tears were filming them.

"Well, but, now's no time to talk of marrying! I'll be leaving very soon on a dangerous mission... I might not return..."

"I don't give a damn!" she said. "No, I don't mean I don't care that you're going to be in danger! I care very much; I don't have to say that. I mean that it doesn't make any difference! I'm willing to take a chance I'll be a widow, and if you love me you would, too. Hank, I want your child."

He gripped the edge of the table.

"But it should have a father."

"Will you marry me? A yes or a no will do. As far as words go, anyway."

"Yes. As soon as I get back," he said. "We don't have time to get married. And I'll be very busy tomorrow getting ready for the journey. We couldn't even have a honeymoon."

"Oh, I think Glinda will manage to marry us, first thing in the morning. After breakfast. As for the honeymoon, you might say that we've had that."

He got up from the chair and walked around the table and picked her up and kissed her.

"I didn't force you to say yes, did I?" she murmured.

"I'd not be much of a man if you could."

"You're a big man, as big as they come and larger," she said. "We Quadlings have a saying: A big man is not necessarily a big man. It has a double meaning, but I'm talking about strength of character. About a strong man."

"Listen, Lamblo. I've got guts enough to tell you I didn't want to marry you if I didn't. I'll tell you the truth. I've not met any other woman here—of course, I haven't met many—whom I'd rather marry. And I do love you."

"But Glinda?"

"She's more goddess than mortal. I realized that some time ago. I just don't want you bringing her up when you get mad at me. It wouldn't be fair. I don't care what else you reproach me with, but just don't taunt me about her."

"That depends upon how angry you make me."

But she giggled.

The marriage did not take much time. Instead of a priest or priestess, Glinda conducted the ceremony. Glinda said a few words, a question to and an answer from each, and the bridegroom and bride exchanged golden rings, Glinda blessed them, and that was that. Later, when there was an opportunity, there would be a reaffirmation, a big formal wedding with priests and priestesses, Lamblo's parents and relatives present, a band, dancing, much drinking, and many bawdy jests.

The honeymoon lasted an hour. Hank had not taken the anti-fertility drink, but since its effects had not yet worn off, he could not make Lamblo pregnant. He would not have to worry about his child being fatherless if he did not return from the mission.

23

The final landing was on a farmer's meadow ten miles north of Wugma, the Gillikin capital.

Hank had flown only at night, and he had followed a circle which took him far west of Wugma over a hilly, thinly populated area. Glinda had arranged for guerrillas and spies to light beacon fires at fifty-mile intervals to guide him. Even with these he would not have been able to fly in the dark if it had not been for Bargma the owl. She was familiar with the mountain ranges he had to pass through, and she guided him safely through them.

The weather had cooperated, though the skies were usually cloudy. Bargma attributed the lack of rain and high winds to Glinda. Hank did not believe this because he could not see how any witch could summon up and control the vast amount of energy involved. But he did not argue with the owl.

Jenny landed between a line of torches. She bounced a little—the meadow could have been more level—and as soon as she was firmly on terra firma, the torches were doused. It took a little longer to put out the big beacon fire with water.

Hank cut the ignition. Figures appeared out of darkness. At his order, they pushed the plane under the branches of a huge oak and turned it around. A man holding a bull's-eye lantern stood by the cockpit. He was as tall as Hank. Sharts the Shirtless. Behind him was the three-foot-two-inch-high figure of Blogo the Rare Beast. His crested head and the knobbed cylinder of his nose were outlined by the dying fire.

Hank greeted them, then climbed out to supervise the refueling of

173

Jenny. The hawks, who had ridden in the rear cockpit, and the owl got onto the windshields. Balthii gave her companion some additional instructions, and Martha flew off with the message that the final landing had been accomplished.

"Everything's set up and going well?" Hank said to Sharts.

The man's tone bristled. "Of course! I made all the arrangements! To the last detail!"

"It was just a rhetorical question," Hank said.

He was already irritated at having to be so careful with this prima donna. The mission was difficult and nerve-scraping enough, and he was in no mood to handle Sharts as if he were a vial of nitroglycerine. Which, in a way, he was.

Some day, he would ask how the giant had earned his title. He certainly would not put the question to Sharts, however. At the moment, Sharts was wearing an elegant brocaded and frilled shirt with a high neck-ruff. An unbuttoned sleeveless jacket hung from his broad shoulders. It looked like leather but probably was not. Leather was far more rare and costly than gold or diamonds and was illegal in all nations unless the owner could prove that he or she had the deceased's permission or the relatives' to skin the deceased. Sharts's pants were jodhpurs; his boots, conventional wooden shoes with felt leggings and rolled tops. These would be replaced later by all-linen shoes

Nearby were eight saddled deer and eight deer attached to a large wagon.

"We'll ride in," Sharts said, interpreting Hank's gaze correctly.

He introduced Hank, Jenny, and the birds to the other members of the raiding party. Five human males, seven hawks, and the deer.

The Rare Beast said in his piping voice, "Sharts and I could do this by ourselves. But Glinda said no, and what Glinda wants, Glinda gets."

"Besides," Balthii said, "if you didn't obey her, you wouldn't get pardoned for your crimes."

"What crimes?" Sharts roared.

The deer jumped, the hawks screeched, the owl hooted, and some of the men backed away.

"How'd you like your neck wrung like a bell?" the Rare Beast squeaked.

"Now, now," Hank said, raising his hand. "There's no need to get upset. I'm sure that Balthii meant no insult. Right, Balthii?"

"Most certainly not."

"Well, it was very personal," Sharts rumbled. "Watch your big mouth, hawk, or I'll twist your beaks so much they'll look like a corkscrew."

"How would you like to kiss the south end of a duck going north?" Balthii said, and she winged off before Sharts could catch her.

Hank moaned, and he muttered, "We'll all kill each other before we get off the meadow."

He spoke to Sharts. "As Glinda's official representative, I apologize for any remarks Balthii made. You know how those hawks are."

Sharts grunted.

Unwaz, the leader of the Gillikin hawks, said, "And just how are we hawks?"

"Proud!" Hank said quickly. "Proud! And also, I mean no offense, somewhat touchy, uh, I mean, very sensitive."

Balthii had flown back to her roost on the edge of the windshield. She said, "We're all, myself included, acting foolishly. If Glinda were here, she'd chew us out. I suggest that, from now on, we stick strictly to business. I am sorry, Sharts, if I hurt your feelings. I won't do it again, I promise."

Hank thought, I'd crack up if I was a professional diplomat. I'd like to bust this guy in the chops. Maybe I will after it's all over. Only . . . that wouldn't be very intelligent. He could probably beat hell out of me with one hand tied behind his back. I might try it, anyway.

"We have to settle one thing before we get started," Sharts said. He glared around him. "There seems to be some confusion about who's in command here. Glinda's messenger told me that I was."

Hank's back was to Sharts because he had been removing the BAR box magazines from the front cockpit. He turned, unable to speak for a moment because of rage. Glinda had made it clear that he was the chief. Sharts was lying. Or maybe he wasn't. Maybe he really believed that the hawk had given him that message. He was such an egomaniac; he would reconstruct the past to fit his self-image.

"You know the territory," Hank said. "I don't. You're the leader. Lead on, Macduff!"

"Makduuf?"

"An English word. It means 'son of a . . . ' I forget of what. Macduff was a great man."

He walked over to Jenny and whispered, "If I don't come back, tell Glinda I died hating her because she fixed me up with these clowns."

"O.K.," the airplane said. "However, I have complete confidence in you, Hank. I'll be ready when you come back."

"If I do, I'll probably be running like Charlie Paddock."

"Who?"

"The world's, my world's, greatest sprinter. Listen. I've instructed the farmer on how to prime your carburetor. It's a good thing you have enough energy to spin the propellor yourself. These Gillikins are too short; he'd have to stand on a stool, and he might get cut in half."

"I'm not stupid, you know. I won't forget."

Hank patted her cowling, said, "Another prima donna," and walked to the wagon. Sharts was on the seat, waiting. Hank climbed up and said, "Excelsior!"

"What?"

"Onward, ever onward and upward! You may fire when ready, Gridley! Let's go!"

Sharts spoke softly, for him, and the deer began pulling the wagon. He was silent for a moment, then said, "If you think you're showing off by speaking in that barbarous tongue of yours, if you think that doing it somehow makes me look less knowledgeable . . ."

"Heavens forbid!" Hank said. "It's just that I'm tense, and when I'm nervous, I tend to use my native language. No offense meant."

Sharts grunted and began whistling again.

They passed from the meadow onto a narrow dirt road and headed south. Blogo the Rare Beast rode a deer ahead of the party and flashed his bull's-eye lantern on the road. The only other light was hanging from a hook in the body of the wagon. Hank, looking back into the wagon, saw some boxes and a large paper-covered package. One box held arrows; the second, his BAR ammunition; a third, three black-powder grenades.

"What's in the package?" he said.

"My shirts."

"There's nothing like being clean," Hank said.

"Is that supposed to be sarcastic?" Sharts said.

"No, I sent my sarcasm out to the cleaners, and it didn't come back before I could leave," Hank said.

The dim light showed the giant's half-scowling, half-puzzled expression.

Finally, Sharts said, "I think you and I are going to have a talk when this is over."

"It'll be nice to know you better," Hank said.

After five miles, the party turned onto a broader but just as rough and rutted road. They began passing more farmers' houses, most of which were dark. Hank was glad that there weren't any dogs in this world. If there had been, the farmers' hounds would have been barking for miles around. Or would they? They would be sentient and so, supposedly, would wait until they were sure that they had something that needed barking at. On the other hand, instinct was stronger in the beasts, and the dogs might be barking their fool heads off.

When about ten miles had passed and another road taken, the caravan halted. Fresh deer came out of a woods to replace the tired ones.

Hank said, "The local animals must know these deer have been hanging around here. Didn't they ask questions?"

"They're not all as nosey as you," Sharts said. "However, these deer didn't come here in a body and so attract undue attention. They were recruited by Glinda's hawks long ago. When they got the word, they left their herds and assembled here."

"I wonder how long ago Glinda made these arrangements."

"I don't know. Probably before Erakna became queen."

The late Witch of the North had been Glinda's good friend. Yet Glinda had set up means to get into the castle undetected. Had Glinda gone by the precept that two rulers can only be friends as long as the political situation permits it? Or had Glinda really trusted Wulthag but had been wise enough to anticipate that her successor might be hostile? Whatever Glinda's reasons, she had been right to do what she had done.

But that made Hank wonder if Wulthag had also been foreseeing enough to have made similar arrangements for secret access into Glinda's castle. However, Glinda would have thought of that. She would have made an intensive search of the castle and the surrounding area.

But if Glinda could plan this, Erakna could suspect it. Thus, Erakna may have looked for secret routes into her castle, found them, and now have them well-guarded or booby-trapped or both.

At this thought, Hank began to sweat even though the mountain air was beginning to be chilly.

They were passing through land where the farms were side by side now, and they went through two small villages. Few of the houses were lit up; almost everybody was in bed. In the distance were some clusters of lights, the torches and big lamps on the towers and walls that surrounded Wugma.

They also passed a sight that made Hank even more nervous. It was a tree from which dangled the stinking bodies of six men and a raccoon.

"Spies or rebels," Sharts said, and he resumed whistling.

"I don't think so," Balthii said from Hank's shoulder. "If they'd been spies, they would have been taken to Wugma and tortured. They must be rebels. Or maybe they're just common criminals."

"What do you know about it, hawk?" Sharts said. "Common criminals are executed by beheading."

"What difference does it make?" Hank said.

"It makes a great deal of difference," Sharts said. "It's the difference between knowledge and ignorance. I'm very anxious to know what those dead people were and why they were hanged. Knowing that might have some influence on my conduct in the near future. It might mean the difference between my being killed or living. Besides, knowledge for its own sake is desirable."

"A brain can only hold so much," Balthii said. "What's the use with cramming it full of trivial junk?"

"Your brain can only hold so much," Sharts said, and he snorted. "Birdbrain!"

Balthii bristled her feathers. There was no telling what might have happened then, a fight perhaps, if they had not been interrupted. Hank heard a flapping, and he was startled when something landed on his other shoulder.

"Bargma! Damn it, you almost made me jump out of my skin!"

"There's a patrol coming toward us," the owl said. "About half a mile away."

"How many?" Sharts said.

"Twelve men on deer and two camels."

Sharts wet his finger and held it up.

"The wind's still coming from the northwest. Pass the word along to turn in at the first gate on our left. Quick, you two!"

The birds launched themselves from Hank's shoulder. His jacket was being ruined by talons, he thought, irrelevantly. Not to mention that it needed cleaning every day.

A minute later, Blogo's lantern was turned toward them, and its bright eye swung. The cavalcade went through a wood and wire gate which had been opened with only a little squeaking. The raiders quickly left the narrow road leading to the farmhouse and cut across the grass to a copse of trees. They waited under its darkness until the lanterns of the patrol had disappeared around the bend a quarter mile north of them.

Sharts asked Unwaz how far they had to go before they reached their hiding place for today.

"A mile."

They went slowly, not wishing to hurry and so make noise which might wake up some farmer or beast. Their destination was a farmhouse where the owner and his son waited for them inside a barn. Unwaz introduced the members inside the building after its doors had been closed. The Gillikins looked with awe at the two giants, Sharts and Hank.

"My family and animals are all right, they hate Erakna," Abraam the farmer said. "You'll be safe while you sleep here. Only..."

"Only what?" Sharts said fiercely.

"Only... there's a mouse in the barn. Barabbaz there," he pointed at a large black tomcat, "hasn't been able to catch it yet. I suppose I'm overly worried. After all, what does a mouse care who's queen or what we humans do as long as it can fill its belly with my stolen grain? But..."

"It might think that if it went to the queen and squealed on us, it would get free food for the rest of its life and not have to worry about cats, right?" Sharts said.

"It's not too worried about Barabbaz," Abraam said. "I'm telling you, that cat is the laziest critter this side of the mountains."

"I do all right," Barabbaz said, and he licked his leg.

"Yes, but not for me."

"Enough of this idle chatter," Sharts said. "The mouse might not be dangerous to us, but we can't take a chance. You, cat, get busy. Flush out that mouse."

"Mouse?" Bargma said. "Where? Where?"

The owl had just returned from a search for a high beam to sleep on.

"You can help the cat," Sharts said. "If he'll get off his dead haunches and do what he's supposed to do."

"I can appreciate your concern," Barabbaz said, his yellow eyes glowing redly in the lantern light, "but, just now, I don't feel like hunting. Some other time, perhaps."

"No perhaps!" Sharts roared.

Barabbaz licked a paw and then sauntered towards a dark corner. He said over his shoulder, "Go screw yourself."

"What? What?" Sharts said. "Look, cat, do you know whom you're speaking to?"

"A pile of manure with funny-looking eyes," Barabbaz said.

Sharts gargled something and ran towards the cat. Barabbaz sprinted up a pile of hay, leaped onto a beam, jumped to another, and flashed onto the loft. There he turned and snarled at Sharts.

"Blogo," Sharts said to the Rare Beast, "you get up in the loft and chase that damned pussy down here. I'll wring his neck like it's a bell."

Blogo was smiling, but whether it was in anticipation of the cat's demise or amusement because his arrogant chief had been insulted, no one could determine. He started up the ladder to the loft, but Hank said, "Hold it!"

Sharts turned and glared at him.

"You've probably scared the mouse out of the barn with all that noise," Hank said. "And if it overheard us, you can bet that it's hotfooting it now towards Wugma with an interesting story for the queen. The cat doesn't matter; the mouse does."

"I'm the chief here!" Sharts said. "I give the orders!"

Hank spoke to the owl. "Bargma, you should get outdoors and see if there is a mouse there."

Hank walked past Sharts, who was standing stiffly, fists clenched. He pushed open one of the barn doors, and the owl flew out. Hank turned and said, "Sharts, my people have a saying. 'A cat may look at a queen.' One of its meanings is that cats are privileged, and their natures are not to be judged by human standards. Anyway, you're too big a man to take notice of such a creature. What would people say if they heard that our mission was jeopardized because you were chasing a cat?"

"That's telling him," Barabbaz said.

"You shut up and keep out of this!" Hank roared. "You've done enough harm as it is!"

Blogo, halfway up the ladder, looked past his long knobbed nose at his leader. He said, "What do I do, boss?"

Sharts unclenched his fingers, and he spoke softly.

"The Earthman is at least half right. The cat is only a minor nuisance, a pest. Why should I, Sharts, bother with it? Though I'll squeeze his head until his eyes pop out if I get hold of him! Very well. Everybody pitch in and look for the mouse. You hawks get up there where we can't go and look for it. We'll ransack the barn if we have to take the hay apart blade by blade."

In a sotto voce to Hank, he said, "We'll have to talk about your manners later on."

Hank suppressed his retort and began looking in a manger. The bull there said, "There's no mouse in here."

"You're probably right," Hank said politely, "but we can't risk overlooking anything."

The search had just started when Bargma spoke from outside. "Open the door. I got it."

A Gillikin, Smiirn, pushed the door out, and the owl flew in. Smiirn closed the door. Bargma lit on the edge of the loft. Her beak held a gray mouse. The creature, one-third smaller than a Terrestrial housemouse, was not struggling, but its eyes were bright with terror.

Bargma had no trouble talking clearly though her mouth was closed.

"It was just leaving the farm and turning onto the road when I swooped down and caught it. It must be your mouse."

"It could be any mouse," Sharts said.

Hank did not like to agree with him, but this time the giant might be right.

The farmer, Abraam, looked up at the cat. He was sitting on the edge of the loft with his front legs folded.

"Barabbaz, is this the mouse?"

The cat yawned and said, "It's a mouse. Any fool can see that."

"Damn it!" the farmer said. "This is no time for your tomfoolery! Is it the one you couldn't catch?"

"Not couldn't," Barabbaz said. "Just wouldn't. I was saving it for when I got especially bored."

"Then it is the right one."

"The mouse doesn't think so, I'd say."

The farmer threw his hands up. "Godalmighty, why do I put up with him?"

"It's the other way around," Barabbaz said.

The mouse spoke then in a pitiful wavering voice.

"Don't let it eat me! Please! Please!"

Hank swore softly. The mouse was sentient and, therefore, feeling all the emotions and thinking all the thoughts of a doomed human.

"I'm innocent," the mouse said. "I wasn't going to tell anyone. I was just getting away from danger. If the queen's men caught you here, they'd burn down the barn."

"It may be telling the truth," Hank said. "Can't we just keep it in a cage until we come back?"

"The laborer is worthy of his hire," the owl said, quoting the Bible.

She opened her beak and caught the falling mouse in a razorsharp grip. She then degutted the creature, but not before it had cried, "Help me! Help me!"

"You've spoiled all my fun," Barabbaz said to the owl.

Bargma was too busy swallowing the mouse to reply.

24

They slept the rest of the night and part of the day in the barn. Hank took his turn as sentinel an hour after dawn. He had trouble getting back to sleep but finally managed. The deer had gone to a woods across the fields behind the farmhouse. They would stay there until the raiders (a euphemism for assassins, Hank thought) returned. If they returned.

Hank was awakened when the farmer's wife and daughter brought in breakfast. He ate the hot cabbage soup, bread, butter, jam, and nuts with gusto and drank the warm milk with less pleasure. The two women took out the chamber pots, emptied and washed them, and brought them back. The humans, a hard-looking bunch, sharpened their weapons and boasted of their exploits. The hawks went hunting but promised to be back by nightfall.

Hank, Blogo, and Sharts went over the diagrams provided by Glinda until they knew them by heart.

Supper was cabbage soup, canned corn, bread, butter, nut pastry, pie made from canned pumpkin, fruit, milk, and barley vodka. The hawks who had failed to catch enough to eat tore into the hard concoction made of nuts and sugar icing. They complained about its taste, but they ate it all.

During the day, Hank observed through a window the hordes of people and animals walking or riding toward Wugma. They were on their way to hear Erakna and others speak at a war rally in the city square. The raiders planned to use the crowds and the consequent confusion to sneak into the city when it got dark.

Hank had plenty of time to satisfy his curiosity about the Rare Beast.

He gave him some Quadling tobacco since the fellow had run out of it during his trek from the south.

Blogo said, "Thanks. This Gillikin stuff rips out your throat."

Sharts was sitting cross-legged in a corner, his eyes closed, apparently going through some sort of mental exercises. Blogo felt free to be friendly with Hank while his chief did not notice them.

Blogo came from an area isolated by mountains in the west where the borders of Quadlingland and Winkieland met. As far as he knew, his people had always been there. They had never been very numerous because, he thought, the females bore only one child during their lifetime.

"I don't know why," Blogo said, looking like a chimpanzee when he grinned.

Hank thought that his original ancestors had been made by the Long-Gones. At least, that was the only explanation he had for this anomaly. He did not voice it, however. Blogo might be offended. Hank also thought that the extreme warlike tendencies of Blogo's people were partly responsible for their diminishing population.

"We seldom leave our kingdom," Blogo said. "But Hama and I, he was my very good friend though too given to practical jokes, he and I decided to see what the outside world looked like. Three months later, Hama was killed by a sow that thought he was after her brood. Actually, he was. Not to eat, understand. We weren't cannibals. I think he was going to stick one of the piglets in my sleeping bag as a joke. He was a great joker."

Tears ran down his hairy cheeks.

"If I may ask," Hank said, "how did it happen that you became an outlaw?"

"Oh, that!"

Blogo shook his head, and the red cock's comb waved.

"It was all because of a joke. After Hama died, I traveled on the road to Suthwarzha. I wanted to see Glinda so I could be one of her bodyguards. I'd heard that it'd be a cushy position, and there were plenty of good-looking women there. But on the way I fell in with some garrison troops, and we all got drunk. They decided they'd play a trick on their commanding officer. They didn't like him at all, and they knew he was with a woman. But when it came time to pull the joke, they weren't so drunk that they didn't have some second thoughts.

"So I told them what cowards they were and said I'd do it. It seemed like fun at the time. I sneaked into the hut where this officer was on top of a woman, and I squirted turpentine on his bare tail. That sure stopped his lovemaking, haw, haw, haw!"

Blogo wiped his eyes and said, "But the joke was on me. Those clowns had barred the door on the outside when I went in. The officer tried to kill me, so, naturally, I had to defend myself. He was a big guy, almost as tall as your chin, but I broke his neck. The woman was screaming, and the soldiers on duty were coming. I couldn't get the door open, so I tore out the planks in the wall and took off.

"If I'd been just a human, I might have gotten away with it. How could those drunks have identified me? But I stand out like a leopard among sheep, a wart on Glinda's face. I was wanted. The government had an intense desire to separate my head from my neck. Governments, you know, take everything very seriously. No sense of humor. So I wandered around in the woods, almost got eaten by a tiger, and then met Sharts . . ." He looked at the giant to make sure that he was concentrating inwardly. ". . . the Shirtless," he whispered.

Hank hesitated, then said, "Uh, Sharts mentioned something about the Very Rare Beast. What's that?"

Blogo's eyes widened, and he bared his teeth. He held his hot pipe by the bowl, and he said, "How'd you like this shoved all the way up to your liver?"

"Sorry. No offense meant," Hank said.

"Well, there's plenty taken. How'd you like to step outside and take me on? I've torn men bigger than you into little strips!"

"That'd be stupid, no offense meant," Hank said.

He walked away shaking his head.

Shortly before sunset, the farmer and his son pushed a wagon into the barn. After the doors were closed, Hank, Blogo and Sharts lay down with the weapons and Sharts's shirts on the floor of the wagon. They were covered with hay over which was piled a few layers of an early-season indigenous fruit. While the three crypto-passengers breathed through cracks in the floor, the wagon was pushed out of the barn and hitched to four of the farmer's deer. And they were on their way.

Hank could hear the crowds on the road and the occasional talk of his compatriots walking behind the wagon. The farmers going to the big rally did not sound as happy as Erakna would have liked. There was no laughter, and there were many complaints, though he noted that no one said anything directly about the queen. Doubtless, there were spies and agents provocateur among them.

After what seemed a long time but was probably only an hour, the wagon stopped. Hank could hear the gate guards asking the farmer some questions. Abraam said that he intended to sell the fruit to the crowd during the rally. If he did not sell all of it tonight, he would tomorrow at the market. Would the guards care to sample some of the fruit? Take some home for their families?

The guards said that they would.

Hank hoped that they wouldn't stick their spears through the fruit to find out if there was any contraband. They did not, and, after they had lightened the load somewhat, they told Abraam to go on and have a good time.

They were within the walls and passing very slowly through noisy obviously drunken crowds. The halts were frequent. But, inside an hour, or so it seemed, the wagon halted, and Abraam knocked three times on the side of the wagon. Hank came up out of the hay and fruit like Lazarus rising from the tomb. Very stiffly and wondering, ''What next?''

It was dark, the only near light was from the windows of a few houses and a tall oil-burning lamp on a street corner half a block away. No. Blogo's lamp, held by Smiirn, was lit.

The street was narrow and smelly, and the narrow houses were three- or four-storied and had high pointed roofs. There were no sidewalks. The house before which the wagon had halted was dark, but a stranger was talking to Smiirn and Unwaz. From what seemed to be far off came the muted surf-dash roar of a crowd.

Sharts went up to the man in the doorway and began talking. Presently, he turned and spoke to Hank.

''This is Audag the Limper. He says we're to go inside now, no loitering, and the wagon will be parked inside the court behind his house.''

Audag was middle-aged, thin, and had an exceptionally long and narrow face. He introduced his teen-aged son, who looked like his father but was taller.

Abraam and his son said their farewells and wishes for the success of the raid. They would go to a relative's house for several days and then return, minus the wagon and deer, to their farm.

The owl and Balthii settled on Hank's shoulders. He took the cloth case containing the BAR; a man carried the boxes holding the box magazines and the grenades. He went into a small unlit room with a steep staircase in front of him and a door on each side. He passed the staircase and turned to go into a doorway on its side. A wet and musky odor struck him. He sniffed. There was something familiar about it. Dead rats.

They were in a cluttered basement which held wooden boxes of all sizes, piles of papers tied together, and broken furniture and toys. Audag and two raiders began removing the boxes stacked against the north wall. When these were out of the way, a mortared brick wall, damp and gray-streaked with some kind of lichen, was revealed.

Audag marked an area on the wall with chalk and then indicated a sledgehammer, some wedges, picks, drills, and shovels.

"You'll have to tear out the bricks here."

Sharts worked at the upper level of bricks, and Blogo removed the lower level when Sharts was done. The hole revealed a solid bank of dirt.

"It's two feet deep," Audag said. "There's another wall behind that. It was constructed that way so tapping on the wall wouldn't bring a hollow sound."

Two men picked at and shoveled away the dirt. Sharts got impatient with what seemed to him their slowness, and he attacked the dirt facade. When it was off, another brick wall was before him. Without pausing for rest, Sharts began tearing the bricks loose from the decaying mortar. A chain of men picked up the bricks and passed them to a corner.

Sharts, not breathing hard after his exertions, said, "We'll wait for a few minutes. The air might be bad."

It certainly smelled dead, but it was moving. There was a means for ventilation somewhere in there.

Sharts thrust his torch into the entrance. Hank, standing close behind him, looked within. The downward-slanting tunnel had been dug from the dirt for about sixty feet. Then it had been hewn from rock. The bricks lining the wall had given way in a few places, and dirt had poured through the gaps. But the wooden beams, though rotting, and the reinforcing steel beams, though rusty, had held.

"It goes under the moat around the castle," Audag said.

"I know that," Sharts growled.

"Thanks very much for your help," Hank said to Audag. "Glinda will see to it that you get your money."

Sharts leading, they filed into the narrow tunnel. There was just room for two pygmies to walk shoulder to shoulder, and the two giants had to stoop. They walked slowly since Sharts still did not trust the air, and he also was wary of traps. When they came to the lowest part of the tunnel, they were confronted with a black pool of water about thirty feet across. The tunnel slanted upward on the other side.

Even as Sharts stood on the edge, the water oozed towards his feet and a few bubbles broke in the center of the blackness.

"A day or two later," Sharts said grimly, "and the tunnel would have been filled with water."

Hank, watching the spreading pool, thought that they would be lucky if they did not have to swim when they returned from the castle. Perhaps Sharts thought so too but did not want to discourage the others.

Blogo was standing just in front of Hank. He carried a sword and a long dagger in sheaths attached to his belt and held a two-bladed ax with a short shaft. A knapsack contained the package of his chief's shirts. What in blue blazes were those shirts? The giant's good-luck tokens?

Unwaz the hawk, sitting on Smiirn's shoulder, said, "What are we waiting for? This place makes me nervous."

Sharts did not reply. He began walking into the pool and presently was up to his chin. Then the water receded as he walked on. He turned when he was out of it. Dripping, he said, "All but the Earthman will have to swim."

"That's obvious," Balthii said. "You're very good at pointing that out. But if you think we hawks are going to get into the water, you are mistaken."

"Don't try me," Sharts said. "Of course, you'll fly. But I won't guarantee what'll happen when you get over here."

Balthii waited until the other birds had transferred from shoulder to shoulder and then flapped off from Blogo's before she flew over the water. By then Sharts had turned away and was proceeding slowly up the tunnel.

Hank assisted each man across so that they would not go under the pool. This put him in the rear, where he stayed. It was too time-consuming and awkward for him to squeeze by all those ahead of him. Besides, he liked the idea of having the way clear if he had to turn tail and run.

Wet to the chin, shaking with cold, he arrived at a chamber which was just big enough to hold the entire party. Sharts, the little men pressing against his back, was squatting and shoving up on a rectangular slab inset in the ceiling. The slab groaned and squeaked as it rose, but it was soon out of the floor and pushed to one side.

Sharts stuck his head into the opening, his torch held high.

"Another room," he said. "Bigger than this one."

He got down on his knees, turned, and held out his clasped hands before him. One by one, the little men and hawks stood on his hands and were propelled upwards and slightly outwards. Smiirn fell back onto Sharts, and there was some screaming and cursing for a while before Smiirn went back up.

Hank knew that he was risking Sharts's anger, but he had to speak up.

"Don't you think that all that noise could attract attention? We'd better be very quiet from now on. Don't talk above a whisper."

Sharts surprised Hank by apologizing.

"You're right. I was stupid to yell like that. However, it did not make much difference. Smiirn was screaming."

Smiirn muttered something. Hank was close enough to hear that Smiirn was going to put a knife into someone's heart after this was all over. Sharts and Blogo glared at him but said nothing.

A thickly painted metal ladder led to a hole in the ceiling twenty feet above the floor. Sharts, his torch gripped by his teeth, went up the ladder rapidly even though it was not built for a man his size. He climbed through the hole and leaned out over it, the torchlight making his eyes look even weirder.

"Come on up."

The birds riding on their shoulders, the men ascended one by one. Hank found himself in another room. This had more space than the one below. It, too, was hewn out of rock except for one wall of huge blocks of dark purplish stone, the wall of the castle. They were outside its dungeons.

This room also had another twenty-foot-high metal ladder leading into another hole in the ceiling. When they had climbed that, they were in a room which had two levels. The upper one could be reached by a ten-foot ladder. It was a narrow platform hewn out of rock, and an iron door with massive hinges and a massive bolt was set within the inside wall.

Sharts went to the upper level and took a can of oil from his knapsack. He oiled the bolt thoroughly and then pulled it, though not without some straining. He had to stop now and then to apply more lubrication. Even so, the bolt squeaked. Having drawn that, he oiled the hinges and carefully pulled it open by a big handle. It required more oil, and it squeaked. But it came fully open.

Sharts looked inside the doorway and signalled that the others should follow him. When Hank went through the doorway, he was at the bottom of a shaft which had been cored out of the massive stone blocks. The ladder was a series of painted metal rungs set into the stone. Hank hoped that the rungs had not rusted away, but those he could see seemed to be unaffected by the damp.

Hank took the BAR from its case and hung it by its strap over his shoulder. He set the middle part of the torch, which had been whittled down, in his teeth. He started climbing.

So far, their route had been exactly as described by Glinda.

He marveled at her patience and planning. The castle was two hundred years old. Glinda must have had the tunnel and rooms prepared before the castle was built. Her agents must have taken twenty years to make this shaft. They had had to chip away very slowly and carefully not to be detected. She must always have had her agents planted in the house in the basement of which the tunnel began. They had nothing to do except pretend to be good citizens of Wugma and to wait for the day when the tunnel would be used. There must have been many generations of agents. But they would have been well paid.

And this was the woman that the U.S. Army was tackling.

The ladder went up and up. Finally, he pulled himself over the edge. A door in the wall only two feet from the shaft was open. Its hinges dripped oil. Hank stooped through the entrance, which was low for the pygmies. The others were in a low narrow room lit only by the torches. The fumes from the burning oil-soaked pine caught at his throat and made his eyes water.

25

Blogo put his fingers to his lips when Hank entered. Sharts rose from the floor, against which he had had his ear. He stooped and gripped a ring set in the floor, and a trapdoor rose. Though its hinges had been oiled, it, too, squeaked.

The drop to the floor below was twenty feet. The two men carrying coiled ropes over their shoulders gave them to Sharts, who tied the end of one to a hooked bolt set into the wall. This was more evidence of Glinda's planning. She had known that the room below could only be reached by a rope, and she had ordered the installation of the bolt.

Sharts let himself down into the room by the rope. The others followed. The room was large and unwindowed, and dust was thick on the floor and the objects stored there.

The only door was locked. Sharts produced a key from the knapsack and unlocked the door. More evidence of Glinda's foresight. She had had a duplicate made from the steward's key long ago.

Outside the door was a long dusty drafty hall. A heavily barred window covered with dust and spiderwebs was at one end. The footprints there were half-filled with more dust.

Smiirn sneezed, causing everybody to jump.

"There'll be no more of that," Sharts said softly.

They waited, hoping that no one had heard Smiirn. After a minute, Sharts led them to the stairway halfway down the hall. There was complete silence except for the shuffling of feet, someone breathing heavily, and a hawk's wings rustling.

The stairway led to another hall the far end of which held the only torch. There were numerous comparatively fresh footprints on the dust-covered stone floor. Sharts, a loaded and cocked crossbow in one hand, peered around the corner. He signalled that they should follow him and went down another hall. Reaching another stairway, he halted.

According to what Hank had learned from Glinda, two human guards and a falcon would be stationed at the bottom of the staircase. If anyone came in from above, and that must have seemed very unlikely to Erakna, the falcon would fly away to arouse the guards on other floors. The two men were supposed to hold any invaders until help could come. Though the two must have known they were actually sacrifices, they would not be uneasy. How could anybody come from above? The windows were few, and all were barred against hawk assassins. Nobody could climb the castle walls.

Sharts indicated that the two men with crossbows should follow him and that two hawks should get on their shoulders. The others would appear about ten paces behind if they heard a hullabaloo. Then they would charge en masse.

In single file, they went down the stairs. Sharts peeked around the corner. When he pulled back his head, he whispered something to the two hawks and the two men. Hank, who was standing near the top of the stairs, could not hear him.

Sharts lifted his hand and sprang out into the hall. The two crossbowmen jumped out after him, the hawks rising from their shoulders just as they did.

There was a spang! as the three bolts sped toward their targets. A choked-off cry.

When Hank got to the bodies, he saw that Sharts's bolt had gone through the falcon as it lifted from its perch. A bolt had hit one guard near the spine, penetrating the chain mail and half-burying itself. Another bolt had gone through the back of the shoulder of the guard, who was lying speechless on the floor, dying of shock. Blogo cut his throat.

Hank felt like vomiting.

There was no noise from the well of the staircase a few feet beyond the dead. The guards below had heard nothing, Hank hoped. It could be that they had stayed silent, had sent a hawk to the guards on the floor below them, and were waiting to ambush the intruders.

Sharts went to the bottom of the next staircase, stuck his head around the corner, and quickly withdrew it. He came back up the steps.

"One guard's asleep. So's the hawk. Same plan. This should be like cutting through pumpkin pie."

It was.

Hank looked at his wristwatch. They had an hour before Erakna was scheduled to return to her suite two stories below. She was said to be very punctual, and she should return on time. But many things might happen to delay her.

The change of watch would take place in an hour and fifteen minutes. There was always a danger, however, that an officer might make a surprise check on the guards. Two of Sharts's men would be stationed to kill the officer if this should happen.

There was also the chance that some of the dwellers in the apartments on the queen's floor might come home early.

The distant but unmistakable rumble of thunder came.

Hank swore. If it rained or there was a storm, the rally would break up.

Sharts, grimacing, went down the next staircase. He raced back up a minute later.

"I almost got caught," he said. "The guards walked down the hall to look out the window, but I ducked back behind the corner just in time."

He told the two crossbowmen and the two hawks to follow him. Hank glanced at his wristwatch as they left. It was exactly sixty-two seconds later when Sharts came back up.

"Done," he said. "Now comes the hard part."

The hawk there had been sleeping. Sharts had trod softly down the hall while the two guards obligingly kept their backs to him by looking out at the thunder and lightning. Sharts had cut the hawk's head off, and the two guards were dead, pierced by bolts, a second later.

Hank, standing at the head of the next staircase, could see some of the hall below. It had a luxurious carpet and a piece of statuary with diamonds for eyes on an ornately carved marble pedestal. A part of a huge oil painting was visible on the gold-filigreed walls.

There would be six guards and two hawks there while the queen was gone. When she returned, she would be accompanied by many guards, ladies-in-waiting, and courtiers.

Thunder boomed closer now. The windows at the end of the hall where Hank stood rattled with a hard wind. He went down to it and saw that it was also raining.

Glinda and Hank had talked about trying to kill all the guards of the queen's suite and then dressing up the human raiders in the uniforms and having the hawks replace the dead ones. That idea had been quickly dismissed, however. There would be an unavoidable amount of noise which might attract the guards on the floor below.

Hank was to wait until Erakna came home and toss a grenade at her before she went into the suite. He would then step out and finish the work with his BAR.

"You don't mind killing women?" Glinda had said.

"I mind killing anybody," Hank had said. "But it has to be done."

Sharts came to him and looked out the window.

"She'll be here soon. It's just as well. Better, in fact. I didn't like the idea of waiting for her. Too much chance of somebody checking on the guards. As it is, somebody will be coming up these steps before the queen gets on this floor. I hope that there isn't more than one."

The bodies had been dragged around the corner of the staircase. Unwaz was occupying the late hawk's perch, and two men had put on the casques of the guard.

Ten minutes later, the hawk listening at the top of the steps turned and fluttered over to Sharts.

"I heard an officer challenge the guards. Must be our man."

Sharts got on one side of the doorway, and Blogo got on the other. As the officer came through the doorway, he was gripped around the neck and the mouth by giant hands. Blogo cut the officer's throat.

There was much noise down in the hall, the grounding of spear butts, hoarse commands, and the shrill voices and laughter of little women and men.

"Holy Thun!" Sharts said. "They're here! Quick, man!"

Hank went down the steps as softly but as quickly as he could. When he got to the doorway, he stood behind the wall and pulled a grenade from his jacket pocket. He had another in the other pocket if the first one did not explode.

"The queen! The queen!" an officer bawled. "Open the door for the queen!"

Hank stepped out into the hallway, pulled the pin on the grenade, got a glimpse of the crowd around the door, heard a warning shout to his right from down the hall, and threw the grenade. He turned then and ran up the steps. The door had been twenty feet away, and the wall would protect him. But there was going to be a hell of a blast. If the grenade worked. If it did not, he would have to run back down and use the BAR. His plan for tossing the second bomb might not work out. The queen could be behind her door by then.

There were shrieks and then a very loud boom.

Air rushed up the staircase. Black smoke followed it.

Hank turned, his BAR in his hands, ran down the steps, and plunged into the hall. Behind him he heard feet striking the steps. Sharts and the others were following him.

The smoke was still dense, but he could see some torn bodies on the floor. A few were still alive and screaming.

Pointing towards where he thought the door was, Hank pressed on the trigger until the twenty rounds were expended. Smiirn at once handed him a fresh magazine, and he attached it to the underside of the rifle.

A guard at the end of the hall charged them. He was a brave man, but he died when Blogo's ax caught him between shoulder and neck.

Hank ran toward the stairway down the hall past the door to Erakna's suite. He hurdled the bodies but slipped on blood, and he fell heavily backwards. Though partly stunned, he got up at once and continued running. He got to the stairway just as a mob of soldiers came up it. The BAR cleared them away.

He looked down the hall. The smoke had thinned enough to see that the queen's door had been blown off. His compatriots were examining the bodies to determine which was the queen's. Blogo looked at Hank and shook his head.

He cried in his piping voice, "She's not here! She must have gotten away!"

Hank groaned and said, "After all this!"

Sharts had plunged through the doorway. Blogo followed him, and three hawks flew in after him. Smiirn came to Hank and said, "How long can you hold them off with that thing?"

"Until the ammunition runs out," he said.

"We may need more time to look for the witch than we thought," Smiirn said. "It's a big apartment."

A helmeted head poked from the doorway below. Hank loosed two shots. The soldier was not hit, but two minutes passed before there was a yell and men poured through the entrance. The BAR crumpled ten before those behind ran, some falling down. Hank let them go. He just wanted to discourage them.

Two more minutes went by.

Another head came around the corner. This time, Hank did not shoot. He thought that his mere presence would keep them back. For a while, anyway.

Another sixty seconds.

All but Smiirn had gone into the suite to help in the search. It was well that Smiirn was there as his ammo supplier. Otherwise, Hank might have been caught off-guard. Smiirn yelled. Hank looked at him and saw that he was pointing past him. He whirled. Two men were at the end of the hall and more were coming through the doorway of the apartment there. Glinda was not the only one who had prepared secret routes.

Their crossbows were pointed at him. He fired as he fell forward. The bolts missed, and his burst knocked the soldiers backwards. He reached forward and pulled the supports of the BAR down and fired from a prone position. Ten men fell. No others followed them.

He got up and beckoned for Smiirn to bring more boxes of magazines. He removed the empty one and put on a new one. Then he told Smiirn to watch the stairway while he took care of this other matter. When he was close to the door, which was open and bore two bullet holes, he took out the grenade, pulled the pin, counted, and threw it inside the door. He ran away along the wall and then dived. The explosion tore the door off and filled that end of the hall with black smoke for a while.

He put the third grenade in his pocket.

Sharts came running out. He stopped when he saw the bodies at the end of the hall.

"So!"

"Yeah, so," Hank said. He had resumed his post at the top of the steps. "Did you find the queen?"

"No. She must have gone into a secret hideaway. Or down secret steps. She's probably on the floor below now."

"We'd better run then," Hank said. "Now."

"I don't like to fail!" Sharts yelled.

"Who does?" Hank said. "There's something worse than failure, though. Death. Let's get out of here."

"Do you think you could shoot your way through to the queen?" Sharts said. "She could be just around the bottom of the staircase. You might catch her before she could get away."

"No, I don't think so," Hank said. "Let's get out of here!"

Sharts snarled, but he turned and went to the door and bellowed for the searchers to come out into the hall.

Hank said, "Do you want the Gillikins to know what we're doing?"

Sharts gave him the finger. For some reason, Hank found that very funny. He laughed until he realized that he was close to hysteria.

Before following the others, Hank half-emptied a magazine just to let those below know that he was there. He turned and ran then, but he stopped when his eyes caught something extraordinary. It was a velvet-covered box which had been blown open when he had thrown the grenade at the queen. Something dull yellow gleamed inside the box. He removed it and looked at it. It was a hemispherical object of gold large enough to fit over the head of an Amariikian of normal stature. He turned it over and looked inside it by the light of an oil-lamp which he took from a table near the window.

There were inscriptions in four rows inside its rim, but the light was not bright enough for him to read them. Even if the illumination had been stronger, he would not have been able to read them, for they were written in the undecipherable script of the Long-Gone Ones. Nevertheless, he knew what the gold hemisphere was.

"I'll be a monkey's uncle!"

26

With the golden object in his knapsack nestled beside his last grenade, he ran after the others. By the time he got to the room where the rope hung from the ceiling hole, he was breathing heavily. He had plenty of time to regain his wind. Four men were waiting for their turn to climb the rope. He guarded the door while they swarmed up. So far, so good. There was no sound of pursuit. The Gillikins would have no trouble tracking them, however, by the footprints in the dust. Even so, the queen's men would be further delayed because they would have to find a ladder.

Sharts was by the hole. He pulled up Hank easily with one hand, while holding a torch with the right hand. The others were out of sight in the shaft.

Those strange eyes missed little. He said, "What's that in your sack?"

"Something that might come in very handily."

Sharts grabbed Hank's arm with a grip that threatened to pop the blood vessels.

"Remember. We all share in any loot."

"Not this. I think this belongs to Glinda. And take your hand off me."

Sharts bit his lip, but he removed his hand. He went down the shaft. Hank crouched by the trapdoor for a moment listening for the Gillikins. He heard nothing, but, when he straightened up and began lowering the trapdoor, he caught a faint sound. In a few seconds, he could hear loud voices. He hesitated. Should he wait until the room below was filled and then drop the grenade? That might make them so fearful that it would be a long time before they pushed on after the invaders. But Erakna would be very angry, and she would drive her soldiers on no matter how reluctant they were. They would fear her more than his fearful weapons.

He decided that he should save the grenade for a more critical situation.

Going down the rungs, he felt very uneasy. If the Gillikins should get to the top of the shaft while he was still in it, they could drop something on or shoot him. He was a comparatively easy target since he was holding in his teeth the torch which had been left for him in the room.

No shouts of exultation came from above. Reaching the bottom, he found his box magazines. Smiirn had wisely concluded that Hank might need them handy now that they were separated. Hank put one in each pocket and the remaining five in his knapsack.

He ran upright through the rooms and stooping through the tunnel. Then he stopped.

"My God!"

The pool had spread at least twenty feet on each side. That was both good and bad. By the time the pursuers got here, they might find the tunnel flooded. On the other hand, he would have to swim holding the torch up above his head with one hand while the BAR and the gold object and the magazines dragged at him.

There was no use hesitating. He walked into the cold water until it was up to his chin and began paddling with one hand. He had to work furiously to keep his nose above the water, but he was soon touching the floor, and he began walking again. He was glad that it was not winter. He would freeze when he left the house.

Sharts was putting on his wooden-shoed boots.

"They're upstairs," he said. "Everything's ready. The wagon is in front of the house. First, though, put on your boots."

They went outside. Many of the houses had bright windows; the inhabitants had all returned from the rally. The rain smote him, thunder rumbled, and lightning did its best to put the fear of God in all living creatures. The storm had shattered their plan to get lost in the mobs returning from the rally while they made their way to the escape point. The hawks, however, had flown away. Bargma, the owl, looked as if he would have liked to go with them.

"The city will be swarming with soldiers!" Sharts yelled.

Hank did not reply; none was needed. He got into the wagon with the giant and Blogo and assumed the fetal position again. The others piled hay and fruit on them in a thin layer. They had removed these and put them on the street, and now they did not think that there was time to completely cover the three.

Audag, his son, and one man would get up on the seat. The wagon began moving slowly, then it picked up speed. Now that there were no crowds and no traffic, there was no use ambling innocently along.

Hank began counting the minutes. One thousand and one, one thousand and two, one thousand and three. . . . Four minutes had just passed when he heard a loud challenge. There was the clatter of iron deershoes on the cobblestones, and the wagon stopped. Hank gripped the stock and barrel of the BAR and waited.

"Who are you?" a hoarse voice said. "What are you doing out in the storm?"

"Please, sir, we're just farmers," Audag whined. "We were turned out of our inn because of a little disagreement with the owner. He charged us more than he had promised he would. We're looking for a place to stay."

"And just where is this inn and who owns it?"

"The Jolly Cheeks. The crook who owns it is Skilduz the Stammerer, may he rot in the ground and worms enjoy his beer-soaked putrid carcass."

"The Jolly Cheeks? That's on the other side of town. Sergeant, probe that pile in the wagon with your spear."

"Yes, sir!" the sergeant bellowed. "You, Izak and Azgo, help me!"

"Nuts!" Hank said. He came up out of the pile at the same time as Sharts and Blogo. He only had time for a quick estimate of the situation. The wagon was surrounded by nine men on deer and three getting off their beasts. None of them seemed to have crossbows. He stood up, yelling at Sharts and Blogo to get out of his fire, and he turned, shooting until he had completed a circle. The officer fell first; eight either dropped from their saddles or fell under the weight of their stricken animals. Then Hank had to attach a fresh magazine to the BAR. Three on the ground leaped up and started to run away. They and the three still mounted might have gotten away in the darkness if Hank's colleagues had not brought loaded crossbows from under their cloaks and shot them.

Blinds went up in the nearby houses, and people looked out through the rain.

"Go like hell!" Sharts screamed.

The wagon started with a jerk that hurled Hank off his feet. Fortunately, the hay and fruit softened his fall.

While the wagon rattled, bumped, and jolted down the streets and skidded around corners, Hank reloaded. A minute later, a patrol spread out across a wide street to block them. The BAR was emptied clearing them out of the way. Hank attached another box magazine. Five left.

The wagon finally stopped below a sentinel tower on the outer wall of Wugma. It was a half-mile from the north gates. While Audag and his son unhitched the deer, Sharts hallooed the guard in the tower. He would be, if all went according to plan, an agent of Glinda. He had been in the Gillikin army for three years, and he was supposed to put his fellow guard out of commission and let down a rope ladder. Every tower had one; they were to be used to admit other troops to the top if besiegers broke through and cut off the access of other defenders to the top of the wall.

Their disadvantage was that they could be lowered to let enemies in or out.

The man in the tower was barely visible by his torchlight. He waved, and, two seconds later, the ladder fell down. Smiirn was the first up; Audag, the last. The deer were gone then. They would hide during the night. When morning came, they would dash through the city gates and be lost in the country. At least, that was what they hoped. The plan to haul them up by ropes had to be abandoned. There just was not enough time for that. The sentinels in both towers on each side were yelling and beating drums now.

A lightning flash showed that a man had left each of these towers and was advancing towards them. Hank killed them with four rounds.

Presently, they were on the ground with the agent, Lukaz, and they were heading north through the village there. Just as they left it and were going across farmland, Bargma lit on Hank's shoulder.

"Give me some warning the next time!"

The owl laughed, then said, "There's no sense in my staying with you. I'll go on to the farm."

"O.K. Tell the farmer to unstake Jenny if the storm quits and if there isn't a high wind. He'd better be ready to run with his family if we're tracked to the farm."

The owl flapped off heavily. A little later, the group left the farmland and took a narrow deeply rutted dirt road which ran northwest. Every step the group took would head them one step more from the main road. There would be cavalry—cervusry?—out on the highway now and perhaps on the sideroads. When daylight came, Erakna's hawks and eagles would be surveying from the air. However, the band only had ten miles to go now and should be on the farm before dawn.

Even so, if this storm continued, the airplane would be grounded.

Hank plodded on, his jacket collar around his neck, the rain trickling down his neck, looking now down at the ruts so he would stumble less, then at the bull's-eye lantern. Sharts would occasionally turn it around so that the others could see him.

They came to a road at right angles that ran to the main highway. They would have preferred to cut across the country toward the farm, but they could easily get lost in the dark hills and woods. They would have to chance encountering the soldiers.

Luck played out on them. Erakna's men were in a copse of oaks ten yards from the crossroads. They had with them what Hank had not expected: hawks and eagles. These had ridden on the pommels of the saddles. They swept out of the darkness and struck the band before it was aware that anybody was within a mile.

The cavalry charged, screaming and whooping, the moment the screeches of the birds and cries of the men notified them that the birds had attacked. They came through single file on the narrow bridge across the ditch along the meadow. Fortunately for Sharts's band, the third deer in line slipped and fell down. Six mounts and riders piled up on top of them. The three behind them managed to pull up in time. Their beasts jumped the low fence and plunged into the ditch. Here two deer fell under the water, but the third got his beast to scramble up the bank.

The eagle that came from behind and sank its talons into Hank's leather helmet was almost as surprised as Hank. It must have been much more disappointed. The strap of the helmet was loose. Though the talons went through the leather and gashed the top of Hank's head, the helmet came off. Hank threw himself on the ground, crawled away, turned, and removed the BAR from his shoulder. The eagle was somewhere in the darkness, doubtless trying to get its talons loose from the helmet.

Others had not been as lucky as he. They were screaming and

battling desperately with the birds trying to rip out eyes and gash faces. Hank decided that it was too dangerous to shoot in the dark. He reversed the BAR to use as a club and brought it down on the back of a hawk that had a man on the ground. Though its back was broken, the hawk's talons did not come loose. Man and bird rolled away into the night.

The three who had cleared the bridge galloped up waving their swords. Hank could not see them very well, but he could make out three bulks. He reversed the rifle again and shot the riders off the saddles. The deer, though disciplined to fight, ran away at the explosions.

Hank located three more battling couples and killed the birds. By this time, the soldier who had gotten across the ditch charged. He cut down Smiirn, who was stabbing a hawk whose talons were sunk into his chest. Hank shot the soldier and his deer.

Sharts and Blogo had managed to slay their attackers and to pull the talons out of their flesh. They aided Hank and soon had put an end to four more birds. Hank came across the eagle with the helmet caught in his claws. He shot it, but he had no time to get his helmet back. Three deer and riders who had struggled up from the mess on the bridge roared in. Hank shot two. Blogo leaped onto the back of one and slashed his throat.

It took a while to kill the other birds, but it was done. Of Sharts's band, all except three were dead, unconscious, or blinded. The only ones who could walk were Sharts, Blogo, and Hank.

From an indeterminate distance to the south came the faint notes of a bugle.

"They must have heard us!" Blogo said. "They'll be ripsnorting up the road now! We haven't got much time!"

Sharts said, "We can't leave them at the mercy of Erakna!"

He pointed at the blinded and the badly wounded.

"Right you are!" the Rare Beast cried.

Before Hank could protest, Blogo had cut the throats of the blind men and was starting on the others.

"I don't like it, but it has to be done," Sharts said.

"Yes, I suppose so," Hank said wearily.

The thunder and lightning had ceased shortly before the attack, though it was still raining. He took Blogo's lantern and searched until he found the eagle. After trying to get the helmet loose, he gave up.

The two men were threatening to leave him behind if he did not stop fooling around. He trudged after them, and they reached the farmhouse within twenty minutes. They had to go at a wolf trot to do it, run fifty steps, walk fifty. Sharts halted when they got to the gate. The light from the lantern fell on a ghastly figure. His face was deeply gashed, blood was spattered over his face and clothes, and his shirt was torn to shreds.

"What's the matter, boss?" Blogo said. "We shouldn't stop now!"

"You know what the matter is," the giant said.

Blogo said, "Oh, yeah. Sure."

He took off his knapsack and removed a paper-covered package. After tearing open the top, he took out a purple-and-gold-striped shirt with an exquisite white lace collar and cuffs. Meanwhile, Sharts had taken off his jacket and the ruined shirt.

"For God's sake!" Hank said.

Blogo looked up at him.

"Every time he gets into a fight . . . well, you can see for yourself. That's why . . ."

"Why what?" Sharts said angrily.

"Nothing, boss."

If he had not been so weary, Hank would have laughed. That was just as well. Sharts would undoubtedly have attacked him, and he would have been forced to shoot Sharts. Shoot Sharts. Alliterative and attractive idea.

The giant, now reattired, said, "Blogo, you go down to the house and tell the farmer that he and his family should take off for the hills. They can watch from there to see if the Gillikins come here."

"Sure, boss, only . . . there isn't any doubt they will. Once day comes, the hawks'll be all over this area like pepper on soup. They'll spot Jenny, and the whole army'll be here."

"They can't do that until dawn," Sharts said, very patiently for him. "If the weather clears by then, we can fly off in her."

"Not if there are a lot of hawks here," Hank said. "The moment we get in the plane, they'll attack. We won't have a chance to get off the ground if they are here in great numbers."

"Do you want to flee into the hills?" Sharts said. "That army will be beating the bush, and the chances are they'll find us."

"It's twelve one way and a dozen the other. No, I don't want to run for the woods. Not until I have to. I'm for waiting until dawn to see what the weather's like.''

"If a patrol finds us, a hawk will be sent to Wugma to bring the garrison army here.''

"There's your patrol now," Hank said.

He pointed at the swinging lanterns far down the road.

Blogo left to notify the farmers. The two men waited until they could hear the clop-clop of hooves and see a dim mass moving toward them. Hank emptied the rest of his magazine and expended five rounds from the fresh supply. Some of the lanterns were dropped on the road, where a broken one burned. What was left of the patrol had retreated, though several wounded men were screaming. After a while, the cries gradually got fainter. The soldiers had sneaked back and carried off the wounded.

The Rare Beast came running and out of breath. "What happened?'' Sharts told him.

"Where's Bargma?'' Hank said.

"Gone hunting. She'll be back just before dawn.''

Hank did not think that Terrestrial owls went hunting in such foul weather. They would not want to get wet, there was so little light that even an owl could not see well, and the prey would be staying out of the open. But here the animal kingdom did not behave exactly as on Earth. Bargma could be walking through the woods now, trying to find some holed-up rodent. Her sentiency would enable her to hunt in a manner her other-world cousins would never dream of.

Sharts sent Blogo after some food and hot berry juice. When he returned with a large basketful, he said, "They're gone.''

Sharts said, "You sound as if you'd like to go with them.''

"Not me!'' Blogo said. He thumped his barrel chest with a fist. "You know me. Did I ever run away from a fight? Hell, boss, you and I have taken on and licked twenty men! And look at what havoc we worked among the Gillikins tonight! They must be filling their britches just thinking about tackling us! Maybe I ought to go down the road and tell them who we are! That'd shake them up!''

"Yeah,'' Hank said. "All ten thousand of them.''

"Numbers don't scare me,'' Blogo said.

Hank had to listen to much more boasting. He was tired of it, but it did keep him awake. That and his mental images of how he would like to kick the two in the rear while they were bent over looking down a cliff.

When dawn was almost due by his wristwatch, the sky was still black. Moreover, the thunder had come back, and lightning was running fiery fingers over the pages of the earth. Hank hoped that it was not looking for his name.

27

Carrying the lantern, Hank walked on the down-slanting road. When he came to the level ground, he cut across the field. He stopped under the oak tree and said, "How are you, Jenny?"

"Fretting and fuming, very worried. I knew that three of you had gotten back because I asked Blogo when he went by. But he wouldn't tell me what had happened."

She sounded hurt.

"Sorry," Hank said. "We've been very busy."

He sketched the raid and then said, "I'm going to untie you even if the wind is still strong. We'll take off at dawn or a little after. We don't have any choice. I'll let you handle the taxiing and the takeoff, but when we're ten feet off the ground, I'll take over. Understand?"

"Yes," Jenny said. "What then?"

"Some action. Maybe."

He patted her cowling and returned to the gate. By then the east was paling, though not much. Hank could see a dark mass of men a half-mile away on the road. He supposed that there were many more under the trees along the road.

Two minutes passed before what he had been waiting for came. A hundred or so hawks and eagles appeared. They did not attack, but settled down a quarter of a mile away on the branches of the oaks to Hank's right and left. One hawk flew back along the road. She would be reporting the number and location of the defenders.

"I'll bet that Erakna is here, directing the army," Hank said. "She'll be furious because of what we did, her narrow escape and all. And she'll want to make sure that her soldiers don't screw up again."

Blogo said, "I hope she doesn't use her magic against us."

"She shouldn't think it's necessary," Sharts said. "She'll want to save her energy."

Hank pointed at the birds sitting quietly but glaring at the three men. He said, "You agree, Sharts, Blogo, that we don't have a mammoth's chance on thin ice of getting off the ground while those birds are still there?"

The giant looked narrow-eyed at Hank. "They'll swarm over us as soon as we get into the cockpits. You can kill a lot of them, but they'll keep coming."

"Yeah, and as soon as I run out of ammunition, which will be quickly, we'll have had it."

"It's evident you have a plan," Sharts snapped. "What is it?"

Hank reached into the knapsack and brought out the hemisphere. Sharts's and Blogo's eyes widened.

"The Golden Cap which controls the Winged Monkeys," he said triumphantly.

Sharts should have been happy, but he frowned and bit his lip and began whistling. He was reproaching himself for not having seen it.

"Wow!" Blogo said. "Maybe we could trade that to the queen for an immediate pardon!"

"I think they call you the Rare Beast because you're rarely intelligent," Sharts said. "Why should she bargain with us when she can get it at the expense of a few lives?"

"Sometimes, I think you don't like me," Blogo said. "But...yes...I see what Hank is getting at. I think."

"This is the main reason why Erakna will be personally commanding the army," Hank said. "She knows what we'll do with it if we have any brains. O.K. Here goes."

The inscriptions inside the rim of the Cap were unreadable by Hank, but he did not need to have to decipher them. At least, he hoped he wouldn't.

"Memory, don't fail me now!" he muttered.

He put the Cap on his head. It was too small to stay on without a helping finger. Feeling silly, he lifted his right leg and stood on his left foot.

"Ep-pe! Pep-pe! Kak-ke!"

"That's from the language of the Long-Gones," Sharts said to gape-mouthed Blogo.

Hank stood on his right foot.

"Hil-lo! Hol-lo! Hel-lo!"

Hank planted both feet firmly on the ground.

"Ziz-zii! Zuz-zii! ZIK!"

Though the anticipated happened, Hank still had difficulty believing that it had. He was facing the west, and there suddenly appeared before him in the air a multitude of winged creatures. It sounded like a vast shooting gallery as they came out of nowhere. The air abruptly displaced by their presence made small explosions, a detail which Baum had neglected to describe when he wrote the first Oz book. Or perhaps he had forgotten it.

The entire horde must be here; it speckled the sky before him as if God had dumped a vast pepper shaker. The chattering and the yelling were terrifying. It shook the three men, and it scared the watching hawks and eagles from their perches.

Glinda had told him that each of the four rows of inscriptions commanded a different type of operation. One called the Monkeys in a limited number to the operator. The second summoned all the Monkeys no matter how widely scattered they were. The third could send the Monkeys in a limited number to a certain spot if the operator had been there. The fourth would send the whole horde to a certain area if the operator had once been there.

Hank knew only one, and that was because he had read the operation directions in Baum's book and his mother had also told him about it. When he was young, he had played at being in Oz and had gone through the ritual with a paper Golden Cap many times.

Baum had mentioned only one row of inscriptions, and he had said that Dorothy could read that. Actually, Dorothy had managed to surreptitiously read the directions in the notebook of the West Witch. The Witch had been very old, and her memory had been drying up as fast as her body. She had had mnemonics all over the castle.

Hank glanced at Erakna's birds. One was flying off to bring the news of the Monkeys to the queen.

A big Monkey landed near Hank and walked up to him.

"I am the king," he said. "King Iizarnhanduz the Third, you son of a bitch."

The king had to obey Hank, but he did not have to like it. It was evident from the loud and bitter complaints of his subjects that they, too, did not care for their sudden displacement. Whatever they had been doing, sleeping, eating, excreting, mating, playing, they had been snatched away to do some hard and probably dangerous task. It must have been very disconcerting to be snoozing away and suddenly find oneself a thousand miles away and falling through the alien air.

Hank told him exactly what must be done.

"For God's sake!" the king said. "If this keeps up, we'll become extinct!"

Hank felt sorry for him, but he said, firmly, "Get going! Now!"

Iizarnhanduz (Iron-handed) jabbed a finger at the simians on the field.

"Women and children, too? Have a heart, man!"

"No," Hank said. "They can stay out of it."

"Sure. And what will they do when all their menfolks are killed?"

"All I want is for those birds there to be killed or run off. And a little holding action. . . . I told you what to do!"

"Yeah, and afterwards, if there is any afterwards, we have to fly all the way back home. You know how *far* that is?"

Whatever it was in the Golden Cap that moved and controlled the Monkeys, it must be losing its power, Hank thought. He suspected that there was some kind of machinery enclosed in the walls of the Cap and this was activated by the words he had spoken. What the energy source was, he had no idea. In any event, the king was showing much more reluctance than he had in any reported situation before.

"The last time the Cap was returned to you, by my mother, by the way," Hank said, "you people were supposed to be free forever from control by others. But you weren't smart. You didn't hide the Cap, and so it was stolen. I'll tell you what. I promise that after you carry out my orders, I'll put it some place where no one will ever find it. Will that make you happy?"

The king grinned, his long sharp teeth a fearsome sight.

"Very."

He turned and ran on all fours to his people. After a lot of jabbering, he arranged his males in formation on the meadow. Then, starting at the southeast corner, going into the wind, they began running. Their wings flapping, they leaped into the air and slowly ascended. Some seemed to be too heavy or too slow; they had to retreat to the corner and try again.

When the lead row had turned and was coming with the wind

carrying them toward the birds now circling nearby, Hank led the two men to Jenny. Bargma, who had been hiding on the floor of the front cockpit, fluttered up to sit on the windshield edge.

"You get back there with Sharts and Blogo for now," Hank said.

Sharts, at Hank's direction, primed the carburetor with ether. He also spun the propellor when Hank yelled, "Contact!" so that Jenny would not have to use so much energy to get the engine started. It caught at once, and presently the 150-horsepower Hisso engine was roaring. Sharts and Blogo waited until the engine was warmed up, then they yanked out the logs that chocked the wheels. They ran to climb aboard while Jenny was moving slowly towards the takeoff point. She had to skirt the edge of the meadow because all of the male Monkeys had not yet gotten off the ground.

The trees protected the plane from gusts, but when she got into the open, she would be subject to ground loops. Hank depended upon her reflexes and the fact that she could use energy to lift or lower her wings to cancel the gusts.

By then the hawks and eagles had closed with the Monkeys. Most of them, anyway. Some of the birds had figured that there was no use being brave against such numbers. They fled, and, within a minute or two, those birds who could extricate themselves did so. None headed towards the east. They made a wide half-circle and sped southward. They did not care to face the queen's anger.

The farmland was on a lower level than the road on this side of the gate. Hank could not see what was happening there. However, he surmised that the Gillikin soldiers had charged. The Monkeys were flapping towards the road. All they had to do was to check the Gillikins' advance until Jenny was airborne.

The plane got to the takeoff point without dragging either end of its wingtips against the ground. She moved slowly into the wind, then began rolling forward swiftly. And she was up.

He knocked on the instrument panel to indicate that he was now the pilot. After clearing the trees on the hills beyond the farm, he banked sharply and brought her around in line with the road. As he passed over the meadow, he noted that the Monkey females and children were jammed into the southeast corner. They were waiting until the plane had gone over before they started the southward migration.

He dipped Jenny's nose until she was only ten feet above the ground. Then he raised it, and he came up over the gate with the wheels a few feet above the fence. To the Gillikins and Monkeys struggling ahead of him, it must have looked as if the plane had been shot by a rocket from the landing field. He brought Jenny up sharply, remembering suddenly that there might be some Monkeys in the air. It would be ironic and not at all funny if he collided with a Monkey.

All of them, however, were on the ground in close combat with the van of the army.

Hank dived to bring Jenny close to the battle. The roar of the engine would notify the Monkeys that they could quit fighting and go home. However, that was not so easy. If they turned tail, they might be cut down from behind. Also, they could not get into the air without a long run, and they had no room for that on the body-strewn road.

Hank could not worry about them. It was every man—every Monkey—for himself. He zoomed down the road and pulled on the cable. Both machine guns fired. Good. He had been worried that they might jam. They had always seemed to do so just when he needed them while dogfighting or strafing over France.

The road was packed with troops. To make consternation, disorder, and panic, he loosed four bursts among them. Those who had not been hit were diving onto the side of the road or trying to.

Ahead near the crossroads on a field was something that stood out. A big white coach with eight moose hitched to it.

"The queen's," Hank muttered.

He lifted up, then made a shallow dive. The people standing around it began running. No. One had not. She was dressed in a long all-white robe. Erakna. Only witches were allowed to wear a dress which was entirely white. She sat on a chair near the coach. The scarlet object propped against it had to be her umbrella, the sign and symbol of a red witch.

Erakna sat calmly, or seemingly so, until Hank fired. Seeing the twin line of bullets striking the earth and racing toward her, she abandoned the chair and her dignity. She threw herself to one side.

Hank brought Jenny up while he cursed.

"Missed!"

He turned and dived again. Erakna was not in sight. She must be hiding on the other side of the coach.

His bullets tore into the coach, and the moose, recovering from their paralysis, or perhaps they had been obeying the queen's orders to stand still until then, pulled the coach away in mad flight across the meadow. Erakna was exposed now, but she had time to run. Lifting her long skirts with both hands, she sped like a rabbit with a hawk after her. She did not make the mistake of trying to run across the open fields but headed towards the mass of soldiers lying on the ground. There, no doubt, she would order some soldiers to throw themselves over her.

When Hank had turned and started another strafing run, he saw that soldiers were indeed clustered around. But when he started firing, the soldiers scattered. The queen was left alone, a white target.

Her hair was so blonde that it looked almost as white as her garment. Hank thought, irrelevantly, Glinda is a white witch with red hair, and Erakna is a red witch with white hair.

The queen threw herself to one side and rolled.

Hank did not know whether or not he had missed again until he climbed and turned again. He felt vibrations behind him and turned his head quickly to see what was causing them. Sharts was pounding on the side of the fuselage and grinning. He pointed downwards. Hank looked down and saw that Erakna was lying on the ground with a red stain on her skirt. She had been hit in the leg.

"This should do it," Hank thought. "I'll put an end to her and the war!"

The queen had other ideas. She rose and lifted her skirts high, showing that she was standing on the unwounded leg. Then she began whirling like a ballerina, her arms stretched out.

"What the hell?" Hank muttered. He had the feeling that something had suddenly gone wrong, that he was dealing with forces that he did not understand. Nevertheless, he pulled on the cable, and the machine guns chattered on the wing above him.

Erakna disappeared.

Groaning, Hank let loose of the cable. He had no idea where she was. He doubted that she had made herself invisible. If she had, she still would have been hit by the bullets. She was probably in her suite in the castle now.

He turned southward. There was no use wasting more time and fuel. Twisting around, he beckoned that Bargma should come to the front cockpit. He could not see Blogo because he was sitting in Sharts's lap, but the giant was evidently raving and ranting. The owl, when she had worked her way to him and clutched his shoulder, yelled, "Tough luck!"

"When I get back to Glinda, my name'll be mud!" he shouted.

"You did your best. Which, I don't mind saying, was better than most men would've done!"

They passed over the Monkeys, flying in a long ragged file, and then Hank saw Balthii below. She had been hanging around somewhere near the farm, observing. Now she'd be taking the message to Glinda that Erakna was still alive.

A half hour later, a storm came from the southeast the like of which Hank had never flown in and hoped he never would again. It was so bad that he momentarily had the crazy thought that Erakna had summoned it up against him. Whatever its cause, it surrounded him with wild black clouds in which he was not sure that he was not sometimes flying upside down. His compass whirled insanely. Updrafts and downdrafts seized Jenny, some holding her so long that he prayed that they would not be dashed against a mountain.

He had perhaps fifteen minutes before the fuel tank was empty when Jenny burst into an open sky and comparatively calm air. He did not know where he was. Neither did Bargma.

28

"That's the ruins of a city of the Long-Gones!" the owl said.

"Hell, we couldn't have been blown that far," Hank said. "Glinda told me that the ruins were in the extreme northwest corner of the land. In Nataweyland."

"I said *a* city. I've heard rumors and stories about other lost ruins."

Hank had been looking for ten minutes for a place to land in the mountains. He alone had a parachute, and so he could abandon ship if he did not find somewhere to set Jenny down. But he would not say goodbye to Jenny and his human passengers until he absolutely had to. There was also the possibility of a deadstick landing on top of the trees, but he did not know if he should chance killing himself for the sake of the unsavory characters in the rear cockpit. Anyway, Jenny was capable of doing that by herself.

Her destruction would make him feel far worse than the deaths of Sharts and Blogo.

"I'll be a hero for Glinda, but not for those two," he muttered.

Still, he was hanging on until he had three minutes of fuel left. But he may not have estimated the quantity correctly.

"There's a place to land," Bargma screeched in his ear.

Hank looked down and saw a level and relatively tree-free place which had suddenly appeared. He turned towards it, noted which way the wind was bending the treetops and bushes, and turned. He rapped on the panel for Jenny to take over. She could handle gusts better than he. Not to mention landings in calm air.

"Good luck," the owl said, and she launched herself up and out.

When the engine had turned off, Hank climbed to the ground, relieved himself, and then spoke to Jenny.

"Well, old girl, it looks as if your passengers will have to hoof it all the way back to Suthwarzha. Unless we can find some alcohol in this God-forsaken area. I didn't see a single village or house anywhere."

"You can't make any alcohol?" Jenny said plaintively.

"Maybe. We'll see. Don't worry. I won't desert you unless there's no other alternative. And I'll come back to get you. I swear I will."

The first thing to do was to push Jenny under the protection of the trees and stake her down. He started to tell the other two that, but Blogo, a minute tempest, stormed at him.

"Why in hell did you land here? Don't you know that the Very Rare Beast is supposed to haunt the Long-Gone ruins?"

"Shut up, stupid!" Sharts said. "If he hadn't landed here, we'd be dead!"

"Maybe we'd be better off," Blogo muttered.

Hank got Jenny taken care of and then asked Bargma if she would try to find her way back to Glinda.

"Who's going to guide you if you do get Jenny up again and do find a familiar landmark?"

"I don't know. But if Glinda knows where we are, she might be able to get us back somehow."

"A fat chance of that. She's a witch, but she's not a miracle-worker. I'm going now but not very far. I have to find something to eat."

That reminded Hank that he was hungry. He took the last of the cheese, nuts, and raisins from the knapsack and devoured them. He was still hungry. Maybe he'd starve to death. No, not if he could kill an animal. He did not care if the others would be horrified. He was not going to die just because meat-eating was tabu. Anyway, they would not have to know about it.

He thought about the pleas of the mouse caught by the owl in Abraam's barn. Could he kill a sentient creature for food?

The empty belly knows no conscience, he told himself.

The question would be answered when he was starving.

He walked to the edge of the plateau from the meadow. A thousand or more feet below the sheer cliff was a river. An equally high cliff rose on the other side two miles or so away. Mountains surrounded this area, those to the west seeming to be the highest. He had been lucky to come through a pass. A mile to the right, a mile to the left, and he'd be dead now. He fingered his mother's gift, the housekey.

To the southeast, near the lip of the plateau, were some hills on which were the ruins of the ancient city. Most of it must be buried under soil and vegetation, but there were enough exposed buildings to indicate that this had once been a populous area. He did not know why the Long-Gones had had a city in this high, remote, and isolated area. Perhaps for the same reason that the city of Machu Picchu, discovered twelve years ago in the Andes, had been built.

His desire to explore the ruins was shelved by hunger. He joined the other two as they set out to hunt. Sharts walked towards the ruins, but Blogo insisted that they go north instead. Sharts said, "Very well. If you're afraid, we won't go there."

Blogo thumped his chest, and his cock's comb got even redder.

"I'm afraid of nothing, I tell you! However, I am man enough to admit that a few things do make me nervous. Only a little, you understand! And that is only because my mother, all the mothers, warned the children about the Very Rare Beast. I, the man, am not afraid. But there's a little child in me that's still afraid. It's that that makes me nervous."

"The child in you must be very little indeed if he can get inside your little body," Sharts said. His grin made his talon-ravaged face look even more horrible.

Hank and Sharts went side by side into the upsloping woods. Blogo was behind them because his short legs could not keep up with theirs. Also, he probably did not want to cause any more remarks about his bugaboo. Sharts was cursing because flies were settling on his open wounds, and then he stopped in the midst of a block-long blasphemous word that would have done credit to a German philosopher.

Hank stopped also. Blogo bumped into him and said, "Why don't you warn a fellow, Giant?"

"Shh!" Sharts said.

They listened and heard, faintly, some piglike gruntings. But when they proceeded stealthily through the brush for thirty yards, they found that the porcine noises came from a big black bear. He was tearing at the carcass of a female moose.

"Meat!" the two outlaws said at the same time.

The stories were true. These men *were* cannibals.

They were close enough that the short-sighted bear could see them. He stopped eating and rose to his hind legs, swaying, his paws held out, his chops bloody.

The bear probably would not have minded being outnumbered if the strangers had been unarmed. But two held loaded crossbows, and one had an object the purpose of which the bear would not know but would suspect was a weapon.

"Beat it!" the bear said. "I killed this moose, and it's all mine. Find your own food!"

Sharts said, "We don't usually kill animals for food. But since you've done us a favor by killing this moose, we'll eat it."

"Over my dead body, freak-eyes!"

"That may be," Sharts said. "However, why don't you just go away? We're not violent men; we'd just as soon not shed blood. There must be plenty of deer and moose in these woods."

"I like bear meat even better than moosemeat," Blogo said. "Why don't we dine on both, boss?"

"Now, wait a minute," Hank said. "That'd be murder!"

"Not if he attacks us," Sharts said. "And if he doesn't move on, that'll be the same as attacking us."

"How do you lamebrains figure that?" the bear said.

"If we start to cut off some of the moose, you'll attack us, right?"

"Right."

"We're going to slice off a hunk."

The bear snarled and said, "Try it!"

"You haven't got a chance," Hank said. "Why don't we compromise, work something out? There's plenty there for all of us. Let's share it. Half for you, half for us."

"I love bear meat," Blogo said, and he smacked his lips.

"And I love to eat monkeys and roosters," the bear said. "Which are you? Or are you a hybrid? Was your father a rooster? What isn't monkey looks like chicken. In fact, you're probably all chicken. Cut-cut-cuh-daw!"

"I'll show you who's chicken!" Blogo said, but he did not step toward the bear.

"I suppose," Sharts said to Hank, "that if we kill this animal, you'll tell Glinda about it?"

"It'd be murder," Hank said. "You'd be outlaws again."

"It isn't such a bad life, boss," Blogo said.

"I prefer the amenities of civilization," Sharts said. "Books, good wine, warm houses, a bath every day, beautiful women, concerts, a laboratory. I'm sick of living like a savage.

"Look, bear, what's your name?"

"It's none of your business, but it's Kwelala the Unbeaten."

"A tough guy, a champ, huh? Well, I'll make you a sporting proposition, you ursine bum. I'll fight you unarmed, no holds barred, and if I lick you, you walk off and leave the moose to us. If you beat me, we walk away. How's that?"

"Yeah? No treachery? Your friends won't shoot me no matter what I do to you?"

"I promise. The word of Sharts."

"I never heard of you, man. But if you want to die, and you must, I don't blame you, you're such an ugly miserable-looking pile of weasel poppy, well, let's have at it!"

Sharts dropped his crossbow and charged. The bear was so surprised that he backed away. Sharts leaped into the air and kicked with both feet. His wooden soles struck the bear's lower jaw, and the bear fell backward, partly stunned.

Sharts landed on his back but was up quickly. The bear got to his feet just as Sharts struck the bear again on the jaw. Cross-eyed, the bear fell once more. But when Sharts leaped at him again, the bear swiped his paw at him. Sharts was hurled whirling away and fell. On all fours now, the bear charged. Sharts, on his back, kicked the bear in the nose and rolled while the animal was bawling with pain. He got up and jumped on the bear's back and applied a full-nelson.

Hank's eyes widened, and he swore softly. He would have said that no man was strong enough to bend the massive neck of a bear. But it was moving downward, and it was going to crack if Sharts could keep the pressure up.

The bear rolled on top of Sharts twice. The giant did not loosen his grip.

"Give up," Sharts said in a strangled voice. "Or I'll break your neck like it's a toothpick!"

"I can't believe this," Kwelala said. "It just can't be happening to me!"

"I won't tell anybody I beat you," Sharts said. "You can keep your pride and your monicker."

"Promise?"

"My word is as strong as my muscles."

"O.K. You can have the damn moose. I think she was sick, anyway. I hope you get sick eating her."

"Shoot him if he tries anything," Sharts said, and he released the bear. Kwelala walked off, grumbling, but he did not look back.

Sharts, breathing hard, said, "That stupid beast tore off my shirt."

Blogo started to take off his knapsack. "I got another one for you, boss."

Their mouths watering, they skinned the moose and cut off a haunch and cut out the kidneys and heart. Sharts chopped off some branches and whittled their ends so they could hold pieces of meat over the fire that Blogo was building. Hank went back to the plane to get the salt and pepper shakers which he always carried because no one ever put on enough for him.

When he returned, he found that Blogo was chewing ecstatically on a small and burnt piece. Hank held his own out over the fire, and, when it looked almost medium-done, he withdrew it until it had cooled off enough to bite into.

But when he brought the meat close to his open mouth, his gorge rose.

After looking at the meat for a long time, he threw it into the fire. He rose and said, "Hell, I can't do it!"

Sharts, grinning, said, "You've been conditioned."

"You might call it that," Hank said disgustedly. He walked into the woods to look for nuts and berries. Two hours later, he returned to the plane, his belly full. He was still dissatisfied.

Bargma was swallowing a small piece of meat which Blogo had brought for her. She got it down and said, "What now?"

"First, the ruins. Then we have to look for somebody or some place with alcohol."

"It's more important to find fuel," Blogo said. "I'll start looking for it first thing in the morning."

They spent the night under a ledge and next to a fire. In the morning, tired, stiff, and cold, they went out for food. Sharts and Blogo did not have far to go since the moose meat was still fresh enough for them. Hank went back to where he had found the berries and nuts and ate the now-monotonous food. When he got back, Sharts and Blogo were smearing a cream over their wounds. These were healing fast and were not, as he had supposed, going to be deep scars.

New skin was growing over the wounds, and the two expected the scar tissue to fall off.

He asked Sharts about the cream. The giant explained that Blogo had brought it with him when he had left his people. Sharts was thinking about analyzing the ingredients and manufacturing it when he returned to civilization.

"He and I, we're going to become rich," Blogo said. "It's a secret remedy which only one of my people knows. But Sharts here, he'll find out what the recipe is and make some more."

Hank thought that if he could get the formula and take it to Earth, he could become a millionaire, too. But it was evident that there was not much chance for returning. Besides, he was not eager to do so.

Shortly thereafter, the Rare Beast set off northwestward along the plateau edge to look for signs of human life. Hank and Sharts walked to the ruins and poked around in the stones and the half-buried buildings. These were made of cyclopean blocks of some white mineral mortared together. Though erosion had crumbled the faces of the blocks, the mortar was untouched by time.

After a while, Sharts wandered off. Hank found a block of stone wider than his parents' mansion in Oyster Bay. About twelve feet of it protruded from the ground. All around it were carved figures of animals and objects and strange-looking bipeds with human hands. Hank thought that they were meant to portray some kind of story. They formed a row running around the block. That this row might be the start or the end of the story was indicated by the tops of figures exposed by erosion below the upper row. A little later, he found a one hundred-foot-long metal obelisk lying on the ground. It was shaped like the "Cleopatra's Needle" in New York's Central Park and bore the shapes of living beings and objects and many inscriptions. He was looking at these when he heard Sharts calling him. Hank made his way through the bushes and trees growing on and along the ruins to the edge of the plateau. Sharts was standing by a place which looked as if an overhang of rock had broken off and fallen into the canyon.

"Look at this."

Sharts pointed at a five-foot-high silvery dome sunk into the earth. At the base where it faced the precipice was an arched hole about ten inches high.

"Interesting," Hank said.

"Wait a minute. I've been timing them."

Fifty seconds passed. Then Hank was startled. A tiny figure, a simulacrum of the bipeds portrayed on the block, walked out. It paid them no attention but marched like a wooden soldier to the edge of the plateau and toppled over it.

"My God, what's that?" Hank said.

"Wait."

Sixty seconds later, a duplicate of the first walked out and, like it, fell into the canyon.

"I think it's a toy-making machine of the Long-Gones," Sharts said. "It's still operating."

"After two thousand years or more?"

"I know it's incredible, but how else explain it?"

When, sixty seconds later, the next figure walked out, Sharts picked the tiny thing up. It still moved its legs and swung its arms as if it were walking on the ground.

"They must have had some control mechanism so that the child could direct it to turn and so on," Sharts said.

Hank thought that he was assuming a lot, but he had no basis for argument.

"There must be thousands on the slope at the base of this cliff," Sharts said. "The others, and there must have been millions, must have been carried off by the river."

The body of the toy was human, and the face would have been human if it had had a nose. Where that should have been was a hole with many fine strands. These may have represented a network of hairs. On closer inspection, Hank saw that the ears were smaller in proportion than a human's and the convolutions in it were different.

The joints of the legs and arms and the fingers and toes could be articulated.

Hank told him what he had found.

"I'd like to try to read whatever story is on that obelisk," he said. "But we'd have to turn it over. The story is a serial one, and it spirals up from the base to the apex."

Sharts went with him to the fallen monument. He felt the red metal, which was unrusted, and looked at some of the hieroglyphics.

"It must weigh from three to five hundred tons," he said. "We could never turn it over to read the other side. We'll have to be satisfied with what we can see. But look at this."

He pointed at a representation of a dome which had an arched hole at its base. Out of it were proceeding figures like Blogo and the Winged Monkeys and other seemingly unnatural beings.

"That adds weight to my theory that the Rare Beasts and the Monkeys are descendants of synthetic *vivants*," Hank said.

29

The exposed sides of the obelisk had the beginning and the end of the story. What was on the underside had to remain hidden, and there was much that they did not understand on the sides they could see.

"Nevertheless," Hank said, "we have enough to know some of the history of the Long-Gones. Including the fact, I suppose it's a fact, that they did not just die out. They left for another world, went through a gate they'd opened between this world and another. If I interpret the pictures correctly, their experiments in trying to open a way to another world is what made weak places in the walls between your universe and mine.

"Maybe I shouldn't say walls. As I see it, the process is more like going up or down from one level of energy or configuration of energy to another. Anyway, the Long-Gones either could not get to Earth or, after a look at it, decided to go some place else."

He did not have to explain to Sharts why the noseless beings had abandoned this world. Sharts had also comprehended that the Long-Gones had decided not to fight any more. They had been pushed into this area, which was about the size of Alaska, and there seemed no way to expand it. They were repelling the forces that had devastated this planet and could do so for a long time. But it was not worthwhile. Not when they could go to a new green world and leave the attackers behind.

The energy configuration of the universe they went to would not permit their enemy to exist there.

"I suppose that they also can't exist on Earth," Hank said, thinking aloud. But I'm not sure. I wouldn't think that the energy entities which possess animals could exist there either. But Glinda told me that she sent a hawk through the opening to Earth, and it came back still possessed.''

"Did she ask you to pass that information on to your people?'' Sharts said.

"Yes. Why? Oh, I see. She may have been lying so that my people would be frightened. I thought of that. However, I won't tell my people . . . those people . . . that I think she's not telling the truth. I wouldn't want them to take a chance that she was.''

It seemed from what he'd read on the obelisk that there were two types of energy beings. One was composed of the giant rolling balls that hurled themselves against the edge of the green land. Most of them perished there because the Long-Gones had buried defenses along the border between desert and oasis. These were pictured as huge poles, subterranean lightning rods, as it were.

A long time before the ancient aborigines had left this universe, they had experimented at making gates to other universes. Their first success had resulted in what was to be disaster. The great balls of electrical fire had poured through before the gate could be closed. Thousands must have entered. And these had propagated their kind by using the earth and atmospheric electricity. They had sucked the electrical energy from all creatures, vegetable or animal.

"They're not demons or souls loosed from hell to ravage on the living,'' Hank said. "Your priests are wrong. They're electrical Draculas. And they exist because the physical structure of this universe is not quite like that of mine. In my world they . . . no. I overlooked something. Why is it that the energy-things originated in another world and can live in this one but not in the world the Long-Gones went to?''

"Perhaps the physical laws of the world they went to are just dissimilar enough so the things can't exist there.''

Sharts might be a near-psychotic, but he was not unintelligent.

"You could be right. No!'' Hank said hastily when he saw Sharts's face tighten and turn red. "You're right! Absolutely right! It couldn't be anything else but!

"However, how do I know that the physical laws of my universe won't permit those things to exist there? I don't. I'll make sure that I put that in the report.''

Sharts's face loosened and regained its normal color.

"The defenses erected by the Long-Gones must be weakening in at least one place," Hank said. "Otherwise, some wouldn't be able to roll onto the green land. I saw some do that one night while I was in Glinda's castle. They were blown up, but I'm sure that it was through Glinda's doing. She was using her own forces to destroy them. What you call magic."

"Perhaps that is why Glinda established her capital at that point," Sharts said. "There is a weak or weakening spot there, and she wanted to be there to guard it."

Sharts looked gloomy and said, "What if Glinda dies or the weak spot becomes larger?"

"I hate to think about that," Hank said.

Maybe he would be better off if he went back to Earth.

"Anyway," he said, waving his arm to indicate the whole oasis, "I can't believe that this is the only alive area and that the rest of the world is a desert."

"Why not? Isn't that made clear on the obelisk?"

"It was true when the obelisk was made. Or maybe it wasn't true even then. My point is the air."

"The air?"

Sharts looked puzzled, and he did not like to be puzzled.

"Yes, the air. The planetary atmosphere. Its oxygen is continually being renewed by plants on the earth and in the sea. But, if the energy-things have destroyed all the plants, where is the new air coming from? This land isn't big enough to keep its inhabitants from asphyxiating. There's air blowing in all the time from the desert, and it would sweep away the oxygen generated here."

"Perhaps the plants in the ocean have not been killed," Sharts said.

"Perhaps. Even so, I doubt that they would be enough. Of course, I really don't know enough about the subject. But I'll bet . . . anyway, I think . . . that all the energy beings are in the desert around the green land. Elsewhere, they'd have no prey, and they would, I suppose, die of electrical starvation.

"So, plants have grown again in many other places, and they've flourished and spread because the energy-things haven't found out about them."

One of the surprises while reading the Long-Gones' cartoons—that was what they were, cartoons—was that the mind-spirits or firefoxes had not come from the universe of the big energy-beings.

These had been created by the ancients after the invasion. They were, if Hank had interpreted rightly, the result of another experiment by the Long-Gones. Using the destroyers' configurations as models, the scientists had made a different type of energy-being. These were designed to transfer the neural-mental contents of a person to a synthetic body. By doing this, the scientists had hoped to become immortal, to pass their minds from one body to another.

Hank did not know why the experiment had gone wrong. But it had. The firefoxes were sentient and, therefore, self-conscious and self-motivated. They had refused to obey the scientists and conduct themselves as laboratory subjects. Also, the hope that the firefoxes would be able to transfer the contents of a mind to another body turned out to be false.

The things could occupy the bodies of animals and human beings. But they could not possess the minds of the latter, though they could those of animals. Something in the structure of the human neural system and, perhaps, the degree of intelligence, prevented the firefoxes from influencing the brains of Homo sapiens.

The firefoxes had escaped and, in a manner similar to that of the destroyers, propagated themselves. They occupied the cerebral-neural systems of animals and birds and reptiles, though they were either unable to or did not care to invest those of fish and insects.

(Hank, learning this, wondered why humans did not eat fish and frogs. Sharts told him that the Quadlings, Munchkins, and Ozlanders did not do so because of religious prohibitions. The fish was the symbol of Christ-Thor and hence sacred. As for the frog, that was forbidden because of the ancient myth that a frog was a fish that had learned how to walk or, at least, hop. The Winkies and Gillikins, however, did not have this tabu.)

What the pictures could not tell was just how the mind-spirits or firefoxes interacted with the neural systems of the occupied animals. Hank had to extrapolate that from what he had observed. Take, as an example, a firefox which had possessed a hawk just after it had escaped from the Long-Gones' laboratory like a voltaic Frankenstein's monster. The firefox was perhaps as intelligent as a human being. But when it became *one,* as it were, with the bird, its physical and mental capabilities were limited by the body it invested. It had to operate through a diminutive brain and a body specialized for flight and without speech organs.

The hawk-firefox could learn language from humans, but it could not utter speech with the bird's oral apparatus. It solved that problem by learning to modulate sound waves with energy output. In some ways, its voice was a telephone transmitter.

There was also what might be called a negative flow. The hawk's nonhuman nervous system affected the firefox's, and the result was an intelligence level that could never match that of the more intelligent humans.

Also, the firefox was, when it first occupied the hawk's body, like a human infant. It had to learn language and to gain experience just like a baby. The difference was that the hawk-firefox learned much faster than an infant.

One of the factors preventing the symbiote's full intellectual and emotional development was the short life of the hawk. It learned much faster than the infant, true, but it did not have a long time to learn.

However, when the hawk died, the mind-spirit lived on. It traveled around in whatever manner circumscribed it, and, when it came to an unoccupied body, it attached itself like iron filings to a magnet.

This process, Hank was sure, caused some kind of traumatic shock. The firefox lost its identity as a hawk, or, rather, it lost its memory of its former life as a hawk. But, like an amnesiac, it retained its memory of language and its unconscious knowledge of its environment.

In some ways, the firefox experienced what the Hindus called transmigration or reincarnation.

Though the firefox assumed a new identity every time it occupied a body, its retention of certain abilities enabled it to grow mentally and emotionally. The knowledge accreted to a certain extent.

Thus, it could be assumed that the firefox did not die. That occupying Bargma, for instance, might be anywhere from fifteen hundred to forty thousand years old. But its intelligence was limited in operation by the avian nervous system. Also, much that it had learned was lost or beyond recall.

Hank did not believe that a firefox could, unaided, invest and make alive an inanimate object. But a witch could do that for a firefox though it probably was not easily done. If it were easy, there would be many more Scarecrows than there were.

Glinda, he was certain, had animated the Scarecrow. And she had managed to transfer a human being's mind-contents, the Tin Woodman's, from a dying body to a metal simulacrum.

Another probably rare phenomenon was the dispossession of one firefox by another. A firefox had been made visible by the electrical potential in a storm, and Hank had seen—well, almost seen—the free firefox oust the entity which occupied the hawk. However, the dispossessor had failed to possess the dispossessed. Instead, it had occupied an inanimate object, the airplane.

Or it was possible that the original entity in Ot, hurled from the hawk-body, had taken up new residence in Jenny?

Whichever event had happened, Glinda had influenced its course.

Why had she effected this? Because, Hank thought, she had a use for a living aircraft just as she had had a use for the Scarecrow and the Woodman and had arranged to put them in Dorothy's path.

Hank explained his theory to Sharts. The giant nodded and said, "That makes more sense than the religious explanations. Though that does not mean that your theory is right and the priests are wrong. It might mean that both of you are wrong. Or half-right.

"I will admit this, though. Despite your deficiencies of character, you are not without some intelligence."

Hank did not know whether he should thank Sharts or hit him. Having witnessed the man overpower a bear, he thought that it would be best to control his fists.

30

They spent the rest of the day exploring and looking for food. When they found a wide deep creek that tumbled over the cliff, they followed it up until they came to a pool. Here they improvised fishing poles and caught three troutlike fish. They also waded around in a small swamp and seized three large frogs. When they returned to camp, their bellies were full of protein. They also arrived just in time to see Blogo's short legs carrying him at his top speed towards them.

Blogo stopped a few feet from them. Panting, looking exultant and proud, he cried, "I've found a village!"

The next day, they followed him to a distant point on the edge of the plateau. There he gestured at a place far down and on the opposite side of the river.

It took a day for the three to climb down and get across the swift rapids-riddled stream. The villagers were not the type of Gillikins expected. They obviously were a nearly pure strain of Neanderthals. They did, however, speak an archaic dialect of Gillikin. The three strangers managed to make themselves intelligible and to make it clear that they wanted thirty gallons of grain alcohol. The villagers had the alcohol, but they refused to give it away. They wanted something in return. They did not know what that something was, but it had to be of equal or superior value.

"Why don't we just take it from them?" Blogo said. "One burst from your gun, Hank, and the survivors will run like mad."

"I won't do that," Hank said. "Besides, we're going to need their help to get the fuel up the cliff."

"It would be a lot of fun seeing the tiny apemen run," Blogo said.

"Tiny!" Hank said. "Blogo, you're the shortest person here! And you look more like an ape than they do!"

Blogo said, sulkily, "In spirit, I meant. In spirit."

They spent the night there, the first half of which was entertainment by their hosts of what must have seemed to them to be rather weird guests. They got up early, however. After a breakfast of acorn bread, fish, frog, nuts, berries, corncakes with wild honey, and a thick, whitish and vanillaish fluid tapped from a milktree, they set out. The headman, the priestess, and six young men accompanied them. They got to the camp just after dusk. Here, by the light of a bonfire, the villagers were shown the toy-making machine.

"You can have this in return for the alcohol," Sharts said.

The Kumkwoots' eyes shone, though with fear as much as with desire. This was a holy, a dreaded place. They had stayed away from here because they feared the ghosts of the Long-Gones. But, since they thought that the strangers were spirits of the ancients who had come down to tell them that the ghosts were now friendly, they had agreed to trespass.

This made Hank grin. If they believed that the strangers were ghosts, why had they bargained with them? He would have thought that they would have given the ghosts anything they wanted. But avarice had ridden down their fear.

"The toymaker is mine, and so I can give it to you," Sharts said. "The other ghosts have agreed to this. In fact, they would like you to visit them whenever you feel like it."

"Where are they?" the priestess said. "I'd like to meet them."

Sharts handled the shrewd woman shrewdly.

"They're off on a visit to the otherworld just now. But they'll be back."

Three days later, they came back to camp with the fuel. The next morning, the Kumkwoot porters bade them farewell. Despite Sharts's reassurances, they seemed glad to get away from the place. Perhaps this was because they were made even more uneasy by Jenny.

Blogo was still sulking because Hank and Sharts had made him stay away from the Kumkwoot women.

"Let's get away from this miserable place," he said. "How long will it take to refuel this thing?"

"Person!" Jenny yelled at him. "Person! Not thing!"

"How would you like apples jammed up your exhaust pipes?" Blogo said.

"I'll be glad when we get rid of that chickenspit," Jenny said to Hank.

He patted her cowling. "Me, too."

However, the black sky threatened rain, and the wind was too strong and gusty for flight. Also, Sharts wanted to explore the ruins some more. Since they could not take off anyway, Hank agreed to this.

"You're coming with us," Sharts said.

Blogo, bristling, his eyes wild, said, "No, I'm not!"

"Yes, you are," the giant said. "You've had this ridiculous and demeaning terror of this nonexistent Very Rare Beast long enough. We're going to go into every place we can get into, and I'm going to show you that there's nothing to be afraid of."

"What good it'll do if there isn't any Beast there?" Blogo said. He swallowed and said, "It could be haunting some other ruins."

"You told me that there's supposed to be one in every ruin," Sharts said.

"I did? I don't remember that."

"Are you calling me a liar?" Sharts said coldly. He stepped forward until Blogo's nose almost touched the giant's navel.

Blogo, hands fisted, trembling, said, "No, but I am saying that maybe your memory isn't perfect."

"What?" Sharts roared. "You know that it's perfect! I never forget a thing! And you can bet your silly-looking nose that I won't forget this insubordination! Maybe you and I should part when we get to Quadlingland! I plan to spend a beautiful life in beautiful surroundings, and you'd spoil the esthetically perfect environment! There's no way anybody as dumb and as ugly as you could fit into anything beautiful!"

"Please, boss!" Blogo whimpered. "Don't make me do this!"

"You have no choice," Sharts said, picking the little creature up by his loincloth. "Really, Blogo, I'm doing this for you because I like you—though how I can stumps me—and it's all for your own good. I don't mind the bother of it, but I'd appreciate it if you'd be more cooperative."

Sharts carried the kicking and yelling Rare Beast into the ruins.

Hank, disgusted with both of them, followed. When they were in front of the first building that had an entrance not choked with dirt and bushes, Sharts put Blogo down. But he held him with two fingers around his neck.

He pushed him into the building. Hank waited. Presently, they came out. Blogo had quit struggling and screaming, but his cock's comb and face were red, and if the bulb at the end of his nose had had a little more blood in it, it would have burst.

"See?" the giant said. "There was no one there except for a few bats. It wasn't so bad, was it?"

"Not bad!" Blogo said. "I left something of me in there on the ground."

"You'd have had to get rid of it, anyway," Sharts said. "Though it was, I'll have to admit, the best part of you."

They went into another building. When they came out, Blogo said nothing, but he was shaking as if he was about to have a seizure. And the blood had drained from his comb, face, and nose.

The third structure could be entered only by a half-buried doorway. Dirt piled around it showed that some large animal had dug into it to make a home there. The stench indicated that animals might still live there. Sharts, however, said that he had run out the wolverine pack that had made their abode there. Hank did not know if he was telling the truth. For one thing, wolverines did not run in a pack; they were solitaries. However, this was not Earth, and the sentient animals might have overcome their powerful instincts.

Blogo, looking as numb as if he had been shot with morphine, walked in ahead of Sharts. No more than ten seconds had passed before Hank heard a despairing scream. A few seconds later, Blogo raced from the entrance and headed towards the edge of the plateau. His eyes were popping, and his head was thrown back. His legs and arms pumped.

Sharts, stooping, came out of the entrance. He was laughing uproariously, but, when he saw where Blogo was running, he shouted.

"Stop him! The damn fool'll run right off the cliff!"

Hank and Sharts sprinted like Charlie Paddock after Blogo. Sharts, though much more heavily muscled than Hank, passed him. He leaped out and, on the way down, caught Blogo's ankle. If he had missed, Blogo would have gone into the canyon.

Blogo fell forward and, for a moment, looked cross-eyed from the impact of his face on the hard rock when he had been so suddenly halted. A cut on the end of his nose spurted blood.

Hank used his dirty handkerchief to stanch the flow.

After a while, Blogo said, his voice quavering, "I saw it! I saw it! Don't tell me I didn't see it!"

Sharts squatted down by him and put a hand on his shoulder.

He spoke quietly. "Sure, you saw it. Now, as soon as you recover, let's go back in there. I'll show you what you almost committed suicide over."

Blogo pulled away from the hand.

"Are you crazy?"

"No. You've been crazy, but there's no reason now why you should stay demented."

"I won't go!" Blogo said, and he burst into tears.

"Sure you will," Sharts said gently.

He picked up Blogo as if he were a child and carried him to the entrance. Setting Blogo down on his feet, he shoved him through. Very curious, Hank followed them into a large chamber dimly lit by sunshafts coming through cracks far above. Rotting meat on gnawed and splintered bones and fragments of fish were the source of the sickening stench. They went past these into a leaning-walled hallway. This, too, was illuminated as if dusk had just come.

Sharts manhandled Blogo into the first entrance on the right. Blogo began whimpering then, but Sharts said, "Now, now, be a man."

The two disappeared around the corner. Hank heard Blogo scream despairingly again, but this time it was cut off. There was a silence. Hank went around the corner and stopped. Though some light leaked through openings high up, this room was somewhat darker than the others. It was not so dim, however, that he could not see that Blogo and Sharts were standing in front of a huge mirror.

"I found it in another room," Sharts said softly. "I cleaned it off and set it here so it would be the first thing you'd see when you came into here. Actually, you didn't see it at all. What you saw was your own reflection."

Blogo sobbed, and he said, "It looked just like the Very Rare Beast to me."

"And so it was. You. Need I say anything more?"

There was a long silence. Then Blogo took Sharts's hand and kissed it again and again. Sobbing, he said, "I owe it all to you, boss. You've cured me!"

Hank was disgusted. The Rare Beast should have kicked Sharts in the crotch.

31

After leaving the two off at a guerrilla base on the Winkie-Gillikin border, Hank flew on to Suthwarzha. They had taken off from the plateau and landed twice, scaring off the locals and stealing their alcohol, before Jenny reached a fuel station. Now Hank, on this August 2, Earth time, was finishing his report in Glinda's castle.

"It sounds as if you had fun," Glinda said, smiling. "I wish you hadn't dropped the Golden Cap in a river. But, after all, you had given your word."

"It was both interesting and educational. There were times when it was downright exciting. I wouldn't want to set it up as a charter tour, though. And I didn't care for the company I had to keep."

"You often have to put up with your partners in business, war, and marriage. I am very pleased with the mission even if you did not kill Erakna. According to my spies, you really shook her up, and the news of what you did to her has caused many desertions from her army. The people know now that she is not as invulnerable as they had thought."

"There's something I don't understand. I thought all red witches feared water. My mother said, and Baum reported her correctly, that the West Witch was so dry that she had no blood. And she carried an umbrella to keep rain, any water, away. I'll have to admit I found that hard to believe. At least, I did until I found out about the firefoxes. Then I supposed that, somehow the red witches used a firefox to keep their bodies and minds alive even though they should have been as dead as mummies."

"You're mixed up. Erakna is a young witch and bleeds even as you and I. You saw her bleed. The old, very old, red witches do start drying up when they pass on. That 'pass on' isn't entirely a euphemism, because, when they are close to dying of old age, they do use a firefox to keep them animated. Its energy is also used as food for the witch. They don't eat after they've started to dry up, you know.''

"I didn't know," Hank said. "What about the kitchen my mother had to work in when she was the West Witch's prisoner? And the food she stole from the cupboard to feed the Cowardly Lion?''

"They were for the West Witch's servants and soldiers, of course.''

"O.K. But why would the West Witch dissolve into a puddle when my mother threw water on her?''

"I suppose that the water broke the electrical bonds holding her atoms together. I wouldn't have any explanation if you hadn't told me about atomic theory. My scientists, by the way, are grateful for your information.''

"Which is pretty elementary," Hank said. "Anyway, I'm glad that you weren't too disappointed in what I did.''

"I can give you a medal," she said, smiling. "I'll have one made up especially for you and the occasion.''

Hank blushed, and he said, "Your thanks will be enough reward.''

"Now, I'll give you something that came through the green cloud while you were gone.''

She picked up a large white envelope with no writing on it and handed it to him.

He looked at it and said, "You didn't open it.''

"Don't be stupid. I can't read English. As yet.''

"You fluster me.''

She smiled but did not reply.

He slit the envelope with a steel opener. It held two sheets on which were handwriting. He recognized the beautiful Spencerian letters, and he verified it by looking at the name on the second sheet.

"How can this be? How is old Stinky Wright involved in this? How . . . ?''

"We'll find out when you read it. First, though, tell me about this Stinkii Rait.''

"We grew up together. His parents' house was near mine. We went to school together; we were best friends. And we were in the same squadron in France. The last time I heard from him, he was a cadet at West Point. That's the American military college. The best. But . . . O.K. I'll read it.''

Dear Hank the Rank:

I'll bet you never dreamed, even with your fertile imagination, that I'd be here and you'd be there and I'd be writing this
to you. I'm writing this secretly, no one around, and I'm putting
my ass on the line to do it. But friendship, true friendship,
triumphs over everything. Besides I don't like at all what they're
doing or what's happened. Maybe I'm a traitor for saying that,
but I don't think so. I'm not your typical West Point wind-up toy
soldier.

I'm a shavetail in the Signal Corps, I got an engineer's degree
even if I was at the bottom of the class. Why they assigned a
dummy like me to this project, I don't know. No explanation
comes to me except that that's the Army for you. Why did I go
to West Point when I'd had all that experience with the military
mind? I'll tell you why. Because the pater wanted me to and I
didn't have guts enough to tell him that I didn't care if I was the
eldest son and the eldest son always went to West Point. I
couldn't tell the old so-and-so that I loathed Army life and break
his heart. But I may resign soon anyway.

I'm in this project but I wouldn't know what was really going
on if I hadn't gotten into the secret files. I may be stupid but I do
have guts. Or is that just another sign of imbecility?

I'm mad as hell, Old Rank, but I can't go around shooting my
mouth off to the newspapers or anybody else for that matter. I'd
disappear, end up in Army prison, probably in solitary. Maybe
I'd even get shot. It'd be an "accident," but it could happen,
believe me, Hank, old buddy.

I wish there was some safe way, any way, that you could
answer this. There isn't. As it is I don't know if you'll get this.
But I'm taking the chance you will. What I'm going to do
tomorrow is take a private plane I've rented and drop this letter
through that green cloud called the Sampson phenomenon. After
Mark Sampson, the brilliant young guy who made the machine
that made the green cloud that opened the way to Oz, though it
was an accident. Oz! I can't believe it!

Anyway, I'll be up there when the green cloud appears if it
appears. It doesn't always and even then they can't be sure how
big it'll be and how long it'll last.

Anyway they're trying some kind of experiment with it, but
they won't be trying to fly anybody through. So I should have
the sky to myself. I'll zoom up there and strike like old
Balloon-Buster Frank Luke himself, drop this through the cloud

in a box with a Very flare attached, and run like I saw Richthofen coming after me. I rented the plane under a fake name, paid cash, and I'll be wearing a fake beard and civilian clothes and using a German accent.

If they find out who I am, I'll take off for Brazil. I always did prefer dark-eyed beauties, remember?

When they heard about what happened to their invasion force, they just about crapped in their whipcords. And they sent off a cipher message to Washington. Whoever's handling this deal there sent a cipher message to the President. He was in Alaska on a tour. The message rocked him, he got sick and had to go to bed. He's in San Francisco now, but he's said to be still sick. He hasn't been much help to the people here. They've been told to make the decision about what to do, but you can bet that if it's wrong they'll be blamed. That's the Army way, God bless it!

The reason I know all this is that I've been sworn to secrecy and though they don't tell me much I overhear more than I should. I make it a point to do it. And as I said I got into the secret files and learned what the hell was really going on.

From what I can gather the big boys are seriously contemplating another invasion. But they're going to have to cover up the deaths of the soldiers and the loss of those aircraft, and they don't want to have to do that all over again. Too many people asking questions.

Sampson, he's not a bad guy at all, is all for telling the public the truth, but they won't stand for that. They're afraid of the public uproar, and the bigshot politicians in this are afraid of the political repercussions. As it is, I've been hearing rumors that some of the members of Harding's cabinet have been caught with their hand in the public till and there's going to be a hell of a scandal and maybe jail sentences.

Hank stopped reading and said, "My father wrote me that he'd heard that the Secretary of the Interior, Albert Fall, and the Secretary of the Navy, Edwin Denby, leased some navy oil reserves to Edward Doheny of Pan American Petroleum and to Harry Sinclair of Mammoth Oil. He said he'd heard that that big crook Doheny had bribed them to give him the deal and 'Clear Sin' Sinclair had taken Fall into some of his financial dealings.

"Dad says that Harding is personally honest though not very bright. Some of the people he gave high positions in the government because he owed them for political support have betrayed him. And the people of the United States.''

"Most people are corrupt in one form or another," Glinda said, "and they don't even know it. Get back to the letter."

"O.K."

Well, Hank, my roommate is about due to return so I'll have to finish this quick. I'm so het up that I've even considered telegramming or phoning the President. He's at the Palace Hotel in San Francisco right now, but he's sick in bed and couldn't handle it even if I could tell him I'd like to blow this sky high. I couldn't get through to him anyway. So I'll just have to keep mum for now. I don't want any "accidents" happening to me. I hope you can understand my position.

I wish you the best of luck, however. Jesus! Oz? Would anybody believe me if I told them about this? I'd probably end up in an insane asylum, that'd be worse than getting shot. So I hope you understand.

Good luck, ave atque vale, vaya con Dios, Un homme averti en vaut deux, and all that. Is Glinda as beautiful as Baum said? If she is give her a big smackeroo for me but watch the hands, Hank the Rank.

Your pal,
William Wordsworth "Stinky" Wright

"*Afe atkei fale, faya kon Diioz,* and the rest?" Glinda said. "What do they mean?"

"Hail and farewell, go with God, a man warned is equal to two unwarned men."

"You must miss him."

"Yes. I miss my parents, too."

"If you gain something you lose something and vice versa. Hank, I have to take care of the Earth situation as soon as possible and that means tonight. Erakna will be attacking me here. I know that, and she knows that I know that. I need every bit of energy that I can summon for the attack, but I'll have to expend much before I can get prepared for Erakna. I'll have some time; I know when she'll come."

Glinda paused.

Hank said, "Yes?"

"I'll give some details later. First, do you have a picture, a photograph, of President Harding?"

Hank thought that there might be one in the copies of the *Current Opinion* periodicals he had brought with him. Glinda sent a servant to get them from Hank's apartment after he had printed the title of the magazines on a piece of paper. When the servant returned with them, Hank leafed through the pages for the photograph. Glinda busied herself with paperwork while he did so.

His eye caught and stored various advertisements, titles of articles, and parts of text. They were like little hooks dragging him back to Earth or like tappings on tiny bells which reverberated through his mind and caused it to salivate images and emotions.

VOL. LXVIII   APRIL, 1920   No. 4

IS THE WORLD ON THE WAY TO BANKRUPTCY?

Inflation as a Means of
Destroying Capitalism.

PARTY POLITICS AND PROHIBITION

THE EIGHTEENTH AMENDMENT BEGINS TO INTRUDE

Prosperous Days in Peoria
and St. Louis.

A SPECIAL investigation has been conducted "with severe neutrality," by the N. Y. *Tribune*, into the effects of prohibition in other lines. It has developed, so it says, in New York City, "enough arguments in favor of prohibition to wreck the white paper market were they printed in detail and with all their far-reaching ramifications."

IS JAPAN CONCEALING A REVOLUTIONARY MOVEMENT AT HOME?

I AM one who thinks that the theories of seapower advanced by Admiral Mahan may be greatly modified, if not completely shattered, by the sinister triumphs of the submarine and the torpedo.

EXPLAINING THE ALLEGED BREAKDOWN OF LIBERALISM IN AMERICA

"AS a body of political and international doctrine, liberalism has practically collapsed." So Harold Stearns, formerly associate Editor of the *Dial* (in its brief ultra-liberal period) declares in a new book, "Liberalism in America" (Boni and Liveright), which is being widely discussed.

"It stands," Lord Morley says, "for pursuit of social good against class interest or dynastic interest. It stands for the subjection to human judgments of all claims of external authority." Militarism is named by Lord Morley in this connection as "the point-blank opposite of liberalism."

Mr. Stearns refers to the triumph of prohibition as an evidence that anti-liberal forces are dominating the scene in America today.

PHILADELPHIA CRITICIZES NEW YORK

NEW YORK SCOLDED FOR ITS MORAL AND OTHER SHORTCOMINGS

NEEDED—A BUDGET SYSTEM TO SAVE TAXPAYERS $2,000,000,000 A YEAR

A BUDGET system in regulating the expenditures of the United States government would save the people $2,000,000,000 this year, according to Roger W. Babson, the expert financial statistician.

The Einstein Theory of Relativity, by Prof. H. A. Lorentz, of the University of Leyden (Brentano's), is a useful little book of 64 pages, intended for the layman and written in simple language. It makes accessible to English readers an article that appeared originally in the *Nieuwe Rotterdamsche Courant*.

THE COMING SCIENCE

Compared with other branches of scientific investigation it might almost be said that Psychical Research in the past four decades has made far more progress than any other branch of learning in a similar period of time.

A FEW OF MANY TOPICS TREATED IN THIS FASCINATING WORK

What Happens at Death, Projection of the Astral Body, The Sexes Hereafter, The Subconscious Mind, Self and Soul Culture, The Three Laws of Success, True Ghost Stories, The Human Aura, Automatic Writing, Haunted Houses, Psychology of Dreams, Messages from the Beyond, Psychic Healing, Hypnotism and Mesmerism, Crystal Gazing, Materializations, Spirit and Thought Photography, How to Develop Your Psychic Powers, etc.

He had gone through one *Current Opinion* without finding the photograph. He glanced at Glinda. She was still working with her documents and messages and did not seem disturbed that he had taken so much time with the periodical. He picked up the April 1921 issue.

NERVE EXHAUSTION

How We Become Shell-Shocked In Everyday Life

Must We Fight Japan? by Walter B. Pitkin (Century), is hailed in the New York *Times* as the most deeply searching and widely ranging study of the Japanese question in its relation to America that has yet been made. Mr. Pitkin is an associate professor in the Pulitzer School of Journalism, Columbia University. He spent several months of 1920 in California. He holds that there *is* a Japanese "menace," and he finds a strong similarity between the temper of present-day Japan and that of pre-war Germany.

OIL ECLIPSING COAL
AS A WORLD FUEL

A MILLION
DOLLAR SECRET

A Sensational Principle and Power that Guarantees Prosperity, Happiness and Supremacy

This subtle and basic principle of success requires no will power, no exercise, no strength, no energy, no study, no writing, no dieting, no concentration, and no conscious deep breathing. There is nothing to practice, nothing to study, and nothing to sell.

WHY EVERY MALE IS A
LATENT FEMALE

TRAILING THE NEW ANTI-SEMITISM TO ITS RUSSIAN LAIR

If You Want Prosperity, Abolish the Income Tax

JURYWOMEN AND MODESTY

SHOULD WOMEN SERVE AS JURORS IN DIVORCE CASES?

In England this whole matter has been widely discussed as a result of a recent disagreeable case in the London Divorce Court. Women were sitting in this Court for the first time. Part of the evidence was in the form of indecent photographs. The Judge was unwilling that the photographs should be shown to the women and suggested that the jurymen should look at the photographs and explain to the women as they thought fit the bearing of this evidence on the case.

EXCESS OF THE SEX-FACTOR IN FREUD'S METHODS

A NEW MENACE

IS BOLSHEVISM GETTING A GRIP ON THE CHURCHES?

Principles of Freedom, by Terence MacSwiney, late Lord Mayor of Cork (Dutton), is the self-revelation of a man who died for his beliefs.... An "illuminating document, revealing the mentality of the Sinn Fein rank and file," is what Mr. Boyd, himself an Irishman, calls this book. It has one single preoccupation, the independence of Ireland from England.

Experts are found who argue that one impression of cancer which had fallen into discredit may have to be revived and examined afresh. This is the notion, prevalent among the laity in some places, that an old house overrun by rats is a spreading center for cancer.

SIGNIFICANT SAYINGS

"My advice to men who cannot stand the sight of the loving meetings of minds and eyes —and in some cases lips—on a Fifth Avenue bus is to ride in the subway. Let the spooners spoon."—*Sheriff Knott, N. Y. City.*

"As a member of the male sex, I protest indignantly against the conclusion that all men are familiar with abominable things, and my sensibilities are less delicate than women's." —*G. Bernard Shaw.*

The Sick World and the Shoplifter

The rabid determination of partizan politicians not to allow the United States to enter into any agreement with the rest of the world to stop war, the outbreaks of violence among the criminal classes, the determined efforts of the liquor interests to nullify the constitutional Prohibition amendment, the depression in business, the increase of unemployment, the strenuous effort of the agitators to make trouble between this country and Great Britain on one side and Japan on the other, all may be grouped with this pathetic spectacle of respectable women turned shoplifters as an indication of that other moral slump from idealism.

32

"Here it is, page 434," Hank said.

Glinda put her pen aside and took the periodical. Hank came around the desk to stand behind her.

"That's President Harding, sitting in the front row, third from the right."

"A handsome but weak man," Glinda said. "He's not as honest as you said."

"How can you tell?" Hank said.

Glinda did not reply. Instead, she pointed to Calvin Coolidge and Herbert Hoover, the Vice President and the Secretary of Commerce, respectively.

"These men should succeed this Harding in office, though in what order I don't know."

She pointed to Denby, Fall, and Daugherty, Secretary of the Navy, Secretary of the Interior, and Attorney General, respectively.

"Except for this one, these men will be disgraced or at least should be."

She indicated Denby.

"He is probably innocent, but he will be disgraced, too."

"Are you telling me that you can determine all that just from their photographs?" Hank said.

"I'm telling you nothing except what I just said."

Having picked up a large paper, she unfolded it and spread it out on the desk. Hank was astonished again. It was a map of the United States of America.

"I took this when I left the letter for the Signal Corps," she said.

"Now, just where is San Francisco on this map?"

Hank put a finger on the city.

"Just where is the green cloud in relation to the map?"

Hank indicated Fort Leavenworth.

"Have you ever been to this Palace Hotel your friend spoke of?"

"Once," Hank said. "When I was sixteen."

"Describe its location as best you can. I want all the details you can recall. And then draw a map for me."

What is she up to? Hank thought.

When he was through, he handed the paper to her.

"Good. Do you have any metal fillings in your teeth or fixed bridges?"

Hank said, slowly, "No."

"Good! Hank, would you like to go with me tonight?"

"Where?"

"To the Palace Hotel."

"Wha . . .? I mean, you mean it?"

"It's possible that we may not get there. But I'll be trying very hard, and if all goes well, we'll get there."

"How?"

"That doesn't matter as far as you're concerned."

"Are you planning to harm the President?"

"No. I will be honest with you, though. What I do may be interpreted as harm to your President. It will be necessary, however."

"I'm your man."

"I'm not finished. Wait until I'm through. You may be in grave danger if you go with me. There is always the chance that we could get lost. Or encounter something that might destroy us. I'll explain what might happen in detail."

When she had done so, she said, "I would not blame you at all if you refused. In fact, I am beginning to regret now that I did ask you to come with me. The reason I did is that I want you to be able to report to your people exactly what happened. If that, with what I plan to do, does not convince them, then they are fools."

"You think they'll be so scared they'll lock up the gate to this world and throw away the key?"

"I hope so."

"I'll go with you."

"You're sure that you're not saying that because you think I might question your courage, look down on you?"

"I'm sure."

"Very well."

He went to his apartment and stayed there alone until 8:30 P.M. He did not even see the servants who brought his meals. They put the trays on the floor, knocked on the door, and were gone before he could get to the door. Lamblo did not come because Glinda would have told her to stay away. He was not to have any sexual relations or to talk to anyone. He exercised, and he lay on the bed trying to visualize the Palace Hotel and its environs. Though he had thought that he was too excited to sleep, he did so while visualizing.

He awoke just as the sun set. Nine minutes past seven. His watch was on standard time, so it would be 6:09 P.M. in California, which was on daylight saving time. The moon was approaching its last quarter here and also in Kansas and San Francisco. Glinda had said that she would have preferred a full moon, but this was better than an all-dark moon. She had not told Hank why.

He brushed his teeth after eating, bathed, washed his hair, and cleaned his toenails and fingernails. Glinda had told him to make sure that he did that. When he was dry, he put on only cloth slippers and a robe. The housekey and the wristwatch were on a table.

He was surprised when he answered the knocks on the door. He had not expected that the queen would come for him. She was wearing cloth slippers and a robe with a monk's hood shadowing her face. She gestured for him to come with her. Silent, Hank walked beside her along hallways, down stairs, and into the southwest arm of the X-shaped castle. There was not a person, animal, or bird in sight, an unusual event. Glinda must have ordered everybody to stay away from this route.

She stopped before a very tall but very narrow door and unlocked it with a massive wooden key produced from a pocket of the robe. She went in, and Hank squeezed through it. He looked around while she shot a thick wooden bolt and laid the key on a table. This was the room into which he had looked when Glinda had gone through that wild ritual. It was vast and dark except for a few tiny lights on the walls and the torch on top of the four-faced sphinx. He felt a chill as if a winter draft was blowing over him.

Glinda led him to the far end where one of the little lights shone. A transparent sphere embedded in the stone held a glowing dust.

There was a huge low bed near the light, a bed the like of which existed nowhere else in the two worlds except in the castles of the Witches of the South and of the North and the castles which had been those of the Witches of the East and of the West. Even these were not quite like Glinda's. It had white sheets and covers and pillows and was canopied by a silvery dome from under which hung an intricate array of mirrors. These would catch the "essence" of the travelers—whatever "essence" meant—and would reflect them from mirror to mirror— building up the velocity and density of the "essences," so Glinda said—and would eject them through a silvery funnel.

The legs of the bed were silver and went through the floors of this room through the ceilings and floors of all below it and deep into the earth into a pool of mercury enclosed in thick glass.

Glinda touched a sphere on the wall, and it glowed as suddenly as an electric light turned on.

She signalled to Hank that he should remove his slippers and robe. He did so and put them on the floor where Glinda had shed hers.

Then she hooked her fingers into her mouth and removed a complete set of false teeth.

Oh, my God! Hank thought. How ugly that fallen face looks!

He should have expected this if he had been thinking clearly. Her body cells might renew themselves, but three centuries of wear would erode her teeth to stumps. Even she, with all her seemingly magical powers, could not grow new teeth.

She smiled at him as if to say, "See! I am no longer the beauty you craved, lusted for, burned with love for. I am, though a queen, also a subject of the worm."

She put the false teeth on the pile of clothes and crawled into the vast bed. Hank went on all fours after her and lay down by her side. She rolled to the edge and lifted from the floor a thin wooden object carved in the form of a three-pointed star. There was a faintly glowing writing on it, but Hank could not make it out clearly in the dimness. She reached out her left hand and took his right. Holding the wood up before her, she looked at it while her lips moved silently. She read the characters on one ray of the star, then whirled it in the air, caught the next ray, read the forms on it, and then repeated the procedure to read the inscriptions on the third ray.

She must have known them by heart, but perhaps the ritual or operation required that she hold the object.

Sighing almost inaudibly, she placed the star on her magnificent breasts and closed her eyes. Hank had been told to close his eyes when she shut hers, and he did so.

He had just begun to visualize the Palace Hotel when he sank—or seemed to sink—through the bed. Though he opened his eyes—or thought he did—he could see only a grayness that seemed to twist in corkscrew fashion. For a moment, he screamed with terror as a baby fallen from its mother's arms might scream. He could not hear his voice, but the crimson square waves pouring from his mouth and speeding ahead of him—downwards—must be screams. They looked like terror transformed into vibrations, a wavy watery route to Hell.

He did not know why he knew or felt that he was falling. Perhaps the silver shafts and the mercury pool were a sort of cannon firing him like a shell toward the glowing nickel-iron core of the planet. Though he had no reference point, he *knew* that he was hurtling downward.

He stopped screaming. At least, he was no longer consciously screaming. But the crimson waves still spewed out and raced ahead of him, narrowing far in the distance and forming a sharp point. As if they made the blade of an ice-breaking ship which was cutting a way for him through the grayness. He might be wrong in thinking that the waves were a "visible" projection of his terror. They could be something else. Or it might be that something unconscious in him was doing the screaming.

He slowed down, though he did not know why he knew that.

Glinda was not with him. But just as he "stopped" and began floating, the crimson waves dwindled, shooting back towards him like a cataract in a movie film running backwards. They did not disappear in his mouth, however, but stopped before him and curved upwards and down to form a bright sphere. And then the sphere became a shadowy semi-transparent Glinda.

She smiled and moved towards him, expanded, and enveloped him. The thought that he was inside her rolled his mind like a snowball racing down a slope.

She had taken him into her "womb" just in time. Something that he did not want to see or even hear about was moving about them now.

Only Glinda kept the thing from closing its "jaws" around him. And she was in extreme peril, though he did not know how he knew.

"Up we go," her voiceless voice said softly.

They "rose," but the thing was close behind them. Hank felt that he was trembling and sweating, though not physically. He could not feel his body. All his Terrestrial senses seemed to be shut down or left behind him, but there were other senses that he could not define.

The grayness became a deep purple through which he could see or sense what seemed to be the intricate network of tree roots, moles digging, and writhing nests of worms and snakes. And there was a flash of a hollow in which the dim wavering shapes of gnomelike things hewed stone and hacked out metal and one seemed to be sitting in a stone chair and listening through earphones to something far below it.

They ascended from the crust of the earth and were inside the hotel, quivering ghostly stuff. He was no longer in Glinda; she was a phantom by him but more solid than the floors through which he was rising like metaphysical smoke.

Hank recognized the room in which they stopped. It was the bedroom of the suite in which his parents had slept when they had taken him to San Francisco. Somehow, Glinda had pointed him—and herself—toward it. They had headed toward it as surely as iron leaped toward a magnet.

What if he had never been here? Could Glinda still have found her way? He felt that she would have been able to do so, though she would have had much more difficulty.

The man in the bed was Warren Gamaliel Harding, the President of the United States of America. The woman sitting on a chair by the bed and reading to him from a magazine was Florence Kling De Wolfe, Mrs. Harding.

There were also two nurses moving around as if they had nothing to do at the moment but were pretending to find work.

On a table by the bedside was a vase with a few long-stemmed roses and a clock. The clockhands were on 7:27.

Harding was much fatter, older-looking, and far less healthy-seeming than in the photograph Hank had shown Glinda. His haggard eyes stared up at the ceiling while he listened to his wife, but he was smiling slightly.

The room and its contents seemed to Hank to be behind thin white veils. Still, he could see everything clearly, though he could not hear, smell, or feel anything. Glinda had told him that she could have activated these senses if it had been necessary to do so, but that would have required more energy. She had also told him that she was in a "form" that differed slightly from his. He could not affect anything; he would be as intangible as ectoplasm. She, however, would be more "dense" and could, when the occasion demanded, briefly handle material stuff. She was floating by him now near the ceiling and holding in one hand an object that he had not seen when in the castle room. She must have picked it up in her right hand when she closed her eyes.

Had she brought the actual object with her or was it an astral simulacrum of the object?

The President said something. Hank, lip-reading, thought that he said, "That's good. Go on. Read some more."

Then Harding shuddered, his mouth fell open, and his eyes looked fixedly at the ceiling, the lids unmoving. His wife rose from the chair and bent over him. Her lips worked in her emotionless face. The nurses came to the bed, and one felt Harding's pulse. Then Mrs. Harding ran to the door and called out something. Several men hurried in, pushed the nurses away, and examined the body. One shook his head; one seemed to say, "Apoplexy."

Glinda moved down. The thing in her outstretched hand, which he now saw was a tiny golden statuette of herself in her witch's robe and holding a shepherd's crook, began being less transparent. By the time she reached the bed—she had passed through the doctor in front of her—the statuette had almost ceased wavering and looked almost as hard as the wall.

She shoved the statuette deep into Harding's open mouth.

Now Hank understood what she was doing. The coroners would find the statuette when they performed the autopsy, and they would notify authorities. These would not permit the public to know about it, and they would make sure that whoever found the statuette would keep quiet. But they would know whom had placed the statuette there because Glinda had sent one exactly like it in the package that Hank had delivered to the Signal Corps.

If, somehow, the public learned about it, so much the better from

Glinda's view. Its true identity would not be revealed; it would always be an unexplained mystery except to a few.

Glinda floated up to Hank, said in a voiceless voice, "It is done," touched him, and they shot downward. The return trip was much like the outward, though Hank felt that they were in even graver danger when they were in what he thought was the center of the planet. As he rose along the silver shafts from the mercury pool, he sensed that great "jaws" snapped shut close behind him, and something "screamed" in frustration.

33

"The figurine differed from the other," Glinda said, "in that it was made of wood, not gold, and it was hollow. A very thin layer of paint looking like gold was on it. I can't transport metal without losing so much energy that I'd be too vulnerable to that . . . thing. Even then, I wouldn't be able to take anyone with me. The mass and the chemical composition of the transported object have to be light and nonmetallic."

She was as pale and as languid as one of Count Dracula's donors. After the return, she had not left her apartment for two days. Hank thought that she had been sleeping most of that time. Her first minister had conducted all governmental business until the third day, and she had not worked for more than two hours then before going back to her suite.

"Did we really go to the center of the Earth or of this planet or maybe both?" he said.

"I didn't know where we were until we got to the basement of the hotel. But I, like you, felt that we were in the molten heart of the world. My theory is that we have to go there to accumulate energy from the great heat so that we can propel ourselves on the second leg of the journey and the return. For all I know, we may have been inside the sun. I don't think so, though. I feel that we are deep under the ground, as deep as you can get."

"I can understand, I think, why your magic works in this universe. But I can't understand why it should work in my universe."

"It's much more difficult and dangerous to work magic in your world. Much more uncertain. I have a theory that it only works there, your world, because, somehow, there's a leak of influences from my

257

world to yours through the weak places in the walls. Or, to put it another way, Ertha is on a higher energy level than Earth. That is why it's easier to go from here to there than vice versa. And, when the way is open, there's a flow of energy involving a temporary and weak influence from this universe. The laws of your universe, you might say, are slightly changed during the opening whether the opening is made by us witches or by your scientists.''

"Which might mean,'' Hank said, ''that the witches and sorcerers of my universe have been able now and then to affect real magic. They've opened the way for the energy exchange or flow or whatever you want to call it?''

"It's possible. However, there's a more important subject to talk about now. Will we or won't we get a message from your people?''

"I don't know. I suppose that Coolidge, he'll be the President now, will have been informed of the project and the statuette. He's a hard-headed, no-nonsense, New England Yankee. I'd say that he's considered all the dangers to Earth, balanced profit against loss, and decided that it's best to close the project down. He'll make sure that the records are either locked up or destroyed and everybody in the know has been sworn again to silence. He's not a man to want to mess around with another world. He's got enough troubles in his own. Also, I doubt that he really believed the evidence even when it was laid out on his desk.''

"Whatever happens there, I can't worry about it now. The news from the front is mostly bad. The Emerald City may fall anytime now. I've suggested to the Scarecrow that he leave the city—he could be carried out at night by two eagles—but he refuses. The Gillikin armies have invaded my country; they're still in the mountain forests and on the rivers, but they'll soon be on the farmlands and the prairies. I've had to replace some of my generals with younger, more flexible-minded men. Those I've discharged only know about war from textbooks; they can't adjust to the realities. The Gillikins in Winkieland have occupied most of the strategically important places there, and they've been replaced by Munchkins and Ozlander draftees. The relieved men will be marching into this country to reinforce the Gillikins here.''

"What's the good news, if any?''

Glinda smiled.

"My guerrillas, led by the Cowardly Lion, captured a dam long enough to blow it up. Fifty boats loaded with Erakna's troops were swept over the edge of the broken dam and were drowned.''

"You permitted the use of gunpowder?''

"For that time only. However, I suspect that there will be some drastic changes made now. Erakna will probably order that gunpowder and firearms be manufactured. She'll be afraid that I'll make them and so gain a tremendous advantage.''

"It won't have any effect on the course of the war,'' Hank said. "By the time that enough ammunition and guns are made and the troops have been trained to handle them, the war will be over one way or another.''

"In thirty-five days, there'll be a total eclipse of the sun. It'll start at 14:10 and end at 16:35.''

Ten minutes after 2:00 P.M. and thirty-five after 4:00 P.M., Hank thought. But that doesn't seem right.

"Only eight percent of the sun will be darkened as viewed from here,'' Glinda said. "That makes me happy, though not overly much. Erakna's powers would be considerably increased if the eclipse were total here, and mine would be proportionately lessened.''

Eighty percent, Hank thought. If a map of Amariiki were overlaid on that of the United States, then this point, Suthwarzha of Quadlingland, would be near the Oklahoma-Texas border. His farmer's almanac indicated that the area near Fort Leavenworth, Kansas, would get a seventy percent eclipse. The green cloud appeared there, but the entrance led to a place farther south. He should not be surprised. Quadlingland was the southern California of this oasis.

The difference in location was what had puzzled him about the time.

"Are you telling me that the sun, the moon, and the stars can influence people?'' Hank said. "I've always believed that astrology was pure nonsense.''

"Everything in the universe is interconnected. It's a vast spiderweb in which one minute fly can't land on a strand without sending shivers through the entire network. However, you're right in thinking that the astrologers don't know what they're talking about—unless they're also witches. Even then, a witch knows only a little of a subject that's cosmically complex.

"But, yes, the amount of the darkness or light of the sun or the moon and the position of the stars can influence witchly powers.''

"I'm in no position to argue with you,'' Hank said.

"In one way, the eclipse is an advantage for me. I know that she'll have to attack then because then is when she'll be most powerful. But, on the other hand, she knows that I know that and will be prepared as best I can.

"I wish, though, that the eclipse would occur much sooner. If her army gets this far south before it does take place, she may storm this castle, and I may have to flee. I'll be much less protected if I am not in my seat of power."

Hank did his best in the following weeks to aid Glinda's soldiers. He strafed the Gillikin columns and dropped small bombs. His efforts did not amount to much in slowing the advance. As a scout, he was not nearly as efficient as the hawks and eagles in the air and the foxes and mice on the ground. Moreover, every time he went up he was in peril of attack from Erakna's birds of prey. He had many narrow escapes during which he reduced the number of the red queen's avian corps, but he also was often grounded for repairs to Jenny.

By September 10, Earth calendar, the Gillikins were within fifteen miles of the capital. Between them and the castle was a large army of fierce defenders vowed to fight to the death, no surrender. The invaders, however, outnumbered the Quadlings by three to one.

34

Lamblo, pregnant and weeping, had been taken by Jenny to a farm deep inside a green forest. Hank wondered if he would ever see her again.

The castle was empty of all life except for some outlaw rodents, Hank, and Glinda. He had been told by Glinda to leave, but he had refused.

"This is the first time in a hundred years that anyone has disobeyed me," she said. "That person was severely punished."

"I won't go. You might need me."

"That is why I'm not going to have you dragged out of here," she said, smiling. "You may well die for your loyalty, but I am selfish enough to let you stay if you insist. I know that, just perhaps, you might be able to help me. When and how, I don't know. But I know that it is possible. It has something to do with your being an Earthman. You are not as vulnerable to Erakna as a native-born."

She was set, however, on his staying in his apartment.

After eating a very light lunch because his stomach seemed to have turned inside out, he paced back and forth. Now and then he went out on the balcony. The sky was clean, but there were low dark banks on the southern horizon. The estimated five-mile-an-hour wind would bring the clouds here long after today's battle was over unless a much stronger wind was behind them.

The wind was hot and dry and blew over an unusually large number of the giant lightning balls.

He was ready for action. The fully loaded revolver was on a table.

261

The BAR had a full magazine box. A sword was in the scabbard attached to his belt.

From the balcony, he could look across and down into Glinda's laboratory. The window drapes had not been pulled shut, and the room was ablaze with glowing spheres and dozens of torches. Glinda sat for a long time in a tall-backed chair near the four-faced sphinx, but, when Hank returned from the toilet, she was gone. It was possible that she was in a part of the room he could not see.

He looked at his wristwatch. Nine minutes after 2:00 P.M. The next sixty seconds seemed to drag their feet; he could almost hear them. Then, as was inevitable, the shadow of the moon began to eat into the sun.

He had expected Glinda to reappear, but she did not. Where was she? She would not run away, not Glinda.

As he paced from the balcony a few feet into the room, the sky became darker, and gloom crept over the earth. Except for the noises he made, he could hear nothing. Even the birds were avoiding the air around the castle.

At 4:10 there were twenty-five minutes left before the eclipse ended. Where was the white queen?

Where was the red queen?

What am I, a knight, or maybe just a pawn, doing here? he thought. For that matter, what can I do against these forces?

Ten minutes later, he looked at the sun through dark glasses. The power of the Uneatable would reach its peak in fifteen minutes. Immediately thereafter, it would begin to wane. Surely, Erakna would attack very soon. But he could not see Glinda.

His mouth was dry, and his heart was beating hard. He had to have a drink of water. Brushing past the drapes, he jumped when static electricity crackled, and his boots evoked more sparks from the carpet. As he passed the table, he thought of putting the revolver in his holster. No. He would do that on the way back.

While the water poured into the cup, he wondered if Erakna had lost her nerve. She might not show. After all, she was young and did not have her foe's centuries of experience and practice. And Glinda's reputation must be near overpowering. Erakna might decide to put her trust in her conquering armies. If Glinda were forced to leave the castle, she would be at a great disadvantage.

He gulped the water and turned to run back to the balcony. Before he reached the bathroom door, what seemed to be a thousand writhing red worms appeared around him. He yelped and jumped back away from the things in front of him but into those behind him. For a second or two, he was covered with them, but he could not feel them; they were intangible.

They disappeared as violent explosions deafened him, and the bathroom door slammed shut. The floor shook beneath him.

He pushed the door out so hard that it bounced from the wall and half-shut again. Black gunpowder smoke poured in, blinding and choking him. He stumbled out into it, his eyes tearing, and opened the two outer doors to clear the air in the big room. When he turned, he saw that the revolver and the automatic rifle had been torn apart by the explosions of the ammunition. Something—the red worms?—had set off the powder. The vibrations of the floor had been from the ammunition dump in a ground floor room going off.

It was a good thing that the revolver had not been in his holster. He would have a ghastly wound in his hip and leg, and, if not dead, he would be out of any fight.

That was something that Glinda had not expected or she would have warned him and have had the dump removed. What else did the Uneatable have to spring on Glinda?

His bed was on fire, touched off by the explosions of three BAR magazine boxes on it. The revolver had rocketed itself off the table and what was left of it was on the floor. White spots showed where bullets had ricocheted from the stone wall.

If he had been on the balcony, he might have been killed. He found himself holding the big housekey hanging from a chain around his neck. His unconscious was telling him that his mother's key was still bringing luck to him.

He ran to the balcony and leaned over its railing. By the lights still burning in the room, he could see Erakna walking around and bending over now and then as if she were looking for something. She was in a long white low-cut gown and wore a scarlet helmet with two goat's horns. In her left hand was a closed blood-red umbrella.

If only he had the BAR now, Hank thought. He could spray the witch with it, shattering the windows and riddling her with .30-caliber bullets. She, however, had somehow known that and had taken care of him. That is, she had disposed of his firearms. But he was still alive and to be reckoned with even if she did not think so.

However, if, for some reason, Glinda had deserted him, Erakna would not have much trouble dealing with him. Where was she?

Erakna had turned her back to him and was poking with the umbrella end at a tall oak cabinet in one corner. Hank blinked and shook his head. Something was wrong with his eyes. The four-faced diorite sphinx was shimmering, expanding, and contracting as if it was radiating heat waves.

Then he gripped the railing tightly and swore. Abruptly, the shimmering had ceased, and the sphinx had risen from its crouching position and was walking toward Erakna.

Just as it came within twenty feet of the North Witch and crouched again as if to spring, its black mouth opening and exposing long sharp black teeth, Erakna turned. Her mouth opened wide—she must be screaming—and she brought the umbrella up swiftly and pointed it at the sphinx. The stone thing sprang, a ball of lightning shooting ahead of it from its forehead. That met the fiery sphere hurled from the end of Erakna's umbrella, and the two merged, expanded, and exploded as if they were kegs of dynamite.

Smoke and a blinding light filled the room. The windows blew out. Hank recovered his sight just in time to see the shards, vitreous snowflakes, spinning toward the courtyard below.

The smoke, red, not black, billowed out of the broken windows.

Erakna was standing in the same position, the umbrella extended, seemingly untouched by a violence that should have hurled and smashed her against the wall. The sphinx was shattered pieces of stone on the floor. Glinda stood in the midst of the fragments, and she too was untouched by the explosion. Somehow, the two women had thrown up barriers around themselves for the very small fraction of a second required.

The torches had been blown from their sconces and were burning on the floor. The huge glass bottles and retorts and the copper and silver tubing on the tables had been fragmented or twisted. Smoke rose from pools of acid eating away the floor.

Hank yelled as loudly as he could.

"Glinda! Behind you! Behind you!"

Thirty feet behind her, the air had quivered, boiled, red steam or smoke rising from the whirling, and then the air had gotten darker, the boiling and steam had suddenly ceased, and a great brown bear was there. It was a short-faced bear, a descendant of the monstrous creatures which had roamed the American southwest until ten thousand years ago and then had died out. This one was a third smaller than its ancestors, but it still was massive enough to take on a Siberian tiger.

Glinda must have heard him through the opened windows. She turned in a half-circle and, without hesitation, pointed one finger at Erakna and the other at the bear. The animal charged, its roar audible to Hank.

Another glowing globe was on its way from the end of Erakna's umbrella. It met an equally large sphere ejected from the end of Glinda's middle finger, but her sphere traveled only a few feet from her when it coalesced with the North Witch's and blew up. The fiery globe expelled from Glinda's left middle finger seemed to strike the bear on the nose, but the brightness blinded Hank again. He could not be sure of the sequence of action; it was too fast for him.

When the darkness slid away, he saw that the bear was slumped on the floor, its nose and lips burned away. It almost touched Glinda, who was lying on the floor. The impact of the charging beast, probably dead when it struck her, had knocked her down. She seemed to be unhurt, however, and she got to her feet just as Erakna shot from her umbrella a huge bubble which shimmered with colors like gasoline on water.

The bubble sprang toward Glinda but slowed in proportion to its nearness to her. She seemed to hold it away with the finger pointed at it. Her left-hand middle finger jabbed at the corner where the bed stood, and from the finger shot a whirling many-angled shining object. It struck the corner above the bed and banked—a magical billiards shot—toward Erakna's back.

Erakna half-turned and pointed the umbrella at the polygon. It bounced as if hitting an invisible wall and struck the wall of the room. At the same time, the glowing sphere sped on a straight line back toward Erakna. Her right hand rose, the thumb and all fingers except the middle finger clenched, and the sphere slowed, stopped, and hung rotating tiredly in the air. It emitted a screeching like an unlubricated bearing.

The shimmering polygon bounced off the wall and shot across the room and out a window.

All this happened so swiftly that Hank could barely follow the offensive and defensive moves. Now he had to quit watching the two because the sphere which had bounced through the window was curving upwards toward him. Though intensely concentrating on her battle with Glinda, the North Witch had seen him. And, now that Glinda had deflected the sphere from the room, Erakna was using it to get rid of him. He was certain that he was the target for the glowing ball.

But it was not swift. The North Witch could not put much energy or thought behind its projection. She had lost much energy when she had transported herself from her castle into Glinda's. She had lost more when she had moved the great mass of the bear from its forest into the room. And she was trying now to cancel the white queen's moves while simultaneously destroying him.

If Hank had had time to consider, he would have admired, however grudgingly, the powers of magic and mental control and nerve-coolness of the Uneatable. He did not have that time, though. He had to do something about the death sliding through the air toward the balcony.

He ran by the flaming mattress, plunged through the smoke carried by the wind, slammed the two doors behind him, stopped, turned, drew his sword, and waited. Sweat soaked his clothes and ran into his eyes. He wiped the stinging fluid away with his left sleeve. His heart beat like the tattoo of a drum just before the trapdoor was sprung by the hangman.

The front of the sphere bulged—oozed—through the door. Smoke roiled from the wood at its edges. Hank threw the sword point-first into the door and in the middle of the sphere. The blade quivered there while the sphere continued to move until it was almost free of the door. Flames burst from the wood around it, and the sword turned from gray to dull red. Hank could feel its heat.

He ran down the hallway to where another angled across it. When he whirled, he saw that the door was blazing and that the sword was bending, the weight bringing it down as the metal inside the sphere softened. Then the sword fell with a clang on the bare stone floor. Smoke from the fire-enlarged hole mingled with smoke from the fire on the inner door caused as the globe had passed through it.

The globe was gone, its energy dissipated by the sword.

He ran headlong down the hallway and down a spiralling staircase until he came to Glinda's floor. He ran until he came to the very tall but very narrow massive door to her laboratory. There he stood, panting, his brain also panting as it raced. What could he, weaponless, do to help Glinda? There would be swords and bows in the armory, but that was on the first floor, and he might not be able to get into it because the explosion of the dump may have blocked the armory entrance. If the armory door was unblocked, it still might be—probably was—locked. He did not have the key nor did he know where the keykeeper was.

He became aware that he was clutching the big housekey hanging from the chain.

The key! There had to be a key to this problem.

He pulled on the handle of the door. Unexpectedly, it swung out. Glinda had not locked it. Had she done so because she had anticipated his coming here? Or had she not locked it because she might have to try to escape through it? Or both?

Thick red smoke swirled out through the half-opened doorway, choking him and burning his eyes. He smelled acid and something else in the smoke. He coughed, but he doubted that he had warned Erakna with its sound. Something or some things bellowed like a bull in the room. That ceased but was succeeded by a series of poppings like firecrackers exploding.

He managed to suppress his coughing just as a six-inch tall creature spurted like catsup from a bottle through the door. He jumped back, crying out, as the thing brushed against his leg. The catsup simile was correct; it was covered with what would have been blood if the blood had been brighter and not so thick. It sped wailing down the hallway, its thin legs and huge webbed froglike feet a blur and a slapping, its thin arms pumping, its froggish saberteeth-armed mouth open, its eyes on top of its hairless and blood-spattered head bulging.

Before it got to the end of the hall, it collapsed with a noise like a wet towel thrown against a wall. It quivered, legs kicking, and then began to swell. Horrified, Hank watched as the thing ballooned and then burst open as if it had been gas-filled. The thick heavy blood and organs spattered the floor and the walls. From it came an odor that seemed to curl the hairs in his nostrils.

Something half the bulk of the dead creature crawled out of the organic ruins and croaked. It grinned at Hank and then scuttled on many legs around the corner, leaving little wet footprints behind it.

Hank gulped and fought an impulse to throw up. Conquering that, he stooped low through the door so that he could not be seen. As he ducked behind a desk, eleven creatures like the unidentifiable but undeniably horrible things that had crawled out of the frog-like thing ran by him, their feet splatting wetly. They stank like mildewed potatoes with rotting chicken, but they were not the source of all that he had smelled at the door. Peering around the desk at the room after the things were gone, he saw stalactites of some whitish, green-flecked, doughy stuff hanging from the ceiling. One dropped, and it quivered for a moment and then began undulating slowly across the floor. The globs were also on the wall here and there as if they had been dough hurled by an explosion. It was their odor, he thought, which was almost making him gag.

They stank like a mixture of dried blood, dog excrement, decayed gardenias, witch hazel, beer farts, Limburger cheese, and an odor that was strange to him and one which he hoped would remain a stranger.

He counted six of the froglike things dead and exploded on the floor. He supposed that if he could see the whole room there would be six more. One of the witches had summoned them in the hope that they would be too many for her foe to deal with. But the other witch had summoned the many-legged things to appear inside the batrachians. Also, one of the witches had brought the mobile doughy things from whatever hellish place they lived.

The witches must be desperate indeed to expend so much energy in these maneuvers.

Breathing through his mouth, Hank went on all fours around the desk and looked around its corner. For the moment, both women seemed to be taking a rest break, an undeclared but silently agreed-upon truce. Glinda, near the windows, was breathing hard, and she was sweat-soaked. Her auburn hair was smoke-streaked, the side of her face looked seared, as if it had come close to a flame, her bare arm was bleeding from many places as if tiny shell fragments had struck her. Her dress was blackened in many places and ripped as if claws had caught it, and she had either kicked off her shoes or been torn loose from them by an impact or explosion.

Her arms hung down as if she were completely exhausted. Her mouth was open, but that might be because of the odors.

Erakna was far from untouched. She looked as if she had been ground through a people-mill. She might be uneatable but something had chewed on her before spitting her out. Her helmet lay on the floor, its goat's horns cut in half. Her white hair, which had been in a Psyche knot when she appeared, was flying loose. It, too, was smoke-smeared, and blood welled from a scalp wound. Her dress, sweat-permeated, clung to her magnificent body, and it was so torn that it was about ready to fall off. A red and blistered sear mark was just above her breasts. One eye was swelling and rimmed with red. A rip from the waist through the hem of her skirt showed a beautiful but tattooed leg. Hank recognized some of the red and purple symbols.

There was silence except for the women's loud breathing. Then Glinda said, "Your power is waning, Erakna. The darkened sun is beginning to brighten. He is emerging victorious from the mouth of the Wolf. Just as I will emerge victorious, and you will go where the Bargainer waits for you."

"But your power has weakened even more than mine, White Witch," Erakna said. "When you thrust those *wilna* inside my *helyafroskaz*, you used far too much energy for your own good. You are weakened, White Witch, and it is too late for you to profit from the rebirth of the sun."

"You are as wrong now as you have been all your life," Glinda said. "Which is near its end—in this world, anyway. Where the Bargainer will send you is where only a soul sick with evil would have agreed to go."

One of the things hanging from the ceiling dropped. Neither of the women looked at it. Hank, however, saw that the first one to drop was oozing very slowly toward Glinda. It was behind her, and she seemed unaware of it.

The second glob did not move. Perhaps it was dead; Glinda may have killed it, though it bore no signs of a wound. Or maybe it had been summoned here by Glinda, and Erakna had slain it. No. If that were so, Erakna surely would have mentioned that transporting the things would also have lowered Glinda's powers.

A third dough-mass plopped on the floor. That also did not move.

Greasy puddles were forming along the edges of the last two dough globs. They were dwindling, melting. But the first one was still undulating toward Glinda.

"What do you know of the Bargainer and the agreements She makes?" Erakna said. "I have made a very good compact with Her."

Glinda smiled and said, "Yes, She told me about that. No, it was not so good. It was better than any other of your slimy kind have gotten, but it will put you where there is no hope. And it will be soon filed away in the Bargainer's unspeakable archives.''

For the first time, the Red Witch lost her composure. Eyes wide, she said, ''What do you mean?''

''You are not the only one who has walked the dread way to the Bargainer. I, too, have gone there, and I have talked with She Who Broods In The Heart Of The Moon. I, too, have agreed on certain terms with Her.''

''You're crazy!'' Erakna screamed. ''No white witch would go to Her! None could even approach Her! You lie! You lie!''

''I am more red than you know,'' Glinda said.

''You're lying!''

The white mass was now within a few inches from Glinda's bare heels. Erakna must see this, but she seemed to have forgotten it in her fury.

He hesitated. If he leaped up and shouted at Glinda to warn her, he would be exposed, defenseless, against whatever the Red Witch might hurl at him. On the other hand, Erakna would have to divert some of her force at him, and that might leave her with a part of her defenses down.

The glob was only an inch from Glinda now. He did not know what it could do to her, but he was sure that it was not desirable. Though it might be capable only of startling her, that would give Erakna a momentary edge. That was probably all she needed to strike Glinda dead.

Erakna—still shrilling, ''You lie! You lie!''—gripped the handle of her scarlet umbrella with both hands and pointed it at her enemy. A glowing red cloud sprang into being from the end, swirled, and then formed a blood-red face which undulated but still had definite features. It was that of an old, old, toothless woman with unusually deep eye-sockets and unusually large eyes. They glowed; one green, one red. A scarlet tongue slid out out from greenish gums.

''Look upon the face of the Bargainer!'' Erakna screamed. ''It's a face you've never seen before, you lying bitch! But it'll be the last face you'll ever see!''

''I have seen it,'' Glinda said calmly.

Hank bit his lip so savagely that it hurt him. He had to divert Erakna's attention to him, but he knew that he would die.

The face was moving as slowly as a sick sloth towards Glinda. Both her hands were up with the fingers extended towards it. He was fighting against it, but she could not stop its inexorable advance.

"She will eat you alive!" Erakna screamed. "Bit by bit!"

Her face was twisted, and sweat poured down her. But the umbrella was as unmoving as if it were in the hand of a statue.

The blob had halted; it moved again. He could not even see the floor between it and Glinda's heel.

He sprang up with a hoarse yell. At some time, he did not know when, he had lifted the chain from his neck. Now he held the housekey in his left hand. His unconscious had done it for some reason, a reason that he knew a second after he was aware that it was in his hand.

Erakna turned slightly, her skin paling, her eyes becoming even larger. She must have thought that he was dead. But she still pointed the umbrella at Glinda. One hand loosened its grip and pointed at Hank.

Glinda flung her arms up as the doughy thing touched her heel, and she jumped forward.

The face shot forward, but it stopped when it was within a few inches of the fingers Glinda held outwards again. Glinda was looking into the eyes of her death, and they were again moving very slowly toward her.

Glinda shouted hoarsely, "If you use your power against him, I will turn the Bargainer against you! She has promised me that I will win! I will go where no one wants to go, but I will have sent you to a worse place, and I will have saved my people!"

Yelling like a Comanche, Hank ran toward the Red Witch.

Erakna screamed, and from her finger sped a fiery globe. It was far smaller than the others, the size of a baseball, and it did not travel as swiftly.

He pitched the key at it, unsure that its path would intercept that of the destroying thing because it was so small. And he did not know that the key, if it passed through the sphere, would do anything. The sphere was ungrounded.

He was aware that Erakna was still screaming, but the cries sounded different. They were not born of hate but of horror and pain.

The key arced and touched the sphere.

Hank was deafened and thrown back by the explosion. His head struck a table, half-stunning him. He got up groggily, saw the key on the floor, and saw what Glinda had done to Erakna.

The face had been turned around and pushed back during that very brief time when Erakna's attention and power had been divided. It was attached to the Red Witch's now. At least, Hank assumed that it was. He could not see it clearly. It was almost invisible from behind and did not look like the back of a head. He did not know what it looked like.

Erakna rolled on the floor and tore with both hands at her own face as if she were trying to rip the thing off. Suddenly, she quit screaming. Her hands fell off her face and lay motionless by her sides. Her eyes looked fixedly and unblinkingly at the ceiling. Her mouth gaped. Her skin turned gray.

Two wisps, wavering and semi-transparent, rose from her head and floated through the ceiling. They looked to Hank—surely, it was his imagination—as if Erakna's face was against the Bargainer's, and the horrible old woman was kissing Erakna.

Hank jumped, and he swore as the corpse gave a tiny scream.

"An echo," Glinda said. "Poor woman."

Her voice was faint, and she looked too exhausted to move.

He leaned on the table, but it was not enough support. He sat on the floor and looked numbly at Glinda. She moved now, though slowly and stiffly.

"It is over," she said. "I knew that you should stay in the castle."

"I'm not sure that you did not plan all this."

She smiled slightly. "No, Hank. I did not know what would happen when she came here. If it hadn't been for you, I'd be dead."

The light outside was getting a little brighter.

"Did you . . . really make a compact with the . . . Bargainer?"

"No, Hank. I lied to Erakna to shake her up, make her less confident, confuse her."

"Glinda the Good," he murmured.

Author's Notes

1. Somewhere out there is somebody who will check up on the weather at Fort Leavenworth on April 1, 1923. Don't bother unless you want the exercise. I got my data from the *Kansas City Star* and the *Kansas City Times*. An interesting item which has little to do with the weather is that the "King Tut Craze" was just reaching its peak. The professional models who appeared on Easter day at the Auteuil races in Paris wore King Tut hats, green robes with slashed sleeves, floppy waists, tight hips, long skirts, and slashed gauntlets. Many had kerchiefs with Egyptian figures around the necks and arms.

2. The circumstances surrounding President Harding's death were mysterious, or so many claimed. One ex-government official even wrote a book in which he claimed that Mrs. Harding had poisoned her husband. This story seems, from all known, to have been a vile canard. Mrs. Harding did, however, refuse to let an autopsy be performed on her husband. Thus we can speculate that the coroners may have missed Glinda's calling card, but the embalmers would have found it. Perhaps they did not. In any event, the Signal Corps project was kept secret. Somewhere in the U.S. government files, though, may be the complete story. It would be as difficult to find as the Ark of the Covenant, also stored by the government.

3. Did the ancestors of the Amariikians diminish in stature because of something in the water? Or was the shrinking caused by the presence of the firefoxes? No one, except possibly Glinda, knows.

4. If the energy beings called mind-spirits or firefoxes could be used by old red witches to keep them animated, why didn't the witches use them to transfer their mind contents to new bodies? The answer is that the body the witch would like to possess had a mind which would have rejected any attempt at takeover. However, it was said that there had been a few times when firefoxes possessed idiots. If this was so, why didn't the witches use the firefoxes to possess idiots? They undoubtedly tried to do this, but they failed. A firefox operating by itself could sometimes possess an idiot. But the combination of a firefox and the mind-contents of a witch could not effect a transportation, though the witch could control the firefox while it was in her own body. In fact, the witch, if she tried to shunt her mind-contents to another body, was likely to have them discharged electrically, erased as a tape is erased. The firefox would then take over the body and mind structure with ease. After this happened a few times, the old red witches avoided this type of attempt at longevity.

5. The Witch of the East was killed by the impact of Dorothy's house falling over her, and she immediately became dust. The Witch of the West dissolved into a puddle of water when Dorothy threw a bucket of water on her. (This action by Dorothy could be called "dirty pool.") I had figured out some years ago just how these two events came about, but it is only fair to record that Doctor Douglas A. Rossman, in an article, "On The Liquidation Of Witches," in *The Baum Bugle*, Spring, 1969, extrapolated much as I had. I was not a member of the International Wizard of Oz Club then, but when I found out about the article in 1981, I had Fred Meyers, the Club's secretary, send me a copy.

Water or violent impact may, under certain conditions, break down the force which holds large molecules together. The old red witches using firefoxes to energize them after they had died had no blood, and it was only the firefoxes which kept them from sloughing away, from becoming dust. I suspect that, in time, the old witches would have fallen apart without the intervention of water or a very hard impact.

6. In Baum's *The Wonderful Wizard of Oz*, the West Witch is afraid of the dark. Was this a neurosis or were all of the red witches fearful of the dark places? Hank never asked about this, but I suspect that, if all the red witches had this feeling, it was because they dreaded

encountering the Bargainer there. Or perhaps they were apprehensive that some thing a white witch might have sent would be lurking there.

7. I regret that I had to cut out a section where Hank, on his way back from the city of Long-Gones, finds the very old and dying Wizard. This might have been a touching scene and would have thrown some light on Oz's career in two worlds. But the length of the novel forced me to make this decision.

8. In *The Wonderful Wizard of Oz,* Baum said that there were no dogs or, at least, the natives had never seen or heard of any. In a later book, he said that no horses existed there. This is strange, since the ancient Goths would have brought both animals in with them. If you accept Baum's premise that the human beings originated there instead of migrating from Earth, the absence of dogs and horses is still puzzling. There are indigenous North American plants and animals there and some types of animals from Africa and Asia. (But I've explained why Dorothy would wrongly identify the lion, mastodon, and sabertooth as the African lion and elephant and the Asiatic tiger. She never saw the mastodon or tiger, and the American lion looked like the African lion, though it was much larger.)

In reality, the Goths and Celts did bring in horses and dogs, and the Amerinds did bring in dogs. However, the newly arrived humans had great difficulty in hunting the sentient animals they found there. Most of these were too intelligent to be easily caught, and the meat-starved tribes ate the dogs and horses. What they did not devour, the beasts of prey did.

During this time, a few horses and dogs must have been possessed by firefoxes, but these sentients were too few to reproduce in large enough numbers to survive.

What about the domestic fowl? The answer is that the ancient Goths, Celts, and Amerinds did not have them. These came into Europe from Asia at a later time. The Amariikians talked some wild fowl into cohabiting with them as egg-suppliers. In return, the fowl were protected from the predators.

9. The Natawey are native Americans, what used to be called Indians or Amerinds. (To me, anybody who's born in the Americas is a native American.) The Natawey speak Algonquin dialects related to

the tongue of the Pequots, Naticks, Shawnee, and Illinois, among others. Their words for tobacco and other indigenous North American plants were borrowed by the Caucasian Amariikians.

I would have liked to have taken Hank into Nataweyland, where he would have observed that their civilization had certain parallel developments to those of the Olmecs, Mayans, and Incas. There would also be many differences. Again, the length of the novel, if I'd done this, eliminated this excursion.

10. The Quadling dialect is the least archaic or most changed of all those descended from Gothic. The examples are not what I would have given if I had had special phonemic symbols available. I used "a," "o," and "u" to indicate two different sounds for each, and I made no distinction between long and short vowels. I also preserved Baum's spelling of Quadling, Munchkin, Winkie and Gillikin.

Hank thought that Glinda's name was derived from a Gothic word similar to the English "glint." He was wrong. If it had been, it would have been Glindo. It was derived from a word borrowed from the pygmy Neanderthals. That the meaning was similar to that of "glint" was a coincidence.

Word-terminal *s* in Amariikian was lost unless it was preceded by a vowel; *s* then became *z*. Thus stains (stone) became stain, and fotus (foot) became fotuz.

The personal name, Sharts, and a few other words were exceptions because they came into the Quadling language after the change.

Word-internal *s* between voiced sounds became *z*. Thus, fraliusan (to lose) became, during this stage, fraliuzan.

Word-initial *i* and word-internal *i*, when followed by *u*, were palatalized and so pronounced like the *y* in "year." Fraliuzan became fralyuzan.

At a later stage of Quadling, *y* (represented in the Gothic alphabet by *j*) became the sound of *j* in the English "jalousie." I have represented this by *zh*. This change is similar to that in some South American Spanish dialects in which "yo" (*I*) became "zho."

Winkie and Gillikin, however, did not experience this change. That is why the Sneezer's name is Nabya, not Nabzha.

Fralyuzhan then became, in Quadling, fraizhuzhan. The *al* became a dipthong, the *i* compensating for the loss of *l*.

Word-internal *t* became *d* between voiced sounds. Thus, bota (advantage) became boda. Bota may be related to the English "booty."

The aspirate *h* was lost except when word-initial followed by a vowel. Aspirated word-initial *w* did not lose the aspiration.

Gothic did not have the sounds which English represents as *sh* (as in ship) and as *ch* (as in church). However, these first came into the language through some Neanderthal loanwords. Munchkin, for example, which was originally Munichikin. At a later stage, *t* and *s* followed by *u* became palatalized and then became *ch* and *sh*.

Thus, tuggo (tongue) became tyuggo and then chuggo. (The first *g* would be pronounced as the *n* in "sink" or the *ng* in "king.") The change of palatalized *t* to *ch* has taken place in other languages, including English.

Kiusan (to choose, to test) became kuzan, became kyuzan, became chuzan.

There were other sound changes which I won't go into here.

Quadling went through a process during which internal syllables collapsed, though not to the extent which Old Norse experienced. Gender and number were almost entirely eliminated. Except for a few forms, all the cases disappeared. The nominative singular case form was kept as the base form for nouns except for a few. The genitive was formed by the addition of *s* after word-terminal unvoiced sounds and of *z* or vowel plus *z* after word-terminal voiced sounds. There were, however, some exceptions to this.

The accusative forms of the personal pronoun were kept, though, when Hank arrived, the mass of people were inclined to use the nominative for the accusative. The academicians were fighting a losing battle against this.

The scholars attributed the wholesale regularization of Quadling to the long and close contact with the Neanderthals and the ancestors of Blogo's people. (His ancestors were not so rare then.) There is no evidence to confirm this theory.

I would like some day to translate *The Wonderful Wizard of Oz* into Quadling, but I have so many similar projects which I've only half-finished or never started that I can't be sure I'll carry out this project.

11. It is possible that Hank's explanation for the animation of the Tin Woodman and the Scarecrow and for the sentiency of animals was wrong. It is also possible that he misread the hieroglyphics on the

Long-Gone obelisk. Notice that Glinda neither denied nor accepted the validity of Hank's reasoning. Glinda, when Hank was not around, may have had a good laugh at his arguments.

Baum did not record her other title, Glinda the Ambiguous.